Amelia Caroline

By

Jon C. Lewis

Cover Portrait by Pat Harrison Lewis

Cover design by Kris Pfeifer, Pfeifer Design

ISBN 978-0615993829

Six Range Point Publishing
New Mexico

DEDICATION

TO

PAT HARRISON LEWIS

INTRODUCTION

Three women lived in the same town and in the same house over a period of two hundred years. They sat on the same porch and in the same rocking chair. The women were related, but their lives were separated by time. Their story begins in the early years of the 19th century with the birth of Amelia Caroline Potter Everitt. Her great-granddaughter, Amelia Caroline Everitt, was born one century later. The two women knew each other through family stories, memorabilia, and through conversation across time. It is through these conversations that their lives are revealed.

The third woman, Dr. Mary Eliza Langdon, a current day descendant of the family, tells their story, which is based upon historical record. Explored are issues related to health care reform, women's struggle for independence and professional identity, religious faith and the impact on the women of war and military activity in a small town, the center of which is an 18th century military installation.

The village was -- and still is today -- quite small, yet the lives of the women were of epic proportion, involving events that ranged from a landmark case argued before the U.S. Supreme Court to securing voting rights for women and the worst military sea disaster of the 19th century. Yet their lives also were of the everyday variety for their times, and encompassed the joys of childbirth as well as the tragedy of epidemic fevers. They celebrated sunrises and sunsets, and they searched for understanding in times of pain.

This is the story of the Everitt family, descendants of Dr. Reuben Everitt who was born in 1762. Over generations, the family included physicians, pharmacists, planters, merchants, and military officers. By necessity, the family's story is entwined with the stories of other families in the community, including descendants of Richard Langdon and Samuel R. Potter.

In addition to these three families, the story includes more than eighty other individuals, actual persons, whose lives touched either the life of Amelia Caroline or her great grandmother. Every attempt has been made to portray involvement of these persons in a manner that is consistent with recorded history. Liberties have been taken in some instances to weave Amelia Caroline into that history, but I trust this has been done in a manner that does not bring discredit either to the individuals or to history.

THE TOWN

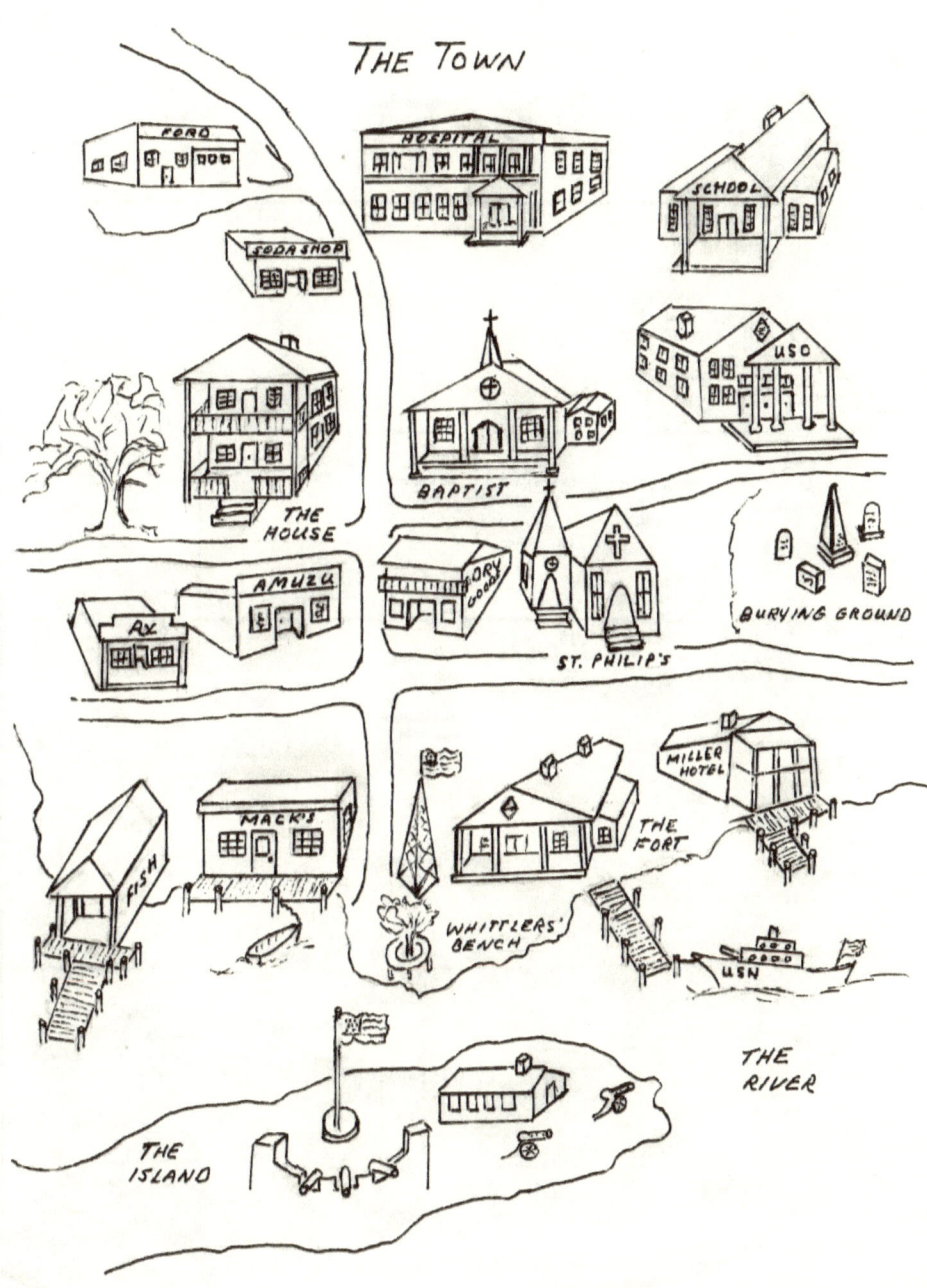

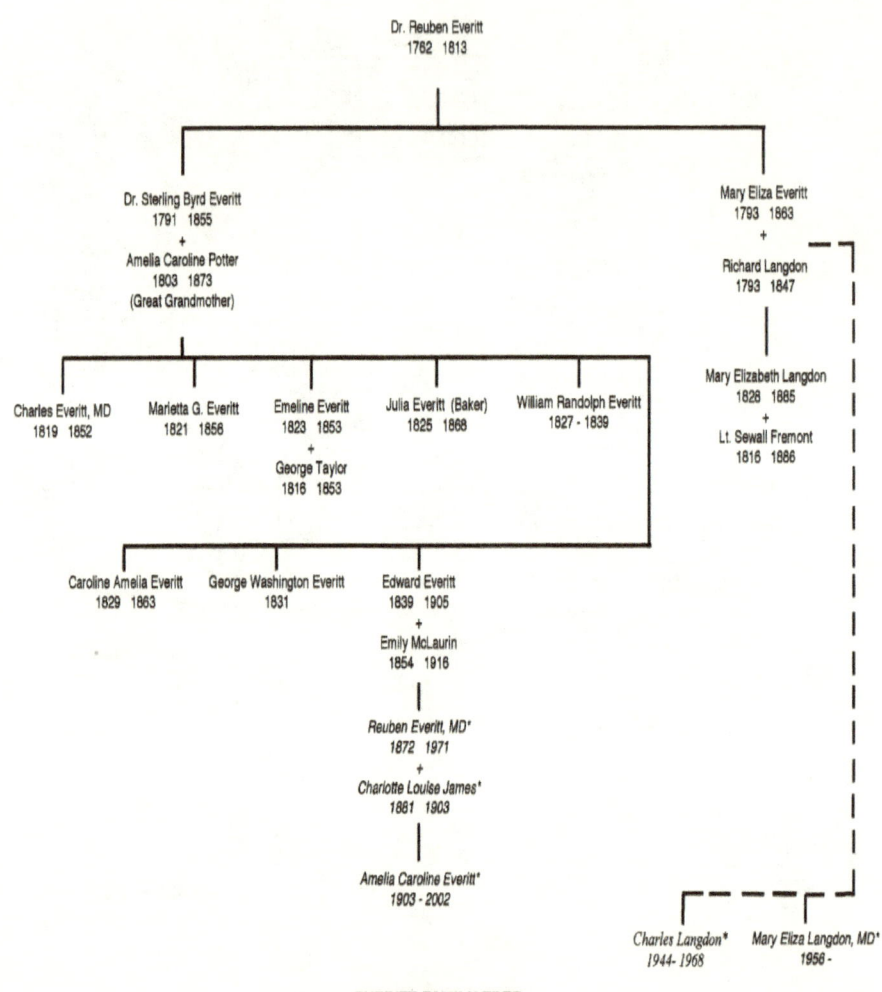

EVERITT FAMILY TREE

*Fictitious

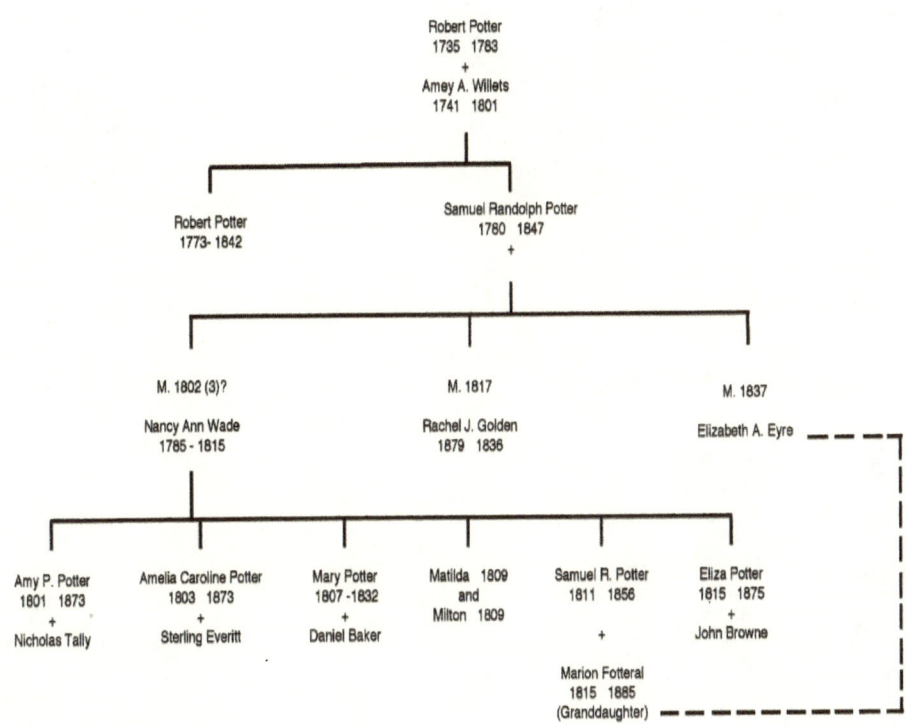

Robert Potter
1735   1783
+
Amey A. Willets
1741   1801

Robert Potter
1773- 1842

Samuel Randolph Potter
1780   1847
+

M. 1802 (3)?

Nancy Ann Wade
1785 - 1815

M. 1817

Rachel J. Golden
1879   1836

M. 1837

Elizabeth A. Eyre

Amy P. Potter
1801   1873
+
Nicholas Tally

Amelia Caroline Potter
1803   1873
+
Sterling Everitt

Mary Potter
1807 -1832
+
Daniel Baker

Matilda   1809
and
Milton   1809

Samuel R. Potter
1811   1856

+

Marion Fotteral
1815   1885
(Granddaughter)

Eliza Potter
1815   1875
+
John Browne

POTTER FAMILY TREE

9

AMELIA CAROLINE

1

BEGINNINGS

The breeze coming out of the south on this September day was warm and moist, as I pulled into the parking lot next to the clinic building where Catherine Arrington, MD, PhD, practiced. I was here to see Dr. Arrington, a twice-weekly ritual that had been going on for the past several weeks – ever since that day late in August when I had finally admitted that I needed help.

That day, August 29, 2002, remains in my mind because a rare midsummer cold front had passed through the region. The unusual drop in temperature, with accompanying high winds, had driven vacationers from the beaches following reports of waterspouts over the ocean. In spite of the turbulent weather conditions, I had driven back from the city of Wilmington, thirty miles upriver, to the small fishing and vacation village of Southport on the southeastern coast of North Carolina where I lived and had my medical practice.

As a family practice doctor, I occasionally travelled to attend grand rounds at the New Hanover Regional Medical Center, where I had spent my early afternoon that day.

Grand rounds are regularly scheduled conferences of interest to the general medical community. Usually the presentations are overviews of recent advances in selected medical topics. The focus of the conference that week had been the relationship of asthma to summer allergies. It was a topic of interest to all who, as in my case, practiced general family medicine.

By coincidence, a prominent researcher from Mayo Clinic had that very month published a review of allergy testing in the journal *American Family Physician*. The journal was one that I regularly read, and I was particularly interested in the article related to allergies for it dovetailed with the conference to a degree. I did not personally know the author of the article, but I had been aware of clinical studies with which he had been involved ever since the days of my residency in family medicine. Now, summer allergies are a frequent problem for vacationers and I saw numerous summer visitors, so both the grand rounds in Wilmington that afternoon and the article in *American Family Physician* had been directly applicable to my practice.

Upon arriving back in town from Wilmington, I had driven directly to the Old Burying Ground, which was located on Rhett Street between Moore Street to the south and Nash Street to the north. I had parked the car at the corner of Rhett and Nash and walked to the northeast section of the cemetery, where an ancient obelisk marked the site of the Everitt family plot.

For the next hour, I had sat at the foot of a decaying, moss-encrusted headstone and wept.

Just so you'll understand, this had not been an isolated incident. I had been on a psychological treadmill ever since the death on August 19th of Amelia Caroline Everitt, an elderly relative who also was my dearest companion. A part of me had passed at her death.

Amelia Caroline and I had family ties that extended back nearly two hundred years. At fifty years my senior, she had been the living link to my family as far back as the early years of the 19th century. At the time of her death, we had been living together for nearly twenty years, a period during which we shared each day's joys as well as tragedies. Our relationship was similar to -- yet even more than -- that of grandmother and grandchild. Through her, as you will learn, I came to know and experience my ancestors. Our lives had become so entwined that I believe our souls were one, and it was through this commonality of soul that we were bonded to those of our past.

The day of her death had also been, as I thought back, the very same day that the allergy article appeared in the journal.

During the ten days between her death and the afternoon when I had sat at the foot of the ancient grave at the Old Burying Ground, I had been quite distressed. My mind would not stay focused and I had been quick to tears.

The conference in Wilmington had concluded just a couple of hours earlier, yet I barely remembered the speakers, and the main points from the journal article were completely lost to me. Though distressed, I was still aware that the state of my mind would be reflected in the care of my patients and I recognized that help was needed.

Now, as I sat in Catherine Arrington's parking lot, I once again took time to remind myself why and how I came to be there. I felt that this would help me maintain my perspective during the day's session.

Southport, the small town in which the cemetery was located, was one in which I have lived and practiced for nearly eighteen years. However, the town had been part of my life for a number of years prior to establishing my practice. In fact, the community had been among my favorite vacation spots throughout my years of medical training.

"Everyone in the Carolinas spends at least one week every summer at the beach," I was told by classmates shortly after my arrival in Winston-Salem to attend Wake Forest University School of Medicine.

That was late in July of 1977. Being from the small Midwestern farming community of Greenfield, Indiana, and recognizing that the Southern culture differed from that in which I had been raised, I was determined to fit in. So, after settling into the new surroundings and prior to the beginning of lectures, I and three other first-year medical students made reservations for a weekend at the beach. Another of our classmates, who had grown up in Eastern North Carolina, recommended the Blockade Runner Motel on Wrightsville Beach, just outside of Wilmington.

This kind of true North Carolina summer vacation, though brief on that first occasion, became the established pattern for our group of friends for the next few years.

Initially, the annual beach trips with medical school friends were like those of other vacationers. Daytime hours filled with sun, salt and sand were followed by dinners of grilled grouper, blackened tuna and freshly boiled shrimp. Sometimes we took side trips to Calabash for delicately breaded and fried shrimp, oysters and flounder.

Then after four years of this pattern, I made the decision in the summer of 1981 to spend one of my vacation days riding the state ferry from Fort Fisher, which is located south of

3

Wilmington near Kure Beach, across the Cape Fear River to the town of Southport.

This particular trip was special, for I was celebrating graduation from medical school. My folks had traveled from Indiana to attend the graduation. They wanted to share the day when I would officially become Mary Eliza Langdon, MD.

Following the ceremonies and all the accompanying celebrations in Winston-Salem, Mom, Dad and I went to the coast together. Dad had recently retired from his position as a research scientist with Eli Lilly Laboratories in Greenfield, and his interests in retirement encompassed a bit of genealogy. He had plans to visit as many old cemeteries as possible while in North Carolina.

We spent several days together in the Wilmington area, then on the final day we checked out of the hotel at Wrightsville Beach and drove down the coastal highway to the ferry. After a short stop at the Fort Fisher State Historical Site, we continued the final couple of miles past the North Carolina Aquarium to the ferry terminal.

The journey across the river was a pleasant forty-five-minute trip, with constant entertainment as seagulls and pelicans soared gracefully over the wake at the rear of the ferry. The birds were responding to a myriad of small fish churned to the water's surface by the boat's passage. In addition, children who had gathered at the stern rail were throwing bits of bread into the air. Nearby parents watched with enjoyment as the gulls swooped to catch the morsels in mid-air, and the pelicans made diving plunges into the churning water to snag fish.

Then along the shore there were numerous sights. Several of these were pointed out to us by an elderly gentleman named Tom, who explained that he had been born and raised in the area. The first attractions were a large U.S. Navy ship and a Coast Guard cutter, both of which were docked at the Military Ocean Terminal at Sunny Point on the west bank of the river.

"The terminal is a major military cargo and ammunition depot. It was established shortly after the Vietnam conflict to serve the Atlantic Fleet, which supports America's military personnel in Europe and the Middle East. Some say the depot is the largest in the nation," Tom said.

Tom spoke with a sense of authority. This introduction was followed by a concise history of the terminal and the role it played both locally and nationally. Tom took great pride in his knowledge and he was quite animated in his explanations. His posture, we learned, was not without justification. Tom had retired following nearly twenty-five years as the captain of an ocean-going tug. Several of those years had been under contract to serve at the military terminal.

As we moved farther down the river, Tom pointed to tankers that were docked to unload cargo at the site of the Archer Daniels Midland chemical processing plant. As the ferry glided past that terminal, Tom again spoke.

"They make citric acid at that plant. Did you know that nearly everything we eat contains chemicals produced by ADM? Most everything has at least some of the citric acid from this very plant."

Dad responded by telling Tom of his career in chemical research for the pharmaceutical industry and, for a brief period, the conversation revolved around their mutual interests.

But the narrative tour quickly resumed, for on the sandy shore adjacent to the ADM dock was a small pre-Civil War lighthouse, namely the Price's Creek Light. The brick superstructure was the only lighthouse left along the river following the fall of Fort Fisher to the Union Army in 1865. Shortly after passing the lighthouse, the ferry turned toward a secluded inshore bay at the mouth of Price's Creek, where the Southport ferry terminal was located.

By that time, Tom had drifted into a monologue about his early days as a member of the crew on a menhaden fishing boat. But it was nearing time to disembark, so I thanked him for sharing his memories and we headed for the car. Tom, as it turned out, was the first of many local "historians" whom I would encounter over the ensuing years.

The town center of Southport was a short drive from the ferry landing. As in the case of many newly arrived, our first stop was at the Visitor's Center. It was located on the main street next to the town library. Volunteers in the center were friendly and they called attention to highlights on the walking tour. We were given a complimentary map and a pamphlet to guide us.

The volunteers also mentioned their favorite places to eat, then they sent us out to explore. Among the stops were a number of unique attractions: historic homes, one of which had been used in a recent Hollywood movie; the local haunts of an 18th-century pirate; and the grounds of the town's fort.

The pamphlet explained that the fort had been established by the British in 1734. At that time, the lower Cape Fear River was a major source of naval stores for the British Navy, and the military presence was necessary to protect the region and its resources from the Spanish.

Leaving the fort brought us to the waterfront park, where we sat in a swing beneath the shade trees and ate ice cream purchased from an ice cream truck parked nearby.

Finally, we headed to the Old Burying Ground to round out the day.

We had been in the cemetery for about thirty minutes, walking among the diverse, aging grave markers, when Dad called out, "Mary Eliza, come over here and see what I've found!"

I walked over to where Dad was kneeling beneath the boughs of a large live oak tree. His hand reached out to a marker with the inscription, "Richard Langdon, March 18, 1793 – January 19, 1847." I don't recall ever seeing Dad that excited.

"Possibly," he exclaimed, "we have found a family link right here in this small fishing village!"

Dad was determined to find out more about the local Langdon family, but his enthusiasm had to be put on the back burner. The day was drawing to a close and our plans were to leave the coast that evening. Mom and Dad spent several more days touring North Carolina and I returned to Winston-Salem to begin my residency in family medicine.

It had been a pleasant occasion, and I felt the day in the fishing village added something special to our family vacation and my celebration. In particular, I found myself fascinated with the old cemetery. Dad's energy had been transferred to me.

My new-found interest was such that every vacation and holiday break over the first two years of my residency included time to roam the coastal cemeteries. In particular, I made a brief visit to the Old Burying Ground in Southport whenever possible. I had become captivated by the lives of the people buried there, some of whom had been laid to rest nearly two hundred years earlier.

Dad, as it turned out, did not get around to following up on his discovery in the cemetery. Shortly after he and Mom returned to Indiana, Eli Lilly announced a major reorganization

6

in the Greenfield Research Laboratories. The company asked Dad if he would fill an interim administrative position to assist with the transition and he accepted the challenge. Both retirement and genealogy were put on hold.

However, during that same time, my non-professional interests were evolving into historical research. This was not a major focus, for my residency was quite demanding of my time, energy and intellect. Nevertheless, several of my short visits to Southport included time spent in the genealogy center in the local library. Ultimately, I was led to explore the State Historical Archives in Raleigh.

It was also during the course of my early residency that a voice in my head began nagging at me. It was like one of those songs that unexpectedly pops into your mind then refuses to depart. You know the experience. One morning, say in 1997, a song recorded in 1957 by Fats Domino is turned on in your head. There you are, forty years down the road of life and unable to take the platter off the mind's turntable. "Blueberry Hill" plays over and over and over. Now to be sure, having Fats Domino inside your head for hours on end can be annoying or even disconcerting, but the nagging voice in my head was more troublesome.

Unlike the music of Fats, which tended to be quite clear, all I could decipher -- or thought I could decipher -- from the platter in my mind was that its roots were somewhere in the Old Burying Ground. In addition, I began to realize that with each trip to the cemetery or with each day spent rummaging through county historical records, my life was somehow becoming entwined with the lives of those who were buried in the little fishing village of Southport.

One Saturday afternoon toward the end of my second year of residency -- it was the spring of 1983 -- I was sitting with friends on the deck behind our rental house near the medical school. The impromptu party included other residents, a couple of senior medical students and related family members.

I was speaking with Bill Benton, the husband of a co-resident. Bill was a junior history professor at Winston-Salem State University. We were discussing my interest in history and my fascination with the coast. Bill asked if I knew from where these interests had come.

All I could answer was, " I'm not sure, but there was the Langdon grave that Dad found."

We sat quietly for a short period, then I added, "I don't understand all of what is happening, but there also seems to be something inside me, like a voice trying to speak out. Whatever it is remains cryptic. Yet I sense it is telling me that I belong at the coast."

On previous occasions during spontaneous gatherings such as on that day, Bill and I had discussed my fascination with the cemeteries. And, more than once, he had suggested ways in which a historian might track down information about the families whose members were lying at rest in Southport.

That afternoon while sitting on the back deck, Bill gave me his best academician smile. In response to my statement regarding an inner voice, he just said, "I'm not surprised."

Although the message (or messages) originally seemed clear enough – "Get yourself to the coast!" – they were more intuitive than rational. I felt a gut-level reaction rather than a cognitive understanding.

There were times when I assumed that the recording was just an emotional reaction to the stress and chronic fatigue experienced by doctors in training. Then there were days when I asked a quiet question just in my head, "Why won't this noise go away? I get the message." But something inside was beginning to tell me that the recording in my head was not as it seemed.

"It's a cryptogram, the decoding of which you will not accomplish on your own," began to come through.

Yes, I know what you are probably thinking, so more about cryptography a bit later. But meanwhile, the noise did end a few weeks later through a significant event.

That which brought my repetitive message to conclusion happened following the conversation with Bill Benton. I had decided to spend my entire summer vacation, the full two weeks, in Southport. Having met several of the town's residents over the previous two years, I contacted a couple of them and asked if they were aware of rooms that could be rented for the vacation period. I was living on a resident's salary and certainly did not have enough vacation money to pay the cost of a motel.

Just by chance, I was told that one of the town's long-term residents was interested in renting a room for a short

8

period. The potential landlady was an elderly woman whose house was a couple of blocks from the waterfront.

"Perfect," I thought. So I made an appointment to meet her and discuss the arrangement.

Both the day and date of the appointment I remember quite clearly. In fact, I will probably never forget them. The day was Wednesday and the date was May 11, 1983. The day sticks in my mind, for I had been on duty at the hospital for the previous thirty-six hours and was quite tired. Yet anticipation of the appointment got my energy going.

I left Winston-Salem about 7:00 AM after coming off call and arrived in Southport shortly after noon. We had agreed upon an appointment time of 12:30, so I had arrived on schedule.

The house was located on the northwest corner of Nash Street and Howe Avenue, the main thoroughfare to the waterfront. It was a large, stately old house with architectural characteristics suggesting pre-Civil War construction. The place was a bit down at the heel in appearance and I was guessing at its age, for the history of architecture was not in my expertise.

I parked at the curb and started up the short walk. The house had an expansive front porch on which were several rocking chairs. The rockers were of the style typical in the coastal Carolinas. Sitting in one of the chairs and rocking slowly was an elderly woman. By elderly, I refer to her apparent age, for she in no fashion appeared infirm. I spoke while climbing the five front steps leading to the porch and the front door.

"Good day, Ms. Everitt. I am Dr. Mary Eliza Langdon. I spoke with you from Winston-Salem."

The woman in the chair smiled warmly. Then she replied in the most remarkable way.

"Yes, Mary Eliza. Please use my given name – Amelia Caroline. We simply can not be formal with each other."

I acknowledged her request with a nod and a smile.

Amelia Caroline continued, "I have known you for many years and I have long awaited this day. Today is my birthday and it marks the eightieth year of my life in this house. In preparation for your arrival, I've prepared a small birthday lunch. We'll visit long into this afternoon, then in the summer you will come to stay here in the house."

After a brief pause, her next statement took me completely by surprise.

9

"You see, we are related."

Later that evening, I sat in one of the rocking chairs on the porch quietly listening to the late spring sounds from the waterfront. Amelia Caroline Everitt was to my right in her favorite rocking chair. The recording in my head had come to its close. And I now knew why my summer vacation in Southport was meant to be.

That beginning was nineteen years ago.

As usual upon arrival at Catherine Arrington's clinic, I debated whether to park the car facing the building or at the side of the parking lot in a space facing a small patch of coastal scrub. The scrub was actually a sandy spot where yuccas, pampas grass, wind-swept live oak trees and a single longleaf pine attested to what the island's character had been before the post-WWII boom years brought cottages and increased population.

Then came the 1960s' shopping centers, where fiddler crabs, salt-water taffy and the latest in beachwear were sold.

The patch of coastal scrub next to the parking lot was a relic from the days of undeveloped dunes and natural beach vegetation. In times past, pennywort, sea oats and arrow-leaf morning glory with its trumpet-shaped flowers heralded the arrival of each sunrise. Back then, the dunes stretched from the island road, which had been just a sandy lane, to the ocean less than a quarter mile away. Most of that distance was now developed with large beach houses that were getaway homes for people from Charlotte, Wilson, Raleigh and other places where summer's heat radiated untempered from brick, concrete and asphalt.

The question of where to park did not require an earth-shaking decision. In fact, one might wonder why it was even an issue. But the mind does interesting things. It presents -- often without warning or provocation -- questions, challenges, memories and distractions. Some of its presentations are significant, whereas others are quite trivial. And the parking lot question was one such trivial situation.

Yet, like the recording in my head that had begun following my first visit to Southport in 1981 -- and more recently the distressed state that had brought me to the clinic -- the parking lot has kept at me.

10

"Perhaps parking is not trivial at all. The act may encompass something deeper than my current state of awareness can perceive," I thought.

These and other such thoughts went through my mind.

"So… should I park to the side of the lot looking out the windshield at the vestige of what once characterized the entire coastal island, or should I simply pull up in front of the building, go up the concrete steps and walk through the full-view glass doors to the reception desk? Then simply announce my on-time arrival for my appointment with the doctor?"

My musing self did not respond, but continued to ponder.

The building was not striking. It was small and its presentation was unassumingly brick. Along the front to each side of the entry steps were gardens – or that which were intended to be representative of gardens. A few yaupon holly bushes and some trimmed-back wax myrtles were surrounded by Indian blanket, golden asters, ladies' tresses and horsemint. Since the early spring had been unusually warm, the ubiquitous azaleas and jonquils had long since flowered. Dog fennel, mainly the remnants from the previous year, volunteered at the corners of the building.

"There is nothing professionally remarkable about this place," went through my mind. "It is standard 1970s and not unlike that place next door."

The next-door building was one of those small centers where summer vacationers purchased beach chairs, sunglasses, boogie boards and supplies such as ice, chips, beer and bait for offshore fishing.

I chose to park facing the sand, the vegetation and the memories of an earlier time.

Deep inside myself, I knew the thoughts about the building and parking were just distraction. After all, I had been baring parts of my soul in these sessions and today I was about to bare another. This day, poetry would be at the heart of my revelation.

I opened the car door and stepped into the warm coastal air. The breeze brushed through my hair as I walked up the steps and entered the office building.

2

MOONLIT MORNING

The reception desk seemed excessively busy as I waited to check in to see Catherine Arrington. And there was a new person, the name Susan on the placard, handling the sign-in. The young woman appeared to be in her early twenties, and several mannerisms suggested that this was a new role for her.

"Good morning, Susan. I'm Mary Eliza Langdon, here to see Dr. Arrington," I offered.

"Yes, Dr. Langdon. Please take a chair in the lounge and I'll let Dr. Arrington know you have arrived," Susan responded.

"Pleasant enough for someone new on the job," I thought, as I sought a location farthest from other persons in the lounge.

It is not that I have a phobia about people in waiting rooms, after all that is one aspect of my own career. Rather, my intent was to remove the poem from its manila folder and review it one more time before sharing it with Catherine Arrington. I was not interested in sharing it with others in the waiting lounge.

So I chose a chair on the far side of the seating area, next to a window.

The dog fennel was just outside at the corner of the building, and its brittle tips from the previous year's growth were blowing across the glass, making a slight scratching noise. The sound was not of the fingernail-on-the-blackboard variety. Rather, it was more like those times in late fall when mice, having left their outdoor lives, take up residence in the attic and, on occasion, can be heard scurrying across the attic floor.

"Another of those distractions," I thought. "Focus, focus, focus! There is not much time left. Catherine has already been notified."

I slipped the poem out of the manila folder.

LUNAR SHORE

The clicking, clacking, crunching sounds
Of shells beneath my feet abound
As I walk night's path beside the shore
Where waves break gently evermore

Soon in the dark of early day
The crunching sound of shell gives way
To quiet steps upon wet ground
Where together sea and shore are found

And in the quiet of my stroll
A soothing voice speaks to my soul
And promises another day
Will soon appear as night gives way

And morning light which barely shines
Shows in the sand the early signs
That day now comes as in the past
And brings the sun with warmth to last

Yet as I stroll along the strand
And waves wash gently o'er the sand
Tis not the sun that lights the shore
But lunar glow which needs no more

I seek the orb and find it high
Where shines its glow in western sky
And ask again that voice to speak
Of warmth and light my soul does seek

An answer comes from where unknown
That warmth of day has never grown
From sun itself, though warm its light
But from the moon, that orb so bright

So as I walk upon the shore
Where waves meet sand forevermore
I greet the moon and praise its light
And know it brings me through my night

About five minutes passed as I read and re-read the words I had written just two days before. I concluded that discussing the poem with Catherine was appropriate.

"Besides, you really have not been inhibited in past sessions," went through my mind.

But until now, it was stuff in my head that had come out. You know the kind – mostly past history, like events from childhood, disappointments in relationships, parental issues and discomfort over decisions made or opportunities missed. The poem not only represented something currently going on, it also constituted a paper trail. It was not unlike the yellow brick road to Oz. It could lead to something. But what? Then I heard her voice.

"Good afternoon, Dr. Langdon. Please come into my office."

This greeting may seem a bit formal, since Catherine Arrington and I normally were on a first-name basis. However, in a clinical setting where patients were present, use of professional titles was appropriate.

One of the little things I appreciated was Catherine's habit of greeting you in the reception lounge, rather than just having a member of her office staff lead you down a hall lined with institutionally tan walls. It was one of those things that made patients feel less apprehensive about being in the presence of the doctor.

I was even considering trying the approach in my own office. Of course, time is precious in a family practice where the waiting room is full of unscheduled patients in addition to those who have appointments. Nevertheless, I have been trying to figure out how to gain a few extra minutes so each patient can be greeted in the waiting area by me.

"Good afternoon, Dr. Arrington," I replied, as I gathered my folder and followed along.

The office was not extravagant, which is another thing I appreciated. After all, patients came to see or be seen by the doctor; they did not come to admire office décor.

Catherine waited for me to enter, then sat behind and just to the side of her modest desk. The position was professional, yet at the same time it created a relaxed atmosphere for conversation.

I selected the more straight-backed of the two chairs that faced the desk. The chairs, both of which were comfortably upholstered, were separated by a small table where I placed my notes and the manila folder.

Generally speaking, I was at ease, as had been the case even during my first formal meeting with Dr. Catherine Arrington. That initial encounter had gone quite well, much to my pleasure. I say this because, though recognizing that I needed help, I had had concerns about sharing my most personal inner thoughts with a colleague who was also a social acquaintance.

In addition, there were some totally unprofessional impressions left over from my college days. The generally held view had been that students who were drawn to Psychology had unresolved personal issues. And by extension, the dormitory consensus had held that all practicing mental-health workers were still dealing with those issues.

Let me assure you before moving on with this tale that I was wrong. Therapists are not the only members of society who have hang-ups, and most likely they have done a better job than the rest of us in working out their issues.

This certainly was my impression following that first session with Catherine and it remains so to this day.

"How are you today, Mary Eliza?" Catherine asked once we were seated.

The sessions always began with polite greetings and inquiries about my previous few days.

"Well enough, Catherine, given the circumstances. However, I have been quite tired, so I decided after our last conversation to temporarily reduce my patient load," I offered.

"That seems like a good strategy," Catherine observed. "The time away should give you a chance to rest and provide an opportunity for introspection."

"That is my hope. I have had a couple of restless nights."

"Why the restless nights? Do you have any ideas?"

"Not anything I can specifically identify. The feelings of distraction keep recurring, and random thoughts seem to clutter my mind." I paused to reflect and we sat quietly for a brief period.

Then Catherine spoke.

16

"Mary Eliza, I have been thinking about the discussion we had last time, particularly your comments about voices pulling you to the waterfront and the old cemetery. This is much more tangible than the vagueness of your earlier experiences. I'm recalling the recording in your head – you described it using a Fats Domino analogy – the one that brought you to the coast originally. Have you been able to go any farther with your own interpretation of these more recent voices?"

Right off the bat, there it was. Dr. Catherine Arrington had a way of getting directly to the core.

So I offered my poem.

"I wrote this between four and six in the morning, two days ago. It was after our previous session on Monday. I had awakened on Tuesday about three in the morning. A very large, full moon was shining through the bedroom window and something was drawing me into its light. So I dressed and walked to the waterfront, where I remained watching the moon's reflection on the quiet water surface," I explained.

"The stream of light extended from where I sat on an old log that had washed ashore at the water's edge. The light stretched across the bay and it seemed to connect with the moon, which was making its descent toward the western horizon. It seemed as if I could feel the moon. We – the moon and I – were in direct communication. In spite of the night chill, I was transfixed by the gentle sound of waves caressing the shore. The moon's reflection penetrated my soul."

I paused before continuing.

"After forty-five minutes or so, I returned to the cottage, sat at the computer and the words just came out."

We sat quietly for a few minutes, then Catherine said, "If you would feel comfortable doing so, I would like you to read the poem."

So I did. The initial stanzas came out easily enough, but toward the poem's end I began to choke. Tears streamed down my cheeks, just as they had a few weeks back in the Old Burying Ground. I had difficulty finishing the reading.

Catherine passed the ever-at-hand box of tissues.

After several more moments of silence, she asked, "Mary Eliza, how do you feel about the experience at the waterfront and about having written the poem?"

"I'm not sure, Catherine. I don't know why it happened. That is to say, I'm not sure where these words came from. All I

17

recall is returning from the waterfront and, while walking home, I was repeatedly saying the first two lines. Those actually reflected what I experienced at the waterfront. The path to the strand was paved with shell. As I walked, there was a crunching sound that permeated the quiet of the night."

Working to express something I didn't really understand, I continued, "And of course, the moon's reflection did extend across the water. When I got back to the house and sat at the computer, the rest just came out. The soothing voice, the moon's warmth, and all ending with 'brings me through my night.' The whole process was a little disconcerting, since it was the light from the full moon that had awakened me and drew me to the water in the first place."

"Mary Eliza, your reading of the closing lines of the poem brought out some powerful emotions in reaction. Do you have thoughts about the phrase 'brings me through my night?' Why 'my' night? And to what do you think 'night' is referring?" Catherine asked in a soft voice.

The ultimate questions had been asked. I had known long before deciding to share my poem that this session would begin to open the box.

"Those are not simple questions, but I do have some vague ideas. They encompass Amelia Caroline Everitt, her Great-Grandmother Amelia Caroline Potter Everitt and, to a lesser extent, my brother Charles Langdon, all of whom are now dead," I said.

Catherine paused to consider for a moment.

"You have decided to reduce your time in the office, Mary Eliza, and I think that is a wise decision. Perhaps you should think about using some of that time to record your ideas in a journal. The writing might help you sort things out."

It was logical to suggest a journal, I knew it was a mechanism often used effectively to reach what was hidden.

I left Catherine's office with thoughts of journal writing foremost in my mind. Throughout my high school and college years I had kept a diary of sorts, so the process was known to me. But thinking back, I realized that most of what I had written was fairly trivial. So the current challenge would be to capture my innermost feelings and the events or circumstances behind the feelings.

Over the next few days, I did record some of my thoughts. However, when looking back over the journal, the thoughts seemed contrived, as if I had been forcing words on to the pages.

Repeatedly, I went to the water's edge, often in the quiet of night and under the moon's glow. I was searching for the voice that would bring me through at least this small part of "my night."

Then one evening, I was focusing upon the river's sounds while sitting in the bow of a small skiff that a friend kept tied at the old city dock when something – a voice – told me that the journal should not be a chronology of my thoughts. It was not from there that insight would come. Rather, the voice suggested that I tell Amelia Caroline's story, for in a way it was also my story and that of her Great-Grandmother and my brother Charles.

So Amelia Caroline's story will be told. I begin on August 15, 2002, four days prior to Amelia Caroline's death.

3

THE CHAIR

Amelia Caroline had been sitting on the porch, rocking, for what seemed like the full 184 years that the house had been in her family. In reality, it could not have been for more than ninety-nine years, three months and four days, that is assuming her nurse brought her into the sun on the day of her birth, May 11, 1903.

Actually, for her, this particular day had begun just prior to sunrise. As is known to all whose call to the encroaching day comes with the early gray light, sunrise in mid-August happens to be very early in the morning. It is that time of day when the fading of stars in the still-dark western sky is answered by a faint orange glow just over the eastern horizon. And as can be attested by all light sleepers and early risers, these celestial events are heralded throughout the summer by the chatter of feathered nestlings, early risers all, as they call out for the day's first meal of bugs, insects and a variety of invertebrates of all shapes and sizes.

Typical to her pattern, Amelia Caroline had remained in bed for a period of gentle wakefulness while she listened to the chirping of dawn's birds and the day's first sounds of life on the river. The deep-throated diesel engine of the Cape Fear Pilot sent subtle sonic waves that permeated the town as the boat pulled away from its slip in the old yacht basin and moved cautiously across the smooth, as yet undisturbed, water.

Following were five short, fog-muffled blasts of the horn from a tanker, the *Yang-San*, as it approached the old quarantine station in mid-river. The ship was awaiting arrival of the pilot who would guide it through the shifting river shoals and across the bar into the open Atlantic. This relationship between international sailing ships and the local river pilots had been going on since before charter of the town in 1797.

The tanker had crossed the bar and entered the harbor a couple of days earlier with a cargo destined for the Archer Daniels Midland plant, located three miles farther up the shore. It now was en route to the Gulf of Mexico, where it would take on cargo destined for the Far East.

I knew why Amelia Caroline valued this time of day so much. Each day the sounds differed. On some days, shrimpers with nets trailing behind in the water would sail quietly across the bay. Often, their harvest of the ocean's yield would be sold quickly in the late afternoon, right on the dock, to folks who came from seasonal homes in nearby vacation communities. In the fall, sport fishermen in sleek twenty-five-foot to thirty-foot fiberglass-hulled boats pushed by dual 250-horsepower outboard engines would roar past the channel buoys and out to sea at the first light. Landing a nice-sized king mackerel or a couple of grouper was their goal.

Listening to the morning sounds was always a pleasure for Amelia Caroline. However, after feeling "her morning wits had been gathered," as she would often say, she arose, put on her favorite terry robe as was her habit and went into the kitchen.

I was just completing preparations for our breakfast and had coffee ready. A cup of jet-black coffee, made palatable through copious amounts of fresh cream and several spoons of sugar, was prepared. Then Amelia Caroline made her traditional trek to the front of the house, out the screen door and into the rocker.

I joined her on the porch a few minutes later. We shared breakfast and shortly thereafter I departed to the hospital for morning rounds. The day was still young, so Amelia Caroline remained in her rocker, where she could watch and listen as the town came to life.

The rocking chair had been in Amelia Caroline's life for her full ninety-nine-plus years, and it was the same one used by her mother and her paternal grandmother. If family stories held any merit, the chair had even belonged to her Great-Grandmother Amelia Caroline Potter Everitt, who had come to live in this very house more than 180 years earlier and for whom Amelia Caroline was named.

According to family legend, Amelia Caroline's Great-Grandfather Sterling Byrd Everitt, a physician in town (and on occasion surgeon to soldiers stationed at the fort), had commissioned a local craftsman to make the chair as a wedding present for his bride in 1818.

The fort, or garrison as it was now called, was located just down the road at the waterfront. Other than for one of those roadside historic marker signs and one or two buildings of questionable history, physical evidence of the fort and the role it played in the early life of the community existed in archival form only.

Yet the family rocking chair, held together with wires that were strung from the rockers, through the seat, then up to the arms and over to the back, was still on the porch. It appeared as if the chair would remain so for a few more generations.

The old chair had so many wires holding it together that Amelia Caroline recalled as a teenager hearing her father jokingly tell folks it was the most wired chair east of the state penitentiary outside of Raleigh. At the time, the chair had already been in the family for over a century.

The comment by her father had been made shortly after electricity was introduced to the penal system. At the time, a lot of attention was being given in newspapers from cities across the state – including the hometown *Southport Standard* -- to the use of electricity and wires as the most humane method for capital punishment. It was a topic often discussed by folks and feelings ranged widely on the matter. Actually, at issue was not how to carry out capital punishment, but whether it should be practiced at all.

But the politicians in Raleigh found it more comfortable to discuss methodology rather than face the more difficult underlying philosophical question. The town, being isolated as it was at the coast, was not directly involved in the matter. However, the town was the county seat, and the number of resident lawyers ranked just below the number of fishermen and farmers. Consequently, political matters of any and all sort were always of great interest within the community.

It seemed ironic that her father, a physician whose life had been dedicated to saving folks from afflictions of every conceivable human making and from those physical discomforts that just come for no apparent reason from the natural world, would make jokes about how society disposed of some members. That is to say, to permanently remove -- for reason of criminal punishment -- persons with whom the general membership no longer wished to share life.

However, her Papa did joke. But it was one of the few times he ever spoke cynically for, under most circumstances, Amelia Caroline's father had been a man of genuine kindness and consideration. His had been character traits of inestimable value for one whose life was dedicated to tending the physical illnesses and emotional woes of others.

So on this special late-summer morning, Amelia Caroline slowly rocked the chair as she sipped her coffee. A warm feeling came to her as she listened to the sounds of the awakening town and thought back over the years she had spent with her father. As would be expected of someone whose life had spanned nearly a century, thoughts of the family and events of the past frequently flooded Amelia Caroline's mind. In fact, she had admitted to me that it was difficult for her to neglect the monsoon of memories that came whenever she sat on that old porch in the chair that had brought comfort to so many of her ancestors. After all, both the house and the chair had shared a lot of life and death in her family.

The chair had always been particularly special to Amelia Caroline. As far back as childhood memories would carry, sitting in the old chair on the porch gave Amelia Caroline the feeling of being linked to the past. Initially this perception had been a mystery to her, but as she advanced in age, the experience of connection with her ancestors and with ancestral events seemed to become both more frequent and more intensely meaningful.

I had first become aware of Amelia Caroline's experiences toward the end of the summer in 1983. My second year of residency in family medicine had drawn to a close, and I was spending my entire two-week summer vacation , as planned, sharing the house with Amelia Caroline. We, Amelia Caroline and I, had communicated several times over the early summer months and, by the time of my arrival for vacation, we were quite close. I had become quite comfortable addressing her as "Aunt Amelia."

We were sitting on the porch one of those mornings when Amelia Caroline turned to me and said, "Mary Eliza, I don't mean to alarm you, but there is something you should know. Often, while sitting here on the porch, I feel the presence of my Great-Grandmother and, on many occasions, she and I have had conversations. This is not just a recent phenomenon that can be attributed to age. It has occurred throughout most of my life."

Well, by that time I had come to know Amelia Caroline well enough to expect most anything, so I was not caught off-guard.

My response was quite direct, "When did you first experience the presence of your Great-Grandmother, Aunt Amelia?"

In a far-off voice, her life began to unfold.

Why, I was just six years old, but I remember it to this day. Papa had made arrangements with a woman here in town, Mrs. Piver, to give me some introductory music lessons. I don't recall much about the lessons, but Mrs. Piver had a daughter, Lillie Drew, who was just about my age. We became regular playmates and the best of friends, as only happens in childhood.

One day as I was gathering things to take over to Lillie Drew, our housekeeper, Mrs. Wescott, came to me and told me that I would have to remain at home. She said Lillie Drew would not be able to play that afternoon. I was disappointed but passed a pleasant enough day in the yard.

Late in the afternoon, Papa came home and asked me to sit with him in the parlor. He told me that Lillie Drew had gone to be with God and that I would not see her ever again. I cried for my friend and the loss of my playmate. Papa held me for comfort and Mrs. Wescott brought my favorite snacks. Then early in the evening, while still quite upset, I went to the porch and sat in what had become my favorite old rocker.

Mary Eliza, there was something about being in this chair that brought great comfort to me that evening. As I think back, it was as if a wise and kindly force was lifting my burden and removing my sadness. Looking back from today with all that has happened in between, I know it was Great-Grandmother who had come to me. She didn't speak, but I know it was she."

Over the years, I have come to believe the experience of communication with the past was directly related to this house and this old rocking chair.

4

THE HOUSE

As I learned over time, the actual date for construction of the house was not known. This was the case with many of the older houses in town, most of which were no longer occupied by either the original owners or their descendants. In fact, most houses were now owned by newcomers from the Northeast, folks who had come south beginning in the 1990s seeking the ideal retirement. They had left successful careers and prominent community positions for life in this small, sleepy "Southern" village.

Hypothetically, tranquility and simpler lives were their retirement goals. However, these goals can be elusive, particularly for those whose working years revolved around dynamic and high-energy lifestyles. Not unexpectedly, therefore, nervous energy was brought to the town in abundance by the retirees. As if having been programmed prior to arrival, the newcomers immediately became active in churches, attended city hall meetings and joined the local historical society. Soon they began to consider themselves experts on local matters and historians of great merit.

Those who considered themselves historians, driven by the energy that had characterized their previous lives, set goals for themselves to record for posterity all that had happened in the town since its origins. Invariably, this process began with great flourish as the newcomers rushed to the county seat in order to sort through dusty records and document the chronological histories of the houses they had recently acquired.

Upon completion of the research, the records were submitted to the Historical Society, which for a modest price issued plaques to be displayed just outside the front doors of the houses. These plaques attested to the ages of the dwellings. As a corollary, the houses were listed among the town's historic properties.

However, with few exceptions, the newly arrived had no prior ties to the town. Furthermore, before their involvement with the historical society, they had little interaction with Amelia Caroline or with others whose lives had been spent in town or nearby in the county. Yet the new residents talked with authority about the past. They spoke of people, events, properties and politics. Most notably, they took great pride in knowing exactly when and where their adopted houses had been constructed. They were quick to point out that their homes had been built using only the finest locally-fired clay bricks and prime lumber that had been harvested from nearby forests.

Ironically, most of the prime timber had been cut, sawed and shipped to places like New York City long before the majority of the houses in the small town had even been conceived. And the local brickyard had been a venture of relatively short life. Yet the newcomers were dedicated believers.

This posture on the part of newcomers amused Amelia Caroline, who knew -- based upon a lifetime of observation while sitting on the porch -- that nearly every man-made structure in town had been moved at least once. Few of the houses remained either at their original sites or in their original configurations.

For nearly a century, house moving seemed to be the chief form of amusement and entertainment in town. As the town grew from its rudimentary roots, properties were divided and subdivided, and businesses were opened or closed or shifted in location. It was a process typical of small-town evolution.

Locally, relocation of houses and buildings had begun prior to occupation of the town by Confederate troops during the Civil War. The activity continued until well after construction in 1913 of the Amuzu movie theater, which still stood all boarded up and neglected less than a block down the street from Amelia Caroline's front porch.

In the case of most houses, the original occupants were no longer on the earth, and their descendents had long since moved away to places like Wilmington or Charlotte. The end result of this process with respect to houses was the loss of documentation other than those few dusty records maintained by the county. In many cases, the chronologies compiled by the newcomers were simply land transfer records, with little hard-core information to verify the origins of the houses or other structures.

Amelia Caroline's house, on the other hand, had been part of the family nearly since the laying of the first hand-hewn, heart-pine floor joist. And if that was not enough to establish longevity, every room of the house was crammed full of memorabilia attesting to family and related residents since long before Abe Lincoln left his log cabin to become president. Included in the piles of stuff were documents, family keepsakes and records.

Of significant importance to Amelia Caroline was evidence that her Great-Grandmother Amelia Caroline Potter Everitt, the one for whom the chair had been made in 1818, had lived out nearly her entire adult life in the house. In addition, many of Amelia Caroline's great-aunts, great-uncles and distant cousins had been born and grown to adulthood while living in the house. Some had even died in the house, the earliest in 1831.

The house now was different from what it had been in those earlier days. Originally, the yard and garden had extended a full 320 feet to the street behind. This was the case for all one hundred of the originally platted properties in town. However in Amelia Caroline's case, some of the back property had been sold off by the family in order to clear the estate shortly after Great-Grandmother Amelia died at the age of seventy during hard times in 1873. Nevertheless, the property had still encompassed over one-quarter acre at the time of Amelia Caroline's birth.

The house originally was a classic two-story design with living room, parlor, pantry and dining area on the first floor. In the early 19th century when the house was built, cooking was done in a small building to the rear of the house. This was to minimize the chance of fire.

There were two rooms on each side of the long hall that extended from the front door through the house to the rear door. Paralleling the hall was a staircase that began just inside the front entry and led to the upper level. Four sleeping chambers on the second floor were arranged much as the rooms below.

Each of the floors had a porch that faced the street to the front. And each of the porches had several chairs in which the family could relax in the spring and the fall or on cool summer mornings. Amelia Caroline's favorite chair held a prominent place on the first-floor porch.

Amelia Caroline and I were on that porch having coffee and toast with orange marmalade one morning toward the end of my first week of vacation in 1983. The sounds of seagulls and motorboats came unobtrusively along with a gentle breeze from the waterfront.

"The local people would use the word 'salubrious' to describe this day," went through my mind. The breezes brought feelings of well being, and salubrious was the term used in the 1790s by Joshua Potts, the town's father, when describing the climate to his friends from Raleigh and elsewhere.

Having breakfast in the rocking chairs on the porch had quickly become our morning pattern together. Actually, I should say my pattern, for Amelia Caroline had been enjoying such mornings long before I came to visit.

We had both finished breakfast when I turned and commented, "Aunt Amelia, when looking around I see that several changes have been made to the house since your Great-Grandmother's days."

"Oh, yes, Mary Eliza. As the years passed and times changed, so did the house."

I leaned closer to capture this fascinating piece of history as she spoke.

Comparable modifications were taking place at many houses. The town had established a water plant shortly after the turn of the 20th century and the new service made indoor plumbing possible. Although water was available from the town, most houses still had wells and hand pumps on the back porches to get water. It was relatively costly to install the water lines to take advantage of the city utility, but Papa finally decided we needed to modernize.

I remember when several rooms were added, including a washroom with indoor plumbing, a toilet and a large claw-foot bathtub. Backyard privies were deemed by the city marshall to be both unsanitary and a public nuisance. I'm sure you can understand that reasoning. Residents, therefore, were being encouraged to modernize as a means of improving the image of the town.

In addition, I recall when the pantry was expanded. Originally the room was used to store food, linens and other necessities for food preparation.

And Papa had decided it was time we had a complete indoor cooking kitchen with a sink, running water and a coal-burning stove. Detached kitchens were becoming relics. By the time of my youth, the safety of cooking stoves had been improved and the improvements greatly reduced the probability of house fires.

So Papa had our home completely updated. However, in spite of the alterations, the house retained its original character.

I was very young at the time, but it is hard to forget all that commotion and excitement.

The house had been the home place for four generations of the Everitt family. And now in her one-hundredth year, it was where Amelia Caroline had lived her entire life – excepting a brief period when she was away for school.

Amelia Caroline's life was intimately entwined with both the house and the chair. This was so much the case that I now believed that, when sitting quietly on the porch in the rocker, she could actually feel the presence of her ancestors.

This perception was very real to her, as she had explained to me during that first summer together. Amelia Caroline apparently carried on conversations with her Great-Grandmother. Yet her Great-Grandmother had departed life during the previous century. In fact, her Great-Grandmother had passed away a full thirty years prior to Amelia Caroline's birth in 1903.

Even so, Amelia Caroline as a child had sensed a special gift bonding her to those in the past. Though she did not in her youth know about all of her ancestors, there was much in the house to bring past family members into her life. There were portraits from the 1820s, ferrotypes that preceded the War Between the States, and photographs from the 1880s and 1890s. The association was particularly acute with her Great-Grandmother, whose oil portrait still hung in the parlor.

The portrait of her Great-Grandmother had been commissioned in 1820 by Amelia Caroline's Great-Grandfather just two years after his marriage. The image, though slightly worn with age and yellowing with varnish, was that of a strikingly beautiful young woman. The face conveyed warmth and love. The soft, caring eyes were captivating and Amelia Caroline had been enthralled from her earliest years.

This was not the only image of her Great-Grandmother: There was also a tintype of both grandparents that had been prepared just prior to the death of her Great-Grandfather in 1855. Though stiff in pose as was the photographic practice at that time, the images were of two elegantly aged persons.

So throughout her youth, while surrounded by memories of family past, Amelia Caroline came to know her deceased Great-Grandmother a bit more each day. And it was this familiarity that gave rise to the feeling of connection when Amelia Caroline sat in the rocker on the porch.

This is what she had first experienced following the death of her childhood playmate back in 1909. But it wasn't until years later that Amelia Caroline experienced what she perceived to be direct communication. That is to say, her Great-Grandmother actually responded in conversation.

I was surprised to learn that the conversations, or rather Amelia Caroline's ability to communicate with her Great-Grandmother, were lost for more than twelve years beginning about 1959. According to Amelia Caroline, the disconnect was directly related to renovations of the house during her father's retirement years. This was told to me one evening toward the end of that summer vacation in 1983, as Amelia Caroline and I were walking along the waterfront after having eaten dinner at the Sea Captain Restaurant.

The Sea Captain Restaurant no longer exists, having been replaced by a condominium complex a few years back. But when it did exist, it was actually part of a mom-and-pop motel complex. The motel was a favorite for out-of-town fishermen and fisherwomen who wished to spend the night.

The restaurant, on the other hand, was of and for the local residents. This was not exclusive, for visiting fishermen also ate at the Sea Captain; but generally they preferred the morning breakfast offerings, which were hearty to say the least.

In the evenings, though, the crowd was of local folks who came to have dinner with friends and neighbors. The special at the restaurant that summer evening in 1983 was broiled flounder. The fish had been caught earlier in the day just offshore in the shallow waters where the river flows into the Atlantic Ocean.

"A seafaring town, comprised of seafaring men and seafaring women, knows where fresh fish are served," I thought, as we waited for our dinners to arrive. We enjoyed the meal and

Amelia Caroline introduced me to several of her old friends. The visits with friends put Amelia Caroline into a reflective mood, and she remained in that state as we began the walk back to the house.

We were walking down Brunswick Street, also known as "the alley," when Amelia Caroline began to speak.

I have been thinking back to the first conversation Great-Grandmother and I had. It was 1918. The time was one of great distress for many, as the nation was in the throws of World War I. One day when we have much more time, I will tell you the full story of what had transpired to lead up to this event.

The short version, however, is that a close friend of mine, a soldier, had died while in training here in the county. I was fifteen at the time, and I felt that his death was the direct result of irresponsible behavior on the part of the military. At any rate, my state of mind following his death was similar to that which I described following the death of Lillie Drew Piver.

As had happened with the passing of Lillie Drew, I went to the rocker. While sitting in the chair, a voice spoke to me and I knew.

"Amelia Caroline, I am here with you," she said.

"Oh, Great-Grandmother, I am so sad," I immediately replied.

Amelia Caroline paused in her story for a moment. It was clear that she still carried pain from those early events in her life. She reached into a pocket in her dress for a tissue, with which she wiped her eyes. Then she continued.

Immediately, a great calm came over me and we talked. The contact that evening was the beginning of conversations which continued over the next forty years. Then in 1959, when I was fifty-six years old, the communication came to an end for reasons I did not understand, at least I did not understand until 1972. I was in my seventieth year when once again Great-Grandmother and I spoke.

The renewal of communication took place one summer evening while I sat on the front porch in the old rocker. I was particularly pleased that evening, for earlier that day in the late afternoon, construction work on the house had been completed. I had arranged for the work a few weeks earlier. In my opinion, *the work was necessary to free the house from what I considered the confines of mid-20th-century modernization.*

My goal was to restore the house to a condition resembling that of my youth. Well, not exactly my youth, but prior to 1959 when I lost communication. I felt certain the state of the house during those earlier years was one in which the family from the past felt most at home.

Amelia Caroline's decision to remodel the house, or de-remodel as was the actual case, had not been made impulsively. Nor was it because she had become disenchanted with the color of the bathroom linoleum or had begun to tire of the pattern in the kitchen cabinets. Such motivations are often the case with folks who wish to bring change to their lives.

In contrast, Amelia Caroline's decision had been made following a suspicion on her part that the house in its 1970s' state was no longer recognized by her ancestors. After having been the common family ground for over a century and a half, something about the house had become a barrier between Amelia Caroline and her predecessors, the very ones to whom she had felt uniquely bonded. But the feeling of closeness, that is the presence of her ancestors, had waned during the busyness of mid-life.

This absence of connection with her ancestors had been somewhat evident to Amelia Caroline for several years prior to the death of her father, with whom she had shared the house for almost seventy years. And although troubled by the disconnect, its source had not been obvious.

Furthermore, Amelia Caroline in the 1960s had reached that stage in life when responsibility for others, her father in this case, was all consuming. Her father, Reuben Everitt, having been born in the early 1870s, was then well on his way to celebrating one hundred years of life. And as most people who approach the century mark, assistance was required for many routine aspects of daily life. Amelia Caroline was pleased to provide such care.

However, since so much of her effort had been spent supporting her father in his advanced years, there hadn't been time either to worry about philosophic matters or to seek answers from the past. It wasn't until a few months after her father died in 1971 at the age of ninety-nine that Amelia Caroline concluded there had to be a problem with the house.

And finally, she concluded that the problem was related to the renovations undertaken by her father during his early retirement years.

5

THE FAMILY

The day I met Amelia Caroline to arrange for my summer vacation back in 1983, she greeted me, and in that greeting she told me three things.

First, she said that she had for many years looked forward to the day of our meeting.

Second, I learned that the day of our appointment was her eightieth birthday, and it was a day we would share as if we had been close for my entire life.

Then finally, Amelia Caroline told me we were related. I was a bit surprised to say the least. As I crossed the porch to where she was sitting, my mind automatically went to the Old Burying Ground and the grave where Richard Langdon had been laid to rest in 1847. That grave was next to a smaller one where Richard Langdon, Junior, was buried. He had died twenty-one years earlier than his father at the age of seventeen months.

"The markings of a family," was my first thought.

"If I am related to that Langdon family of 150 years back, how does that link me to Amelia Caroline Everitt?" was the next thought.

As it turns out, Amelia Caroline is not actually my aunt. She and I are cousins of sorts. I say "of sorts" because our family linkage goes back over 180 years.

Determining how two people are related in contemporary time, when thinking back to ancestors who were directly related nearly two centuries ago, is complicated at best. However, I did learn later in the day that Amelia Caroline's Great-Grandmother is the key link between Amelia Caroline and me.

Although this seemed quite clear when explained to me, other relationships among the various branches of the family over many years have become complex. I'll attempt to describe the major aspects of our relationship as they were explained to me. Bear in mind, the linkages may seem a bit confusing. The confusion stems both from time, nearly two centuries, and the many gaps that exist in the genealogical records.

Amelia Caroline and I were finishing our birthday celebration lunch on the day of my initial appointment with her. Just a few hours had passed since she had told me we simply could not be formal with each other. We were enjoying pineapple-upside-down cake, which she said had always been her favorite. Interestingly, it also was among my favorites.

I turned to Amelia Caroline and thanked her for including me in the special occasion, then said, "When I came up the steps earlier, you announced that we were related. I have long suspected a link between my family and the Langdon family members who are buried in the old cemetery. I also have noted, during my many brief visits here over the past three years, the Everitt family plot.

"I'm now pleased to know that Amelia Caroline Potter Everitt, who died in 1873 and is buried in the family plot, is your Great-Grandmother. But I don't have a clear understanding of our relationship."

Having completed our celebratory meal, Amelica Caroline sat back and began to fill in the blanks for me.

As you can tell, Mary Eliza, my entire life has been spent in the midst of family mementos and memories. My father often shared his recollections of the past, and in my youth there were in town a number of elderly people who still recalled my Great-Grandmother and her sister-in-law, Mary Eliza Everitt. The two women are the keys to our relationship. But let me start at the beginning.

The family, meaning the Everitt family, first came to the region before the town existed. To my knowledge, the exact year is not known, but it was late in the 1780s. The nation at the time was just a few years old. The original member of the local family was Dr. Reuben Everitt who, as well as I can determine, came from the region of Litchfield, Connecticut. For reasons you will come to learn, I will refer to him as Dr. Everitt, Sr.

He was related to the military and was assigned to be surgeon to the troops stationed at Fort Johnston. At the time of his arrival, Dr. Everitt, Sr. was about twenty-five or twenty-six years of age and he was married.

During the early years here, Dr. Everitt, Sr. and his wife had two children. The first, Sterling Byrd, was born in 1791; the second, Mary Eliza, was born in 1793.

I have never known who their mother was. Perhaps she died during childbirth. I do know that some years later, actually in November of 1800, Dr. Everitt, Sr. married a young widow, Judith Flare, of Wilmington. The family remained here and the two children grew to adulthood.

The important point from this is that Sterling became my Great-Grandfather and his sister Mary Eliza became the wife of Richard Langdon. This was the same Richard Langdon who died in 1847 and lies at rest in the Old Burying Ground.

Viewing the family from the most simplistic perspective, Mary Eliza Everitt Langdon is your Great-Grandmother, whereas her sister-in-law, Amelia Caroline Potter Everitt, is my Great-Grandmother. Looking again at this relationship from a most simplistic viewpoint, you and I are cousins.

Though our linkage is quite clear when seen in this most simple light, many of the family relationships are a bit obscure. This is particularly true for the Langdon branch of the family. After all, there are fifty-some years' difference in our ages, and many decades have passed since the days of my Great-Grandmother and her sister-in-law.

On the other hand, I know the Everitt family lineage with absolute certainty. Edward Everitt, the son of Amelia Caroline Potter Everitt, is my grandfather. His son Reuben is my father. The linkage between generations is documented by all that exists in this house. We have always been right here.

The Langdon family, in contrast to the Everitt family, began to drift away from town even before the death of Richard.

Mary Eliza, your Great-Grandmother many generations removed, even left town to be with one of her married daughters following Richard's passing.

Over the ensuing decades, others moved westward into Tennessee, Ohio and even Minnesota. In the century and a half since Richard died, many of your predecessors have been unknown to those of us who remained here. As a consequence of the migration, the Langdon family archives are scattered from here to Greenfield, Indiana, your hometown.

During the course of that first day, Amelia Caroline and I touched on many other topics, mostly unrelated to family matters. She was determined to secure the bond between us, and to assure me that I would feel at home with her in the house while vacationing later in the summer.

Our conversations about the family resumed during that vacation of 1983, and the dialogue took an interesting turn toward the end of my two weeks with her. The surprise came on the evening of our dinner at the Sea Captain Restaurant.

I have already mentioned the revelation by Amelia Carolina of conversations with her Great-Grandmother and the details of the first conversation that she shared as we were leaving the restaurant. Since I wanted to learn more about the conversations and since Amelia Caroline felt quite at ease being out that evening, we spent about thirty minutes on the waterfront.

The tide was low, and we paused to watch children playing in the sand at the water's edge. Some of the youngsters were probing the sand with dried shafts from reeds that grew in the low tidal pools and against the berms where the front edge of high tide melted into the strand.

Amelia Caroline, sitting next to me in one of the park swings, smiled as she watched. The activity was one she had seen on many occasions over her lifetime. Then she spoke, not directly to me, but as if she were verbalizing her thoughts of the moment.

"How nice to be young once again and to play in the surf or dig in the sand with full expectation of finding treasure at any minute. Youth finds such joy in its freedom to pursue simple pleasures," she observed.

It became clear to me that Amelia Caroline was still in a reflective mood, so I decided to bring up a topic that had been on my mind ever since our interview day.

"Aunt Amelia, when I arrived at the house back in May, you greeted me and said 'I have known you for many years and I have long awaited this day.' We have never talked about how you knew me, knew of me, or knew that one day we would meet," I said.

Amelia Caroline replied almost instantly. "Why Mary Eliza, I was told about you and your family by Great-Grandmother!"

"When did that happen, Aunt Amelia?" I continued, hoping she would elaborate.

It was not so long ago, Mary Eliza, you were a teenager at the time. The conversation was one of several that Great-Grandmother and I had following my father's death. I don't recall the exact date, but I do remember the circumstances.

Earlier in the day I had been on the sidewalk down the street from the house when our neighbor, Mr. Perry, came out of his door. He lived at the other end of the block. We had known each other for most of our lives and I had enjoyed company with his wife for many years.

Mr. Perry had just returned from Tabor City where he had gone to attend the funeral of his younger brother. The brother was a confirmed bachelor who passed away unexpectedly at the age of fifty-five. The brother's death had left Mr. Perry alone in the world. Though he had been married for over thirty-five years, his wife had passed on a few years earlier. Their only child had died of diphtheria at an early age.

When Mr. Perry saw me on the sidewalk, he came over to me and, out of the blue he said, "Amelia Caroline, it looks as if we are the last of the Mohicans."

For many, this comment might have seemed a bit inappropriate, but it was the kind of statement I had come to expect from Mr. Perry. He had, throughout his life, been one of those people who cover their pain with flippant remarks. We spoke briefly about the loss of my father and the loss of his brother. Then I walked back to the house.

Later that evening, while sitting in the chair, I began to think about what Mr. Perry had said.

I was the last of the family living in town. Furthermore, as far as I knew there were no living relatives elsewhere either. A sadness came over me, as I thought of all the family history that would be lost upon my death.

I sat in the rocker and remained in that state of mind for some time. Then without expectation on my part, Great-Grandmother spoke.

"Amelia Caroline, you have been deep in thought this evening. I sense a sadness. Would you like to talk?"

"Oh, yes, Great-Grandmother," was my response. I then told her of the encounter with Mr. Perry and why I had become so upset.

"But you will not be alone, Amelia Caroline," was her reply.

41

So I came to know you, Mary Eliza, as a result of that conversation.

6

FATHER AND DAUGHTER

Amelia Caroline and her father had been especially close, the kind of closeness that comes from a lifetime of sharing each day's joys as well as sorrows. In addition, the two had similar educational experiences and professional lives.

At the time of his daughter's birth, Dr. Reuben Everitt had recently completed his studies at the Louisville Medical College in Kentucky, and he had returned to the family home in Southport to begin practice. Accompanying Reuben was his young wife Charlotte Louise James, a native of Louisville.

Reuben was approaching thirty-one, an age that was quite a bit older than most who were just entering the profession. This late entry into the profession was not due to any deficiency on the part of Dr. Everitt. Rather, it was the result of economic hard times that had befallen the nation during the latter years of the 19th century.

Reuben had known since his earliest memory that medicine was to be his calling. After all, the family had had at least three prior generations of physicians. The earliest of them, Reuben's Great-Grandfather and namesake, Dr. Reuben Everitt, Sr., had been physician to the town in addition to being surgeon for troops at the fort.

For a while he had even operated an apothecary in Wilmington. Dr. Everitt, Sr. had been quite enterprising, for his apothecary had offered considerably more than medications, as I had learned from Amelia Caroline.

One day in 1986, after I had completed my medical training and moved to Southport to begin my practice, Amelia Caroline and I were rummaging through family documents that had been kept in an old cedar-lined shipping trunk. I remember the year, because I had recently been notified of my Board Certification in Family Practice.

43

Among the myriad of papers, the trunk had shipping bills dating to the middle of the 19th century, as well as pages from two volumes of the *Wilmington Gazette,* dated 1804.

The newsprint was brown and shredded somewhat at the edges. The paper was extremely fragile. One hundred and eighty years is a long time. Amelia Caroline was extremely careful as she handed the pages to me.

"I first learned of the items in this trunk just prior to my sixth birthday," Amelia Caroline explained. "Until that time, the trunk had been locked. Papa, however, had decided that I could read well enough and that I was old enough to appreciate some of the old family documents. As a birthday surprise he opened the trunk and, just as you and I are doing today, Papa and I rummaged through the treasures."

Both of the news volumes, one dated Tuesday, August 7, and the other dated Tuesday, November 6, had advertisements placed by Dr. Everitt, Sr., Amelia Caroline's Great-Great-Grandfather. The headings in themselves bespoke much of the family and the times. I was amazed at what followed.

The August 7, 1804, advertisement read :

FOR SALE AT THE STORE OF

R. EVERITT

BRANDY, *Cogniac*
Madeira, Sherry, Port
Cordials of Many Kinds
Pickled Walnuts, Capers, Preserved Pine Apples
Currents, Raisins in Boxes, Turkey Figs
Almonds, Soft Shell
Mustard
Sweet Oil
Split and Whole Peas
Tongues and Sound in Kegs
Salmon, Cheese, Chocolate
Leaf sugar, Best Philadelphia
Soap, candles, Spermaceti Oil
Maccabau Snuff
Hingham Ware, consisting of Tubs, Sifters,
Measures, Boxes, Barrel Covers, etc.
Hyson Tea
Shrub - Vinegar
NEW - ENGLAND **RUM** in barrels

Best Philadelphia Butter, by the Firkin or
less quantity
*Chamber Lamps, of very safe kind, and low
price*
Essence of Spruce
and
MEDICINES AS USUAL

That initial advertisement in the *Wilmington Gazette* was followed three months later, on November 6, 1804, by the following announcement:

JUST RECEIVED
By the Schooner Hope, from New York
AND FOR SALE AT THE STORE OF
R. EVERITT

REAL Cogniac Brandy
Madeira, Port, Sherry and Claret
Brown Stout, Best Strong Ale
India White Sugar
Muscadel Raisins
Turkey Figs, Prunes
Mustard
Brown Soap
Windsor Do.
Best English Ketchup
Quince Sauce
Nutmegs

While I was reading, Amelia Caroline said, "Papa's Great-Grandfather was not the only member of the family to be so distinguished and successful in his profession. Charles Everitt, Papa's uncle and oldest brother to Papa's father Edward, was the first physician from the town and from the family to earn a formal degree at a college of medicine.

"Uncle Charles had completed his education a full decade prior to the beginning of the Civil War. The distinction brought to the family by Uncle Charles was to be expected, for he was following in the footsteps of his father. Great-Grandfather Sterling had been practicing medicine for over twenty-five years at the time Uncle Charles entered medical school.   Furthermore, Great-Grandfather Sterling was highly regarded both for his skill as a physician and for his contribution to the town through service in many governmental and civic roles.   It was no surprise, therefore, that medicine was to be Papa's career."

These remarks by Amelia Caroline, as it turned out, were just a lead-in to the story of her father's early life. Amelia Caroline shared the stories she had learned of his marriage and told me how her unique relationship with her father came to be.

Papa was born in 1872 and, to the best of my knowledge, had an uneventful childhood. At the age of six, he began studies at the Smithville Academy. Though erratic in its operation, the Academy did provide an adequate educational foundation.

Then at the age of sixteen, Papa started a three-year apprenticeship under the joint tutelage of Dr. Walter Curtis and Dr. D. I. Watson, both physicians in town.

Dr. Watson also operated one of the local pharmacies. Dr. Curtis, in addition to his medical practice, served as chief medical officer to the Federal Maritime Quarantine Station. The quarantine station, with its isolation facilities and hospital, was located in mid-river a short distance from the town.

As a result of these experiences, Papa was exposed to numerous aspects of medicine while an apprentice. In addition to operation of a pharmacy, Papa had a unique experience that few aspiring doctors could boast: he was introduced to the brand new field of Medical Epidemiology.

Information regarding the worldwide spread of disease was being accumulated by the Federal Maritime Quarantine Service, and Papa had spent many days with Dr. Curtis at the quarantine station out in the river.

Toward the end of his apprenticeship, Papa enrolled at Wake Forest College. He was nineteen at the time. As you know, Mary Eliza, Wake Forest College in Papa's day was not located in Winston-Salem as it is today. When Papa attended, it was a small but progressive school located in Wake County just outside the state capital of Raleigh. Papa was drawn to Wake Forest College because a few years before, in 1886, the school had introduced a two-year course of studies preparatory to the formal study of medicine. Papa's intention was to transfer to the Louisville Medical College following completion of the two-year preparatory course at Wake Forest College.

I don't know if you had an opportunity during your years in Winston-Salem to look into the early history of Wake Forest College. By early, I mean prior to the relocation of the medical school and later the undergraduate college to Winston-Salem. To my understanding, the pre-medical curriculum of 1886 was one of the first of its kind in the nation, and it had become outstanding even in the short time before Papa enrolled in 1891. Papa told me he attended classes in Physics, Chemistry, Physiology, Botany, Mathematics and Latin while there.

I suspect, had Wake Forest College begun its formal medical school prior to 1902 when it was actually chartered, Papa probably would have remained right there in Wake County for his full medical training. However, the timing was not right and Papa followed the advice given by his mentors.

I'm getting a bit ahead of myself, so let me step back to the early 1890s when Papa, as a young man, was initially considering his educational options. As I mentioned, foremost on his list at that time was the Louisville Medical College. The school was one of seven medical colleges that were located in Louisville in the 1890s, but it was the most highly regarded at the time. Today, it no longer exists as a free-standing college, for it was purchased in 1909 by the University of Louisville and became part of the modern University of Louisville School of Medicine.

The decision to study at the Louisville Medical College had been made by Papa under the advice and with the support of Dr. D.I. Watson. Dr. Watson had studied and received his medical degree from that school some years earlier.

Had things gone as planned, Papa would have been twenty-two at the time of matriculation. This desire, however, was put on hold for several years. The nation was devastated by a financial collapse in 1893.

For the most part, the townspeople were immune to the financial crisis. Daily needs were met through local farming, fishing or forestry. Papa said that years later the town would pride itself on the fact that not one of its citizens went cold or hungry as a result of the hard times. The town, however, was not entirely exempt from the downturn. Several regional banks closed, including the Bank of Hanover in Wilmington.

It was this failure and a concurrent run on the Wilmington Savings and Trust that resulted in dashing many dreams. Included were aspirations of local leaders who envisioned a dynamic city growing from the small town.

On a much less grand scale, Papa's desire to complete formal medical training was delayed. The time, however, was not lost. Papa simply continued working as an apprentice under Dr. Watson and Dr. Curtis, and he learned much about hands-on medicine. Ultimately, financial conditions improved and, in 1899, Papa entered Louisville Medical College. As a reward for the years of service to them, both of Papa's mentors help pay the educational costs.

Papa's graduation from medical school and his return to the town in 1902 were heralded by the entire community. This I learned from many friends and neighbors as I grew up. The community had, since the earliest days, taken pride in the fact that physicians resided here even before the town existed. Papa was one of their own.

By the time Papa began practice, the town knew that his career choice had been no coincidence, and they knew that three prior generations of healers occupied major branches on Papa's family tree. In fact many folks, particularly those attuned to history, knew that the family's medical service in the community began when Great-Great-Grandfather Reuben settled in the region just a few years after the War of Independence.

Amelia Caroline's story continued for nearly an hour as we sat amidst various old documents we had taken from the trunk. Her narrative included several side anecdotes. Many of these were not directly related to the story being told, but I had grown to love our discussions, and I always found something new and interesting in the reflections. So I sat quietly while she continued.

Shortly after my father and his young wife, my mother Charlotte Louise, returned to town in 1902 and took up residence in the family homestead, the promise of a child was fulfilled and I began my journey into life. However, my birth was not without tragic cost, as was often the case at the time. I learned many of the details through Mama's midwife, Hattie Frink, during my late childhood years.

Mama's pregnancy had been uneventful, except for a brief period during which she experienced episodes of abdominal discomfort and nausea. At such times she took counsel from Papa and advice from experienced women in the community, including her mother-in-law. Under this counsel, she acquiesced to her burden. As was the case with most women of that era, Mama accepted discomfort as the normal price to pay when honoring God's expectation for women.

As a general rule, Mama's discomforts were mild and the inconvenience was relieved by taking lime water. If she felt poorly late in the day, iced champagne was the preferred remedy. When the symptoms persisted, thus disrupting her normal daily routine, she would be offered oxalate of cerium. This was one of the old remedies, a mild anti-emetic, which served to curb the nausea.

Occasionally, however, the symptoms progressed to include excessive pain and vomiting. At such times Papa, with concurrence of Hattie Frink and in consultation with Dr. Watson, would prescribe more aggressive treatment.

I should point out that, although quite different from today's standards, Papa's ministrations were in accordance with the highest medical standards of the day. So Mama was administered tincture of nux vomica. This was a general tonic containing strychnine. The treatment was considered useful in virtually all conditions of debility. According to the chemical manufacturer, this included "those debilitations particular to the female condition." When on rare occasions this intervention failed, relief was guaranteed through administration of laudanum.

It was with this care that Mama progressed through her pregnancy. Then during the early morning hours of May 11, 1903, I announced my intention to leave the security of the womb and embark upon independent life. The delivery, carried out by light from an oil lamp and the light provided by a yet-to-wane full moon, was without incident. Both Grandmother Everitt and Mama's mother, who had traveled from Louisville to attend the joyous occasion, were present. The delivery, as planned, was attended by Hattie Frink, who was a skilled midwife. Mama was in good hands, for Hattie, over the previous five decades, had delivered nearly seventy-five percent of the town's babies.

According to Hattie Frink, Mama was quick to recover from the immediate trauma of delivery. For three days, she shared the joy of my birth with the many neighbors who came to call. Apparently I was strong, healthy and active. Hattie said that both my presentation and my birth under the radiance of the *full moon were portents noted by those sensitive to such. But their full significance would not be realized for many years.*

The euphoria following my birth evidently grew with each new visitor, and by all reports Papa was the most proud father they had ever known. All were convinced that the family had been blessed with my life. But that joy did not last, for within a few days great sadness fell upon the house.

Though every care had been taken to protect Mama during pregnancy, and she seemed so well following my birth, a fever came on suddenly.

On the fourth day after the delivery, she was overtaken by violent chills. These were accompanied by a great thirst. The following day Hattie Frink, who had agreed to remain in attendance as a nurse, noticed a uterine discharge. It was the dreaded sign of childbed fever.

Three days later Mama's mind became clouded and delirium set in. When Hattie told me this tale, she was aware of the sadness it brought me, and she was quick to point out that the delirium mercifully relieved Mama of the knowledge that she would soon depart this world. And it spared her the realization that she would be leaving behind an infant daughter whom she hardly knew.

It was, therefore, under this tragic circumstance that my life began. And it was this fateful beginning that colored the course of my life and that of my father for the next sixty-eight years.

At this point in the recitation, Amelia Caroline paused, which provided an opportunity for me to ask, "Aunt Amelia, how did you feel when you heard the full story?"

Oh, Mary Eliza, so many years have passed, it is hard for me to recall exactly. Indeed, as Hattie Frink perceived, I was quite upset. And as a child, there were thoughts of my having been responsible for Mama's death. But I never knew Mama, except through conversations with the many women who helped raise me, so my feelings were mixed. Still, there is even today a small residual question, perhaps even sadness, and I sometimes wonder how life would have been if circumstances had been different.

REUBEN'S STRUGGLE

The death of Charlotte Louise was devastating to Reuben. He was well aware of the risk for childbed fever. Many young women -- and often their newborns -- died during or shortly after childbirth. However, Reuben could not imagine such a fate for his wife.

He was plagued with soul-wrenching questions, "Hadn't the child, my own daughter, been delivered with the greatest care? And my beloved Charlotte Louise had entered her confinement with good health and in a cheerfully expectant frame of mind. Then following the delivery, Charlotte's general constitution was evidenced by a seemingly quick recovery and the immediate return of her good spirits. How could she ever succumb to such a fate?"

Reuben, with all of his medical training and experience, agonized. Yet the townspeople, those who had little knowledge of medicine and lived life as it came, one day at a time, usually seemed to understand or at least accept.

I came to realize this dichotomy during my first year of practice in town. Thomas Hankins, one of my elderly patients, was in the office for a check of his heart, which was entering an irreversible state of failure. During the exam, Mr. Hankins could tell that, as a young physician, I was distressed in the knowledge that little could be offered in the way of relief for his condition.

He looked me in the eye and said, "Dr. Langdon, death has no favorites and takes what it can. Often this is in spite of our intentions and ministrations to deny death its victory."

The statement and the manner in which it was delivered took me by surprise. Here was a man whose education was far less than my own, yet he clearly understood his own physical circumstances and philosophically had come to grips with life's ultimate reality. I was unsure how to respond, so I simply placed my hand gently on his and thanked him. The conversation was a lesson for me, and it was one upon which I have reflected numerous times over the years.

Upon seeing the early signs of childbed fever – the onset of chills, flushing and fever -- Reuben acted as his profession had prepared him. However, though applying all the skill and knowledge available to a young physician of that time, he was powerless to save his wife.

Reuben labored tirelessly for three days directing the care. Hattie Frink and Charlotte's mother remained at the bedside. Continuously, cold sponges and alcohol were applied to Charlotte's body to relieve the fever. Every few hours, freshly prepared doses of quinine and strychnine sulfate were administered. Yet in spite of Reuben's efforts, his wife's condition deteriorated, until death brought release.

The loss of Charlotte left Reuben in a deeply saddened and troubled state. His anguish increased with the passage of time. Again and again, the events of Amelia Caroline's birth passed through his mind. The death of his wife came to represent failure: both failure on his part as a physician and failure of the medical profession as a whole. After all, throughout the ordeal he had consulted with the most experienced physicians in town, yet to no avail.

The torment was so all-consuming that Reuben came to question his chosen role as a physician. For several weeks he saw no patients, fearful that his ministrations would be inadequate. He even began to entertain thoughts that medical intervention into the human situation might be detrimental under any circumstance.

Reuben's mind drifted to the extreme, "Should I even continue as a physician? Perhaps there is a valid reason why most folks distrust doctors. After all, home remedies, folk medications and patent medicines are always the first treatments tried when sickness comes. I know from experience that folks, more often than not, recover from illness without the assistance of doctors. Are the services we offer, other than for setting bones and stitching wounds, of any value?"

At the time, families often consulted physicians only after all else had failed. The medical profession was considered by many of the less-educated to be a final resort. And folks knew that physician intervention frequently culminated in death.

"Is the profession simply a handmaiden for the Reaper? And am I just an implement of its purpose?" were the thoughts in Reuben's mind. Irrational as the thoughts were, he remained in this frame of mind for some time.

Reuben knew, of course, that the great distrust of the medical profession pertained mostly to the outlying county where poor farm families lived in relative isolation. It was also the case in that part of town bordering the waterfront docks where a population of downtrodden folks lived. This knowledge, however, did not serve Reuben in his distressed state of mind. He overlooked the high esteem to which he was held by the townspeople and his mind remained mired in negative thoughts.

Reuben's only escape from these thoughts during the early days following the death of his wife came while giving attention to his young daughter, for whom daily care was necessitated. Initially, Charlotte Louise's mother and her mother-in-law, Emily Everitt, had provided much of the care. Charlotte's mother, being greatly saddened over the death of her daughter, felt she could not remain in Southport, so she returned to her home and family in Louisville following the funeral. However, Reuben's mother agreed to provide help until permanent arrangements could be made.

Immediately following the birth, a wet nurse had been engaged by Hattie Frink. This had been to allow recovery time for Charlotte Louise. Then following the death, the wet nurse agreed to remain and tend Amelia Caroline's needs on a long-term basis. After several weeks, a mature woman, Mrs. Emma Wescott, the widow of a fisherman who had drowned during a storm at sea, also came to live in the house to care for Amelia Carolie and serve as housekeeper.

So time passed, and Reuben's pain over the loss of his wife slowly eased, but questions regarding the adequacy of the medical profession in general and his own training did not fully go away.

Then one day, some months after the death of his wife, Reuben found his young daughter in a distressed state. He had been having breakfast on the front porch when Mrs. Wescott approached and said, "Doctor, you must visit the nursery. The child is listless and she turns away from the wet nurse. She neither takes the breast nor accepts other nourishment. Her cheeks are flushed and she seems feverish."

Such symptoms, particularly when of short duration, were not unusual in a young infant. Amelia Caroline's condition, however, was one which Mrs. Wescott felt required medical attention.

Several diseases had recently been reported in the county. Early cases of whooping cough and scarlatina had been rumored in the region of Town Creek, a dozen or so miles upriver. And smallpox was always a concern when ships came into the harbor.

Reuben was torn between his fear of failure as a physician and the agony he experienced upon seeing the discomfort of his child. Amelia Caroline was the only link to his beloved wife. Finally acknowledging there was no alternative, Reuben reached within himself and found the strength to intervene as a physician on Amelia Caroline's behalf. Yet his ministrations were basic and conservative. Within a brief period, Amelia Caroline returned to a normal happy state.

Some time later, thinking back to the event, Reuben realized that his care for Amelia Caroline had been less medical than it had been simply reaching out to touch the life of another. Reuben found that simply being present and holding the child seemed to help. He was conveying, without specific intent, the healing power that comes simply from human care and love. His infant daughter was comforted and she soon returned to health.

It was, in fact, this single interaction that established a unique and enduring relationship between Amelia Caroline and her father. A special bond had evolved from the experience, and it was this bond that guided their shared lives until Reuben's death in 1971.

Interestingly, the interaction between Reuben and his daughter during her time of illness gave direction to the manner in which Reuben would approach his entire professional life. The practice of medicine had, for nearly two decades, been evolving as scientific knowledge provided answers and direction to the profession. In many situations, the classic model of the physician as a healer was being displaced by science.

Yet Reuben realized, based upon interaction with his young daughter, that the skills of the classic healer, which encompassed understanding, care and compassion, were as important as the newly identified scientific interventions. It was this realization which directed the balance of his life.

So it was for sixty-eight years that Reuben and Amelia Caroline would share not only their lives, but also the front porch and the rockers.

As is often the case in small, rural communities, the majority of events comprising those years were as mundane as the sandy soil and live oak trees which dominated the local environment. Townspeople for the most part were born, enjoyed an uneventful childhood marred only by a few broken bones or a bad case of chicken pox. Ultimately they married, raised a new crop of children, then became old enough to while away their remaining days on the waterfront or the back stoop of the house, all the while anticipating the final reward that awaited them.

Amelia Caroline's life, however, would not follow the expected pattern.

8

MESSAGES

"Charles died in Vietnam, and so did Louis Gabral, his closest friend in the unit!" I finally blurted out.

I felt as if a howitzer charge had just exploded somewhere in my deepest mind, and the projectile came out in the form of this emotionally charged statement.

The day was Tuesday, following our break-through session on the preceding Thursday, and Dr. Catherine Arrington and I had been talking for a little over thirty minutes when the explosion occurred in my head.

Our session this day began with polite inquiry by each of us about the other's weekend activities.

In the intervening days since our previous session, I had spent numerous hours walking about town and repeatedly strolling through Franklin Square Park. The park, located in the center of town adjacent to the courthouse and other city administrative buildings, was designated in the 1797 town charter to be used for "civic, fraternal and religious purposes."

Over the weekend, the first arts and crafts fair of the fall season had taken place in the park. Amelia Caroline and I had always enjoyed seeing the exhibits at the fair, although we rarely purchased anything. Yet the art fair was a place and a time when friends could meet, and that always was pleasurable. Typically after spending time at the fair, she and I would walk to the waterfront to enjoy ice cream, children and sea gulls.

I repeated that pattern this past weekend. Perhaps it was in memory of Amelia Caroline.

Catherine's weekend had been consumed by time with her two children. They were six and nine years old, ages which require considerable hands-on attention. School had begun just after Labor Day, so there were all those little school-related

57

demands and activities. Her youngest child, Erin, had entered the first grade, which can be a traumatic event for some children and Erin was no exception. So over the weekend, Catherine had devoted a fair amount of energy stoking Erin's confidence and enthusiasm.

This neighborly interaction between us lasted just a few minutes. Then we turned to matters at hand -- my status and progress.

The opening discussion seemed to me to be benign in nature. Catherine inquired about general, but pertinent, topics such as physical health and sleep patterns. She asked whether there had been some relief from the mental distractions I had described during our earlier meetings.

As we talked, however, the discussion gradually shifted from my health to my writing. This brought us back to the poem I had shared with her during our meeting five days earlier.

Catherine became more pointed in her questioning. "How are you doing with your journal, Mary Eliza?" she asked.

"I try to write for a few minutes each day, Catherine. Most of what I've written has focused upon Amelia Caroline, her life in, and her relationship to, the house with the rocking chairs on the front porch. I've also touched upon family relationships, but just to a limited degree."

"Has the exercise been beneficial for you?"

"I'm not certain. When I left you following our last session, my plan had been to just record my thoughts as and when they came. I interpreted your suggestion that I write a journal as being a mechanical exercise. The physician/scientist in me concluded, 'That's easy enough, just keep track of what is going on in your head.'

"This approach, I soon learned, was not getting me anywhere. Journal notations regarding the day's weather or thoughts about converting patient files in the office to a computer format – thoughts that do take up a lot of space in my head -- seemed unproductive."

I continued, "So I began spending more quiet time at the waterfront. I decided that reflection or meditation would be more helpful than writing a journal. Mostly the quiet time has been early in the morning, around sunrise. The idea is to be there before arrival of the waterfront coffee drinkers and the tourists.

Often, I stop in the Old Burying Ground while en route to or from the water."

At this point I paused, "As I have said, the intent was to find an alternative to writing a journal, but that has not actually been the case. I am writing, just not in the form of a journal."

My next thoughts came out with difficulty.

"I hear their voices while at the waterfront or in the cemetery, and they seem to tell me what to write. The instructions, as I will explain, have not been precise. Consequently, most of what has been recorded so far is background in nature. I feel as if I am dancing around the real stories that they want me to tell."

"When you say 'they,' to whom do you refer?" Catherine asked.

My response was immediate, "Amelia Caroline, her Great-Grandmother, my brother Charles and his friend Louis Gabral."

Catherine continued to probe, "You mentioned your brother after reading the poem. As I recall, the poem ended with the phrase 'it brings me through my night.' When I asked how you interpreted the phrase 'my night,' your response included a reference to Charles, but before today you have not referred to Louis. Can you tell me about them? How are they related?"

So I began to open the "secret box," the one that each of us has locked away deep inside. The box contains aspects of our lives or the lives of others that we unconsciously choose not to acknowledge, for to do so results in great pain.

Fear of what would emerge from the box and how I would react began to grip me. Shakily, I began to speak. Immediately, as the first words left my lips, tears began to flow down my cheeks. I knew this conversation would take me back in time to an experience that was among the worst of my life.

Catherine waited patiently, as I slowly continued.

"Charles, my older brother by twelve years, was born in 1944. Like all young girls whose brothers are much older, I idolized him. He was my teacher, my protector, my buddy, my confidante, and all other things that a wonderful brother could be. When I was six years old, Charles, along with Mom, held my hand as I walked to public school for the first time. He taught me how to use a baseball mitt and how to stand at the plate with bat in hand. We fished together in the lake, and he helped set up

59

camp for my overnight stays with friends in the backyard. Memories of one-on-one basketball are with me even today. Charles always cheated to make me look better at the game than I actually was."

Recalling for Catherine my early memories of Charles was difficult, not because of the relationship he and I had, for that had been wonderful. Rather, the difficulty came because my mind could not separate memories of those early years from the knowledge of what was yet to come.

I had to pause momentarily while Catherine passed the box of tissue. When recomposed, I continued.

"When I was just going on seven, Charles finished high school and enrolled at the University of Indiana. During high school Charles had played several sports, but basketball was his favorite. He had always followed the Hoosier basketball program, so Indiana was the only school on his short list of choices.

"He was an excellent student and he selected electrical engineering as a major. I missed Charles while he was away, but the university was near enough for us to meet several times during that first year, and Charles was home for holidays and family celebrations. It seemed that life was on track, but it was during the winter break of Charles's freshman year that the course of our lives would actually become charted.

"As you know, Catherine, the early 1960s were turbulent years for the nation. The cold war was near its zenith and anti-communist zeal dominated much of the national psyche. For young men such as Charles, the times were particularly stressful. The nation had compulsory draft registration for military service, and all young men were required to serve at least two years of active duty. There were exceptions, of course, but many young men felt a sense of obligation to honor their country. Charles was among them.

"One of our neighbors at the time was Colonel Jacobson, who was retired from the U.S. Army. Though no longer affiliated with the Army in an active-service capacity, he had remained involved in various Army-related organizations. In particular, he took interest in recruiting young men for the Army Officer Corps. Just by chance during the holiday break, our family met Colonel Jacobson at one of the neighborhood gatherings, and he spoke with Charles about becoming an Army officer. They discussed the Army's R.O.T.C. program at the university and Colonel Jacobson mentioned opportunities for scholarship support through the Army. Charles already was aware of the R.O.T.C. program and he told Colonel Jacobson that he was considering enrollment. Then in January, under the continuing encouragement of the colonel and with the support of Dad, Charles enrolled in his first Army R.O.T.C. course.

"Charles, as it turned out, enjoyed his student military experiences and he advanced in the Corps. Late in the spring of his sophomore year, he was offered and accepted a contract for a military scholarship. A few months later, during the summer break, Charles attended a basic training program for officers. By that time, I was approaching nine years old."

Once again, I had to pause to collect my thoughts.

"Although I was still quite young, I was happy for Charles. My big brother clearly had found a niche he enjoyed and I shared his pleasure. Charles continued to excel both in the engineering program and in his military training. Initially, Mom and Dad shared enthusiasm with Charles, but as the months passed a subtle change was noticeable in their attitudes.

"The nation was slowly being pulled into the political upheaval of Southeast Asia. Vietnam was becoming known even by folks in Indiana. Dad expressed concern that Charles might become involved in an escalating conflict, but Charles was confident about the future. 'After all, electrical engineers do not live in foxholes,' he would say to Mom and Dad.

"The summer following his third year at college, Charles went to Fort Benning, Georgia, to participate in the Army's paratrooper training program. He earned the basic paratrooper badge, which he proudly called 'his wings.' Charles graduated from the university in 1966 and was commissioned as a second lieutenant in the U.S. Army.

"The commissioning ceremony during graduation brought pride to all of us, but the celebratory atmosphere was overshadowed by news of the war in Vietnam. Mom and Dad did their best to keep their concern suppressed, and they did take small comfort from the knowledge that Charles had no intention of making the military his career. Having given Mom assurances of his safety, Charles left Greenfield to attend several highly specialized training programs.

"Ultimately, Charles was classified as a communication electronics officer and assigned to Headquarters Battery, Division Artillery, 101st Airborne Division. It was there that he met Louis Gabral, a warrant officer in charge of tactical data systems.

"Louis was originally from the East Side of Los Angeles. At the age of twenty, he joined the Army to beat the draft. Louis had decided that by enlisting he would have more selection regarding job assignments. Prior to enlistment, he had completed two years at a technical college where he majored in electronics and communication technology. Louis had just the right training and skill after a few years in the service to apply for the warrant officer commission. Officially, Louis was in charge of electronic systems maintenance.

"He and Charles quickly became friends. They worked closely together, and each had highly specialized knowledge related to ultra-sophisticated cryptographic communication. They were entrusted with the military's most sensitive intelligence, and theirs was a world of enciphering and deciphering messages in secret codes."

I paused in my story, as it seemed Catherine wanted to comment.

"Mary Eliza, I am beginning to appreciate the origins of your focus on secret and encrypted messages," she observed.

"Yes. I speak as if I'm an expert on all of this, Catherine, but you have just heard my limits. What little I know is based upon the few visits Charles made home to Greenfield during the early months of his active duty. Then, when he was assigned to the 101st Airborne, we saw him more often. Fort Campbell was just three hours away by car, so it was relatively easy for Mom, Dad and me to drive down just as a day trip. We also met Louis while there, and on two occasions both Louis and Charles came to Greenfield for home-cooked meals and an overnight stay. I was approaching twelve years of age and, in my opinion, I was sufficiently old enough to both love my brother Charles and be in love with his friend Louis."

"My life seemed idyllic. Then early in 1968, Charles came home to visit for a weekend and brought disturbing news. He and Louis were both being sent to Vietnam. The 101st Airborne had been assigned a major role as part of President Johnson's commitment to the government of South Vietnam.

"As the military conflict intensified, the number of troops sent into combat escalated. More troops were needed;

Charles and Louis were among those selected to go. This news brought by Charles placed a cloud over the family. Still, we were determined to enjoy the weekend. We laughed over family stories while recalling school days, hikes, vacations, holidays and ball games. Mom baked Charles's favorite cake saying, 'You won't be here for your birthday, so we will celebrate today.'"

"As the weekend drew to a close, I promised Charles I would write frequently, and Mom made a plea to talk if and whenever possible. Charles again said to Dad, 'The Army does not assign electrical engineers to foxholes.'"

"But Vietnam was not a foxhole kind of war!"

I paused for what seemed like forever. As I neared the next part of the story, the fear of unleashing pain brought me to a state of near paralysis.

"I cried for days after Charles returned to Fort Campbell, and I cried again on the day he actually departed for Southeast Asia. Little did I know that those same tears would be falling decades later as I retold the events.

"Shortly after their arrival in Vietnam, Charles and Louis were transported to the Tay Ninh Province near the Cambodian border. A few weeks later, their headquarters and command center came under heavy mortar and rocket fire."

I had to stop and I was unsure whether I could even continue. Anger, pain, disillusionment, sadness of the darkest kind, and tears all came out. The story had emerged from my "secret box," the one that had been locked away in some remote cellar of my mind.

Then ......the explosion came!

"Charles died in Vietnam, and so did Louis Gabral, his closest friend in the unit!"

A long time passed and Catherine sat patiently. Then she asked, "Mary Eliza, do you feel well enough to continue, or would you rather put this on hold until we next meet?"

"I'll continue, Catherine, not because I feel up to it, but just to bring closure."

"Don't hurry, give yourself a few more minutes."

I tried to relax, but finding that to be impossible, I just decided to continue.

"Originally, we did not know of Louis's situation. Following the death of Charles, Mom and Dad were contacted by the Army. I was completely devastated and required counseling for several months. Slowly the pain became less and our lives returned to a semblance of normal.

"Approximately eighteen months later, on a Saturday afternoon while Dad and I were watching a ball game on television, the phone rang and Mom answered. A couple of minutes later she came into the room with the most surprised look on her face.

"'You won't believe who just called,' she exclaimed.

"Breaking away from a ball game takes effort, but I turned, and in my best teenage voice said, 'OK, Mom, tell us.'

"'Louis Gabral' was her reply. And that got our attention.

"She continued to explain the unexpected call, 'He phoned from Fort Campbell where he has been ever since being wounded back in Tay Ninh. He's scheduled to depart for another tour in Vietnam and he wants to visit briefly before going. I invited him to have dinner with us tomorrow.'

"We had a wonderful visit that Sunday, and it was through Louis that we learned the circumstances under which Charles had died. Later in the afternoon, we wished Louis well, and Mom promised another dinner upon his return from Vietnam. I was sad to see him leave, but I had gotten over my infatuation of two years earlier.

"Louis never came back for the dinner Mom promised. The war was lost, the years drifted by, our pain faded, and so did my thoughts of Louis – that is until 1984.

"The end of my residency program was drawing near and I was preparing for my move to the coast. However, before packing my things in Winston-Salem, I had to travel to Anaheim, California, to present a research paper at a clinical research meeting. The paper essentially reported the results from a small clinical trial involving a new drug used to treat childhood asthma.

"Just by chance, before flying out to the West Coast, Louis popped into my mind. I remembered that, years back during the Sunday visit to our house in Greenfield, Louis had written the names, address and phone number of his parents.

"I wondered if Mom still had that information, so I phoned home.

"Dad answered the phone and, after hearing my explanation, he said, 'Mary Eliza, you know your mother. She has kept every piece of paper since the day we were married, and the papers are all neatly filed away.'

"Dad was right, as usual. I got the details, flew to Anaheim, gave my research paper, then called the phone number Louis had left those many years earlier. His mother answered the phone and, upon hearing who I was, she invited me to visit.

"Mrs. Gabral had met Charles during a visit to Kentucky back in the mid-sixties and she knew what a good friend he had been to Louis. Mrs. Gabral at that time lived in Garden Grove, not far from the convention center where our meeting took place. The taxi trip took less than ten minutes.

"Mrs. Gabral greeted me warmly at the door and I stepped into the entry hall, which was lined with family photos. Louis was on display from childhood to handsome Army officer. In one photo he was standing arm in arm with Charles. Both were in full combat paratrooper uniform; they were a two-man band of brothers.

"'Mom and Dad have a copy of this same picture,' I commented.

"Mrs. Gabral smiled as I stopped to look at the smiling faces of my brother and his friend. We then entered the parlor and sat together on the sofa. I asked about Louis.

"Her response was quick and pained, 'Oh, Mary Eliza, I thought you knew! Louis died near the city of Hue in 1970. That battle, one of the final in the war, took place in the Thua Thien Province next to the border with Laos. The outcome was costly for our boys and in particular for the 101st Airborne. It was especially tragic for Louis's father and for me.'"

Now that the story had been freed from my "secret box," my heart rate was slowly returning to normal. One final point had to be made.

"Catherine, to this day, Charles, Louis and I have conversations in my head. There is some secret communication code, a cipher, that keeps us in touch. And, more than three decades since their deaths, I wonder how our lives would have evolved had it not been for the folly of that war."

After a moment, Catherine quietly asked, "Mary Eliza, are you all right?"

"I'm sorry, Catherine, my mind just seemed to drift off for a moment. This is difficult for me to explain, but to some degree my 'night' is related to Charles's Army days and his friendship with Louis. I know that Charles and I don't actually talk, nor do I actually hear his voice; but he and Louis are with me these many years later. I am beginning to understand the 'noise' in my head as the vague messages that remind me of them and the cryptograms they dealt with.

"But just as I hear Charles and Louis, I also hear Amelia Caroline and her Great-Grandmother. Amelia Caroline's story comes out a little each day. It emerges spontaneously following my trips to the waterfront or my stops in the cemetery. I don't always know from where much of the story comes, nor do I understand the code in which it is sent. I refer to voices, but in actuality I just sense the presence of encrypted messages.

"Upon return to the cottage, the messages remain a mystery until I sit at the computer. Only then does the cipher emerge. The computer is my cryptograph."

9

THE YEARS OF YOUTH

Amelia Caroline's childhood years, as would be expected from small-town life, were unremarkable. The major exception in her case was the presence of Mrs. Wescott and various neighborhood women who served to fill the void created by the death of her mother. Amelia Caroline as a toddler often spent hours hanging onto the skirts of kindly neighbors. These were salt-of-the-earth women whose days involved doing wash, feeding chickens, milking cows and slopping pigs. These daily chores were in addition to tending a brood of their own children.

All of this I had learned during the eighteen years I had spent with Amelia Caroline between 1984, when I began practice, and August 15, 2002, when, upon returning from my office in the evening, I found Amelia Caroline still sitting on the front porch.

She was either asleep or deep in thought as I started up the steps, for she did not acknowledge my presence. So I went into the house to wash and change into comfortable outdoor clothing. While inside, I prepared a light snack of cheese, crackers and dried fruit, and I poured two small glasses of wine. Then I returned to the porch and my rocker.

As I opened the screen door, Amelia Caroline spoke, "Did your day go well, Mary Eliza?"

Evidently, she had known of my arrival but did not wish to break her train of thought as I entered the house.

"Yes, Aunt Amelia," I replied. "Mostly I saw scheduled patients, but one child came in with a serious cut on his foot. He had not been wearing protective footwear while playing in the river shallows, and he stepped on a large piece of glass.

"The family was vacationing out on the island, but came to town to enjoy the waterfront park, which for children always means playing on the strand and putting their feet in the river.

Unfortunately, the family was unaware that the river hides nearly three hundred years of history, some of which is treasure, but most of which is trash.

"The child's mother was quite distressed, but Jennifer, my clinic nurse, calmed her while I stitched the wound. The youngster, though in a bit of pain, was brave throughout the entire episode. I suggested they return in a week to have the sutures removed, but the mother said their vacation would end in two days.

"I insisted they report to their family doctor upon arrival at home. I even offered to forward the clinical record to their physician so she would have the details upon their arrival."

I placed our snack and wine glasses on the small porch table, then sat.

"Aunt Amelia, you were up early and out here on the porch even before I left this morning for hospital rounds. Have you been out here talking to Great-Grandmother all day?"

I had, during the initial years we spent together, gradually began to refer to Amelia Caroline's Great-Grandmother as if she were my own. This was primarily for convenience, but it also was due to the fact that our lives had become quite interlaced. At times I actually felt as if we had a common lineage.

After a few moments, Amelia Caroline responded to my question.

"Heavens no, Mary Eliza. I went into the house before the day's heat, prepared a small salad using some of the shrimp left over from last night, and then enjoyed a long nap. I've not spoken with Great-Grandmother today, but I have been thinking back over the early years and the events related to my father's retirement. You have already heard most of the stories."

I eagerly responded, "I know, Aunt Amelia, but I enjoy hearing them repeated and there is always something new." So Amelia began her tale for the evening.

Although my circumstances at home were different from those of most of my friends because of the absence of my mother, my early recollection is that I fit in as just one of the gang.

I had a number of playmates as a young child, and several schoolgirl friendships evolved from the times we had spent playing together. While schoolgirls, we passed many afternoons in the park teasing the boys and playing games that only a group of young girls enjoy. You understand what I mean.

Those early friendships were deeply meaningful and many have remained throughout my life. Even upon entering our senior years, these same friends and I often spent time on the waterfront visiting and enjoying summer afternoons.

Choices for schooling were limited when I was very young, but along with many of my friends, I attended a local academy. It was not the same school that Papa had attended, for the Smithville Academy of his day had closed during the hard times in the 1890s. But in 1901 following the economic recovery, a new private academy for younger children was opened. Mr. H. B. Early, a newcomer to town, served as headmaster. The cost for tuition at the academy must not have been much, for many of my friends were from modest homes.

Some years later, the town opened a new public high school and Mr. Early became superintendent. The high school offered the usual topics of History, Grammar, Elementary Mathematics and Geometry, Latin and Literature. Papa made sure that I studied each of them.

I was an enthusiastic student and did well in all of my classes.

The time of my youth was one of prosperity for the town. The economic slump had abated and financial stability had returned to the region. The fishing industry was booming, and plans once again were afoot to establish a great port with service to Europe.

Work also was progressing on the Panama Canal, so local speculation included numerous trading partners in the Far East. Financiers from New York, Chicago, St. Louis and Cincinnati were contemplating investments in our local economy. Plus there was much in the way of modernization. The town had its own water works. A private electric company had been founded and telephones were available for local calls. As you will remember, I told you of when my father made these updates to our house.

Then the railroad came to town. Though not a major event in most communities, the railroad guaranteed communication and shipping links between the town and the great markets of the Midwest. Following nearly twenty years of politicking and financial manipulation, the rail line south from Wilmington was completed in 1911.

I was eight years old when the first passenger train arrived at the newly constructed station on November 23, 1911. It was a day to remember. Mayor Guthrie declared a town holiday and he named it "Railroad Opening Day."

The train was scheduled to arrive at noon, but by midmorning nearly the entire town had turned out to meet the train and celebrate. Among the distinguished travelers on the first train were the governor and two representatives to Congress in Washington. Several U.S. Navy vessels in the harbor saluted the day and talk of a great shipping port dominated all conversation.

Even I, as a young child, could sense the energy. The town was clearly on the upswing. Papa later told me that a new neighborhood was being platted for the woods north of the town gate. He also said plans were afoot to widen the streets in town. The goal was to be more city-like.

The street work actually did happen and it was a time of fun for my friends and me. Each day as the roads were newly graded, we looked for treasures in the freshly exposed dirt. Old marbles and buttons from Civil War uniforms were plentiful. Occasionally, one of us would find an ancient coin or a token from the Wilmington trolley system.

This led to speculation regarding when construction would begin on our very own local electric trolley system. Even we children were aware of proposals being considered by the town council for a multi-track service with rails extending into all the - as yet non-existent - outlying suburban neighborhoods.

The mayor, during his speech on Railroad Opening Day, announced that twenty-five to thirty new buildings were under construction. In addition to the twenty houses and four or five new stores in downtown, there was to be a new bank, which was to be the town's first.

This prosperity continued over the next several years and, although welcomed and celebrated, it was not all domestically driven. As the year 1917 approached, the town had been abuzz for nearly three years with activity related to the "Great War" in Europe.

Eventually, the war would impact my life and the lives of others in town.

The fort, which had been in a state of neglect and disrepair for decades, once again was brought to life. Shortly after celebration of the railroad, city fathers had petitioned the

U.S. government to establish a public park adjacent to the fort. After all, other than occasional military exercises, not much use had been made of the garrison grounds.

However, as the war in Europe intensified, the U.S. Senate Committee on Military Affairs cancelled all plans for public use of the property.

Fort Johnston, at the time nearly 200 years old, would once again play a role in defense of the nation. At the same time, extensive work was being done to improve the coastal defenses on the island across the bay. Gun batteries were improved, new barracks were constructed, and the latest rapid-fire three-inch guns were installed to repel torpedo boat attacks. Locally, the officers' quarters at the fort in town were revamped and new chapters of the Red Cross were chartered.

The townspeople in general were excited about the economic boost that would come from having sailors and soldiers in town. So the community rallied to defend the nation's shore, or at least that small portion of the shore which was in sight when one stood on the high ground overlooking the river and its exit out to the open ocean.

As anticipated, the war brought soldiers, sailors and their families, swelling the community to more than twice its pre-war size. Nearly 1500 military personnel were stationed at Fort Caswell on the island. Their presence was complemented by several officers of high rank whose duty was in old Fort Johnston.

Then in January of 1917, Major General Leonard Wood, Commander of the U.S. Army of the East, visited the region. The nation was going to war.

Mary Eliza, the town positively became overrun with people. The influx of new residents included family members and their friends. These were wives and children, and occasionally sweethearts. It was so exciting, for nearly every day new students joined our school classes.

Housing became a problem, as military support groups such as Red Cross workers, entrepreneurs and speculators all took lodging in the town. But their presence spelled prosperity, so every effort was made to accommodate their needs.

Papa, by that time, had become a successful businessman and leading citizen. In addition to his medical practice, he operated one of the local pharmacies. It was no *surprise when he assumed responsibility for providing medical services to many of the new residents and their guests.*

At the outset I was enthralled, particularly with the attention given to me by the new residents. I was the doctor's daughter and I was the envy of every other young girl in the community. Though initially swept up by the romantic aspects of my stature, a response to be expected of any young teen, I tried diligently not to succumb to self-indulgent vanity. Rather, following the example set by my father, I quietly made a commitment to help in any manner possible those who suffered due to the war.

These military activities coincided with my final years of high school, so I was quite busy.

When not in school or doing home assignments, I spent every free hour either out in the community or at Papa's side. He was constantly trying to alleviate that which he referred to as "the invisible pain enshrouding the town."

On the surface, everyone seemed enthusiastic and supportive of the war. It was a public show of unity in support of a process that was tragic at its core. However, as was explained by Papa, the people, during quiet moments of nighttime wakefulness, nearly all dreaded the pain and misery to be faced each day. The pain, he said, was due to a fear that they would hear of loved ones who had been killed or lost in battle.

Papa also said, "Nearly everyone dreaded having to endure the distress of welcoming home young men whose bodies and minds had been mutilated on the field of combat."

The time for me was one of maturation. The carefree days of childhood gave way to the uniqueness of wartime. As the months passed, more and more of the typical teen life was replaced by adult matters. More of my hours were spent working with the Red Cross or assisting my father.

Picnics became infrequent, as did playful days in the park and outings to the waterfront. This transition, subtle as it was, had an impact on my psyche. I found that my normally outgoing, cheerful and somewhat carefree nature was at times overwhelmed with concern for others.

In my youth I would ask, both in my own mind and of my father, "Why are young men of our quiet little town being sent thousands of miles across the ocean to fight a war that has been started and perpetuated by others?"

Of course, there are no absolute answers to such questions, and youth often can not extrapolate to rationalization. So the result for me, and to a lesser extent my friends, was a quiet and somewhat confusing pain. I don't mean to imply that my friends were less sensitive than I, for that was not the case. It is just that through Papa, and the small role I played helping him, I had greater exposure to the suffering of others than did many of my peers.

Irrespective of the degree of exposure, we all did feel pain. And the pain was not the sort that life normally holds, such as routine illness or disappointment in some social or economic aspect. Those were burdens of the natural world. What I and many of my peers experienced during those years was pain that was as unique as the wartime experience itself. It came at the hand of man, and it was for reasons I as a young person could not fully comprehend.

Had it not been for the strength I saw in my father and the comfort I derived during my brief moments on the porch in the rocker, I might have been pulled down into the depths of youthful despair, but I endured.

Then following the armistice, which brought the war to a close in November of 1918, and upon graduating from school shortly thereafter, I traveled to New York City to study nursing at the Teachers' College of Columbia University.

The decision to become a nurse was based upon a number of factors, some of which were personal and others simply a reflection of the times. Of course, my close relationship with Papa was a key contributor to the decision. Then, there were events which stemmed from the war that took place during my final years in school.

The nursing course extended over a period of two years, and it was both challenging and rewarding.

I felt that my call to serve was being answered and, living in New York, the nation's largest city at the time, was an exciting adventure. Yet I did miss being at home. In spite of the stimulating classes and the excitement of life in the city, I always looked forward to holidays and the end of each term when I boarded a train in Grand Central Station for the welcome ride on the Atlantic Coast Line to Wilmington. Then there was the short ferry trip across the river to Navassa, where I boarded a local train for the final twenty-eight miles to home.

During each of these return visits, the bonds with my father, the town and my heritage would be redoubled. I came to understand that my life would be lived out in this small coastal town.

So it was that upon completion of my training in 1921, I returned to town, the porch and the rocker. I immediately became involved in my father's practice.

At this point in the recitation, Amelia Caroline fell silent. But I had learned enough through our many previous conversations to offer a sketch of her father's life and how Amelia Caroline became integrated into his practice following her training in New York.

Reuben Everitt, MD, upon the return of his daughter, encouraged her to assist with his female patients. Intellectually, Reuben understood the medical issues unique to women, but he could not fully appreciate those needs in the manner that another woman could.

This willingness on Reuben's part to extend such responsibility and independence to his daughter was viewed with some skepticism, primarily by men. The town at the time was a typical conservative Southern community and, based upon historical precedent, women were confined to limited roles. Apart from a few years in the teaching profession prior to marriage, they were expected to be homemakers, wives and mothers.

However, the post-war years were bringing changes even to entrenched communities. Amelia Caroline, when challenged by someone who questioned her professional role, would reply, "Hadn't Annie Mae Woodside, just a few years older than I, recently been named assistant cashier at the newly established Bank of Southport?"

This reply by Amelia Caroline often brought an end to the challenges, for Annie Mae Woodside was the daughter of a prominent and highly respected town leader.

Reuben persisted in his encouragement and he used his influence to advance Amelia Caroline in the profession. After all, his daughter had studied at the Teachers' College of Columbia University, one of the nation's premier academic and medical institutions. She had assisted in surgery, done primary care, and mastered technical topics such as Physiology, *Materia Medica* and Therapeutics.

His daughter was familiar with the latest concepts ranging from Psychotherapy and Hydrotherapy to serums and vaccines. All of these concepts and interventions had evolved since his studies had been completed more than two decades earlier. Reuben knew, from years of practice and encounters with both peers and more senior colleagues, that Amelia Caroline's scientific knowledge and skills, though professionally those of a nurse, greatly outstripped the majority of local practicing physicians.

Reuben and his peers had been trained during the 19th century. Physicians of that era, for the most part, had completed prolonged apprenticeships and attended a few months of medical lectures prior to entering private practice. Often their knowledge of contemporary science-based medicine was limited.

Furthermore, the apprenticeships in many cases had been under the tutelage of post-Civil War practitioners who used centuries-old, unsubstantiated, marginally effective and often detrimental treatments.

Thus, medicine had changed radically during the first two decades of the 20th century. Both college education and full attendance at a two-year medical school were becoming the standard for physicians. Scientific knowledge of Physiology, Chemistry, Pathology and Nutrition, the very topics Amelia Caroline had studied, were required to understand and effectively treat illness.

Over time, the medical practitioners and the men of town came to appreciate the medical skills of Amelia Caroline. She became a partner both in her father's practice and at the pharmacy.

10

REUBEN'S RETIREMENT

So it was in the dual relationship, father to daughter and colleague to colleague, that Amelia Caroline and her father remained for over thirty-five years, until the time of Reuben's retirement in 1955. He was 83 years old.

Reuben had been a healer in town for more than five decades. His service had been unprecedented and, although he was still agile, alert and professionally dedicated, the time for retirement had arrived. However, Reuben's decision to retire was not based entirely upon longevity, for events during the fall of 1954 were contributory: Hurricane Hazel had arrived in mid-October of that year.

I remember quite distinctly the conversation in which Amelia Caroline shared with me those days. We were having tea and scones on the porch. It was Sunday afternoon, September 16, 1984. I had moved to Southport to enter practice a few weeks earlier, and Amelia Caroline and I were beginning to settle into a routine that we would share for many years to come.

My early weeks in town had been enjoyable. Clear skies and crisp clean air had promised a beautiful fall season. Then on September 13, a monstrous hurricane named Diana headed for the Southeast coast of North Carolina. The storm had sustained winds exceeding 130 miles per hour and the mouth of the Cape Fear River was at the center of the storm's track.

For several days prior to September 13, we had worked with others in town to prepare for the probability of a direct landfall. The early weather reports warned that the storm was the strongest one to target the Carolinas in over twenty years, and the weather service said that, if the trend continued, Hurricane Diana might even match the force of Hurricane Hazel.

The storm did make landfall at Cape Fear on September 13 and the town took the brunt of its fury. Luckily for all, however, the winds subsided and, just before landfall, they were at ninety miles per hour. There was no major damage, although significant flooding resulted from rainfall, which over thirty-six hours totaled nearly nineteen inches. By Saturday, September 15, the storm had moved inland then off to the northeast.

On Sunday, clear skies and sunshine brought good spirit to all. The scones – spiced pumpkin -- were a special fall treat in celebration of our good fortune.

As we sat on the porch, neighbors passing by stopped to share greetings. "We just missed the bullet on that one," was a frequent comment. Amelia Caroline shared this sympathy with her friends, and a few times she recalled similar close calls from the past.

Then as the day was drawing to a close, she turned to me and began to talk about "the storm" that will never be forgotten by the folks in town.

Mary Eliza, that hurricane of 1954 was the worst weather-related event of my life, as well as the lives of everyone I knew. We had all weathered hurricanes several times in prior years, and our fishermen knew that death was lurking inside storms at sea, but Hurricane Hazel was the most intense storm ever to hit the town until then. And the impact of the storm was to influence my life for years afterward.

Perhaps if I tell you about the fall of 1954 and the winter of 1955 you will better understand what I mean. I think you will also see why I came to the conclusion nearly seventeen years later following Papa's death in 1971 that the house needed to be changed in order for me to resume converstations with Great-Grandmother.

The approach of Hurricane Hazel had been heralded for several days. Reports had arrived from Haiti that hundreds had died in the storm's path.

Hurricane warning flags were raised on the Weather Bureau flagpole at the waterfront. The storm warning system had been introduced during the latter years of the 19th century with the intent of alerting mariners in coastal waters of impending danger. Over the decades, the warning system had resulted in saving the lives of numerous fishermen.

Thus, ample advance notice of the storm was posted, so all were ashore prior to the disaster. As expected in a seafaring community, measures were taken to protect property, particularly the fishing fleet. However, few anticipated the pending fury.

Throughout the day on October 14, Papa and I, along with most other folks in town, watched as clouds gathered. Warm tropical winds came off the water and barometers fell. Then early in the day on October15, that storm of unprecedented magnitude struck.

For over fifteen hours, the wind often exceeded 150 miles per hour. The accompanying torrential rain and a tidal surge approaching fifteen feet wreaked havoc. The entire waterfront including shops, hotels and the town's vibrant fishing industry were devastated.

Miss Kate Stuart's House, once visited by senators, poets, governors and presidents, had been a landmark for over a century; but it was damaged beyond salvage. Shrimp trawlers were washed ashore where they crushed cars and were thrown into houses.

During the storm, and for days and weeks following, neither Papa nor I slept more than a little at a time. Our days were spent in neighborhood homes, at the hospital or in Papa's clinic treating the injured. The pharmacy remained open long hours, meeting the needs of those seeking first aid supplies and medications.

Many residents had sustained injuries, including lacerations, sprains and broken bones, during the storm. Many other townspeople incurred injuries during the prolonged period of waterfront restoration and reconstruction. Water supply to many homes was compromised, resulting in additional illness.

House calls seemed endless. Fishermen, bankers, carpenters, store-clerks, children, wives, mothers, the elderly and those who had been infirm before the storm all needed additional care. No one was exempt from the pressures brought by the hurricane and, as the weeks went on, Papa slowly acknowledged his own tiredness.

The fury of the storm and the devastation both in human suffering and property loss nearly overwhelmed the entire town. In fact, the aftermath of the storm was so demanding that Papa and I both became exhausted.

He had been practicing for more than a half century. Over his years of service, the hospital staff had grown. The pharmacy, by then primarily under my supervision, was doing well.

I told Papa, after the post-storm activities had subsided, that it was time for him to enjoy a bit more leisure. So he agreed to retire, but insisted that early 1955 would be the best timing. I agreed, for I knew that the remaining weeks would give him time to emotionally phase out of his work.

Papa retired soon thereafter and this, on top of the storm's impact, brought great change to our lives in a very short period. I was experiencing considerable emotional upset while coming to grips with adjustments, both personal and professional. And of course, I saw on a daily basis reminders of the risks that are inherent to life at the coast.

Then one day in 1955 some weeks following the storm and Papa's decision to retire, while sitting on the porch as we are now, a poem began to formulate in my head.

A few days later, as I began to write, the pressure from the previous days and weeks began to lift. I was coming to grips with my own circumstance.

Life either at the coast or on the open ocean is a special gift and offers much to those who live it. At the same time, however, trials and death are always on the horizon. And in the end, those of us who come to old age have memories of all that we have either celebrated or endured.

WHITTLERS and DREAMERS

They come each day and tell their tales
Of days before when ships wore sails
And men risked lives in wooden hulls,
Went out to sea amid flocks of gulls

They talk of time, of sharks and whales
When ships and men in sun and gales
Risked life and limb beyond the shore
For fish to catch, some less, some more

Despite the risk, 'twas out to sea
The darkest depths, where fish would be
Yet men they were, and catch they would
If providence beside them stood

They spoke of days and waters fine
When holds soon filled with many kind
Flounder, pogies, shrimp and squid
'Twould be a purse, small coin and quid

But there were days, remembered well
When gentle seas gave way to swell
And they stood fast, faced tempest's roar
Then prayed to be once more ashore

They talk of friends and neighbors bold
Who went in ships, tho' winter's cold
Swept down the sails, brought ice to line
And promised death with frozen brine

As mates they went, but many stayed
'Twas fate and sea, some never grayed
Their lives were gone, the darkest deep
Became their rest, their tomb to keep

But most returned, to anchor stay
Their lives would wane, the years bring gray
And with the age, most days would be
To whittle, and talk of life at sea

With friends now gathered near the strand
They dream and speak of times so grand
When ships with sails and wooden hulls
Were filled with fish and flights of gulls

They sit and whittle, and dreamily gaze,
Think things they knew in other days
Of fish and friends and mates before
When ships of wood sailed from the shore

Amelia Caroline Everitt
1955

*In retirement, Papa soon assumed his rightful spot at the
waterfront. He was welcomed by lifelong friends whose days
during their senior years were spent on the Whittlers' Bench.
This was a special spot at the waterfront, a simple wooden*

bench under the shade of ancient cedar trees. It was where elder statesmen, whose lives had been lived in town or out at sea, gathered each day. With a pocketknife in one hand and a piece of wood in the other, memories were shared of times past and all that had changed in the town.

It was a pleasant period for both Papa and me. I continued to do a little nursing, but mostly my work time was spent in the pharmacy. Each day, after having prepared a simple morning meal for Papa, I would leave for the pharmacy to review accounts and discuss store issues with Jim Watson, the new pharmacist.

Jim had received his pharmacy training in Chapel Hill, and he had taken a position with a national chain of drugstores for several years afterward. Like many in town, Jim loved fishing and the smell of salt air. So when the opportunity came to move here and operate the pharmacy in conjunction with my father and me, Jim jumped at the chance. He was a good colleague and his presence had served to ease demands on me.

Following time at the pharmacy, I often would stop at the hospital, or perhaps I might check on one of the patients who had been with Papa over the years.

Much of my time, however, was spent with Papa. Together we would have lunch at Mack's Café at the waterfront. The café had been a town landmark since the late 1930s. Mack initially had come to Southport to serve at Camp Sapona, the CCC camp located just northeast of town. During his time with the CCC, Mack met a local girl and they married.

Mack's place became a town fixture. The café was ideal for those of the "whittling set," including Papa. Breakfast, lunch or a cup of coffee and pie with friends were all available right next door --only a few steps away from Whittlers' Bench.

So our lives evolved with these simple activities. At the close of our days or in the early morning hours, we two would sit together on the porch to discuss the day's events and to share our concerns and joys.

Papa, though initially strong both in body and mind, began after a dozen years of retirement to show signs of his age. Thus it was during the late1960s that we made the decision to sell the pharmacy, which by that time had been a family business for six decades.

The sale freed me to focus more attention on Papa's care at home. Over time, his needs had became more acute, so I

82

gradually relinquished the majority of my outside nursing activities, which by that time included working part-time on the surgical unit at the hospital. Except for those instances involving the medical needs of close friends or neighbors, my time was spent assisting Papa. I suppose my attentions to him were similar to those he had given me during the early years of my life.

Here Amelia Caroline paused, but I knew that the memories of her father's last years went deep. It was in the role of caregiver that Amelia Caroline filled her days until her father's death in 1971.

Reuben's death left his daughter with a great emptiness. Following the funeral for her father, Amelia Caroline returned to the house. She fully anticipated resuming life. There would of course, she reasoned, be an adjustment with her father gone, but in time a familiar pattern would be restored.

So the next many days were spent wandering through rooms devoid of voices other than her own. The house presented a quietness she had never experienced and a deep loneliness ensued. Amelia Caroline was aware of her aloneness, but she comprehended neither its depth nor its sources.

I now understand that she was grieving not only for her father but also for the lives of the many who over the previous 150 years had lived in the house.

To my surprise, Amelia Caroline began to speak where my thoughts had left off.

As weeks passed, I listened to the house, but the only sounds were those of the ancient wood and the echo of my own footsteps through the empty rooms.

At times I would sit on the porch in the ancient rocking chair and talk, with the full anticipation of receiving an answer from the adjacent empty chair. Nothing came!

I knew that the death of my father had left me in a deeply troubled state. Grief, after all, is common to those who suffer great loss. And hadn't I, as a member of the medical community, shared the pain of many?

Yet the degree of despair I experienced suggested concerns that went beyond my own immediate past life. I was apparently seeking answers to questions which themselves were a mystery.

I deeply longed for serenity. I wished for a state of inner calm and strength of surety that I had known in the past. And this longing brought to mind my childhood and younger adult years.

Those were years during which the rocking chair had provided a feeling of continuity with the past and, while sitting in the rocker, I had perceived a sense of communication with my predecessors.

Somehow, these experiences in past years had helped me understand life in the present. Yet now in my time of grief over the loss of my father, there were no such perceptions. I missed talking with Great-Grandmother. After all, she had comforted me following the death in 1909 of Lillie Drew Piver. As I mentioned before, we had our first conversation in 1918, when William Banes, my young soldier friend, died. And there were many other times during the years of my education and early professional life that Great-Grandmother had come to me.

As the days, weeks and months went by following Papa's death, I came to fear that my lifelong ability to touch the past and, by so doing, gain insight to the present had truly been lost. But I kept telling myself that surely there was an explanation. Great-Grandmother, after all those years, would not simply leave me.

So I began to think back over our conversations, with the idea of identifying when they had ended. I could not actually pinpoint when the disconnect had occurred, but I realized that we had not spoken for several years during the time of Papa's retirement.

That was a difficult period for me, Mary Eliza, and I struggled for months.

Then one day in early spring of 1972, after sitting for a short while in the chair on the porch, I entered the house and closed the front door, which is something I rarely do during the daytime hours.

Suddenly, the intensity of silence came to me. While standing there in the entry hall, I acknowledged both the absence of companionship and my isolation in the closed house. But more significant was the realization that the house itself was isolated from everything that over the years had brought life to its walls.

Immediately, as if someone had spoken directly to me, I came to the understanding that, due to changes in the house, past members of the family -- including my Great-Grandmother -- shared my isolation.

The many ancestors with whom I, as a child and as a younger woman, had felt unique bonds no longer recognized the house as the home of their lives. Furthermore, as a direct result of this isolation, my predecessors no longer came to me as I sat on the porch in the rocker.

Mary Eliza, as I stood in the deafening silence of the closed house that afternoon in 1972, I was struck as if by a bolt of lightning. Suddenly, I knew when the wrong turn had been taken. It had been following the events of Hurricane Hazel and during my father's retirement years.

"Of course," I thought, "now some of my own questions will be answered."

11

REMODELING AND DE-REMODELING

Amelia Caroline's father had retained his faculties into old age. In fact, he still had long-term patients calling at the house for medical advice nearly a decade after giving up his practice in 1955. He had remained active in the community, meeting daily with friends at the waterfront. But there had been more to his retirement years.

So I was pleased that Amelia Caroline wanted to continue the story.

During retirement, Papa had had many ongoing interests, among which were the state of the fishing industry and local politics. These had been major topics of daily discussion among the men at Mack's Café and on the Whittlers' Bench. Papa was always in the know and his opinions were freely expressed. This, of course, was true of all the whittlers.

He had also paid attention to matters related to the house and gardens. He had taken pride in the condition of the family home, so it was no surprise in 1959 when he had talked with a salesman who was in town selling new siding for houses.

In the late 1950s, most of the town was a bit shabby. It had been that way ever since 1954 when Hurricane Hazel destroyed the waterfront and the fishing industry. The latter had been the town's main source of income, so full recovery from the storm was slow.

However, nearly five years after the storm, the local economy was beginning to pick up and money was again available to invest in home improvements.

Home improvement salesmen of all sorts came to town. Asbestos siding, guaranteed to last forever in the coastal climate and requiring almost no up-keep, was sold to nearly every homeowner. At the same time, many folks became convinced that the siding, when installed along with the newest air conditioning units that fit snugly into partially opened windows, would ensure lifelong comfort.

Papa had concluded that eighty-seven years of swatting flies and sweating on the front porch was sufficient reparation for any wrongs he had done in life.

"Now," he had often said, "is the time to relax in secure, cool comfort."

Being among those convinced by the sales pitches, Papa had parted with $2,114.63 to purchase asbestos siding and window air conditioners. The house had become insulated -- and isolated from the rest of the world.

Immediately following completion of that work, while sitting in the rocker on the front porch, I had perceived a change – although I did not understand it at the time -- one that transcended the physical condition of the house. The source of the perception, which I had experienced as a loss of connectivity with the past, did not become apparent until after the death of my father.

So it was on that spring day in 1972, some months after Papa's funeral, that upon entering the silent house, I had the revelation. Cool breezes no longer came through open windows on warm summer evenings. The calls of birds no longer announced the early dawn. The laughter of children playing on the sidewalks and in the streets was shut out. Silence had replaced the sounds of a midday rain as it pattered on the roof then dripped into the flowers eagerly waiting relief from the summer's heat.

And it suddenly occurred to me that the silence of the house was related to the absence of the family past.

Just as this revelation came to me in the silent house, I made a decision to act -- instantaneously. I would hire a contractor and have the house restored to its pre-1959 condition. The house would be de-remodeled.

There was to be no compromise. Open the house, get rid of the siding and the air conditioners, raise the windows and reconnect with the natural world.

So it was done. The cost was far greater than Papa had originally paid, but once again I felt completely at home.

The house, after removing the asbestos, was not a pretty sight to anyone but me. The ancient pine siding had numerous multicolored remnants of paint. To me, the random mosaic was

88

evidence of loving care given over the years of family ownership. There were areas with sagging, stained boards. Some were suggestive of early wood rot, others just reflected the house's age.

Overall, the place looked a bit askew, with irregular alignment where rooms had been added over the years to accommodate needs of the family. The effect was to give the house an ancient and, in the eyes of some, a neglected appearance. Yet the windows were open, the midnight breezes came through, and once again I experienced the presence of those from the past.

I sat in the rocker on the ancient porch and the conversations resumed.

"Amelia Caroline."

At first the gentle voice just called out to me, but as was the case with our first contact, I did not become distressed. I sensed this was the very connection which, though experienced in my youth, had been absent in recent years.

The voice brought comfort, a feeling of being securely grounded, at once both in the present and in the past. And it was from this feeling of being one with the past that I was able to speak. The words came without thought, spontaneously, as if I had always known the source of the voice.

"Yes, Great-Grandmother," I responded eagerly.

"Amelia Caroline, it warms my heart to be with you again," she said to me with a smile in her voice.

"Oh, Great-Grandmother, it has been so long. I've been in this house for fifty-nine years and Papa has been gone for seven months now. I have sat in this chair every day since his death wondering where my past had gone. It is just recently that I realized what the barrier between us has been."

"Well, Amelia Caroline, once again we are both here, and in time you will find all of your past, or that part of your past from which you seek answers. We have much to share. I believe you will find some of that which you seek in the lives of others from the family, particularly those whose years were spent in the house."

"Great-Grandmother, I know the family stories, at least those recalled by my father and those you shared with me in past conversations. With regard to the town, a lot has been written, and I have experienced much during my lifetime."

Great-Grandmother hesitated for just a moment before responding, then her next comments reached into my heart.

She said, "It is true that you have read, heard and experienced much, but I sense that you are still striving to understand why some of the events in your life have occurred as they did. We have talked along these lines before, and vivid in my mind is our first direct conversation, the one following the death of your friend who was a young soldier.

"Also, you and your father were very close, and he did his best to give you insight by sharing his own experiences and stories of the family . However, your longing has remained unsatisfied.

"You know that your father was not even two years old when I left this life in 1873. He was just an infant at the time, and you were just a toddler when your grandmother and grandfather moved away to Charlotte. Then your Grandfather Edward died in 1905. What I am suggesting is that neither your father nor you had an opportunity to learn from your grandparents.

Also, I know the sudden death of your grandfather just two years after the death of your mother Charlotte Louise would have added to the burden carried by your father. Much of what you learned from your father carried that burden, so the stories have given little to comfort you in your time. You now sit in the rocker and seek answers to questions which perhaps have not even been identified by you."

"What should I do, Great-Grandmother?"

"We will talk as we used to. I can tell you of that which has been. It will be up to you to understand it and integrate it into how you live the present. The future will follow in its time," Great-Grandmother said.

Amelia Caroline paused at this point in her reminiscing. She had been talking for nearly one and a half hours. Our wine glasses were nearing bottom and we had nibbled our way through the snacks.

I turned to her and said, "Aunt Amelia, you must be getting tired. Would you like to stop now, then resume our talk tomorrow?"

I knew what her reply would be, because in the past she had always wanted to reach a closing point before ending her stories.

"No, Mary Eliza. I would like to continue for just a few minutes longer."

So we did.

12

REUBEN'S DEATH

I do not know whether the conversation between Amelia Caroline and her Great-Grandmother on that spring day in 1972 was actually dialogue between persons (or souls) or if it was simply one distressed soul crying out to a force beyond -- or within -- itself in an attempt to find comfort. But to Amelia Caroline, the presence of her Great-Grandmother was reality. It was this reality to which she turned and the reality responded.

"Amelia Caroline, tell me what you are thinking," said Great-Grandmother.

"Great-Grandmother, I have felt unhappy ever since Papa died."

"But why should that bother you to such an extreme? Your father's life was full and satisfying. He was comfortable with his mortality and knew his own ultimate fate was to be no different than the many whose deaths he had attended. He was ready to accept the transition out of the present life and into the life which follows, knowing of the peace he had witnessed with the passing of others, many of whom were close personal friends in addition to being patients.

"As you are aware, he had long since come to grips with the loss of your mother, and ultimately he found in her death insight that carried him through the remainder of his life," said Great-Grandmother.

Mary Eliza, I had to sit and think for some time before responding. I knew my father was aware of the body's limitations and was not uncomfortable with the knowledge. His view of death had always seemed so reasonable to me; with aging, the body approaches the time when organs, tissues, blood and cells loose the ability to act in synchrony, thus resulting in chaotic physiological expressions. The highly integrated system devolves. Entropy increases until the point is reached where randomness surpasses order and death ensues.

I knew that my father's years had been characterized by philosophic insights, ideas put forth by ancient seekers and substantiated by advances in modern physics. In his later years, insight from the nascent field of Cellular Biology also influenced him.

Papa was aware that his knowledge about the newest fields in biomedical research was limited. Nevertheless, he did his best to understand the scientific data from those disciplines. More importantly, he strove to apply evolving concepts to his understanding of life's fundamental basis.

These intellectual exercises he shared with me. In fact, we spent numerous pleasurable hours on the porch exploring such ideas.

This sharing of ideas was not simply an intellectual exercise. Both of us attempted to apply the knowledge to our own lives. The real intellectual challenge was to better understand the physiological and psychological changes each of us experienced as the years passed. By extension, this awareness of self gave greater insight to the evolving needs of our patients.

It was due to this awareness that both of us knew that Papa had entered a stage of rapid physical decline. We accepted this as the natural physiological response to aging, and we attributed the decline to basic changes in biological chemistry and cellular biology. In Papa's case, the human machine's limits were being approached. He was, after all, well into his tenth decade of life.

Papa actually viewed the change in himself as an experience in medical research. He was, at the same time, both the subject of an experiment in approaching death and the medical observer of the process. The outcome posed no threat.

I remember having to take several minutes with these ideas going through my mind before I could articulate to Great-Grandmother what was really bothering me.

I spoke to her. "Yes, Papa was comfortable with his situation, and when we talked on the porch, he often said his life had gone on long enough. Release from the demands of a worn-out body would be welcome. So it was not his death that brought me to this state of distress, though I dearly miss our times together, and the house has cried out for conversation to fill the void resulting from his departure. Rather, it is the circumstance surrounding his final days that has plagued me for these seven months and has brought me to ask why it had to be as it was."

"What do you mean by 'it'?" Great-Grandmother queried.

"Why, his death, of course, or rather the manner in which it occurred. Ever since the day Papa died, I have imagined that he is still lying in the bed at the hospital asking to return home. Papa was worn out. He knew the end was imminent and he wanted the end to be on his terms. Papa's end-of-life plea weighs heavily upon me."

"Tell me about his final days," Great-Grandmother encouraged.

So I recalled the story in its entirety to Great-Grandmother, and I share it with you as well, Mary Eliza.

Papa knew it was his time to leave this life. Over the years, he had become increasingly frail, but we were still able to share the porch. The exceptions were on those dog days when the sweat would run down our backs or trickle off our fingertips to form puddles for flies to enjoy before they commenced to gnaw at our bodies. On those extremely hot and humid days, as well as on the bleak winter days when the river's damp would creep into his bones to aggravate his arthritis, Papa preferred being inside the house, which he had outfitted for his physical comfort.

I'm sure that the controlled conditions did alleviate some of the weariness for which the medical profession had no answers, yet for which many of his colleagues prescribed numerous medications, many of which Papa and I both knew were of limited value.

Papa believed that aches and pains in the very elderly are just the body's natural way of letting us know that days are limited. When he had his real bad spells -- we both knew his heart had become weak and his kidneys were beginning to fail -- I mostly would stay inside with him, providing whatever relief could be obtained through direct human contact. Companionship, in our belief, was about the most compassionate and useful thing that any one body could give to another who was embarking upon that final stage in life.

This pretty much had been our pattern for over five years, right up until the day that Papa remained in bed long after his usual 4:30 AM awakening. By nine o'clock, he was still feeling poorly and he declined my suggestion to sit on the porch for breakfast. The morning was a bit cool, in spite of what the calendar dictated should be the case. However, the day was still comfortable. I decided in view of Papa's listless status that it might be useful to phone a local doctor.

I did just that, although it was against Papa's wishes. He continued to believe firmly, as he had for his entire life, that simple caring was the answer for most ills, particularly those of the elderly, whose entire bodies were wearing out.

Although Papa had gone through much of his life ministering to the needs of others, he still believed that excessive medical intervention disrupted normal and natural body processes. He often expressed the belief that many of the modern ministrations simply stole from the recipients those few moments of pleasure left to them in this life.

But in spite of Papa's views, I made the call. Dr. Tillier, a young internist from here in town, agreed to stop by the house to check on Papa.

Dr. Tillier was a nice enough young man, probably in his late thirties at the time. We had known him for several years, having initially met while he was still a resident in medicine at the New Hanover Medical Center in Wilmington. He had moved to town and joined the staff at our local hospital following completion of his residency. Being young, Dr. Tillier was respectful of Papa, whose reputation Dr. Tillier had come to know from all the friends Papa had gained over the years.

As is the case with doctors these days, Dr Tiller spent a few minutes checking over Papa's body, mostly thumping him on the back and using his stethoscope to listen to Papa's heart, carotid arteries and lungs. There was little conversation, but throughout the exam Dr. Tillier's expression suggested concern.

Finally he and Papa talked, and Dr. Tillier expressed the opinion that Papa should go to the hospital where he could receive more intensive care and a more thorough work-up. There was some evidence of a lung infection, and it was clear by the swelling in Papa's legs that his heart and kidneys were under strain. Dr. Tillier was certain that these conditions could be brought under control with proper hospital care. In a moment of lightness, he said that Papa "would soon be back home, on the porch, and fit to the extent that an old fiddle could be considered fit."

Papa smiled, but I believe it was just out of politeness.

I agreed with the doctor's recommendation, but it was met with some resistance on Papa's part. He kept insisting that "a time comes when even old fiddles must go to the landfill."

I reminded him that he was not an old fiddle in my eyes or in the eyes of the many people for whom he had cared all of his professional life. Furthermore didn't he, during the aftermath of the Great Depression, work alongside Dr. Dosher to establish the community hospital for situations exactly like his? And hadn't he admitted many of his own patients for care in the hospital knowing that, in certain circumstances, adequate treatment was not possible in the home, even though giving home care had always been his, and by extension my, preferred choice?

Papa and I both believed that people as a general rule seemed to respond to care better when in a familiar space surrounded by those whose lives they shared. But there were, we both knew, occasions when hospital care was both necessary and appropriate.

So the three of us talked until Papa finally agreed, and he acknowledged that there were limits to the medical care I could provide at the house. Neither his years as a physician nor my experience as a nurse was sufficient to alleviate his condition at home. He had, after all, been getting worse. Papa finally relented, and he consented to a short stay in the hospital. This was to be just until we had "gotten the upper hand" against the lung infection.

Dr. Tillier said he would make all the arrangements, then he took his leave. Almost immediately Papa reminded me of the old fiddle.

"My old fiddle diagnosis," he said, "is based both upon my professional experience and the knowledge I have of my body. I have spent years communicating with this body. I know it quite well."

There was a premonition in Papa's voice.

Two hours later, the ambulance arrived. Papa was transported seven blocks up the street to the hospital, where he took up residence in a large private room overlooking the main street in town.

Papa could not see the house from his hospital room, and there were no rooms located in the building that would give such a view. He could, however, see the Ford dealership a couple of blocks away from the house and, if he glanced at the proper time -- usually ten minutes before 12:00 noon -- he could observe Mr. Perry on his way home for lunch. Papa and Mr. Perry had been friends since the dealership opened in 1923 and, over the years, each had provided a measure of care to the other. Papa looked after Mr. Perry's ills and Mr. Perry looked after the ills of Papa's cars, all of which had been bought in that very building right down the street.

Papa wasn't at home, but being in a familiar setting, surrounded in the hospital by friends and former colleagues, put him somewhat at ease. Deep down, Papa knew he would be receiving excellent care under the watchful eye of the hospital staff, but the old physician in him would not give up. He took every opportunity to express opinions regarding his medical treatment. And, if given total freedom of choice, Papa would have elected to return home to spend his final days.

The first two days following his admission were uneventful. However, Papa's condition did not improve; in fact, it worsened slightly in spite of all the pumps, lines and antibiotics. Papa became more listless and somewhat detached. The doctors and nurses came and went. They talked little, other than to each other and occasionally to me.

If expressions could tell stories, this was one tale not headed for a happy-ever-after ending.

Well aware of Papa's age, Dr. Tillier finally admitted his concern for the decline over the previous forty-eight hours. He suggested that more specialized expertise might be beneficial. On the fourth hospital day, Dr. Tillier proposed transporting Papa to the larger hospital in Wilmington where several groups of specialists practiced.

Papa, however, would not hear of it, saying, "My life has been in this town and I've tended the needs of thousands of people right here. I can receive adequate care without being sent thirty miles up the road to be treated by a team of strange physicians."

Most of the new, young specialists in Wilmington knew little of Papa or his professional life in the small town.

Furthermore Papa believed that, at his age, if care could not be provided locally, it was time to face the future. By this he meant the future we all ultimately share, but whose character and whereabouts are unknown except for those who have gone before.

Papa knew medicine, he knew himself and he knew when life had reached its culmination. He repeatedly suggested it might be time to return home.

Dr. Tillier, however, did not concur. He and Papa discussed several of the new medications and interventions that had become standard since Papa's retirement, and he reminded Papa of the role that the new breed of hospital-based specialists played in acute, critical care – partiularly that of the elderly. Papa, of course, knew all of this -- in theory, if not in practice.

Still, he did know himself and he probably knew more of his own status than did I or Dr. Tillier or members of the hospital staff. Home, surrounded by a lifetime of memories and loved ones was the proper setting for those who knew the end was near.

Yet many physicians in those years were reluctant to discharge hospitalized patients when there was a chance that additional care might be beneficial. The opinion of the day was that, if kept in the hospital, many patients such as Papa could possibly improve. Release from the hospital on the other hand ensured rapid decline and this was not an acceptable outcome.

But Dr. Tillier knew the history of Papa's general approach to patient care, and he also knew of Papa's belief about treating the elderly. So Dr. Tillier said to Papa, "I will consider the matter of letting you go home, but only after another day or two of hospital treatment. Let's see what we can do right here."

Dr. Tillier, to his credit, struggled with the conflict between compassion for the wishes of his patient and the current position of the medical community. He had been taught to be a soldier in man's never-ending war with mortality. His belief was to use all modern medical weapons in the battle against death. Two more days of intervention was his attempt to appease the opposing forces.

So Papa stayed, but he got no better. Thirty-six hours after the decision to remain in the hospital, a dramatic change occurred. Papa's kidneys began to go down hill rapidly. Dr. Tillier was even more distressed, as nothing was alleviating the condition.

Papa, however, did not share Dr. Tillier's state of mind. He knew what the outcome would be, and for that reason insisted hospital care was no longer necessary. Papa pleaded his case for returning to the house. He explained to Dr. Tillier *that the house for over 150 years had been the family home place, where both life and death had been honored.*

Dr. Tillier, in response, insisted more emphatically that it would be a significant breach of professional standards if he allowed Papa to go home in such a condition. Papa's death, he said, would be assured following the strain of traveling to the house. This was something he professionally could not allow. It was as if Dr. Tillie believed that the medical profession had the ultimate say in -- or control over -- whether Papa lived or died.

That very night, while still pleading the case to be sent home, Papa slipped into a coma and was gone in a few hours.

Now, both Papa and I had been fully aware of the burdens placed upon those whose loved ones spent their final weeks, days or hours at home. It was an experience well familiar, and it had been the usual pattern in my youth as well as throughout most of Papa's professional life.

But something happened during the Second World War to change this custom. Following the war, people in decline were for the most part transferred to hospitals for their final days. Perhaps it was the pattern of heroic intervention by physicians on the battlefield that created the belief in intensive intervention through which all lives could be saved. Or it may have been the fact that during the war so many young men had died in remote locations away from the people and places they knew. Loved ones back home had been removed from the dying process.

Death and the care required by those facing death during the war years became foreign experiences. The end of one's life was something to be tended by others in appropriate settings away from home. The general populace after the war came to believe that doctors had the knowledge and skill to save anyone, no matter how old, feeble or ill. Hospitals were the place for this to occur.

Having finished the story as she had told it to her Great-Grandmother, Amelia Caroline sat for a long while quietly rocking in the late evening warmth. Tears streamed down her cheeks, but she clearly had been comforted in the belief of her Great-Grandmother's presence.

Amelia Caroline had known, as had her father, that his time was limited. Being transported home would not have been a burden to either of them. It was simply his wish to say good-bye while in familiar surroundings. He had, after all, lived in the house with the rocking chair on the porch for his entire life.

However, his desire to experience life's ultimate transition in that familiar setting with his daughter at his side was not to be. Amelia Caroline was to be haunted by the decision of the hospital caregivers, many of whom had been her colleagues, to deny this final wish.

I could tell from her demeanor that Amelia Caroline had reached her limit. The day, August 15, 2002, had begun quite early, and Amelia Caroline's recollections had placed a great strain on her.The hour was approaching 7:30 PM, a time when Amelia Caroline normally prepared for bed. I decided to give her a few minutes alone. She always enjoyed a cup of hot chocolate before retiring, so I entered the house to prepare some.

Upon my return to the porch I said, "Aunt Amelia, since tomorrow is Friday, I have made arrangements to take the day off. Sarah, my receptionist, has rescheduled appointments, and Jennifer, being a registered nurse practitioner, will see the non-emergency patients. You and I will have a three-day weekend."

Amelia Caroline responded eagerly, "How wonderful, Mary Eliza. I will enjoy our additional time together."

The decision on my part to remain at home on Friday was for reasons other than just having a holiday. I sensed on the part of Amelia Carolina a somewhat urgent need to visit more than our regular routine would have allowed. My awareness of this had been heightened by observations I had made over the preceding weeks.

Amelia Caroline's health, as had been the case with her father at a similar age, was failing.

13

INEXPLICABLE FORCES

BURYING GROUND

Stones and shells and bricks abound
Scattered 'bout this hallowed ground
Where lie beneath in dirt decay
Those who before saw sun in day

Yet now they lie here in the sand
In graves that once bespoke lives grand
Tattered, shattered, thrown about
Tombs decayed, not brick nor grout

And those whose lives, more modest then
Had conch to mark their spot and kin
The shells had laid respectful grace
To give in death those gone a face

Stones which were in death a voice
Are silenced now, bones had no choice
Nor means to stop the slow decay
As setting sun marked day and day

So o'er the years both clay and sand
With life did meld beneath the land
While high above among grass and leaves
The ONE looks down, weeps tears, grieves

For those reposed beneath this place
Forgotten now all but for Grace
Both years and memory with sun have fled
And left behind those now long dead

Now here they lie 'neath hallowed ground
No voice have they, neither sign nor sound
For stones and bricks, shells, random be
No longer they speak, nor us to see.

The room seemed uncharacteristically quiet as I sat gathering my thoughts. All the while Dr. Catherine Arrington sat patiently.

She and I had been discussing the poem "Burying Ground" which I had written a few days earlier. The poem, I explained, came from my feeling that I had been chosen to speak for those who could no longer speak for themselves.

In particular, I was referring to the Everitt family, but I was also referring to my brother Charles and his friend Louis. Catherine remembered our earlier session in which I had mentioned having conversations in my head with Charles and Louis.

As our discussion about the new poem was winding down, Catherine asked if I felt there was any relationship between this new poem and the earlier poem that ended in "brings me through my night."

She sat quietly awaiting my response, while I tried to sort out the various factors that contributed to the state of mind which that phrase reflected.

This was a dilemma for me. It had been several weeks since I had written the poem "Lunar Shore." Of course, voices and cryptic messages were part of the explanation, but there was more. So as we sat, I turned my mind back to the time when I had experienced the earliest sensations.

During my residency in the early 1980s, I had sensed that forces of an unknown nature were pulling me to the town of Southport. Ever since then, I had suspected a link between those forces and cemeteries, particularly the Old Burying Ground.

Now nearly two decades had passed since the years of my residency, and I had come to know the relationship of both Amelia Caroline and her Great-Grandmother to the cemetery.

In addition – and initially this was hard for me to admit even to myself – I had come to suspect that the forces pulling me to the town emanated specifically from the Everitt cemetery plot. Conceivably, those who were buried in the family plot, principally Amelia Caroline's Great-Grandmother, had permeated my being nearly twenty years back and stayed with me today.

"Perhaps," I pondered, "that is where my explanation should start."

So I began to articulate these thoughts.

"As we've discussed, Catherine, I repeatedly have felt that forces of an inexplicable nature, including voices, were acting upon me. The incident when I was drawn to the waterfront by the moon's brightness, which was the stimulus for the first poen, was just one in a long string of such experiences. This all began some years back following the first visit with my parents to the old cemetery. Originally, the sensation of being drawn to the cemetery was just chalked up by me as 'historical fascination.'

"This interpretation was reinforced by visits to other old cemeteries. One such visit stays with me and serves as an example.

"Several years ago during my undergraduate college days, while on a trip to visit friends in Southeastern Georgia, I stopped into a small shop on the coast outside Savannah. The shop was one of those eclectic, locally owned places which specialize in regional artists. Included were local writers, particularly those whose works encompassed local history.

"While there, I purchased a copy of a book written by Frances Anne Kemble. The book was a journal of life on the Butler Plantation in Georgia prior to the Civil War.

"I was impressed with Ms. Kemble's experiences, so her story stayed with me for some time. In fact, I used her book as a key reference for an essay I wrote for an upper-level course on Southern history.

"A few years later, by coincidence, while traveling the low country of Georgia, I stopped at one of those country store/gas stations where beer, fried pig skins and hot dogs are the main grocery items. While relaxing and having a soda out in front of the store, I happened to glance across the street to a field of scrub trees and tall weeds. Nearly lost in the tall grasses and scattered among the pines were neglected cemetery markers.

"Over I went, and for the next several hours I was enraptured. The graves were those of folks who had lived and died on the Butler Plantation. Some had been alive at the time of Frances Kemble's residence there.

"It was as if I had discovered my own roots, and as if I was walking among and visiting with my own ancestors.

"I also describe the experience that day as 'historical fascination.'

"Thinking back, my original experiences in the Old Burying Ground were quite similar, thus my initial conclusion that I was once again under the influence of the same kind of attraction.

"But that conclusion did not hold. And the reason it did not hold I now attribute to Amelia Caroline and her Great-Grandmother, who was buried in the Old Burying Ground in 1873. Let me explain.

"My decision to see you, Catherine, as you know, was made toward the end of August. I had just spent part of an afternoon in the cemetery, sitting and crying at the base of an ancient, moss-covered headstone in the Everitt family plot.

"This behavior was not entirely unexpected. I had, after all, been mildly depressed ever since Amelia Caroline's death ten days prior to that event in the cemetery. My state of mind, however, was not due just to that loss. I had for many years felt an influence coming from and drawing me to the cemetery. This feeling became more acute after Amelia Caroline died.

"I use the word 'influence' because the nature of the drawing force remains a mystery. Ever since my first encounter with Amelia Caroline in 1983, I have tried to understand what has been transpiring, but to no avail.

"However, I have come to believe that the Everitt family actually called me to the Old Burying Ground those many years ago and they have continued to do so since then. There is an inexplicable force behind the calls from the Everitt plot and it is that force which influences my life.

"Originally, in death the family called to me. Now, perhaps as mediated by that unknown force, they speak through me so their story can be told. I have been chosen to be their voice."

Once again we sat in silence.

Then Catherine said, "When you say the family speaks to or through you, I assume you are referring to the voices that come as cryptic messages. Also, I continue to sense there is some distress on your part as a result of the communication."

As usual, Dr. Catherine Arrington saw my dilemma clearly.

I responded, "I'm still not certain how the family voice speaks to me, but my reference to cryptography does apply. I can say that the communication is not the same as Amelia Caroline had with her Great-Grandmother. Theirs seemed to be actual dialogue.

"My experiences are quite different, but they follow a recurring pattern and are related to the poem 'Lunar Shore.'

"Each day, as you know, I spend time at the waterfront. Some days I make several trips to the water. As on the day when the poem "Lunar Shore" came to me, my time at the water is often very early in the morning, and on that day it was prior to daylight. It is a special time when the water is calm, before daily boat traffic begins in earnest. Shorebirds dart into and out of the surf, otters playfully move about in the shallow water, and occasionally dolphins swim and dive just offshore in the deeper channel. On some days, light fog over the water dampens nature's sounds and adds to the serenity.

" Usually there are no other people present, but once in a while a small boat might glide along the water's edge with fishermen seeking flounder in the shallows. I believe they share the quiet.

"My experiences at the waterfront always bring me to a state of inner serenity. In this state, conversations begin. I suspect that being in a meditative state of mind is the key, but – and I know this will sound a bit unusual -- it is as if the river serves as a medium between me and the others.

"The conversations are not overt, for that would change the ambience. I worry that the sound of my own voice might disrupt my state of mind and affect the dialoge. So the conversations are more in my head, and while at the waterfront the dialogue is not always clear to me. As a general rule, the clarity comes only after I return to the house.

"But let me return to the pattern of the communication experience.

"Initially, the thoughts going through my mind involve unresolved matters from my own life, but invariably my mind's eye drifts to the Old Burying Ground and the Everitt family plot.

"Generally, I envision the central obelisk, which was placed in 1855 in memory of Amelia Caroline's Great-Grandfather Sterling Byrd Everitt. The marker at one time must have stood proudly in the cemetery; but now it is a bit tattered, and it lists ten or fifteen degrees from vertical. Large roots from the adjacent live oak tree push the ground from beneath.

"Then the ancient headstones of other family members come into view. Most of these have been broken, and many lie neglected on the ground where dry leaves, acorns and dirt obscure the markings.

"Finally, I see in my mind's eye the modestly elegant but moss-covered marker for Amelia Caroline Potter Everitt. It is there, at the Everitt plot in the Old Burying Ground that my mind remains until I return to the house.

"Immediately upon my return, I go to the computer and Amelia Caroline begins the day's tale. Sometimes she speaks of her own life, but on occasion her Great-Grandmother speaks through her.

"The pattern of conversation is as if Amelia Caroline were on the front porch and speaking both for herself and for her Great-Grandmother. Words, phrases, descriptions of people and events simply are transferred through me to the keyboard. I am part of a process, but I am not 'of' the story. This is because the majority of events happened long before I came to town."

Again I paused and, during the break in my explanation, Catherine spoke.

"During our previous sessions, you described to me some of the many conversations you had with Amelia Caroline over the years. Is it possible that the voices or cryptic messages are spontaneous recollections of those conversations?" she inquired.

"Yes, I'm certain that is part of the explanation," I said. "However, the story being told through me includes incidents and details which I had not previously known. So the daily entries are a combination of that which I do know and the content of the cryptic messages I receive each day while at the water.

"This sequence, now happening on a daily basis, is at the same time both intriguing and disconcerting. The intrigue grows from the realization that this is happening to or through me. As a scientist, the process holds some fascination for me. Scientifically speaking, I am both a participant in and the observer of an interesting phenomenon. This, by the way, parallels the experience Dr. Everitt, Amelia Caroline's father, had as he was approaching his final days.

"However, in spite of the fascination, I am disconcerted at the thought of being directed by a force which I don't understand.

"Somehow, the events of Amelia Caroline's life and the lives of her ancestors, particularly her Great-Grandmother, intersect with -- indeed are part of -- my own life. By extension, the joys of their lives are my joys and the pain of their lives is my pain. This is true even though the events behind the joys or the pain may have occurred years, decades, or even a century before my birth. I experience both the past joys and the past pains as each day's story unfolds before me on the computer screen.

"But then maybe I misspoke when I said that I was not 'of' the story. Perhaps through the influence of these inexplicable forces, I am part of their story.

"All of this goes through my mind on a daily basis. So you see, Catherine, interpretation of the phrase 'my night' is quite complex."

I paused to take a few deep breaths and regain my perspective. After a moment, I continued.

"At present, that explanation is as close as I can come to conveying the meaning of 'brings me through my night.'

"I wrestle daily with two questions. Is possession by the dead an illusion, simply a manifestation secondary to obsession with an ancient cemetery? Or, alternatively, have I truly been chosen to be the voice of those who lie neglected and forgotten beneath the stones, shells and bricks that are scattered about the Old Burying Ground?

"Going back once again to our session several weeks ago, much of what I have tried to describe also applies to my brother Charles and his friend Louis. I seem to have become their 'voices in death,' as well.

"The unanswered questions inherent in what I have just said, and the emotions I share daily with Amelia Caroline and her Great-Grandmother, are nagging sources of distress. They are intimately related to 'my night,' so I search for understanding and wish for serenity. I look where I can, even to the moon, as expressed in the poem.

14

CAREFREE YEARS

It was hot on Friday morning, August 16, 2002. Amelia Caroline's night had been restless, but she was fully awake as the sun began its ascent over the river.

The nighttime temperature had stayed above eighty degrees and little relief had come from the waterfront. This was a rare situation for a town that for over two hundred years had been characterized by cool ocean breezes even on the warmest summer days. On nights such as the last, Amelia Caroline rarely slept more than a few fitful moments at a time.

Frequently, as was the case that day, she spent the final hours of darkness in the rocker, enjoying the quiet sounds of early morning. Though the air was still, the porch offered relief from heat that had accumulated in the house over the preceding weeks.

The weather for most of the summer had been unusual, with excessively high temperatures. And for a coastal town, the season had been particularly dry. So little rain had fallen that folks throughout the town were concerned for their gardens.

In spite of the drought, the air on this particular morning had a heavy feeling. It brought sensations of primordial moisture and warmth. And it came with a slightly acrid odor associated with a ground suspended between inland swamps and coastal marsh. It was a familiar aroma, pungently salty, and one that brought memories of life in the coastal community.

In earlier years, upon finishing her coffee, Amelia Caroline would have walked the few blocks to the waterfront to watch as the gray morning sky gave way to the reddish-orange glow in the east. Over a period of minutes, the sun would feel its way through clouds low on the horizon, finally bursting with radiance into the open sky over the water.

It was a sequence so common she had seen it thousands of times. Yet that simple beginning to the day had been anything but mundane to Amelia Caroline. She approached the river as one would approach an altar, with a sense of awe tempered by an attitude of reverence. It was at such times that Amelia Caroline, who had long since ceased to participate in formal church activities, experienced a worshipful feeling -- but to what, she did not know.

Amelia Caroline was now ninety-nine years, three months and five days old, and I was to spend another day with her on the porch in conversation.

I had awakened quite early, also. My day began in the kitchen making coffee and laying out everything necessary to make biscuits. We had a small amount of country ham left in the pantry from our Fourth of July celebration, and Amelia Caroline had requested ham biscuits for breakfast. Now, ham biscuits are not on the preferred food list distributed by the American Heart Association, but they are a Southern tradition going back to the earliest days of the Colonial Carolinas.

I took two cups of coffee, one prepared exactly as Amelia Caroline liked it, and went to the porch.

"Good morning, Aunt Amelia," I said and kissed her gently in greeting. "I'll sit with you for a few minutes and enjoy my coffee, then go in and prepare the biscuits."

"Good morning, Mary Eliza. The coffee smells wonderful, " Amelia Catherine responded, and to my surprise she moved smoothly into a continuation of her story from the previous night, when she had recalled for me the circumstances surrounding the death in 1971 of her father.

Memories of other conversations also had been going through Amelia Caroline's mind during the night. So, as she slowly rocked in the warm morning air, her hands delicately wrapped around her coffee cup, she began to speak.

I have been thinking over our conversation last night, Mary, Eliza, which focused upon the resumption of conversation with Great-Grandmother following my father's death. Her return was a comfort to me at that time and it has remained so over the past thirty years.

These thoughts then took me back to 1918 when the very first conversation with Great-Grandmother took place. I mentioned that communication to you briefly before and promised that I would explain it all in detail when we had time.

That period was particularly trying for me, as so many significant changes were coming about in my life. I was just a teenager, yet due to the war in Europe I was confronted with very complex situations. Over time, my actions during the war became adult, yet emotionally I was still an inexperienced young girl.

As the country prepared for entry into the war in 1917, the town underwent radical change. Then over the next two years, the tragedies in Europe reached across the ocean and touched us here. I experienced the war's impact, but I did not understand much of what was occurring. As a consequence of those times, I started to question my religious beliefs. Some years later I stopped attending services and, as you know, I eventually gave up church membership altogether. In addition, as a result of those war years, I began to realize the limitations placed upon me as a young woman growing up in the parochial environment of a small, conservative Southern town.

To say that Amelia Caroline did not attend local worship service was to put her into a fairly small minority. Most of the town's residents had been born into, raised under the watchful eyes of, and planned to be buried by one of the town's Christian congregations.

In fact, church affiliation for many was the major source of social contact as well as personal identity. Churches dominated on Sunday and held both Wednesday-evening study groups and Saturday prayer meetings. By the time the men's Bible study or the women's worship society had been attended, there was little time left for activities other than earning a living or doing home chores.

Many of the townsfolk were so involved with religion that they identified themselves not by their own personally intrinsic qualities and characteristics, but rather by church affiliation. They saw themselves as Methodists, Baptists, Episcopalians or Catholics. Furthermore, it was common for them to feel that a major charge in their lives was to bring others into their particular congregational fold.

Newcomers to town, even before exchanging pleasantries common to new acquaintances, were accosted with invitations to come visit the church. Not just any church, but

113

only the specific congregation of the person with whom the newcomer happened to be speaking at the moment.

I had first learned of Amelia Caroline's religious leanings during the summer of 1983, while visiting on vacation. This morning's recollections allowed my mind to briefly fall back to that conversation of nineteen years ago.

As you know, Mary Eliza, I have little use for established religion. Yet I do not look with distain at the religiously focused. I simply don't identify with their priorities. This has been the case for my entire adult life, and it has been so in spite of extensive religious training during my early years.

Our family, as far back as knowledge of it goes, had affiliated with the Episcopal Church, either the one here in town or the one up the river in Wilmington. This lineage extends back as far as my Great-Great-Grandfather. Dr. Reuben Everitt, Sr. was an Anglican by birth and, based upon what I know of religious practice in Connecticut in the late 18th century, he probably was quite devout. What I do know for certain is that, following his relocation from Connecticut to the fort here in town, his Anglican orientation was maintained. He became affiliated with the congregation of St. James in Wilmington. This remained the case until his death in 1813. Of course in those days, church attendance could be sporadic, for travel from this area up to Wilmington was not a simple venture.

The religious orientation of the Everitt family was shared by the family of Great-Grandmother, who was a daughter-in-law to Dr. Everitt, Sr. Great-Grandmother's parents, Samuel Potter and his wife Anne, were also affiliated with the Wilmington church.

In addition, when the local Episcopal Church, St. Philips, was chartered in 1843 as the Chapel of the Cross, members of the Potter family as well as those of the Everitt family became founding members.

Later that same year, both families participated in construction of the first church meeting hall. The land for the church was located adjacent to the northern boundary for the garrison. In fact, even today on the street near the St. Philips Sanctuary are markers which delineate boundaries for the garrison property.

Construction of the first church building was carried out primarily by troops from the garrison and Colonel Thomas Childs, commander at the fort, served as overseer on the project.

Religion and the military, from the outset, were woven together.

This was the religious heritage that I came to share, at least until the war in 1918. Throughout my childhood and young adult years, I attended St. Philips Church and my father served as one of the church elders. When the town became involved in the war, I was well steeped in religion. That, however, changed."

During that first conversation in 1983, Amelia Caroline had given me a thumbnail sketch of what had transpired during the 1918 war and explained how the events stemming from the war had brought her to question her own religious beliefs.

This August morning, it was becoming clear that she wished to return to the years of her youth and the war. The events of that time had remained foremost in Amelia Caroline's memory because they led to the first actual conversation with her Great-Grandmother.

I went into the house for the biscuits, small slices of ham, preserves and some juice. Upon my return, we again settled into our respective chairs on the porch, then Amelia Caroline's tale for the morning began.

My early years, those preceding the war, were pleasurable. Life in our small riverfront town was unencumbered by stresses from the outer world. Virtually everything we needed, and most things just desired, were available in local stores.

The town in 1910, when I was seven years old, had a population just over 1200. We had three dry goods stores, a bakery, a livery, a small dairy, two pharmacies, two doctors – one of whom was my father -- a dentist and various establishments to support the local fishing industry. Fishing, along with crops being grown in the surrounding county for shipment to places as far off as Philadelphia and New York City, provided income for many of the residents.

The years were a time of prosperity. I have already told you about the railroad that came when I was eight years old. Over the following two years, the rail service enhanced the town. A special railroad pier was built out over the water to accommodate ship-borne freight. The pier extended nearly 350 feet into the channel and, at its end, there was a wharf that could accommodate ships up to 400 feet in length. Ultimately, a coaling station for ships was added, and the town leaders began to speculate about a major port with numerous shipping terminals.

Rail lines were envisioned that would extend from the town's waterfront to the agricultural and manufacturing centers of the Midwest.

It wasn't long after the train came that a modern electric plant was built. This, in turn, made it possible to install streetlights in the downtown area. Shortly thereafter, an ice-making company was opened just down the street from the depot.

Even local agriculture benefitted from the rail service, as the prospects for more distant markets became evident. Mr. B. F. Stiffler purchased agricultural land in the county northeast of town. Formerly of Michigan, he recently had relocated to the town to help with the electric light industry, but he soon realized the opportunity presented by the railroad. His intention was to establish a fig orchard on the high ground paralleling the river. About the same time, Mr. Thomas Thompson announced that forty acres of his farm would be dedicated to fruit production, including grapes and citrus.

The train also brought visitors who came from throughout the country. The town, after all, was being touted as the newest up-and-coming city of the South. But travel to the area, particularly during the hot summer season, was not a new phenomenon. The region had been recognized for its salubrious climate since just after the American Revolutionary War

The town was abuzz. Although I was just entering my pre-teen years, I was swept along with the excitement. Each day when we were out of school for lunch, my friends and I would run to the train station. There, along with others from the town, we would greet the incoming train. A few years later, I remembered the joy of those days and, for a school project, I wrote a poem about the train. Papa and my school teacher decided that the poem was good enough to share with others, so

Papa showed it to the newspaper editor, who agreed. My memories became part of the town's folk history.

NOONTIME TRAIN

Click-ity clack, click-ity clack
And wheels go roun' and roun'
Children run, they shout with joy
The noontime train's near town

Cross the fields, down the lanes
They hop and skip, they race
To be there first, the one see
The train stop in its place

Through the alley, jump a fence
The race goes on each day
For every child wants to be
There waiting at the quay

The station master rings a call
So all nearby can hear
The noontime train is on the mark
Its whistle sounds out clear

And so they gather at the rails
The young and old, alike
They came by horse, some by foot
A few arrived by bike

The children jockeyed to the front
Got close so they could see
The engineer who drove the train
And each wished that he could be

Inside that engine, pulling strong
The throttle close at the hand
And reaching up, the whistle line
To caution those who stand

While gathered there upon the quay
Eyes focused down the track
They watched the mighty engine work
With smoke thrown from the stack

Excitement ripples through the crowd
The engine rounds the bend
They see it steaming toward the town
Know soon its trip will end

The children skip and dance about
They clap their hands, so free
For moving toward them, down the rails
It's this they came to see

With screeching brakes, metal grinds
Of wheels upon the track
A coach pulls slowly to the gate
The noontime train is back

Billowing steam beneath the cab
The boiler gives a sigh
Again the noontime train has stopped
The sun high in the sky

As in the past, the crowd remains
To see who will alight
Perhaps some family or a friend
It is always such delight

They welcome in the little town
All who've ridden on the track
Perhaps to have a pleasant day
Then catch the outbound back

The clock moves on, the children go
They've seen what there's to see
But, as on many days before
They leave with shouts of glee

And others move across the town
But know they'll come again
When whistles sound and children shout
"Here comes the Noontime Train"

Amelia Caroline Everitt , 1916

From the time it was first settled, the small town surrounding the fort had been a destination during the summer season for wealthy families. They came from inland plantations to escape the oppressive heat in the sand-hill region of the state. And they came from along the northeastern stretches of the river, hoping to escape from the malaria which plagued the wetland plantations.

Travel in those early days was almost exclusively by ship, though horse-drawn coach service was sporadically available to the more adventurous travelers. All of this changed dramatically with initiation of the train service.

Soon, as the railroad schedule became established, casual visitors could comfortably make day trips to our town. So they came in a constant stream. Folks from Wilmington, Richmond, Raleigh, Halifax and Greenville came to enjoy the sea breezes and fresh fish. They came from all walks of life and from the far reaches of the nation.

Included among these was the Honorable Ira A. Abbott, who had been appointed in 1904 by President Theodore Roosevelt to serve as Associate Justice of the Supreme Court of the New Mexico Territory. In 1915, Justice Abbott came to the town at the invitation of his lifelong friend, Colonel Stride, but while in the community he visited with many of the notable families, including ours.

He was an enthralling dinner guest. I learned during the course of the evening that he had been an infantry officer during the Civil War. After the war, he entered the legal profession in his home state of Connecticut. Most fascinating for me, however, were the tales he told of his eight years serving as a justice on the Supreme Court in the New Mexico Territory.

At the time, the New Mexico Territory was part of the legendary Wild West. Justice Abbott described his early experiences there, which began in 1904. Images of cowboys, gunslingers, stagecoaches and range wars went through my

119

mind as he talked. After all, my friends and I had read many of the stories of the West that were being published in the five-cent magazines.

Justice Abbott retired from the court in 1912 after New Mexico entered the Union as the forty-seventh state.

In addition to my fantasies, I was enthralled with the stories of Spanish culture and daily life in the still untamed Western territory. Justice Abbott actually had met many famous Western lawmen such as Wyatt Earp and, over dinner, he told stories of his association with Pat Garrett, the sheriff who captured Billy the Kid. The next day, I was the envy of all my friends at school.

The riverfront, with its remnants of the old fort, was the center of activity for most visitors. The garrison grounds and gardens offered shady areas for walks or relaxation. Flanking the garrison and extending into the water were fishing piers, docks with pleasure boats for leisure sailing, and a pavilion where parties, receptions and community dances were held. There were numerous accommodations, including several small hotels and boarding houses, to welcome visitors who came to vacation in the seaside resort atmosphere.

One of the most famous of the boarding houses was that of Kate Stuart, who had for decades been considered "the hostess" of the community. Ms. Stuart's house had long been a waterfront attraction. The house had welcomed presidents of the United States, U.S. Army generals, senators, famous actors, financiers from New York and Chicago, musicians of all sorts, and everyday travelers who just happened to be passing through town. Its history and fame for hospitality extended back nearly fifty years – having been opened by Kate's mother shortly after the War Between the States.

Another favorite spot for townspeople and visitors alike was the Miller Hotel, with its spacious porches overlooking the water and a restaurant that served the best food in town. The proprietor of the hotel was Leonhard Miller, one of Papa's good friends. Mr. Miller boasted that the billiard room at the back of his hotel was one of the finest to be found on the East Coast. This was not lost on the men of the town. Many Saturday nights found most of the male population crowded into the billiard parlor, where the aroma of home brew mixed with tobacco smoke, while money changed hands around the tables. It was often said that some of the nation's best pool players had enjoyed the hospitality at the hotel. The Whittlers' Bench crowd, on most Monday mornings, shared stories of the billiard room and how the local boys had outplayed the best.

You have to realize, Mary Eliza, that most of my knowledge of the pool room came from Papa. We often dined at the hotel and, after dinner, we would sit together on the hotel veranda. At those times, Papa would share with me the goings-on inside the pool room. After all, the back room of the hotel was not considered a fitting place for women or young people.

Occasionally, some of the boys would be allowed in, but for the most part, church activities were considered more wholesome.

Much of my social life involved participation in activities at St. Philips Church. However, when not at church or attending one of the many church-sponsored social activities, we could spend pleasurable days in the shade of the live oak trees that canopied the city park. We could also enjoy refreshing afternoons on the strand or in the water at the town beach. But one of the greatest pleasures came when adults from the church took us on outings to the oceanfront on Caswell Island across the bay.

For these excursions, moderately sized skiffs, sharpies and other small sailing craft would be loaded with beach paraphernalia and picnic baskets early in the day. Then, with one eye toward the weather and the other on the tide, our flotilla would make the three-mile journey to the island, with the intent of returning on the evening tide.

As Amelia Caroline fell silent, quite absorbed in a private part of her memories, I wondered if she was remembering some of the events that were about to change both her life and the world at that time.

It had been natural for Amelia Caroline, who was quite popular among her peers, to spend her days with others her age under the guiding hands and watchful eyes of church members. But events that occurred during her teen years brought significant change to this church relationship. War lifted the town from the idyllic and thrust it headlong into the chaos of world events.

Over the course of time, involvement in this war and others that followed created a schism between Amelia Caroline and the faith in which she was raised.

15

A MILITARY TOWN

After years of waiting and reading news reports from across the ocean, the town's people were proud to learn, in 1917, of President Wilson's decision to commit to an active part in the war effort.

For years, the Kaiser had marched his armies across Europe, bringing widespread death and destruction. Finally, after much hesitation, the United States had relinquished its position of neutrality, declared war against Imperial Germany and pledged support for its allies in Europe. Young soldiers from cities, rural villages, farm crossroads and small coastal towns were soon joining the effort.

Amelia Caroline's hometown also felt the war's impact as its young men clamored to join the ranks. But it also became a focus for support of the war effort when attention turned to the local fort as a potential partner in the coastal defense network. Within a matter of weeks, the seaside resort and fishing village again became a military town.

I gently asked, "Aunt Amelia, are you remembering the First World War? Do you want to talk about it?"

She smiled. She both knew and was pleased that I had read her thoughts.

So many changes came in a very brief period, Mary Eliza. Soldiers arrived in town from across the nation to man the fort, while others reestablished defenses on the island.

Our church picnics across the bay came to an end, and church socials were replaced by evenings at the local lodge, which had been converted to a servicemen's club. It was a home-away-from-home where the soldiers could go in the evenings to spend a few hours forgetting the pressures of military life.

During the daytime, the soldiers were also welcomed at the "Dainty," a small lunchroom operated by the ladies of St. Philips Church. Home-cooked meals were offered, including a number of local seafood dishes and a wide selection of breads and other baked goods.

Everyone seemed anxious to help support the "boys." Papa even gave permission for Mrs. Wescott to spend some of her "work time" away from the house so she could help out at the Dainty. The fried chicken, which she prepared each Wednesday, was a particular favorite of the soldiers. And Mrs. Wescott's involvement was my ticket to help serve meals after school on those days.

The changes in town were exciting and they promised adventure for me and my friends. As you would expect, being in our teen years, we were flattered by the attention we received from the soldiers. In addition, I had a special feeling of importance, for I often assisted Papa, who had assumed partial responsibility for the health of the troops. This was no small task for Papa. Many of the young men suffered from camp fevers, intestinal disorders, flu and other diseases common to close quartering of people whose prior lives had been spent in relative isolation.

Unbeknownst to me, as the months passed and evolved into years, I slowly left my childhood perspective and activities behind. Through events related to the war I, even at my young age, was beginning to assume a professional attitude. Much of this was due to the fact that, in a limited sort of way, I became a colleague to my father.

Initially, Mary Eliza, I sympathized with the war and, in many ways, I felt great pride in the support shown by virtually everyone in town.

The Miller Hotel and several of the boarding houses had lowered their rates to ease the financial burden on the soldiers and their families who had been displaced from life elsewhere and brought here.

Several of my friends and I volunteered time after school to help the Red Cross. The Red Cross chapter was newly established, so there was a lot of enthusiasm and support. We spent that time helping the women who were making bandages for shipment overseas. The work was tedious, but we knew the medical supplies were desperately needed to treat men who had been wounded in battle. Not to be outdone by the White community, members of the Black community established a parallel Red Cross unit through the AME Zion Church.

When not busy in school and also not involved with other pressing needs, such as helping Papa or working with the Red Cross, I spent many hours visiting with soldiers at the Army-Navy Club. I, along with many of my friends, became totally immersed in the military culture that swept the town.

The Army-Navy Club had been established by local volunteers in conjunction with the Salvation Army and the War Camp Community Service (WCCS), the latter being a national organization authorized by the Council for National Defense in Washington, DC. The goal of the national program was to provide social and recreational facilities in support of soldiers.

The club was located in the park, so it was just a short walk from our house. The setting was pastoral, as the park back then had even more ancient live oaks than it has today. The stately trees surrounded the fraternal lodge in which the club was located. Also in the park were two churches and the town school.

Administration of the club was under the chairmanship of Mr. Jens Berg, a former teacher. He was a distant cousin to Sven Berg who worked as a druggist in Papa's pharmacy.

Jens Berg was a man of great energy and intelligence and he was involved with numerous business ventures. He also served as supervisor at the Federal Quarantine Station located just offshore in the river.

Originally the club had been managed by the Salvation Army, but their operational guidelines discouraging dances were not appreciated by the soldiers. As a result, attendance at the club was not as anticipated.

Soon, in recognition of the problem, management was changed. The club came under the less restrictive guidelines of the WCCS. Jens Berg took the helm as chairman and James Culton became the director for day-to-day operations. Following the administrative transition, and with loosening of the restrictions, the club became extremely popular.

Spending time in the club was particularly enjoyable for all the young women, as almost every evening the dance hall was crowded with soldiers looking for a good time. The club was an overwhelming success and was supported by the entire town. A canteen was established and managed by Miss Laura Larson. Townsfolk donated a "Victrola" with records. Books, magazines and newspapers were kept current and, on numerous occasions, local musicians played for the dances.

Our program was so popular that, over time, the Army-Navy Club became a model for the entire nation. Was the town ever proud! Following the war, Mr. Berg and Mr. Culton were recognized by the Council for National Defense. They were cited for outstanding service in support of the war effort. Ultimately, Mr. Culton joined the executive staff of the WCCS and our program became known throughout the nation.

War, it seemed, was an exciting activity, one that brought fascinating people and interesting events to our rural community, which until that time had been a pleasant, but sleepy village. So dramatic was the transition that Mr. John Colter, who worked with the WCCS and visited the Army-Navy Club during the war, wrote of his experience for the Community Service Bulletin, *a national publication. In the article, "The Town That Found Itself," Mr. Colter stated, "It took a war to wake up Southport."*

The community had become a flagship in the national armada. Buntings and flags were hung from porch rails, patriotic speeches were regularly delivered from the courthouse steps and military marches were played at concerts in the park.

Military aircraft flew over the town to drop leaflets we referred to as "timely messages from the clouds" that encouraged the purchase of war bonds. "Victory Bonds" were sold at the Army-Navy Club.

Soldiers from the fort across the bay and those stationed at the garrison on the waterfront, while proudly walking the streets in their newly issued and snappy uniforms, were warmly greeted by friends and strangers alike. The presence of a government dock with an official U.S. Navy vessel at the waterfront signified the community's commitment and involvement. In the beginning, it was all very glamorous.

Initially, Mary Eliza, everything was new and exciting. Then the real war began to come home.

Here Amelia Caroline paused in thought for several minutes.

Finally, I broke the silence and asked, "Would you enjoy another cup of coffee, Aunt Amelia?"

"Yes, that would be nice, Mary Eliza," she replied.

So I entered the house, went to the kitchen and warmed the coffee. A few minutes later, I returned to the porch, and Amelia Caroline had obviously collected her thoughts because she immediately resumed the story.

Early in 1917, Joseph Miller, whose parents operated the Miller Hotel, was killed in an explosion at the U.S. Arsenal in Frankford, Pennsylvania. Joseph was a few years older than I. Still, we had been childhood friends and had shared school experiences, church picnics and days swimming with other friends at the beach. Like many of the older boys, Joseph volunteered for service shortly after the war preparations began in 1916. He was assigned duty in the arsenal on the East Side of Philadelphia.

At the time, the Frankford Arsenal was one of the nation's largest and oldest armories, having been in operation for over one hundred years. Joseph's assignment to the arsenal was in response to an order issued in March of 1917 by Secretary of War Newton Baker. The order directed Colonel George Montgomery, then commander at the arsenal, to significantly expand production of artillery ammunition to be used in Europe. In response, the number of workers was increased to over 3600 and all worked extended hours.

Pressure was intense. Then on April 12, 1917, an explosion occurred. Joseph and another man were killed.

Joseph's death was the first local casualty of the war. A notice describing the explosion, stating that Joseph had been injured, was published on that day in the evening edition of the Clearfield Progress *in Clearfield, Pennsylvania.*

Joseph's parents, however, were later notified by the military that Joseph had died in the explosion. The rest of the town learned the details through numerous news articles sent by various friends who lived in Pennsylvania. We also learned that the explosion at Frankford, although taking two lives and injuring several others, was not considered particularly severe.

Initially the explosion was attributed to carelessness. However, the Frankford event occurred close after a similar incident at the Eddystone Munitions Plant a few miles away from Frankford in Chester, Pennsylvania, on April 10, 1917.

The death toll at the Eddystone Plant exceeded one hundred, and the Chester Times *reported as many as 130 killed on that day.*

On the day of the Frankford event when Joseph Miller died, the Chester Times *reported that "German or Austrian Plotters are Responsible for Munition Disaster in Opinion of Many." The following day's headline read, "Government Agents Working on Many Reported Plots in Conjunction with Ammunition Disaster."*

Speculation in Pennsylvania and throughout much of the nation was rampant. German or Austrian plotters might have caused the explosions at the arsenals, and it was suggested to The New York Times *by a special agent of the Justice Department that the perpetrators might have died in the incidents. Several weeks later, Russian socialists were added to the list of suspects.*

These speculations on the part of the press brought suspicion to the minds of some in town. Mind you, there were no overt accusations; but in those days, small, relatively isolated Southern towns often had a few small-minded folks. "Back-room, country-store gossip" regarding the explosions was not unknown.

Joseph Miller's father, Leonhard, was an Austrian immigrant to the U.S. In 1906, shortly after the first Russian Revolution, he had joined the Socialist Party of America. This was not an unusual action for, at the time, many people throughout the country -- and the world for that matter -- supported the political and social values of the socialist movement.

Nearly everyone knew of Leonhard Miller's background, but it had no bearing upon the high esteem in which he was held. He was, in fact, recognized as one of the town's leading citizens. He had been a candidate for the governorship of North Carolina in 1916 and, just one month prior to Joseph's death, he was elected to serve as a member of the Executive Committee for the Southport Commercial Association.

Yet, identification with "foreign political views" was incriminating to those who were small minded. Anti-German and anti-socialist sentiments were not unknown here, even though they were subtle. Even prominent members of the Black community, good loyal citizens, were suspected by some of harboring German sympathies.

Both Leonhard and his son Joseph were patriots beyond question. The overwhelming majority of residents realized that there was no basis for such talk and were aware that the finger-pointing reported from Pennsylvania was pure speculation.

Joseph had gone to Frankford out of loyalty to his country. His death had come as the result of a patriotic act on his part. Neither he nor his father had been part of a sinister plot but, in times of trial, small minds lose sight of reality.

Mary Eliza, this incident was perhaps my first realization that even here, a town that for me had been a child's paradise, prejudice and suspicions were often not far below the surface. And I knew that some who harbored unfounded suspicions were members of various churches, where loving kindness was a focal teaching.

Soon after receiving notice of their son's death, Joseph's parents and his sister Anna traveled to Pennsylvania to accompany Joseph on his final journey home. At the church funeral a few days later, I listened carefully to the minister's words and searched the hymns for relevance. Yet neither the minister's words nor the hymns satisfied me.

Questions raced through my mind over the following days. "How could a loving God take such an innocent young man?" And, "By what justification could some of my neighbors, who professed belief in the teaching of Christian religions, harbor unsubstantiated suspicions about an innocent young man?"

I was approaching the age of fifteen, yet I felt that my carefree teen years were being swept away. I was being plunged headlong into adulthood and was having thoughts and experiences that should have been reserved for my later years.

Mary Eliza, through events of that time and over the ensuing months, I began to realize that the doctrines of my religion often were inconsistent with the practices and lives of its congregations.

We had been on the porch for quite a while, and the August 16th late-morning sun was high in the sky. Our biscuits had long since been eaten. It was time for a stretch, so we entered the house to do the dishes and tidy the kitchen.

While working, Amelia Caroline said she would like to take a short walk, so we did. As we were walking, I turned to

Amelia Caroline and asked what had become of the Miller family.

After a brief pause, she responded.

Mr. Miller continued to operate the hotel throughout the war, then in 1920 he decided to retire to Upstate New York, so ownership of the hotel was transferred to Anna and her husband, David Davis. They continued to operate the hotel until 1946 and, over those years, the hotel remained a center of social life in town.

Anna, following in the footsteps of her father, became quite active in the community. She was the first woman in town to register as a voter and, after registering, she participated in a series of citizenship lectures presented for women.

Following sale of the hotel, Anna and her husband remained in town. Their only daughter Elizabeth had married a young man from Norfolk. The hotel went through a series of owners and, in the 1960s, it burned. That fire brought to end a major chapter in the life of the town and, having spent many evenings of my life sitting with Papa on the veranda of the hotel, its loss brought some sadness to me. Ultimately, the land on which the hotel had stood was dedicated as part of the waterfront park.

We walked a few houses down the street to the corner, where we stopped for a moment. As we stood there, Amelia Caroline turned to me and said, "I have known this sidewalk since my earliest days when the roadways and walkways were paved with sand and shell. Here I am in the year 2002, more than ninety-nine years in age and, other than for the concrete surface, the walk feels the same as when I played here as a child. And just as in those days so long ago, the sea breeze is coming up Lord Street from the waterfront. Can you smell the salt marsh, Mary Eliza? The tide must be low. I have always loved this experience."

I put my arm around Amelia Caroline and smiled at her pleasure. "Yes, Aunt Amelia, I love it also."

Our walk was not long, but it was refreshing. We soon returned to the porch and our conversation.

16

DISILLUSIONMENT

For Amelia Caroline, the seeds of disconnect between the formal teachings of her religion – as she understood them – and its practice by many in town were planted during that early war. But those seeds did not fully bloom until the early 1970s, more than five decades and three wars later. The final schism occurred between Amelia Caroline and organized religion after yet another conversation with her Great-Grandmother.

Now, as she sat in her chair on the warm August morning in 2002, Amelia Caroline's mind went back to that pivotal conversation about religion and war. Although the two conversations were separated by so many years, the circumstances of the two times evoked similar emotions in Amelia Caroline. The latter of the two conversations occurred about two years following her father's death and a different kind of war dominated the news.

Amelia Caroline, despite her advanced age, needed no hints from me to remember where she had left the discussion earlier in the day, and she resumed as if we had not taken the break for our walk.

Unlike the war of my youth, the one weighing on me in the 1970s was, as you know, being fought in the far-off jungles of Southeast Asia. It was not glamorous, nor did it engender widespread patriotism. Rather, it drove a wedge through the heart of the nation and created animosity between brothers at levels not experienced for over a century. Not since the War Between the States had there been such divisions within the local population. Paradoxically, it was a war that did not directly involve our small town of Southport, except for the families of the boys who went to war and never returned.

The town in the early 1970s was not a military encampment as it had been in the past, but six years of seeing news reports from Vietnam brought sweeping memories of my teen years and the events of 1917 and 1918 that had so fundamentally influenced my life.

Mary Eliza, as the conflict in Vietnam dragged into its seventh and eighth years, my mind was drawn more and more to question how our society, which professed such strong religious underpinnings, could allow the war to continue. Why were the basic tenets of faith not strong enough to overcome the inertia which permitted the government to pursue the conflict? So many lives had been lost and that small country had undergone such destruction. These thoughts were not new to me, for they paralleled those which had been in the back of my mind ever since the war of my youth, and again they brought me into conversation with Great-Grandmother. I think you will understand the significance of that conversation, which I remember in great detail and will share with you.

Words of acknowledgement from me were not necessary, so I just nodded. Actually, I was hesitant to speak, for my own experiences during the Vietnam War had left scars on my psyche. I was concerned that any comment on my part would redirect the conversation to me, my brother Charles and his friend Louis. This was a time to focus on Amelia Caroline, so I remained silent.

Amelia Caroline closed her eyes, and a thirty-year-old conversation began again. Her Great-Grandmother immediately began speaking through Amelia Caroline.

"Amelia Caroline, I sense once again that you want to talk.

"Great-Grandmother, the turmoil over this war in Asia has kept me awake nights and, with the unrest, come thoughts that have been with me for such a long time. They keep going over and over in my mind as if on some sort of track. A treadmill without end that just keeps cycling and recycling."

"What kind of thoughts?" Great-Grandmother asked.

"I'm not sure whether they are thoughts or questions, but the recurring theme has to do with how people treat each other. It all goes back to the First World War when it occurred to me that what was being said and done by many in town was

132

contrary to what they professed to have learned in church and, for that matter, what they had been taught at home."

"Can you tell me what comes to mind from that time?" Great-Grandmother gently questioned.

"Yes. I was, as you are aware, just a child when The Great War began and, with its beginning, I was swept along with most of the town into a patriotic frame of mind in support of the country. It was all so much larger than we either individually or as a town could imagine. A great tidal wave of energy swept us up and carried us unquestioning -- both figuratively and in many cases literally -- to the battlefield. The war became life and patriotic furor became its religion. We did not question.

"In the beginning, apart from the death of Joseph Miller, involvement at the Fort Johnston garrison here in town and at Fort Caswell on the island was mechanical, dealing primarily with logistics. Mostly, the town was prepared for the influx of troops being assigned either to Fort Johnston or to the post on Caswell Island. Both the fort and the post had been upgraded to accommodate a large number of soldiers. In town, apartments had been readied for wives and children of the married men. Then the full impact of the war became apparent.

"In 1917, the government called for a military registration day for the enrollment of men. On a fine day in June, the courthouse was decorated in flags and banners, and women of the town, members of various church groups and civic clubs, were on hand to assist with the registration.

"Though the town was small and the county sparsely populated, 184 registrations were recorded. The next month, following a July 4th celebration filled with patriotic speeches, parades, dances and games, three leaders of the town were elected to the County Council of Defense. Then the town chapter of the Red Cross began to make arrangements to meet the needs of war casualties. There was great enthusiasm.

"During August the first two draft calls were issued, and thirty-four young men left the town to fight a war about which they knew little. Some of them never returned. Others, though eventually back from the war, carried both physical and mental scars for the remainder of their lives.

"On many occasions, the drafted men were given farewell parties. These on the surface were rousing send-offs intended to honor the men who were leaving home. They were

being sent to South Carolina and Georgia to be trained as soldiers and then to fight in far-away countries. But at the same time, these were rallies planned as a means to fuel public enthusiasm and ongoing support for the war.

"In a fashion, it was paradoxical to have young people from town being shipped elsewhere for training, while at the same time hundreds of recruits and officers from other parts of the country were being stationed locally. Most of the newcomers were out at Fort Caswell on the island across the bay where they served in the coastal defense corps.

"With the influx of recruits, Papa's activities increased as he helped tend medical needs of the troops. Mostly he treated cuts, broken bones and other minor injuries acquired during routine training. But as the number of soldiers increased, ultimately swelling the town and surrounds to more than three times its original population, so did the number and severity of the problems.

"Much of this was due to crowded conditions and poor facilities under which the soldiers had to live. As a result, epidemics routinely swept through the camps. Before the first year ended, soldiers at Fort Caswell had been quarantined to the island. This measure was taken to protect the town from the threat of measles that was running rampant among the troops.

"The quarantine compounded matters for the healthy soldiers as well, for they were isolated among their sick comrades. The quarantine also contributed to emotional strain here in town, as the married soldiers no longer had the liberty to cross the bay to visit family members, wives and children who had taken up residence in town.

"Though news readily came from Fort Caswell, as there were daily couriers and new soldiers being transported across the bay, there was great anxiety in town among the family members who found it difficult to get specific news of their loved ones.

"Papa tried his best to bring news back from the island each evening. Generally, his news pertained to the most serious of his cases. A few families did receive reassuring news, but with a great many of the soldiers being sick, he could not satisfy everyone's need. It was a prolonged and unpleasant time, which according to my father could largely have been avoided had the Army simply made better provision for the soldiers.

"Less than a year after the influx of soldiers began, an epidemic of Spanish Influenza swept through the Caswell post. Over time, the flu extended into town, then into the county. Within days the number of afflicted soldiers had reached 500. Almost half of those stationed on the island were sick. Every morning Papa would rise before dawn and travel across the bay. He would then return home in the early afternoon to tend his patients in town. Invariably, he would work until ten or eleven P.M. before arriving home exhausted.

"Papa was being worn out with all these demands and he needed help. So I began to petition him to take me along to serve as a nurse. After all, I had been around his practice and in the pharmacy all my life. Ever since the war began, I had helped with some of the patients in town.

"Initially, he objected. He called attention to my studies and to the fact that I was already helping in the pharmacy while he was away. But he also was worried that I would be more at risk for the flu if I went to the island.

"However, I was persistent, and I pointed out that I was already being exposed to the flu here in town, and besides my entire life had involved exposure to the many diseases he treated. I also pointed out that he could hire one of my school classmates to assist Sven Berg in the pharmacy. After all, my role in the pharmacy was not complex: it was simply to keep items on the shelves and help at the sales counter. Occasionally, I would deliver medicines to the homes of those too sick or elderly to come into the store. This, I argued, could be done by any one of my friends, and whoever was hired would be excited to earn a little spending money to use at the Amuzu movie theater, in Willie McKenzie's Ice Cream Parlor, or at the concession counter in the Army-Navy Club.

"Finally, after much persuasion on my part and with the subtle support of Mr. Berg, Papa relented. Providing my studies were kept up, he agreed to my missing one day of school in the middle of each week to help him on the island. In addition, I would accompany him on Saturdays and also whenever he went on Sunday after church.

"As I think back, the experiences I had during the flu epidemic probably were among the deciding factors in my later choice to attend nursing school.

"Papa did not expect me to be involved with the worst aspects of patient care, as my skills were limited; but I did

135

provide another hand for him, and I was ready to fetch, hold, clean and give comfort when instructed.

"Shortly after I began my adventure in nursing on the island, the deaths from the flu began and they continued long after the armistice was signed to bring the war to a close.

"Great-Grandmother, I was shocked at the conditions under which the soldiers had to live and the limited medical resources that were available to them. I had learned through history lessons at school that soldiers during the Civil War endured great privation. But I really had had no concept of what it meant to live as did the soldiers either back then or as I now observed on the island. The deadly flu was much more severe and more widespread among the soldiers than among the townspeople or those who lived out of town in the county. And Papa explained that much of this was due to the conditions under which the soldiers had to live.

"I also came to realize, some years later during my nursing training, that during the war many more soldiers were casualties of deprivation and disease than of combat.

"It was also during the influenza epidemic in the fall of 1918 that I met William Banes, who had been drafted six months earlier. He was barely over the eligible age when he was called up and had to leave his family's farm in the mountains of Western North Carolina .

"Shortly after induction, he was shipped to Fort Caswell for artillery training. However, his assignment to the island resulted in his contracting a number of the diseases which were constantly spreading among the recruits. Ultimately this led to his death. It was through William that I had my first direct exposure to life in the miliary and the horrors of war. We met on the island, but not under circumstances that either of us would have chosen.

"I had accompanied my father one Wednesday afternoon, as we had agreed, to tend the troops. The number of ill soldiers by that time had clearly become too great for the resident military doctor to handle even with my father's help, and nursing care which normally was provided by the Red Cross was woefully insufficient in the face of the epidemic. So I began to assist the few soldiers who were assigned nursing duty in the wards.

"William was among those most seriously sick. His illness, when the autumn chill and dampness were added on top

of an inadequate diet and marginal living conditions, had advanced to pneumonia. His breathing was labored as he struggled for air and feverishness had brought him near to delirium. His condition, though grave, was still not quite as severe as some around him whose jaundiced appearance and low kidney function were suggestive of pending death.

"Over the next several days and weeks, we – my father and I, that is -- tended the troops numerous times. By the end of the second week, we were gratified to see that some, William included, were showing signs of improvement.

"It was during these latter days that William and I began to visit more as friends than as patient and nurse. He talked longingly of his home and life on the farm, and it was during those conversations that I learned that he had suffered other illnesses, including measles, fluxes, fevers and infections, almost from the time of his arrival on the island. In fact, he had been of little service to the Army and it had not served him well, either.

"To cheer William, I shared some of my life, telling him of the enjoyable activities in town, in which he as a new recruit -- if that term applies to someone who has been enlisted involuntarily -- had not been able to partake.

"So it went, and we continued as friends until my father felt that I was no longer needed to help tend the troops on such a frequent basis. However, with his permission, I did invite William to visit some Sunday afternoon when he was able to come to town. However, we agreed this should not be in the immediate future; although greatly improved, William was still mildly feverish and weak.

"I spent the next two weeks back in town. My father continued his trips to the island to tend his usual patients, but he also took care of a few soldiers from Fort Johnston just down the street. I became busy with schoolwork and resumed my after-school tasks in the pharmacy. When not busy there, I tried to help the Red Cross and, when possible, would go to the Army-Navy Club to visit with soldiers.

"Then one Sunday, much to my surprise, Papa and I met William as we were walking home from church. William had no duty for the day and he had decided to accompany others from the island for an afternoon in town. Papa insisted that William join us for dinner and he hinted that I could show William around town afterward.

137

"I was excited about the prospect of having my very own soldier for a day, so after dinner and the proper amount of polite conversation, William and I set out on a walk to the soda fountain at the Miller Hotel for ice cream. Then we went to the pavilion at the waterfront.

"We had a wonderful time and, as would be expected of a young girl, I was so proud to be showing William around.

"However, it became apparent to me as the afternoon progressed that William's condition had not improved greatly since I had last seen him. By late afternoon, his fever had returned. Papa, upon seeing William's state when we got back to the house, went to the duty officer at Fort Johnston and requested permission to keep William in town for care.

"However, officials at Fort Johnston said that such an arrangement would be inappropriate. William was assigned to a unit on the island, therefore care could and would be given to him back at the post. William, they said, would have to return to his unit on the island, which he did.

"Papa's negotiations over William's condition, though done with the best intentions, were unfortunate in that they delayed William's return to his unit and he arrived after post curfew. This tardiness brought William to the attention of the duty sergeant.

"William, as it turned out, had been free from duty as he had told us, but he had not obtained a pass to leave the unit. In my view, going three miles across the bay for a few hours on an afternoon when you are essentially free to do as you please seems a minor infraction. To do so in the Army without first obtaining a pass to leave the grounds apparently can be construed as a criminal offense. In William's case, it was.

"William, though still recovering from illness, was confined to the post stockade. He was held there under conditions far worse than those which initially had contributed to the progression of his disease.

"About midweek, Papa traveled to Fort Caswell to check some of the cases with which he was involved. While there, he inquired about William. It was at that time that he learned of the stockade confinement, which he shared with me later in the day.

"Papa, out of concern for William's health, asked to visit the stockade, but he was denied access and told that Army personnel were providing care. Later that week, only six days after his visit to our house, William died in the stockade."

Sharing the story of William's death with her Great-Grandmother had brought tears to Amelia Caroline's eyes in 1973. Retelling the story to me that August morning in 2002 brought the same response. The pain had not subsided, although nearly eighty-four years had passed since William's death.

As Amelia Caroline sat with me on the porch, she again quietly wept. Her sadness was due to the death of a young man, a friend, who had died for no reason other than the Army's need to control all aspects of his life.

I understood that the duty sergeant in 1918 had acted from a framework of power similar to the one that had determined the actions of Dr. Tillier in the death of Amelia Caroline's father in 1971. Rules of decorum and professional conventions were brought to bear in situations where simple human kindness, compassion and reason were greatly needed. Yet the latter were pushed to the side.

It was clear that Amelia Caroline's recollection of events in 1918 had been precipitated in 1973 by the graphic news coming out of the war in Vietnam. And this had led Amelia Caroline to the conversation with her Great-Grandmother.

It was also quite clear to me that the emotions from William's death eighty-four years earlier had not lessened, for here they were once again welling to the surface on a day when Amelia Caroline was ninety-nine years, four months and five days of age.

Over the next few minutes, I could see Amelia Caroline's tears slowly give way to anger that the lives of two persons important to her, her father and William, had been unnecessarily compromised. In both situations, the outcome had been death under what she considered unnatural circumstances.

Amelia Caroline recognized that the underlying motives were different in the two situations: William had died at the hands of an archaic and repressive military organization committed to causes that accepted death as a natural outcome, whereas her father's death had been managed by Dr.Tillier, a good man, whose life was dedicated to the restoration of the health and the well-being of others. But mixed within Dr.Tillier's decision making was an unconscious desire to protect the image of his profession – it was an image accepted by the general populace that, through multiple medical interventions, all patients would benefit .

Amelia Caroline could accept neither of these motives.

She remained caught up in her thoughts for several minutes. Time was of no significance to her as she struggled with memories and emotions that had come repeatedly over the years.

Finally, I decided to break the silence.

"Aunt Amelia, as I understand what you are saying, your very first conversation with your Great-Grandmother followed the death of William in World War I in 1918. I can appreciate your state of mind at that time, and I understand that your Great-Grandmother's presence was consoling to you.

Yes, Mary Eliza. Great-Grandmother's presence was a comfort to me, for I was quite upset and somewhat confused following William's death. And of course, Joseph Miller's death was still on my mind. Great-Grandmother and I talked generally about life and death, and about religion. There were no major resolutions to my thoughts following that first conversation, but I felt much more at ease with myself – particularly with respect to thoughts regarding religion.

"Have you any thoughts about why your conversation with your Great-Grandmother in 1973 reverted back to the events of 1918? Was there a particular event that precipitated that conversation?" I asked, then fell silent as Amelia Caroline provided explanation.

Yes, Mary Eliza, I had many thoughts racing through my mind that day in 1973, and at the core of the thoughts was William's death in 1918. But also, I was still dealing with emotions stemming from Joseph Miller's death and that of my father. I think Great-Grandmother knew that before I could come to any resolution regarding events from so far in my past, I had to untangle the many thoughts in my mind. She also realized that in order to do this, I had to relive the early war years and William's death. She encouraged me to do this in that conversation.

Concerning your question regarding the timing of the conversation in 1973, I remember quite clearly. I had been shopping earlier in the day at Harrelson's Market, which used to be across the intersection from where we are now sitting.

While there, I met Sarah McKeithan, a cousin of Aleine McLaurin, with whom I had been friends for many years. I think

140

*Aleine and my grandmother Emily were somehow related –
perhaps as distant cousins, but I'm not sure. Anyway, Sarah and
I were remembering Aleine's grandson John who had died at
the age of twenty-three in Vietnam in 1968.*

*I bring this up because John's death had weighed on
everyone following his military funeral here in town. There was
extensive television and newspaper coverage of the war every
day at that time, and as a result we came to know more details of
that war than we wanted.*

*Now that I think back, John's death was in Tay Ninh
Province, very near where your brother Charles had died just a
few months earlier. So our grief here in town was paralleling
that of your family in Greenfield.*

*The talk that morning at Harrelson's with Aleine's
cousin brought back all of those memories and they stayed with
me until my return from the market.*

Out of interest as well as curiosity, I couldn't resist
interrupting the flow of Amelia Caroline's thoughts.

"What was Great-Grandmother's response to all that you
said?" I asked. Then, as I awaited her response, I noticed a
change in Amelia Caroline's demeanor. Whether she was
experiencing anger or sadness I could not tell at first.

"She asked a question!" was Amelia Caroline's
somewhat blunt response. Unsure if she was upset with me for
interrupting or at her Great-Grandmother for her response, I sat
totally still as she moved back into her conversation.

*"Amelia Caroline, I see your pain and anger, and I
understand the reaction to your father's death," Great-
Grandmother said. "Your lives had been entwined for almost
seventy years. But what was it about William, a young man you
had known for only a few weeks, that has left you for so long
with an unhealed wound?"*

*"Great-Grandmother, your question has been my
struggle. William and I were just casual friends, but at an age
when I was impressionable, so the friendship probably seemed
more than it was. But how can the depth of a relationship be
measured, particularly one that was formed under such
extraordinary circumstances?*

*"Thinking back to when I learned William had died, my
mind became a wellspring. From its depths flowed memories*

141

and feelings that had been accumulating inside me during that war. What came bubbling out were thoughts of Joseph Miller's death, other events both here in town and far away in the war, and the people those events involved.

"Each of the events had impressed me at the time of its occurrence, but individually they did not bring me to reaction. News of William's death I now know was the key that opened the cap on the well.

"I realized following William's death, as other individual memories began to slam against my awareness, that there was a common thread to my emotional reactions. The thread was the wastefulness of war and -- equally important -- how both the town and the nation with their Christian foundations were reacting to the tragedies of war.

The hour was well past noon and it was time for lunch. I knew without asking, however, that Amelia Caroline wished to continue relating the conversation with her Great-Grandmother. A long Friday afternoon on the porch was in store.

17

BUT GOD IS OVER ALL

Night closes in with threat'ning skies
And hoarsely moans the gale
Without, the trees like spires rise
Encased in wintry mail

From glowing grates we turn, to think
On whom these rigors fall
And who their deathly cup shall drink --

BUT GOD IS OVER ALL

How fare they in the distant camp --
The father, brother, son?
Oh, many brows with death are damp
With many life is done!

O mothers, wives! Distraught with fears,
Lest your beloved should fall
Remember, in this rain of tears,

THAT GOD IS OVER ALL !

M. H. Cobb, 1865

Having had the ham biscuits for breakfast, neither of us was excessively hungry, but we both knew that skipping lunch would result in fatigue later in the day. So we prepared a tuna salad and some iced tea and returned to the porch, lunch in hand. It was then that I asked about other events from the war in 1918.

"Aunt Amelia, this morning you referred to additional experiences during the early war that had come to the surface during the conversation with your Great-Grandmother in 1973. Had they also been an aspect of the first conversation you had immediately following William's death?"

"No, Mary Eliza. My distress during our first conversation was solely due to having lost William as a friend. Great-Grandmother came to me offering comfort. I suspect, unlike the day in 1909 when Lillie Drew Piver died, Great-Grandmother thought I was old enough in 1918 to converse, so we did."

"Can you tell me of those other events from the war that were so meaningful that they stayed with you for over a half century?"

"Yes, I can and I will. Perhaps, following my explanation, you will have a better understanding of why I came to question the teachings and the practices of fellow Christians. I can share the rest of the conversation with Great-Grandmother that I began to relate; it is still vivid in my mind."

Amelia Caroline again reached into the past.

"Great-Grandmother, on the surface, the war in 1917 and 1918 seemed to engender the best in people. Young men cheerfully went before the draft board and joked about the pending adventure. Local officials presented a unified front pledging support both locally and abroad, and church groups gave parties and receptions to recognize the boys who were leaving and to let them know that the folks back home were behind them all the way.

"The first group of local boys to be drafted was given an official send-off at the courthouse. Among the speakers were Judge E.H. Cranmer, Sea Captain J. J. Adkins, and the hostess of Southport, Miss Kate Stuart.

"Prayers and blessings were offered by both Rev. Lloyd Holloway from the Baptist Church and Rev. Thomas Vickers of the Methodist Church. Ministers from all the other faiths, including the rector of St. Philips, Rev. J.M. Bynum, were in attendance. Each of them endorsed the message of God's Love and God's Will, and each hinted that efforts to support the war would be rewarded on the day of judgment."

I remember that I paused briefly, gathering thoughts about the implications of my last statement. It was in this moment that Great-Grandmother spoke again.

144

"Amelia Caroline, it was the same in my time. Preachers always seemed to support official policies. And this support often seemed at odds with the beliefs they hoped to convey to their congregations. There was little or no questioning. This was particularly so when it came to war. It was as if the preachers believed that God Himself was the Author of the war and its pending tragedies. That God Was Over All!"

"Yes, Great-Grandmother, and we all accepted their words. Then reality began to set in as news trickled in from abroad.

"Family friends, young men I had known, suffered during that war, and the actions of many townspeople – good Christians in their own beliefs – serve as examples of why I was reacting.

"Bobby Mintz died during the bombardment of a trench in which he had lived for several weeks near Ypres, Belgium. Bobby was eighteen at the time of his draft. He had finished high school and had plans to study at the State College to become a teacher. But those plans had to be put on hold until after the war. Instead of a trip to college, Bobby was sent for training to Camp Sevier near Greenville, South Carolina, where he joined the 30th U.S. Division.

"This assignment actually was a source of pride for Bobby and his family. The division, referred to as 'Old Hickory,' had been named to honor President Andrew Jackson. It was comprised of boys from the Carolinas and Tennessee. Bobby was among friends!

"In the beginning, Bobby's parents were proud of his service. Within the division, he was assigned to the 120th Infantry Regiment, which actually was the old 3rd Infantry Regiment from North Carolina. Many of the town's old timers had memories of the famous North Carolina 3rd.

"The training in South Carolina lasted several months. He wrote home frequently, telling of his training experiences and his excitement over the prospect of seeing other parts of the world. Bobby's folks shared most of this news with family friends, including Papa and me.

"In May of 1918, the division traveled to New York, then on to England and ultimately the battlefields in Northwestern France for more focused training.

"Letters from Europe, for the most part, indicated that Bobby was doing well. However, there were a few unpleasant *aspects to his ventures. Among these was a fifteen-day voyage on a troop transport across the turbulent North Atlantic in the cold, gray weather of late spring. He described the sickness experienced by most of the men for the entire voyage, but pointed out how advice given him by one of the seasoned sailors had kept him from becoming sick.*

"In another letter, Bobby told of the thrill of actually being in Europe.

"News then came that the 30th U.S. Division had been sent to the front in early July, at a location along the dreaded Hindenburg Line. It was a sector of trenches that the British had held for nearly four years and the North Carolina boys were sent in relief.

"Soon the tenor of Bobby's letters changed. They became cryptic, and they relayed stories of life and death in the mud, of filth and destruction on the battlefield. His parents' pride became tempered with concern and fear.

"Then notification came from the War Department: Bobby had died with valor in service to the country.

"The news of Bobby's death devastated his parents. They had lost their only son to a far-away cause. Bobby's family was not wealthy and his parents would never be able to visit his resting place.

"Their son was gone. Neither official expressions of gratitude nor descriptions of his bravery in the face of battle could salve the hurt. The pain would lose its edge over the years, but it would be present for the remainder of their lives."

I remember that I had to stop here for a few moments, the sadness of the memory preventing me from continuing. Great-Grandmother, gratefully, respected my silence until I could continue.

"Shortly after learning of Bobby's death, news came of a battle in which James Bell and Thomas Gore were both injured. Both James and Thomas had been drafted as part of a call-up that came some months after the one that took Bobby.

"As in Bobby's case, both James and Thomas were sent to the 30th U.S. Division at Camp Sevier. Fortunately, upon reporting to the training camp, they were assigned to the same company within the 120th Infantry Regiment and, following training, they shipped out to Europe. Although their assignment was to the same regiment as Bobby Mintz, they had little contact

146

with him. Bobby was in a different company – one that had formed months earlier.

"As was the case with Bobby Mintz, their letters home had originally been filled with anticipation and adventure. In late August, news came from Europe that they had made it through those first months in the trenches near Ypres, but the letters were short on details of what had actually been experienced in battle. James, however, did write that he was looking forward to being pulled back from the front lines.

"As James had anticipated, the 30th withdrew from the 'Poppy Fields of Flanders.' Left behind were several more of their comrades in addition to Bobby Mintz. Over 150 members of the North Carolina regiment had been killed or wounded.

"After withdrawal from the trenches, the entire U.S. 30th Division, including the North Carolina regiment, was sent to the rear for a few weeks of convalescence and letters home became less cryptic. They included humorous events, such as being dipped in a delousing tank prior to getting a shower and new clothing.

"However, late in September, the units were redeployed in France near the town of Bellicourt. Once again Thomas and James faced the dreaded Hindenburg Line and, once again, tragedy rippled through our small town of Southport.

"The North Carolina 120th Infantry Regiment was ordered 'over the top.' They were to cross No-Man's-Land and take the German positions. It was during this terrible battle where machine guns rained death that a German shell exploded, taking with it all the excitement and glamor of war.

"Both James and Thomas were among the casualties."

I paused a moment at that stage, for the memory still carried its pain. And, as I sat, Great-Grandmother spoke.

"Amelia Caroline, the news of their injuries must have saddened the entire town, coming so soon after news of Bobby's death."

"Yes, Great-Grandmother, the news brought great sadness, but it was not news that we received immediately. Bobby's family was notified of his death as soon as verification was completed and the offical notification of his death could be transmitted from France. But the families of James and Thomas were not informed of their injuries, for the two were sent to Army hospitals in France with full expectation that they would eventually return to combat.

147

"Initially, the two were treated in a field hospital just behind the lines. However, fighting at the front became quite intense, so within days, they were transferred by rail to the base hospital at Beau Desert near Bordeaux.

"Thomas's wounds were most severe. His left leg was shattered at the knee and there was a compound fracture. Though surgically treated at the field hospital in an attempt to save the leg, gangrene soon set in. Upon reaching Beau Desert, his leg was amputated just above the knee. Luckily, the infection had not spread. Nevertheless, Thomas was to undergo a convalescence lasting nearly two months.

"Ultimately, Thomas was transferred from the Bordeaux area to Base Hospital 65 at Kerhoun near Brest. It was here that he was to be processed for transport back to the States. But upon arrival at Kerhoun, it was determined that his leg was not sufficiently healed to undertake the long ocean voyage. So the decision was made by the medical staff to retain him in the hospital.

"Needless to say, Thomas was disappointed at the delay. This was just one more disappointment, in addition to ongoing concern about what his life would entail as a 'war cripple.'

"Thomas's retention at Kerhoun was out of the ordinary, for the hospital was designed as the major center for deportation of personnel back to the States. As such, most of the soldiers, the majority of whom were ambulatory, were assigned to transit wards and soon processed for transport. Thomas, however, was assigned to a ward in which greater attention could be paid to his medical needs.

"In one sense, the delay was beneficial for Thomas's spirits. Among those working at Base Hospital 65 were nurses, nearly one hundred in number, from North Carolina. They were young women who, at the encouragement of Governor Thomas Bickett of North Carolina, had joined the Red Cross in support of the Army Nurse Corps.

"Ultimately, the goal was to have 450 nurses from North Carolina serving with the Red Cross. Those who met Thomas at Kerhoun were among the nation's first to serve in Europe.

"As might be expected, the young women from North Carolina became particularly attentive when boys from 'down home' entered the wards. Recognizing the emotional struggles of their patients, the nurses worked hard to lift the spirits of the *wounded. So during the delay, Thomas became less fretful about his condition, although he did not become whole.*

"When Thomas arrived back home, the flu epidemic was raging, and Papa was among those to see him first. So we had firsthand knowledge of the treatment Thomas had received. Surprisingly, though in a wheelchair, Thomas was complimentary of his medical care. In particular, he spoke warmly of the nurses from North Carolina who served at Kerhuon.

"I saw Thomas another time or two shortly after his return, but he soon left town for rehabilitation at a military hospital. That was a few days before I met William.

"James eventually recovered in France from his battle wounds and, during convalescence at Beau Desert, he wrote home repeatedly. In the letters, James told of his apprehension about returning to combat. His mother, father and younger siblings lived in a small cottage just down the street from us. Periodically, on warm evenings following supper, Papa and I would stroll down to visit the family on their porch and, on such occasions, we shared James's letters, as friends do.

"Even to me, James's concern was real and, as the time grew near for his redeployment, the magnitude of his distress became amplified. Of course, there was nothing to be done other than wait out the war and hope for the best. But there was a dark cloud over the family and, through friendship with the family, the cloud entered my world.

"James did return home several months following the armistice. He arrived in town along with several discharged soldiers whose homes were nearby in the county. The train was greeted by the local band. It was a glorious reception, as all were happy to have the troops back, and many of the town's old men looked forward to hearing of the frontline experiences.

"Those who had been inducted into the military but had never been in combat talked freely of their Army days. But much to the surprise of most people, neither James nor Thomas would talk about what they had seen, heard or done.

"For the most part, people in town did not understand why reliving the experiences, even through memory, was so painful. Thomas, whose days were spent in a wheelchair at the military hospital knew. So did Elias Hewett, another of the young returnees."

As I spoke Elias's name, my voice caught in my throat and tears came to my eyes.

Great-Grandmother expressed her concern, "Amelia Caroline, you seem particularly touched by the memory of Elias. Was he a close friend?"

"Yes, Great-Grandmother. Elias was a few years older, but we overlapped in school. However, he dropped out of school in 1916 and shortly thereafter he joined the Army.

"As a youngster, Elias was big for his age and a little advanced in maturation. During his early school years, he simply had difficulty fitting in. It seemed he was always getting into trouble, most of which was at school, but some in the community. None of his episodes was serious and, for the most part, he was liked by all of our schoolmates. But he just seemed out of step with everyone else.

"At first after leaving school, he worked at a small dairy operated by an uncle, but this arrangement soon came to a close. Feeling that Elias needed more discipline, he was encouraged by family and former teachers to enter the Army. The suggestion proved to be attractive and it suited him well.

"Within eighteen months, he had made the rank of corporal in a company of mounted cavalry that was stationed at a post just outside of El Paso, Texas.

"Elias's service was exceptional and, as a result, he was selected to be a member of a special squadron under the direction of General John Pershing that made extraordinary raids across the Mexican border in attempts to capture Pancho Villa.

"It was at this time that Elias met Sgt. E.M. Hallyburton who was originally from Western North Carolina and later became a national hero. Though stationed fairly far from home, Elias's rank afforded some privileges, so he was able to return home a couple of times to visit. Articles about his visits were always published in the town's paper, and invariably these called attention to his military accomplishments and the honor he was bringing to the town.

"Elias's early achievements as a soldier were a source of pride to his family, all of whom were relieved to know he had turned out so well in spite of his rocky beginnings.

"Whenever he was at home on leave, Elias would sit at the waterfront on the Whittlers' Bench with the town seniors. He shared tales of adventures in the Mexican campaign and he

150

listened while some of the old men relived times during the Civil War.

"Young people were always excited when he joined them on a beach excursion or showed up at one of the dances in the pavilion. Elias was something of a hero."

Great-Grandmother warmly observed, "It sounds as if Elias had redeemed himself in the eyes of the community during those early years of military service."

"Yes, Great-Grandmother, that is true. Then late in 1917, General Pershing was ordered to mobilize the 1st Division for deployment in Europe. It was to serve as the spearhead of the American Expeditionary Forces. Elias, as a member of the 16th Infantry of the 1st Division, was sent to France.

"The division landed in Southern France at St. Nazaire, but soon moved northward toward Verdun, where they immediately went to work in the trenches.

"They had been on the front for a very few days when the position of the 16th Infantry was overwhelmed by German shock troops. Several American soldiers were killed, others wounded and twelve were taken captive. Among the latter was Sgt. Hallyburton, who became a national hero following his exploits on behalf of fellow soldiers while they were in captivity. The twelve, as it turns out, were the first American prisoners of that war.

"Elias was not among those injured, at least physically, during the battle. In fact, he was promoted to the rank of sergeant within a few weeks.

"Yet over the ensuing months in the trenches of Verdun, a toll was taken. Elias withdrew from his companions and his squad members became uneasy with his leadership.

"This came to a head in the summer of 1918 when Elias received a minor wound while on night patrol amidst the barbed wire entrapments of No-Man's-Land. Upon returning to the trenches, he was treated then transferred to the Hospital Center at Bazoilles-sur-Meuse, south of Verdun.

"The staff at the hospital was very familiar with mental conditions stemming from battle fatigue and, apart from his wounds, Elias presented all the classic symptoms. He clearly could not be returned to the front. So Elias was bound for home for medical reasons unrelated to his physical condition.

"His was a psychological problem for which the Army had no answer and, although serving as an exemplary soldier, Elias apparently was no longer of use to the military.

"Within days, he was transferred to Hospital 65 at Kerhuon where he was given a red tag indicating a mental condition. This was the same hospital to which Thomas was assigned, but Elias' s experience at the hospital was quite different from Thomas's. Elias had no contact with the young nurses from North Carolina, for he was assigned to a different ward, not of medical patients, but rather of those who suffered mental disease.

"Two weeks later, he boarded the steamship Leviathan for the journey to the States and discharge from active service.

"When Elias arrived home from Europe, there was little fanfare, and it was clear that he was no longer going to fit in either at the waterfront gatherings or at the pavilion. He just moved into his parents' house.

"He remained inside throughout the day and roamed the streets at night, often talking to himself. Even before the war ended, folks -- including good Christians and local officials -- were referring to him as 'that crazy guy down the street,' the guy who even in youth had seemed a misfit. It was as if they had forgotten the pledges they had made to Elias during his visits home, and the pride they had felt knowing how well he had done in service to the country seemed to have dissipated.

"On the rare occasions when he came out in the daytime, folks meeting him would cross the street to avoid contact.

"He committed suicide a few years later.

"Throughout all of this time, the town band held regular concerts. The music of George M. Cohen and John Philip Sousa was played over and over. During the concerts, townspeople carried patriotic banners around the park and down the streets to the sounds of military marches. They sang out in rousing chorus, 'Over there, over there, send the word, send the word over there, that the Yanks are coming, the Yanks are coming.' Flags were hung from front porches as if in competition to see who would be the most patriotic.

"Even the Black community was involved, although their young men were denied the full honor of service that was granted to the Whites. On several occasions, under the auspices of the War Camp Community Service, groups of Black singers *held patriotic rallies and sang spiritual songs, many from the slavery days prior to the Civil War.*

"All the while, through songs and speeches and flag waving, the pain at home was being suppressed. The full human price of war was being denied.

"And in churches on virtually every Sunday morning, praise was given to God for supporting the war. The faithful prayed and, in their prayers, asked that the boys be kept safe and returned intact to their homes and loved ones. Invariably the services would close with rousing hymns including a chorus from 'Onward Christian Soldiers' or 'The Battle Hymn of the Republic'.

"Then in the churchyards following the services, folks would visit. Those who were secure in their homes and protected from the war either because of age or influence would approach the uniformed soldiers with a show of support. Conversations would always include the belief that God was on our side and His Will would be done, thus guaranteeing victory. The soldiers would be congratulated on their dedication to the cause and they would be assured that the folks back home would be behind them all the way."

Knowing we had come to the crux of my story, Great-Grandmother spoke up, "Amelia Caroline, it sounds as if you came to believe that the assurances were just empty conversation."

"They were, Great-Grandmother, at least from my perspective. There was much discomfort, almost xenophobia, surrounding those who had already been 'over there' and returned less than whole. And it was obvious that many in the congregations simply avoided conversation with those whose conditions called attention to the less attractive aspects of war.

"It seemed to me that the wounded and the scarred were evidence of God's failure; a failure to take care of those who, prior to entering combat, were assured by their ministers that all would turn out for the best.

"I began to see that much of the war support was a public display of bravado as if anything less would be a transgression unforgivable in the eyes of others in town and perhaps even in the eyes of God. But in quiet conversations to the side, concern about the war was expressed by these same people.

"It was all so confusing, as if there were two entirely different people in each body. The first, a public person, who openly professed a belief in God's endorsement for the war, and the second, a private person, who questioned, feared and wept alone in silence."

"Did you also weep in silence, Amelia Caroline?" Great-Grandmother asked.

"No. Mostly I was confused and somewhat angry. Then all of this, Bobby's death in combat, Thomas's loss of his leg, James's inner agony, Elias's emotional state and the dichotomy in the churchyard came crashing together following the death of William.

"And I have not been able to forget for these fifty-some years."

Amelia Caroline slowly sat back in her rocker and returned her focus to the present. Her eyes were misty with tears as she glanced down the street to the cottage where James Bell had once lived. The Miller Hotel was gone, as was its son who was taken in that Frankford explosion eighty-four years earlier.

She knew that this pain had not been hers alone, nor had it been exclusive to her small town, which had become so dominated by the military. Four thousand, eight hundred and twelve North Carolinians were wounded or killed in battle during that war, and another nineteen hundred and sixty-one had died from diseases or accidents while on military assignments.

Amelia Caroline knew these numbers. She also acknowledged the reality that, for many living today, the numbers were just statistics, particularly from a war that was so long past.

But she continued to carry the pain, along with the wives, mothers, sisters and lovers who had remained at home and would forever weep over those who lie in Flanders Field.

Repeatedly over the decades, she had asked herself, "Where was God at this time of mankind's great need and why did his spokesmen not speak?"

18

LEST WE FORGET

Amelia Caroline's death was now more than two months in the past and again I was meeting with Dr. Catherine Arrington. The conversation with Amelia Caroline during that August afternoon just prior to her death had been going through my mind for the previous few days. She had told me of the many friends -- Thomas, Elias, James and Bobby -- who had either been maimed for life or died as a result of the war in 1918.

Why that particular conversation had been on my mind was a mystery to me, so on this afternoon I was sharing some of the details and what observations I could muster with Catherine. And while speaking, I had become more and more distressed.

I was sitting there across the room from the desk, the small quartz clock ticking quietly. The minutes passed slowly as I now tried to regain composure.

Catherine, as she always does, reached across to offer the box of tissues.

After a moment, she asked, "Mary Eliza, can you tell me what you are experiencing?"

Immediately, my mind asked, "How can that possibly be answered in a way that sounds even marginally rational? But try I must."

"A number of years after Amelia Caroline entered my life, I came upon an internet document that altered how I perceived our relationship. I began to see that the bonds between Amelia Caroline and me went beyond those which normally would be expected when two distantly related persons choose to live together. Initially, we came together as the result of a common ancestry and, as would be expected in such circumstances, much of our time together was spent talking about and, in a sense, reliving that history.

"However, the internet document opened my mind to the thought that perhaps our conversations were more than just communication between two distant relatives who had found each other during adult life and as a result of family ties, however remote, chose to live together. My thoughts regarding this are complex, but I'll try to explain.

"The internet document that I found was included among historical records offered through the University of North Carolina in Chapel Hill. It was an address entitled *North Carolina in the World War* delivered by Captain Walter Clark before the North Carolina Bar Association in 1923.

"Most of the address pertained to Captain Clark's personal experiences during the war, but it concluded with several penetrating questions. They paralleled the questions that began to smolder in Amelia Caroline's young mind during the war in 1918 and continued to haunt her some fifty-five years later when she again spoke with her Great-Grandmother about the war. Indeed, the questions remained with her throughout the balance of her life. They came up repeatedly during our conversations over the long weekend just prior to her death.

"What Captain Clark asked in his address applied specifically to the horrors of that time, but the focal questions profoundly apply to each of us, even today. And, although it took many years to come into focus, the questions were at the core of Amelia Caroline's struggle with the past.

"And have they died in vain? Have the leaders of the nations of earth failed to catch the vision and heed the warning uttered by the soldier who lies in Flanders Field?

> 'To you from falling hands we throw
> The torch. Be yours to hold it high!
> If you break faith with us who die,
> We shall not sleep, though poppies grow
> In Flanders Field.'"

I paused a few moments to gather my thoughts, with the hope that what I was about to say would be coherent.

"You see, Catherine, there was a commonality, almost a bond, between Captain Clark and Amelia Caroline. It seems as if a 'Universal Mind' was expressing itself through each of them and, as a result, they were each part of the Universal Mind. By

156

extension, through the Universal Mind each was part of the other.

"To my knowledge they had never met. But both, in his or her own way, had experienced the war. Their experiences, though distinctly different, had brought them to the same ground. It was a fundamental position of deep questioning.

"Since finding the document, I have wondered about its applicability to my own life, and to the questions I continue to ask such as, 'Why did Charles have to die in that faraway land?'

"I also have wondered, 'For what end or for whose purpose was I led to explore that website? Was Amelia Caroline or perhaps her Great-Grandmother directing my activities -- and if so, why?' Perhaps the Universal Mind was working through one or the other of them – or both.

"Then over time, I began to think that perhaps through this Universal Mind, if there is such a thing, a melding of our souls had been brought about. In some way and to some degree, Amelia Caroline and I had become one.

"This is not to say that I am Amelia Caroline nor that she now inhabits my physical being. What can be said is that I share with Amelia Caroline the emotions she experiences as her story unfolds.

"Over our years together, I have come to share her sadness. Intuitively, I know her questions, I celebrate her joys and I cry at her pain. Conversely, Amelia Caroline perceived and shared the pain I have carried ever since the deaths of my brother and his friend Louis. It is in this way that our commuication goes beyond family conversation.

"During one of our earlier sessions, Catherine, I said that Amelia Caroline's story was being transferred through me to the keyboard. As such, I was part of the story process but I was not directly 'of' the story.

"I now am coming to believe that perhaps in some way I AM part of the story.

"A few minutes ago, you asked what I was experiencing. Well, I was not here with you. I was on the porch in the rocker and I was inwardly shedding Amelia Caroline's tears.

" For we, that is Amelia Caroline and I, know that faith has not been kept with those who lie in Flanders Field."

19

MEMORIES

Nearly a week had passed since my conversation with Catherine regarding Flanders Field. The period had been one of introspection for me. After all, thoughts of the Universal Mind or conversations with persons long dead are not trivial.

As that session drew to a close, Catherine had asked: "Mary Eliza, have you considered the possibility that the ongoing relationship you perceive with Amelia Caroline and her Great-Grandmother might be just an extension of close family ties and your knowledge of family history?"

Indirectly, Catherine was suggesting that perhaps I was not hearing voices or receiving cryptic messages after all. I did not have an immediate answer to her question, but I assured her that I would give it some thought before our next meeting.

I was attempting to sort all of this out while once again seeing patients on a full-time basis. The days with half-day schedules, originally arranged so I could rest and reflect, had ended. I was back in the clinic, and it was busy.

The calendar was moving toward fall, school children were passing viral diseases as if sharing candy, and everyone who practiced family medicine was busy. My reflection times and sessions at the computer writing in the journal were now truncated. Yet I did try to see each sunrise and each sunset, for those were the times that Amelia Caroline and I had shared, and they now were the times when she and her Great-Grandmother came to me.

Today was Sunday, however, and I was not on call for the hospital. Knowing some days ago that the weekend would essentially be free, I planned to spend the days working on my journal.

Yesterday, I awakened early and walked to the waterfront to welcome the sun. Shortly following the sunrise, I headed toward the marina. The morning was one of those only experienced during the days of Indian summer. Comfortable temperature, clear sky and crisp air carried the hint of fall. There were numerous other residents out for the early morning and, by chance while walking, I met a couple of friends from the hospital.

We hadn't had time to visit for several weeks and wished to do so. However, my mind was on matters related to Amelia Caroline and we were all intent upon continuing with exercise. We agreed to meet later in the day at the Provision Company near the yacht basin for drinks and an early dinner. I knew that I would welcome a break away from myself by that time.

The evening was enjoyable, as was our meal. We chose conch fritters and salads with grilled grouper. We talked, shared stories and laughed over an excellent wine until after seven PM, at which time we parted. I then walked around the yacht basin to a point where a long pier extended into the salt marsh. There, at the end of the pier, I sat quietly until the sun set.

It was just as the sun was dipping behind the distant marsh grass that the voices came. Amelia Caroline was reminding me of her Great-Grandmother's final comment on our last Friday evening on the porch before she died. The comment had come at the end of Amelia Caroline's story regarding what she had experienced during World War I. Essentially, she had been describing for me why the events during the war had brought her to question the tenets of her religious faith.

I didn't remember the exact comment her Great-Grandmother had made to Amelia Caroline that Friday, but generally it was to the effect that the military presence here had preceded the town. Consequently, from the very beginning, the lives of the townspeople had been influenced by the military. This was particularly true for the Everitt family, and not all the influences had been for the better.

I say that her Great-Grandmother commented to Amelia Caroline, but in reality Amelia Caroline conveyed her Great-Grandmother's comments to me. This, of course, had bearing on my response to the question asked by Catherine.

With the message from Amelia Caroline still in my mind, I left the waterfront and returned to the cottage and my computer. What unfolded in my journal, much to my surprise, was a continuation of Amelia Caroline's story. My entry began by returning to that Friday evening, August 16.

Amelia Caroline finished her story that day about mid-afternoon. We had eaten our tuna salad lunch while she was speaking. At the end of her recitation, she was clearly exhausted, so I recommended a nap. I planned to make good use of the free time, as I had brought home the charts from several of my patients. The intent was to bring the charts up to date before Monday. This, of course, was not just off the top of my head, as each of the charts contained abbreviated notes I had made during the last appointment with each of the patients.

Amelia Caroline rested for an hour and a half. By the time she was up and about, her normal dinner hour was approaching. She expressed a wish to have dinner at Captain Charlie's Restaurant on the waterfront, so shortly before five PM, we drove over.

The restaurant was family owned and operated. Amelia Caroline had known the family forever. She had seen the births of their children and grandchildren, all of whom helped at the restaurant. We were greeted warmly by the receptionist, who was one of the grandchildren, and taken to a prime table next to a window that looked out over the water.

The timing was perfect, for the river pilot boat was just returning to dock, and not far behind it was a large cargo-container vessel coming into the shipping channel.

Our dinner that evening was fresh flounder stuffed with crab. We agreed to share the entrée because Amelia Caroline wished also to share a small serving of the low-country shrimp and grits, which was a specialty of the house.

Following dinner, we walked a short distance to one of the waterfront park benches, where we remained for quite some time. Then upon returning to the house, Amelia Caroline again said she was tired and wished to retire. This was not too surprising, since she had awakened so early in the day and since so much energy had been expended telling her stories.

I remained on the front porch, from which I could see visitors who had arrived for the weekend. As I sat there, my mind slowly drifted to the numerous evenings that Amelia Caroline and I had shared over our eighteen years together. The stories of her life came to mind and they continued to be with me long into the night.

This past weekend, I recorded in the journal much of what went through my mind that night. The focus was upon conversations Amelia Caroline and I had had over our years together regarding various stages of her life during the two decades following World War I. The conversations encompassed her professional training, her early career, political involvement and social awakening.

As I recorded my memories of those conversations, the thought came that perhaps something about the town during those years should be written to serve as a backdrop for the events that followed. As should be evident by now, Amelia Caroline, her house and her rocker were integrated with the town. And for the town, the years in question were interesting to say the least.

So I wrote a short journal entry.

20

POST-WAR PROSPERITY

Amelia Caroline's faith had been shaken by events in 1917 and 1918, and as a result she began a journey for which there would be no end. It was the journey of a seeker. She was one whose fundamental beliefs or the practice of those beliefs had come into question. This was no trivial matter, as the questions were of the kind for which there were no fixed answers.

Other than the very private experience of haunting memories, Amelia Caroline's search was not manifested in her daily life until many years later. In fact, the journey had not reached its zenith until those days following the death of her father in 1971, when she realized upon entering the house that her lifestyle, particularly how she lived in the house, had to undergo fundamental change.

The years following that early war were busy ones for Amelia Caroline and for the town. Throughout 1919, soldiers returned from the war. Many of them had not seen combat, but rather had been inducted late in 1918 and had served overseas as part of an occupation force.

Unlike those who had been in combat, such as James Bell and Thomas Gore, the occupation troops had returned home with grand stories of life in Europe. They had been welcomed, viewed and treated as liberating heroes. Their days had been spent helping restore order to the lives of those whose world had been destroyed by the war.

During off-duty hours, they enjoyed the hospitality of their hosts. The war for them had been an enriching experience. Their stories at the waterfront upon returning to the town were more of celebration than tragedy and these stories influenced the way in which the townspeople came to view the war. Waterfront stories were dominated by glowing tales of exciting exploits "over there." Soon the maimed, the injured and the lame were totally forgotten, at least in public.

By the war's end, the town had grown accustomed to having troops around. In view of the prevailing public attitude about the war, most of the permanent residents were pleased to have the soldiers remain. They were, after all, young and enthusiastic. They brought vitality to social life in the small community. The effect they had on the local economy was unspoken but widely appreciated: each of the men spent a significant amount of his monthly pay in local establishments.

The dry goods business owned by J.B. Ruark was booming on the edge of the downtown shopping area. More toward the center of town, a modern two-story brick building had recently been constructed by Henry Hood and his son, and their store, like that of J.B. Ruark, was constantly filled with the troops and their families in search of everyday needs. In addition, there was a large demand for special-occasion items, which included flowers, boxes of candy and perfumes, as well as home furnishings, books and hobby crafts. With the closing of hostilities, more time was spent in leisure activities, so the necessities for boating, fishing and hunting were also in demand.

The Miller Hotel, the Brunswick Inn, and Kate Stuart's boarding house were always full. Often the guests included military officers or government officials on leave from their assignments elsewhere in the state. The local economy was doing quite well.

It was, overall, a dynamic period. Airplane service had been established between New York and Miami. Southport, with its sheltered harbor and extensive commercial waterfront, including a U.S. Navy dock, was centrally positioned on the air route. Talk about town included speculation that a permanent fueling station might be established for the seaplanes carrying mail between the two distant destinations. Then in 1920, seaplane passenger service was initiated from New York via Miami to Havana, Cuba. The prospects of participating in the country's first international air service fueled even more excitement. Hadn't the first two seaplanes, owned by Aeromarine West Indies Airways and intended for the Havana service, landed in the town's harbor?

Not all the speculation was of new things to come. Great attention was given to the traditional industries of fishing and agriculture. In 1920, the Ocean Seafood Canning Company was celebrating four years of successful operation. The previous year, its fifty employees had produced 28,000 cans and 1,500 barrels of fish. Oyster canning was soon to be initiated. The canning industry was soon supplemented with cold-storage transport for the town's fresh seafood. And plans were in the works to build a large cold-storage warehouse and shipping dock on the waterfront.

In addition to seafood, local agricultural products such as lettuce, strawberries and other summer produce could be shipped to distant locations. This was to be complemented by cold shipment of products from the West Indies. The town was to become a regional center for distribution of tropical fruits and other commodities.

All of this was in addition to the economic boost provided by the presence of the soldiers.

There was, therefore, a collective sigh of relief – perhaps even quiet celebration -- when the town learned of the U.S. War Department's intention to authorize a permanent contingent of nearly 1000 men at Fort Caswell on the island.

The town's post-war prosperity had an impact on Amelia Caroline, although it was indirect. Her father's pharmacy was located on the main street in the center of town, just down the way from the Hood Building. As was characteristic of the time, the town drugstore offered a variety of items and services. Dr. Everitt's pharmacy had become a regular stop for folks of all ages. The soda fountain was popular among the young people, including the soldiers, where freshly mixed sodas and ice cream treats of all shapes, sizes and varieties were created and sold. Children were constantly drawn to the glass-enclosed counter where peppermint sticks, chocolates, licorice, cherry drops and honey-flavored candies were on display.

Parents who had come to make more mundane purchases were constantly defending themselves from the onslaught of requests for pennies with which to buy treats. It was impossible to avoid the temptation to buy items not necessarily in mind when they had entered.

From the front entry to the rear, the pharmacy was lined with cabinets displaying items of all sorts and adults were not immune to temptation. But it was to the rear of the drugstore that adults typically would go. The back of the pharmacy was the location for preparation of medicines of all kinds, and it was here that Mr. Berg spent his time mixing formulas, either those known to him by experience or as uniquely prescribed by Amelia Caroline's father.

Sven Berg was not professionally trained in either pharmacy or medicine, but his years as an assistant to Dr. Everitt and the study he did on his own had proved to be profitable. Many residents of the town considered him almost as knowledgeable as the doctor. And it was not surprising that a number of his friends and customers addressed him as Dr. Berg. This title was a quietly bestowed honor given respectfully by those who held him in high regard.

Although the townspeople knew he was not truly a physician, it was quite normal for folks to seek his advice on medical issues. This was particularly true for ailments that did not require hands-on attention by the doctor but were beyond the scope of home remedies most families kept at hand.

The relationship between Amelia Caroline's father and Mr. Berg was one of friendship in addition to professional respect. Dr. Everitt trusted the advice given to his customers by Sven Berg, for he knew in the majority of cases the guidance offered was both appropriate and beneficial. And in those rare cases where the outcome was not beneficial, Dr. Everitt and Mr. Berg recognized the advice given was in accordance with standard practice of the time. Medical art was not without limitations.

Over her early teen years, even Amelia Caroline had learned much about medical care while assisting in the store. She also had become familiar with a myriad of products available to cure ailments of all kinds. Proprietary and patent medicines had always been major offerings in the pharmacy. As a part-time clerk, one of Amelia Caroline's assignments had been to assist with inventory. This involved both maintaining records and keeping shelves stocked in an orderly fashion. Though not obviously so, the responsibility was significant, particularly where patent medicines were concerned.

Patent medicines had been staples for virtually every pharmacy in the South since the close of the War Between the States. In many respects, it was the presence or absence of particular patent medicines that affected how folks viewed an establishment. Over the previous half-century the image of pharmacies, including her father's, had changed. Initially, the pharmacy was where patients went to have compounds uniquely blended, ground, rolled, packaged or bottled. This service slowly gave way to that of the drugstore where customers went to select from among the latest, or most commonly accepted, prepackaged patent medicines.

So Pine Brothers' Cough Drops, Scott's Emulsion, Groves' Tasteless Chill Tonic, Electric Bitters, Hood's Sarsaparilla, Dr Fletcher's Castoria and McElree's Wine of Cardui filled the shelves. Attention to maintaining this stock occupied much of Amelia Caroline's time while she helped customers, including the many young soldiers.

The patent medications, though popular, rarely met the claims of the manufacturers. It was common for various patent medicines to be advertised multiple times in the *Weekly Standard,* the newspaper published in town. Through such multiplicity of advertisements, claims would be made for success using a single product to treat disorders ranging from neuralgia and weak heart to those discomforts unique to the female condition. Often, purification of the blood and revitalization of liver function were given as the basis for such a broad spectrum of success.

Not insensitive to the potential for profit, each pharmacy also placed announcements in the paper describing its own proprietary medicines. The goal of these advertisements was to remind readers of the wide selection of products, both proprietary and patent, being offered.

In many respects, Dr. Everitt struggled with this enterprise, for he had been committed to a practice of medicine based upon the best interests of the patient since the time of Amelia Caroline's birth. He knew that his philosophy of practice was diametrically opposed to one based upon the promotion and sale of largely worthless products. The products, however, were immensely popular home remedies. And Doctor Everitt knew that, had they not been available in the pharmacy, customers would have taken their trade elsewhere.

Though constantly struggling with this conflict between his professional philosophy and the dictates of merchandising, Amelia Caroline's father took consolation in the belief that his own proprietary products were effective when used as described and for the ailments intended. He was, after all, careful to associate his name only with treatments having known and proven effectiveness.

So his personal offerings were limited to aspirin-containing analgesics in the form of powders prepared by either Sven Berg or himself, senna compounds for relief of abdominal distress, and opium-based tonics and bitters for use in cases where pain was severe.

He and Mr. Berg, and Amelia Caroline as she matured in knowledge, would talk with customers about the benefits and promises of the various options. Needless to say, the townspeople had developed great confidence in the doctor and his pharmacy. This community confidence was transmitted to the soldiers and military families.

The pharmacy prospered and, because of this prosperity, Amelia Caroline was able to expand her dreams for education beyond that offered in a small town. Her fondest dream was to study medicine and become a physician, thus following in the footsteps of others in the family who had served in that profession.

Her dream, however, was not to be, for at that time women generally were not well received in the profession. This was particularly true in conservative, rural Southern communities. Her home town and its population fit that description.

21

CAREER OPTIONS

Nationally, women had not been entirely excluded from the practice of medicine. During the latter decades of the 19th century, a number of medical colleges were opened where women could study medicine and North Carolina had several pioneering women in the field.

Included were Dr. Elizabeth Blackwell, the first female to study medicine in North Carolina; Dr. Susan Dimock, the first female member of the North Carolina Medical Society; and Dr. Annie Lourie Alexander from Mecklenburg County, who became the state's first licensed female medical doctor. Dr Alexander soon became one of the state's most respected physicians and, in 1909, she was elected the first female president of the Mecklenburg Medical Society. During the Great War, she served as assistant surgeon to the troops stationed at Camp Greene near Charlotte.

Clearly, the role of women as physicians and surgeons had been validated. However, the acceptance of women into the profession overall was to take a step back during the early decades of the 20th century.

This period was one of great reform in medical education. The centuries-old philosophy of medicine as an art based upon long-standing yet unsubstantiated therapies came under attack. Medicine, it was argued, must be derived from a rational, scientifically based understanding of the human body. The evolving disciplines of Physiology, Anatomy, Histology and Chemistry were to be its foundation. The nascent fields of Microbiology, Immunology, Pharmacology and Radiology, in combination with an understanding of disease pathogenesis, would form the basis for Therapeutics. As the result of this trend, small, poorly equipped and inadequately staffed medical schools throughout the nation suffered.

The impact in North Carolina was dramatic. The Leonard Medical College at Shaw University closed in 1918 and the medical college in Davidson could not be sustained. Only the small college at Wake Forest and the University of North Carolina Medical College in Raleigh were to survive the purge. Neither accepted women applicants.

Across the land, medical colleges for women came under attack. Most were deemed academically inadequate and they were forced by economics to close. Even the New York Medical College for Women, one of the nation's most prestigious, closed in 1918. The breadth of opportunities in medicine for young women, including Amelia Caroline, rapidly dwindled.

In addition to providing fewer opportunities for education, the medical field was formulating a more humanistic role for women. Women, it was argued, belonged in less technical roles. They were viewed as being too emotional and less well suited to comprehend scientifically based medicine. Nursing, education of children, social work and public health, on the other hand, were considered to be more compatible with both the temperament and the intrinsic skills of women.

To some degree, this perspective on the role of women was espoused by the male-dominated medical world in reaction to the general demand of women to be more fully recognized in society. Even the reaction by men to the movement for women's suffrage was being extended into the medical world.

I had just completed this journal entry, and I was sitting before the computer screen when Amelia Caroline began to intercede with my thoughts. By this stage in my life -- meaning eighteen years of life with Amelia Caroline and an additional two months since her death -- I thought that I had received every possible surprise from her. I had experienced Amelia Caroline's conversations with her Great-Grandmother while Amelia Caroline and I sat on the porch. And following her death, Amelia Caroline -- and even Great-Grandmother -- repeatedly came to me through some mysterious means while I sat at the waterfront or visited the cemetery. This, however, was the very first time I knew for certain that the entry I was about to make was not just from my memory. Amelia Caroline was not simply guiding my thoughts as in the past: she was speaking directly through me.

My response was simply to record the voice that I was hearing in my head.

Papa was sensitive to the general trend regarding the role of women in society, and he was aware that physician training, even for men, was undergoing dramatic evolution. Papa did his best to explain all of this to me.

During that time, we talked about the socially conservative perspective held by the local townspeople, and we knew that our own representatives in the legislature in Raleigh were taking a stand against voting rights for women. This attitude was not just a local matter, for across the state, the role of women in society was being challenged.

There were a few who argued on behalf of women. Walter Clark, a justice on the North Carolina Supreme Court, argued throughout the state on behalf of equal rights for women. However, the position taken by Justice Clark was not received well by most men, and when townsmen gathered either at the waterfront or in the billiard room at Miller Hotel, great animosity was expressed toward Justice Clark.

Papa, even before the war years, had come to the belief that my professional life as a physician would be a constant battle against such views. In light of this, he suggested, and rightly so I suppose, that a career as a physician would be less than satisfying for me. Consequently, Papa began counseling me to consider nursing as a career.

During my early high school years, I often thought of my future, and Papa and I frequently discussed my plans while we sat on the porch in the evenings. Usually, our conversations included the prospect of attending the State Normal and Industrial College for Women in Greensboro. The Greensboro college was highly regarded throughout the state, and several young women from the town including Annie Mae Woodside, the daughter of Jens Berg, had attended classes there to prepare for traditional careers. Many of the career paths were related to teaching, homemaking, administrative work and nursing. So as the war years passed and I became more involved as an assistant in Papa's practice, I came to be more accepting of the idea of a career in nursing.

Then in the summer of 1918, I learned of a new government initiative to enlist 25,000 young women as student nurses in support of the war effort. The young women volunteers were to become members of a new organization, the United States Student Nurse Reserves.

Under the program, nursing students would volunteer part time in local hospitals under the direction of the Red Cross while still doing their clinical training. By having volunteer student nurses serve in this capacity, more fully trained graduate nurses would be free to serve critical roles either at home or abroad during times of national emergency. I later learned that this strategy had been used in France to staff hospitals such as the one in Kerhoun where Thomas Gore and Elias Hewett had been treated.

Though still in high school when I first heard of the Student Nurse Reserves, I felt that I was already a participant, although unofficially, through my work with Papa. Then, by coincidence, one day while walking at the waterfront, I met Lelia Williams and her sister Susan, who were sitting in the sun on the hull of a skiff that had been pulled onto the strand. Lelia and Susan had grown up a few years behind Papa and had remained family friends of ours over the years.

The friendship was of the kind typical to family and relations. The Everitt and Williams families had been associated for nearly one hundred years. Captain James Williams, the father of Lelia and Susan, was born in town in 1845, just a few years after the birth in 1839 of my paternal Grandfather Edward Everitt. The birth of James Williams, in fact, had been attended by Dr. Sterling Everitt, my Great-Grandfather.

Later, during the War Between the States, both my Grandfather Edward and James Williams had served as members of the Confederate Forces. James was with Company G, 3rd North Carolina Cavalry, and Edward was a member of the 10th Regiment, North Carolina Volunteers.

Following the war, both men participated in reunions of the Confederate Veterans of Brunswick County and maintained their friendship through this kind of camaraderie.

It was no surprise then that, following the death of my mother, Charlotte Louise, Lelia Williams had been among the cadre of women who contributed to my guidance. So following our initial greetings that afternoon at the waterfront, the conversation quickly turned to my plans for the future.

Both Lelia and Susan were delighted to hear my thoughts about a career in nursing. Though Lelia had remained in town over the years, Susan had come under the inspiration of Florence Nightingale and had entered the nursing profession in 1899.

As we sat at the waterfront, Susan told stories of her days in France. She had just returned from Europe where she had served as a member of the American Expeditionary Force. The stories were exciting. Susan expressed support for the United States Student Nurse Reserves and she encouraged me to pursue that prospect. Then Susan suggested that I consider studying at Columbia University Teachers' College in New York City. She had just accepted a position as head of nursing at the hospital maintained by Metropolitan Life Insurance Company in New York. Susan was certain that the nursing program at Columbia was affiliated with the Student Nurse Reserves program. She also pointed out that if I chose Columbia, I would have a family friend in the city and, conceivably, my clinical training could be arranged through the hospital. where she was head of nursing.

I was thrilled at the prospect and could not wait to talk with Papa. Susan agreed to meet with us to explain the role she could fill while I was studying in New York. Immediately following Papa's consent, I wrote and obtained information regarding Columbia Teachers' College and the nursing curriculum.

The literature was impressive, but New York City was much farther from home than Greensboro. I was concerned because the cost of attending Columbia Teachers' College was quite high, comparatively speaking. Still, Papa encouraged me to apply. Going to New York became my dream and Papa in his quiet way began to make plans.

Amelia Caroline's voice in my head fell silent for a few moments and I found myself thinking once again about evolution of the town.

The town was prospering and the pharmacy was doing quite well with all the business from soldiers and their families. Over the ensuing months, Dr. Everitt carefully invested profits from the pharmacy in the local savings bank. Then, as Amelia Caroline's graduation from the academy neared, he told her of the provisions he had made. There was money not only to cover the basic costs of attending college, but the savings were sufficient to permit study at the school of her choice.

So it was that Amelia Caroline and her father traveled for a short visit to New York City late in the spring of 1919.

Our first stop in the city was to call on Susan Williams and, with Susan as a guide, we toured the MetLife hospital. Then time was spent at the Teachers' College for interviews both with the registrar and with the director of nursing. My application to Columbia had been approved, and Susan had arranged for clinical training to be carried out under her supervision.

Five months later, I returned to New York and enrolled as a student nurse. I also enlisted as a member of the Student Nurse Reserves. I admit to being somewhat overwhelmed upon my arrival in that big city, but at the same time it was among the most thrilling events of my early life.

Amelia Caroline was soon to become a professional; her youth was left behind.

22

AN ENFRANCHISED WOMAN

The next years passed quickly. Amelia Caroline was immersed both in the excitement of life in New York and the challenges of her studies. Some aspects of the nursing program were mundane to her. These encompassed the more practical aspects of patient hygiene and diet, in addition to routine hospital or clinical care. Changing dressings on wounds, assisting with bedpans, collecting laboratory specimens and distributing medications were hardly captivating. Furthermore, much of this was already familiar to her, since she had carried out many of these same duties while assisting her father during the war.

However Susan Williams, as head of nursing at the hospital, was able to arrange several more meaningful experiences, such as observing in surgery and assisting in obstetrics. So Amelia Caroline was constantly stimulated even in the face of the more basic activities that predominated during the first year.

As the months swept by, the two women became more than mentor and student. On short holidays, weekends and academic breaks, Susan invited Amelia Caroline to join her for outings in the city. Included were theater engagements, shopping, museum visits, dining at small out-of-the-way restaurants and days in the park.

At such times, the relationship could be characterized more as that of mother and daughter. Susan enjoyed sharing and guiding Amelia Caroline into full womanhood. The role was not unlike the part-time mothering that her sister Lelia had enjoyed during Amelia Caroline's early years.

Upon finishing the entry of those comments in the journal, I was feeling a bit fatigued, so I took another short break to the waterfront. There was a lot of small-boat traffic in the bay, as the fall fishing season was nearing its peak. As usual, Sunday morning was busy. The sport fishermen who had come for the weekend from Raleigh, Charlotte, Wilson and many other towns were getting in the final hours of fishing before returning to their homes and workday activities. I watched the semi-frantic movement of the boats as they scurried to get prime spots at the mouth of the Elizabeth River. It was the favored fall fishing area, where fish in large schools moved out of the Elizabeth River and into the Cape Fear River. Before long, as the traffic slowed and the water calmed, my mind drifted to Amelia Caroline. I knew that upon my return to the computer she would be with me.   As anticipated, I once again became a transcriptionist.

My time in New York with Susan Williams did much to influence the remainder of my life. Though still relatively young, I matured both through personal growth and by gaining confidence in myself as a professional. There were parallels between my path and that which Susan had followed. As in my case, she had left Southport in her late teens to become trained in nursing. Over the years, she had become financially and socially independent. This was at a time when few women achieved independence in the male-dominated world.

Susan supported all aspects of independence for women, and she was an outspoken supporter of a national law guaranteeing full voting rights to women. Needless to say, I came to share her views and I pledged to support the suffrage movement.

The late spring of 1920 was a pivotal time for the suffrage movement. The proposed 19th Amendment had been sent to the states nearly one year earlier for either ratification or rejection. New York had been one of the first states to ratify the amendment in June of 1919. Yet in several states, the amendment remained under attack. Mississippi, South Carolina, Maryland and Virginia had all defeated ratification. North Carolina and Tennessee were among the states still undecided.

Many people, including Papa, cautiously felt that North Carolina might vote in favor of women, for several powerful legislators had expressed support. Included among them was Governor Thomas Bickett. Optimism, however, was tempered with the knowledge that strong anti-suffrage sentiments existed among many old families of wealth and power. There was, throughout the South, a lingering heritage of Southern aristocracy that wielded great influence.

Then on March 23, 1920, Washington State voted ratification. It was the thirty-fifth state to do so. Only one additional state was needed to pass the amendment. Activities of the amendment's supporters increased throughout the country. Pressure was being applied to the hold-out states. Both North Carolina and Tennessee were in the limelight, for both states had scheduled votes within a few months.

I was immersed in the cosmopolitan atmosphere of New York and I felt the surge of womanhood in the promise of enfranchisement. Conversations in restaurants, on the subways, among friends and family members invariably included speculation about the prospects for final passage. Susan Williams and I wondered if North Carolina would be number thirty-six in support of the vote and, by so doing, close the door on a repressive male-dominated past. Would it vote in favor of full citizenship rights for women?

As the summer months approached, suffrage supporters swept North Carolina and Tennessee. There were parades, rallies and community meetings. Even Southport was under siege. Letters from home kept me informed of the developments but, as the weeks passed, the news became less and less encouraging. The situation in North Carolina was so different from the attitudes and opinions expressed in New York. Whereas in New York, the vote for women had been enthusiastically supported, in North Carolina great opposition was being organized.

Given the situation, I was anxious to be home for my summer break. For several months I had been looking forward to conversations with Papa and Mr. Berg concerning new concepts in Therapeutics, but now there was an overriding issue. There was need for additional voices in support of women.

Finally, with the close of the term at the end of May, I returned home. Timing was perfect for, within a week, members of the North Carolina Equal Suffrage Association, in collaboration with the National Woman's Party, arrived in town for a meeting at the courthouse. The meeting was to be a rally in support of North Carolina's ratification of the 19th Amendment. The 6th Congressional District in general and the town of Southport in particular were the targets. Our town was, after all, the seat of government for one of the state's largest counties.

177

The courthouse was packed to capacity that afternoon. Women hoisting posters and banners had traveled from all corners of the county. Many had made the day trip down from Wilmington to visit with the guest speaker, Lola Trax, who had come from Baltimore. Ms. Trax was an activist member of the Congressional Union for Woman Suffrage, an arm of the National Woman's Party. Though she lived near Washington, DC and the headquarters for the Congressional Union, Ms. Trax had spent the previous four years traveling the country in support of the vote for women. She had helped establish an office in Kansas City, Kansas, and had visited Charleston, Columbia, and Aiken, South Carolina, several times.

In spite of these efforts, South Carolina voted to defeat the amendment. As a result of these efforts, Lola Trax had become well known to the Southern press. Her participation as a keynote speaker on women's suffrage and as a representative of the national organization brought great attention to our rally.

More than half of those in the audience were men. Lawyers and businessmen in suits talked quietly among themselves about the legal and economic impact of women's vote. Would this change the attitudes of women toward their roles as homemakers? Might they enter the political arena and introduce other legislation not necessarily of interest to men?

The mayor and members of the Board of Aldermen gathered around the distinguished guests. Politics dominated their conversations. Farmers, builders and day workers in their coveralls and jeans clustered with fishermen and dockworkers in their waterfront-stained khaki pants. These were the hard-working, everyday folks for whom the present status was just fine. Their comments indicated little in way of support for the movement.

Members of the Black community gathered in the halls outside the courtroom, though a few of the more prominent members were allowed to stand along the back walls of the courtroom or were given seats at the rear of the audience.

Papa and I arrived early. His status among the townfolk was acknowledged and we were given seats at the front of the room near the podium. The atmosphere was electric as tensions on both sides of the issue ran high. There was a subtle suggestion of disruption as had happened at gatherings in other cities and states. At some rallies, particularly those in Southern states, the keynote speakers had been shouted down. More than

178

a few rallies had resulted in the arrest of women speakers. Arrests had become so common that members of the Congressional Union were given special recognition by their peers for time spent in jail.

The meeting that day, with the exception of a few shouts from the audience, went well.

Following the main presentation, comments were offered from both sides. Men, for the main part, spoke out against ratification, but they were not alone in this position. There existed in North Carolina a large and politically powerful anti-suffragist movement comprised of women who claimed that the pure, nurturing nature of women would be compromised if they were given the vote and allowed to enter politics. Many of the anti-suffrage women were from wealthy, influential families whose "aristocratic" lineage was threatened by an empowered lower class. Black women and poor White women posed threats to the historical social order and all efforts were made to deny them the right to vote.

The meeting closed with an announcement that a vote on the amendment would come before the state legislature later in the summer.

I came away from the rally energized. Papa and I talked throughout the evening about the day's events and my passions for women's rights were fully expressed. I asked Papa for permission to spend much of the remainder of the summer serving as a volunteer for the Equal Suffrage Association. That, of course, was in addition to helping in the pharmacy. He agreed to this arrangement, and he promised we would travel to the state capital in Raleigh for the vote on ratification, if the vote came at a convenient time.

So the next few weeks passed until mid-August, shortly before my scheduled return to New York at the end of the month. The North Carolina vote was set for August 17th and it was a critical vote for the amendment. Thirty-five states had ratified the amendment and only one more state was required for full passage.

Recognizing the significance of the vote, and knowing that North Carolina would be in the national spotlight, Papa made arrangements for a three-day trip to the capital. On the day of the vote, we were among the throng that lined the galleries of the senate chamber. The debate on the amendment continued for over five hours and it appeared that the anti-suffragists had done their work well.

In a surprise move late in the day, a motion was made to table the amendment until the next session of the legislature. In effect, the legislation was allowed to die. North Carolina took no formal position, yet by this action the message was being sent that the state did not support the vote for women.

I was very disappointed. How could this chamber, comprised exclusively of men, be so out of touch with the rest of the nation? Had the legislature no knowledge of the progressive attitudes shared by much of the country?

Voting rights had been granted nearly two decades earlier to women living in many of the Western states and, in New York, it had been nearly four years. Even prior to approval of the proposed amendment by the United States Congress, voting rights had been granted to women in fifteen of the forty-eight states. Were women less valued in North Carolina? There seemed no answers. Papa could only suggest that long-held prejudice often refuses to die.

The final insult in the matter came shortly after the vote to table the amendment. Members of the North Carolina Legislature composed a telegram that was addressed to the Tennessee General Assembly. The cable, signed by sixty-three members of the North Carolina House of Representatives, urged the State of Tennessee to vote against the 19th Amendment.

The cable stated that a positive vote in Tennessee would be detrimental to North Carolina. Tennessee's vote, if positive, would be the thirty-sixth vote and the final one needed to make the 19th Amendment part of the U.S. Constitution. Consequently, such an action by Tennessee would force voting rights for women onto the State of North Carolina.

However, Tennessee, acting from its own best interest and in concert with much of the nation, ratified the amendment on August 18, 1920.

North Carolina did not join the ratification until 1972, more than a half century after the rest of the nation. Papa was correct in saying, "Long-held prejudice often refuses to die."

23

BRINGING CHANGE

An exciting chapter in Amelia Caroline's life had come to a close. The date arrived for the return trip to New York to complete her training. Though too young to vote in the upcoming presidential election, she was pleased to know that in a few years she would be a fully voting citizen.

Yet the summer's experience was double edged: Amelia Caroline was quite disappointed at the attitudes of her fellow North Carolinians. In particular, the calloused position of men on the role of women in Southern society would remain with her for years to come.

By this time Sunday was nearly half gone and, with the exception of the one morning break at the waterfront, I had been writing for nearly five hours. My night had been short, as I had awakened early and was anxious to cover a lot of ground before returning to the clinic the next day. Mondays were always busy and I knew that the journal would be put on hold for several days after that. Nevertheless, fatigue was again setting in and it was time to have some lunch. So I stepped away from the desk.

I thought of returning to the Provision Company for a seafood lunch, but realized that friends might be there, and I would be drawn into conversations which would take me away from my train of thought. I needed to remain focused, so I opted for a homemade sandwich, which I ate while sitting on one of the benches at the far east end of the waterfront park. It was one of my favorite quiet places.

Upon returning from lunch, I sat at the desk, and immediately Amelia Caroline resumed her narrative.

I was disappointed about the position North Carolina had taken, but my disappointment was eased by anticipation of returning to New York. The routine experiences of my first year quickly disappeared during the second. Clinical training on the various hospital wards predominated.

In addition, the academic challenges of studying Therapeutics and Materia Medica kept my mind actively focused. These topics were studied using an outline prepared by Dr. Cary Eggleston, a highly regarded member of the faculty at Cornell Medical College, and Linette A. Parker, a registered nurse who had taught Nursing and Health for several decades as a member of the faculty at Columbia Teachers' College.

Ms. Parker was a noted author on the topic of Pharmaceutics. I was challenged and had to work quite hard, but I was gaining scientific insight to an area that had always been part of my life. As the months rushed by, I looked forward to the midwinter trip back home when I could discuss the latest hypotheses on Therapeutics with Papa and Mr. Berg.

Amelia Caroline's narrative continued, but later in the day, as I looked back over what she had said, I decided that some observations on my part might be useful. So I simply inserted what follows into the middle of her comments.

Paradoxically, the knowledge Amelia Carolina was gaining was as disturbing to her as it was enlightening. The medical field was undergoing radical change, particularly as applied to the areas of greatest interest to Amelia Caroline. The basis for Therapeutics being taught in the early 1920s was radically different from that of the past. The resulting changes would influence not only Amelia Caroline's role but also that of her father and Mr. Berg.

Movement in the new direction actually began about the time of Amelia Caroline's birth. It stemmed from action taken by the various medical associations to bring more stringent controls over the profession which, until that time, had been based upon centuries-old concepts and practices. There was now extensive awareness that the causes of disease could be learned and it was scientific study that would lead to that understanding. By extension, Therapeutics would be based upon scientific knowledge. Medical schools clamored to strengthen their scientific faculty. Both the Columbia Teachers' College for Nursing and the Cornell Medical College were on the forefront.

One of the texts that Linette Parker shared with us was "The Propaganda for Reform in Proprietary Medicine,"

182

published by a committee of the American Medical Association. The book, based upon studies which had been carried out by the AMA's Chemical Laboratory, called attention to the ill-founded claims made by manufacturers and distributors of proprietary and patent medicines. In addition to questioning the efficacy of many "drugs," the book pointed out the dangers presented by several of them. Nostrums and quackery were given as examples of the need for reform.

The book called attention to the fact that, in many regards, physicians and others of the medical profession were responsible for perpetuating the use of harmful or worthless products. Much of what I was learning brought medical products and practices from the past into question.

Armed with this new knowledge about Pharmaceutics, I was anxious to begin discussions with Papa and Mr. Berg. While in New York, I frequently thought of the soul-searching Papa must have done over the years. I wondered if he would have the will to radically change the kind of products sold in the pharmacy and, by extension, alter how the pharmacy operated. After all, everyone in town expected the pharmacy to provide the home remedies with which they were most familiar. I asked myself whether long-standing customers would go elsewhere if the pharmacy changed. There were no answers to these questions.

My concern regarding Papa's position on the matter and his ability to implement change in the pharmacy ultimately was put to rest. Through conversations we had during my winter break, Papa gave me assurance that he was fully apprised of the trend. He had known for some years that medical societies were calling for change, particularly in the relationship between physicians and manufacturers of bogus drugs. As had been pointed out in society literature, physicians in many cases had become handmaidens of the patent medicine industry by offering endorsements for products which essentially were of no benefit.

Papa knew the relationship between many of his colleagues and the manufacturers of compounds had become so tangled that often physicians were seen as "unpaid peddlers for wretched nostrums." This was to the extent of becoming "particepts criminis" in exploitation.

In these conversations, Papa reminded me of the care with which he and Mr. Berg presented medications to customers. Yet he conceded that there were some questionable remedies, *patent medicines that folks had been taking for years, which were well stocked in the pharmacy and were profitable to sell.*

Over time, Papa and I reached agreement. Upon completion of my studies in New York, I was to tackle this matter in our pharmacy and, by so doing, become a true professional partner in the store.

So it was in May of 1921, with luggage in hand, I boarded a train in New York City's Grand Central Station for the final trip home. The journey had become quite familiar to me. The train made stops in Philadelphia, Washington, DC and Richmond, in addition to a plethora of small towns along the way before reaching Wilmington, where Papa met me. After a restful evening in the city, we were ferried across the Cape Fear River for the short trip to Navassa where we boarded the Wilmington, Brunswick and Southern Railroad for the final two-hour trip home.

A wide front porch, the family rocker and family members from the past awaited Amelia Caroline's return.

24

BECOMING ACCEPTED

I was thrilled to finally be home for good and I looked forward to beginning my professional activities. But before doing so, there was much to see and do, many old friends and neighbors to visit. Father was sensitive to the fact that I needed to reintegrate with the town. He encouraged me to spend a few weeks just experiencing and catching up on friendships. So I did, making trips to the beach for fishing and picnics, and boating along the riverfront with friends.

We traveled into the tidal creeks and salt marshes where egrets, herons, seagulls and kingfishers made their homes. One of our favorite spots was deep within the channels of Dutchman's Creek, where oyster beds came to view and offered themselves for harvest at low tide. Then there were afternoons of quiet fishing in the shallow creeks of the Elizabeth River. Fish fries and oyster roasts were regular events. Frequently, we collected several bushels of oysters in burlap bags. When back on the sandy shore, the burlap bags were soaked in seawater then placed over beds of hot coals to steam the oysters. Dinner consisted of salt crackers and oysters on the half-shell.

While spending warm evenings on the swings at the waterfront, I watched porpoises play in the bay. In the early morning hours, I found otters cavorting at low tide in small wooden skiffs stranded among the reeds in the mudflats. There were wharves to walk, fishing boats to visit and menhaden fishermen to talk with.

The sun rising with spectacular beauty over the water began my days. Then at day's end, there were dances and parties in the Miller Hotel or at the pavilion, where we watched the setting sun slip beneath the hammocks of coastal grass at the western horizon.

185

For a brief time, Amelia Caroline's homecoming seemed like a return to her childhood days when concerns of the world played little role in her life. But Amelia Caroline, though just nineteen, knew the difference between true childhood and this period of self-indulgence. Soon she was ready to reenter the adult world, a world she had first experienced three years earlier with the events of the Great War.

This period of relaxation lasted about two weeks, after which I plunged into the challenges of my new status with the energy typical of a young adult. Though I was eager to help Mr. Berg reorganize the pharmacy, Papa suggested that it might be in my best interest to begin by reaching out to the community. He felt I could apply my newly acquired knowledge in the general areas of health, nutrition and hygiene to help folks understand some of the relationships between lifestyle and disease. Papa had long been aware of the need to provide guidance in these areas, particularly as they applied to health concerns of women and children.

Though this need had been recognized for years, Papa had been hesitant to act upon the matter. He had concerns that addressing such topics in the clinic or while making house calls might be a cause of embarrassment for patients. After all, some of the townspeople, particularly the women, considered matters related to lifestyle to be highly personal. They were much too sensitive for discussion with the town doctor, particularly since the doctor was a man. I, on the other hand, could begin to approach the matter with less discomfort on the part of the townswomen.

However, this was not a simple assignment, for in many respects most people in the town were living a lifestyle not too different from what had been the fashion a hundred years earlier. Few homes had electricity and those that did were under restrictions regarding the time of day and amount of use. Typically, that meant one or two light bulbs being illuminated for a few hours each evening. Indoor plumbing other than for channeling well water to the kitchen was as yet unfamiliar to the majority of residents and privies still lined the rear yards of most houses. Household waste was commonly thrown into the streets to the attention of free-roaming hogs. Cattle were an annoyance as they meandered the waterfront and soiled the sidewalks of town in search of morsels. Everything green was at risk.

I fear my description portrays the town as being unsavory in appearance, but it was not. The town did, however, represent a lifestyle that was fast disappearing from more urbanized areas where the relationships among diet, sanitation and health were becoming recognized. The time for change had come even for remotely located rural communities.

I realized, as had Papa, that many physical ailments routinely seen in the clinic or at the pharmacy would be alleviated simply by altering how families lived. Then, by extension, the need for home remedies -- few of which worked anyway -- would decrease.

In effect, I could be addressing two issues at the same time. On one hand, I would be helping women appreciate the relationships among diet, sanitation and hygiene and how these affected disease or resistance to disease. On the other hand, I would be helping them understand the need to use effective, proven treatments when disease did occur.

Thus began Amelia Caroline's campaign for modernization. This would have been a daunting task for most people, yet she began with the energy and determination of youth. The initial strategy was to meet with groups of women through various church societies and social clubs such as the Garden Club or the Library Society. In such settings, the audiences were comprised of mature women from the more affluent and established families.

Whenever possible, however, Amelia Caroline preferred having individual discussions with women who consented to meet with her in their homes. These meetings were primarily with young mothers. Many of them had married early in life, some even in their mid-teens, so from the standpoint of age, they were Amelia Caroline's peers.

The women who attended the church groups and social clubs were from the town's better homes. They generally felt little need for information in matters related to nutrition and hygiene. Mostly, they expected to be given recent information about common diseases which frequently swept the town. Being well familiar with this expectation, my information was tailored accordingly.

Yet I did not feel limited by the expectations of the audiences. There was, after all, a lot of new information regarding the relation of diet to health. And I knew that even the better homes were inadequate when considered in light of modern plumbing standards. Therefore, my presentations, though focusing upon the expressed interests of the audience, included information that the attendees would have denied needing if they had been consulted beforehand.

These gatherings, for the most part, were rewarding. The exception perhaps was with extremely conservative congregations where the prevailing philosophy held that mankind must pay for its sins. Illness in the eyes of such folks was considered to be part of God's plan for atonement and was to be accepted. Presenting arguments counter to such beliefs was not easy. But when confronted with such attitudes, I still did my best to convince the attendees of the need to improve general hygiene in the town.

The greatest reward for me came during the individual meetings when I could touch upon the needs of specific families. In these more personal settings, concerns routinely were expressed about excessive childhood illnesses and infections.

Diarrhea, boils, head lice, ringworm and intestinal disorders, colds, flu, sore throats and fevers were and still are common experiences of those who live in the poorer sections of town. Some of these maladies, though normally benign, could become life threatening.

In addition, more serious diseases including cholera, diphtheria and typhoid fever were not infrequent. Then there were ever-present concerns about the rare but devastating outbreaks of malaria and yellow fever. Though it had been nearly half a century since the last major local episode of the latter in the mid-1870s, I still felt compelled to inform mothers about ways to protect themselves and their families.

It was in the poorer areas that my messages regarding diet and cleanliness had the greatest impact. In earlier years, little attention had been given to the living conditions of those whose means were limited. I recalled that it had been during my final school years that several cases of typhoid fever occurred in the poor area a short distance north of the town center.

Similarly, in the isolated community of Funston, a couple of miles east of town, living conditions were particularly tragic. An epidemic of smallpox had broken out. Fear concerning *spread of the disease into the center of town had resulted in quarantine restrictions being placed on those who lived in the Funston community. This was a great hardship. Not only were residents struggling with the disease, but the restrictions forbade them from entering the town without first having obtained a health certificate from the county physician, who did not reside in the community.*

Pellagra, though no longer a major issue, was among the most pressing concerns during that period. The disease had first appeared in great numbers during my childhood and many of my schoolmates had been affected. The disease seemed ever present. Throughout the years of my schooling, the number of cases had risen and fallen several times.

There seemed neither a pattern nor a cause. Many doctors in the Southern medical community believed pellagra was infectious and that it was caused by a bacterium. There was no evidence to support such a belief. Quite to the contrary, this belief on the part of Southern physicians ran counter to the most recent research results. Evidence had been accumulating to document that pellagra was due to a deficiency in diet.

Even in the South, pellagra patients were treated through confinement and rest, a period during which they were given a balanced diet containing meat, milk and fresh vegetables. This convalescent diet differed dramatically from the diet typical to poor Southern households where milled corn, molasses and greens were the staples. Yet the relationship between recovery of the patients and the much-improved diet during confinement was not apparent to many doctors whose outdated training lacked scientific insight.

During my training at Columbia Teachers' College, I had learned about some recent research into the disease from studies being carried out by Dr. Joseph Goldberger. He was a nationally recognized expert who worked with the U.S. Public Health Service.

Dr. Goldberger had long rejected the hypothesis of an infectious agent as the cause of pellagra and he carried out numerous experiments to substantiate his beliefs. The results of his studies were published in the most noted medical literature.

At Columbia, the main conclusions from the research had been presented in summary form by the instructor of Nutrition courses. She stressed the concept that by maintaining a properly balanced diet, pellagra could be controlled. This conclusion, I also learned, was neither shocking nor original. Nearly two centuries earlier, Don Pedro Casal, a Spanish physician, had linked the disease to poverty and the limited diet among the lower classes.

Dr. Goldberger, through carefully designed scientific experimentation, verified the observations of Casal. The data were unequivocal. I firmly believed, as I had been taught, that by simply changing dietary patterns the disease could be prevented.

Yet Southern society, including much of the medical community, remained steadfast in its disbelief . Field studies were carried out in South Carolina, but the authors reported having found no relationships among poverty, diet and pellagra. Southern researchers were insisting that the infectious agent would ultimately be identified and research was focused toward this end. Meanwhile, the number of affected individuals had increased dramatically and, by 1920, nearly 100,000 new cases were being reported each year.

This Southern position was not based upon evidence. Rather, it reflected a reluctance on the part of politicians and those of influence to admit that poverty, which was endemic to much of the South and had been since the days of Reconstruction , was the true source of disease. The Daughters of the Confederacy wrote in position papers that neither poverty nor famine was endemic to the South. The epidemic of pellagra was denied.

However, like Dr. Goldberger, there were those in the South who acknowledged the true conditions. Papa and I were among the believers.

Paradoxically, many of the poorer rural families were free from the disease. I knew this was because these families lived from the land. They raised large animals and poultry, and they grew garden crops. Their diets were varied in content and were balanced from a nutritional standpoint.

Other families, however, had restricted diets. Primarily this was the case among those who were poorly educated, were sharecroppers or worked for minimal day wages. These families lived day to day, always on the verge of one disease or another. Pellagra lived on their doorsteps. I knew the distinction between those who were susceptible and those who were relatively free of the disease. It was to the at-risk families that much of my attention was directed.

190

While in nursing school, I had learned that the incidence of pellagra had increased dramatically following the introduction of finely milled corn to Southern diets. Through this process, the corn germ was separated out, leaving a starchy but nutritionally inferior product. By substituting old-style, coarsely milled corn in place of the new finely milled corn, some of the disease could be prevented.

Improvement also came by simply adding small portions of meat, eggs and vegetables. I worked hard to convince the in-town folks to plant small gardens. If enough space was available, I suggested they raise poultry in their rear yards. Both kitchen gardens and backyard chicken coops had been common during Great-Grandmother's life and pellagra had not been an issue.

The work I was doing, particularly meeting with women from the poorest of the struggling families, often was emotionally draining, and my heart went out to those of limited means, ability and prospect.

Amelia Caroline's voice paused for a moment, and I sensed that the pause was a direct result of empathy which had remained with her throughout life.

The issues with which Amelia Caroline was dealing were not entirely due to economic status. She knew that social choices also contributed to the quality of health. On the western edge of town, the low-lying tidal marsh and swamp gave rise to a downtrodden area known as "Bowery Hills." It was a part of town long known to soldiers, sailors and transients of all classes as the place to visit when relief was sought from the tedium of everyday life. The area was one in which several preventable diseases were near epidemic levels.

Studies completed by the United States Public Health Service immediately following the First World War found this to be particularly true for venereal diseases. Fully ten percent of military personnel were affected and the epidemic promised to continue unless social conditions were altered.

The circumstances in the area surrounding Bowery Hills were well known to the permanent residents of the town; with the exception of the occasional clandestine visits by upstanding citizens, consort with some residents of the area was frowned upon.

However, in spite of the stigma associated with the area, the residents there were people whose plight called to Amelia Caroline and she responded. It was there that her message stressed social change as a means to overcome diseases long associated with the transient lifestyle in military and maritime communities.

Conditions in that westernmost reach of town were further compounded by geography. Much of the area was low-lying and, as a result, the properties frequently were subjected to flooding. This was particularly true during storms or very high lunar tides. The flooding was not in itself an issue, except when the waters brought excessive river debris onshore. The problems were due to excess water in inappropriately placed privies.

This situation paralleled that found upriver in the city of Wilmington. In the larger city, dire sanitary conditions existed due to the misplacement of nearly 7,000 outhouses on ground that tended to become saturated with water. The situation in Wilmington had been documented following an extensive study carried out under the direction of Colonel C.W. Stiles, Chief Zoologist at the Hygienic Laboratory of the U.S. Public Health Service. In his report, Dr. Stiles stressed the relationship between poor sanitation in Wilmington's low-lying areas and the levels of typhoid, cholera and diphtheria found there.

Dr. William Boeck, a pathologist at Harvard University, had published a similar study. Dr. Boeck's work had linked inadequate sanitation in Southern towns to the prevalence of parasite infestations and hookworm.

Clearly, improved sanitation would reduce many of the diseases that plagued the South.

While in school, I was not familiar with the details of the studies being done by Colonel Stiles in Wilmington, but I had been made aware of the general issues during my time in New York. Poor sanitation was, after all, a major health concern throughout the nation and New York City was no exception.

Hookworm was at epidemic levels throughout the South in those years so, upon returning to town, I began reading the local literature. As it turned out, our regional newspapers were publishing information from the Wilmington study, and I recognized the parallels between the conditions in Wilmington and the conditions that existed here in the low-lying tidal areas. I also knew that solutions were not simple. The matter of sanitation extended well beyond the mere efforts of a consulting nurse. Primarily, these were matters for city fathers and county health officials, but it was to the residents, those who suffered, that I spoke.

My approach to the sanitation situation differed from the approach used in the past. Others, primarily rigid churchwomen, periodically attempted to bring reform through public condemnation of the downtrodden residents. This approach was highly insensitive, but it was done with the expectation that embarrassment would result in change. In contrast to this approach, I recognized the need for respect. After all, this had been Papa's approach his entire professional life.

I realized that many, if not most, of the residents had few options in life. They were simply living as best they could, given the lot life had provided for them. It was from this perspective that I tried to present compassion and understanding. Now, compassion was not the full extent of our interaction, for I relied upon carefully conveyed information to impress residents with the need to improve their circumstances.

Though dramatic change was not instantaneous, Amelia Caroline perceived a feeling of respect on the part of those with whom she spoke. This perception gave rise to a belief that, over time, change would come both in the lifestyle and health in the neighborhoods.

As suspected by her father when he suggested she take up the cause, Amelia Caroline indeed was becoming recognized as a compassionate and trustworthy member of the medical community.

25

POLITICAL AWAKENING

Southport, upon Amelia Caroline's return from New York, was different from what she had anticipated. Two years earlier, when Amelia Caroline had departed for New York just at the Great War's closure, a war-related military atmosphere predominated in town. Expectations on the part of the townspeople had been that the economic boost created by the troops and their families would continue well into the future. Prosperity had been the word of the times. However, that did not last.

The War Department, during the time Amelia Caroline was away, had reconsidered its position with respect to maintaining a semi-permanent force in or near Southport. Concepts of coastal defense had changed in recent decades and small, strategically placed installations were no longer considered necessary. The garrison on the waterfront, though nearly 200 years old and steeped in the history of the nation, was now superfluous.

Similarly, coastal batteries as they existed on the island were also outdated. Much to the distress of the business community, the immediate post-war promise of 1,000 or more troops did not materialize. Rather, the garrison located at the waterfront, which throughout the war had a contingent of fifty to one hundred naval personnel, was once again deserted.

In addition, the number of troops on the island had fallen below 200. Then shortly after Amelia Caroline's return to town in 1921, the fort on Caswell Island across the bay was abandoned except for a small crew to do routine maintenance. Military officers were reassigned to locations elsewhere in the country. All that remained on the island were fifteen soldiers and one sergeant. Their assigned task was to dismantle the fortifications for surplus or scrap. An historic era was drawing to a close.

Streets in the town were no longer filled with men in snappy uniforms. Military children no longer played at the waterfront and wives of soldiers no longer visited shops in town. Many businesses struggled in the face of these reductions. Dances and theater productions other than those at the pavilion ceased and the Army-Navy Club was closed. Social life, primarily for the young adults, changed dramatically.

The town, once again, was on track to become a quiet fishing and resort village. But it would not fully return to its pre-war status, for aspirations had changed over the years. After all, they now had regular rail service. And phone communication, which originally was a single line to Wilmington, was being extended into the county and began connecting the rural communities.

Additionally, there was a renewal of more traditional non-military enterprise. Processing of seafood and farming were both expanding as commercial endeavors. Once again, the waterfront became the town's economic engine. The population of the town was smaller, as well, having returned to the pre-war level of slightly under 1,700. But the town would survive.

The limited social life for young people had little impact on Amelia Caroline, as she was by now fully immersed in her professional activities. At the end of each day, she was content to sit in the rocker on the front porch and visit with her father. Friends and neighbors out for evening walks or en-route to weekday church activities would stop for a few minutes, and conversations would drift from weather to family news, with occasional political observations. The latter, for the most part, focused upon local concerns, as national politics had become less interesting following withdrawal of the troops.

Several of those who stopped by were former schoolmates who would pull Amelia Caroline to the side porch, where matters primarily of interest to unmarried young women were discussed in hushed tones. Clearly, the number of desirable and eligible men had fallen. Speculation about future prospects, though not particularly an issue for Amelia Caroline, was often on the minds of her friends. Jokingly, the interrelationship of families would be acknowledged, and often it was said, "If you want to be married, it will have to be to one of your own cousins."

However, for Amelia Caroline and her friends, talk was not limited to marriage and social life. The community had become more aware of itself and the world as a result of the wartime experience. No longer could it be just another small, isolated fishing village. Furthermore, its position as the county seat put it at the hub of local politics.

Women had been granted the right to vote, and their interests were placing pressures on government at all levels. Amelia Caroline, as a direct result of her experiences in New York, became involved in political issues at the local level. She volunteered on behalf of the League of Women Voters to help register women. And when possible, she spoke in support of legislation of interest to women. This was particularly true for the Sheppard-Towner Maternity and Infancy Act, which was established to provide prenatal and postnatal care for women and medical support for young children.

Interest in care specifically for women and children had been building throughout the country during the first two decades of the century. Statistics compiled by the United States Children's Bureau had documented that the nation had one of the world's worst records with respect to maternal and early childhood deaths. This was particularly true in rural areas and areas of low income. Among the nation's poorest residents, infant mortality during the first year of life approached twenty percent; and within the first five years of life, nearly thirty-five percent of all children died.

Internationally, the United States ranked seventeenth in maternal death and eleventh in infant mortality. Amelia Caroline's small town, as evidenced by events surrounding her own entry into the world, mirrored those statistics.

Through the Sheppard-Towner Act, federal funds were to be provided to establish health clinics to serve both the rural and urban poor. Public health nurses would be supported and limited funds would be available for physician services.

The act was aggressively opposed by both the American Medical Association and the Woman Patriots. These were the same anti-suffragists who had argued against voting rights for women. Both opposition groups argued that the act was an infringement on personal liberties, and each associated the bill with socialist and communist movements. At the core, however, economics was an underlying issue. Physicians felt their autonomy and income were under threat. After all, nurse practitioners would be paid to act as independent healthcare providers, although in a limited sense.

Papa and I were both aware of the opposition, so we remained steadfastly supportive of the act. At the same time, he was distressed at the position taken by many of his conservative colleagues. Provisions in the Sheppard-Towner Act actually paralleled the role he had envisioned for me in the community. I was already providing guidance exactly as specified in the legislation, and there had been early indications of the positive impact my efforts were having.

Clearly, the programs outlined in the legislation would be beneficial. Furthermore, Papa had not heard comments regarding loss of income to any local physician as a result of my activities. In fact, Dr. Arthur Dosher, Papa's most respected colleague, was highly supportive of what I was doing.

We worked very hard to muster support. Papa and I lobbied the local politicians, and we wrote letters to our senators and members of the House of Representatives in Washington. Papa spoke with colleagues at every opportunity, and I did my best to convince women of the need for their voices in support.

Getting the legislation through Congress was a major uphill battle, but the battle was important. This was the first government program directed specifically at the needs of women and children. Thinking back over the past seventy years, we were working against the same negative voices that had spoken against legislation for Social Security, Medicare and Medicaid and Civil Rights.

Amelia Caroline's voice paused once again, but my mind remained on what she had just been saying.

There always seems to be a hard core of conservative individuals who lack sensitivity to the needs of society as a whole. They adamantly oppose any legislation that speaks to social programs. Child welfare and women's health even now come under their attack. It is unfortunate that those who support social progress must contend with such blindly negative forces, but with enough energy and broad support, the negative voices can be overcome. When Amelia Caroline resumed, I learned that such was the outcome in this case.

Ultimately, the groundswell of support for the Sheppard-Towner Act prevailed and the legislation was signed into law. Following passage of the bill, I applied for the position of County Health Nurse and I became one of ninety-four such nurses in the state. Though my appointment was a part-time position, affiliation with an official program of the U.S. Public Health Service gave authority to all my efforts.

This primarily was how the time passed over the next several years. Efforts toward bringing change in the town and in the way individual residents lived seemed to be having an effect.

The work, though rewarding, also took an emotional toll. Infectious diseases would be brought under control in one season only to reappear the next. Children continued to have severe illnesses. Scarlet fever, diphtheria and whooping cough took their toll each year. I knew that in many of these cases, the illnesses still were made worse because of poor hygiene and inadequate diet. The death rate for those below the age of fifteen years remained high and, throughout the decade of the 1920s, the average age at death was below thirty-five. Appendicitis and tonsillitis were ongoing challenges. The former, when severe and not caught in time, resulted in massive infection and death.

The tragedies did not spare any family and none seemed even marginally immune. Within the first years as county health nurse, I experienced the deaths of Caroline Newton, Henry Davis, Ella Mae Smith, Upshaw Reaves and Bessie Hancock, all below the age of two.

These losses were in addition to young teens such as Carrie Price, Victor Wilson, John Jones, Eddie Swain, and Vida Spencer. Dorothy Smith, just eleven years old, died following the rupture of an infected appendix: The ensuing gangrene took her life. On such occasions, I would just sit in the rocker and weep.

And it was at such times that Great-Grandmother would come to me, just as she had following the death of William Banes. Mostly, Papa was home and, while sitting with me, he would share my distress. Death had been ever present for his entire professional life. But on days when Papa was away and I was alone on the porch, Great-Grandmother came and her presence brought comfort to me.

Papa and I knew that in addition to poor hygiene and diet, many of the deaths could be attributed to inadequate standards of medical practice. Many of his more senior

199

colleagues had been trained under the antiquated system of the 19th century and often they refused to accept the latest standards of care.

The new and evolving area of medical science, Epidemiology, was providing insight into how diseases were transmitted. Much of this information was being compiled by the U.S. Public Health Service at facilities such as the quarantine station located just offshore in the middle of our river.

At the time, Dr. Dosher was medical director at the quarantine station. This was a position he had assumed following his return from France at the end of the first war. The facility was unique, as ships carrying cargo from all ports of the world stopped for inspection prior to entering the state port upriver at Wilmington.

Under the direction of Dr. Dosher, Jens Berg worked as manager of the station. Over time, Jens Berg became one of the nation's leading experts on the maritime transmission of disease. Information compiled by him formed much of the basis for global Epidemiology as we now know it. Yet among many older physicians in rural Southern towns, the attitude remained that "the spread of diseases among sailors had little relevance to those who live on shore."

Papa, however, was aware of the expertise at the quarantine station. He and I often met with Dr. Dosher and Jens Berg to discuss ways in which data and techniques from the station could be applied to healthcare in the community.

A unique aspect of the quarantine station was provision for retaining and treating mariners who were ill. The station provided hospital care for transient sailors; however, at the time, there was not a hospital available to residents either of the town or the surrounding county. Both Dr. Dosher and Papa were acutely aware of the need for a community hospital. Had one been available perhaps Carrie Price, Vida Spencer and others would not have died at such early ages.

Soon a campaign to build a county hospital gained momentum. Dr. Dosher was the spearhead for the campaign. Papa and I joined company with Dr. Broadway and Dr. Goley, both physicians in the surrounding area, to provide key support for the effort.

The relationship between Dr. Dosher and Papa was both personal and professional. The two had been born during the early 1870s. They had attended the local school and grown to manhood in the town. In addition, our family and the Dosher family had been prominent for several generations. The two men had chosen to enter the medical profession at approximately the same time. Papa, under the encouragement of Dr. D.I. Watson, had chosen the University of Louisville, whereas Dr. Dosher had attended the University of Maryland. They had graduated from medical school within a year of each other and returned to Southport to enter practice.

The approaches they took to their individual practices differed slightly, however. Both Papa and Dr. Dosher were fully aware of the need to base therapeutics on the latest medical science, and they both were involved with professional organizations. The differences came in the type of practice. Papa focused almost exclusively on community and family health issues. Dr. Dosher, though maintaining an extensive basic practice, chose also to develop expertise in the field of surgery. Over time, he became recognized as one of the nation's more skilled surgeons.

This orientation on the part of Dr. Dosher was directly related to his interest in establishment of a community hospital. Surgeries, particularly those of a more intricate nature, required a proper hospital setting. Consequently, more complicated local cases had to be treated at a hospital in Wilmington.

This had been the case in the spring of 1923 when Dr. Dosher successfully carried out an intricate brain operation at St. John's Sanitarium in Wilmington. Though arrangements for complicated operations were possible with planned surgeries, as was the case with the brain surgery, acute care was a different matter. Emergency situations such as Dorothy Smith's appendicitis, required immediate attention. Clearly, a local hospital with modern surgical theaters and convalescent facilities right here in town was the answer.

The argument was also made that the hospital could be used for more routine surgical care, such as tonsillectomies and adenoid treatments. In addition, patients with childhood diseases who were being seen by me and being treated by Dr. Dosher or Papa, on occasion, required care that went beyond that available in the home.

So momentum began to build, with the goal of establishing a county hospital in Southport. As is usual with projects requiring significant funding from external sources, progress was not rapid at first. To complicate matters, a mild *economic downturn in the mid-1920s slowed the process. Several wealthy and influential investors were forced to withdraw temporarily from the project.*

However, a formal charter for the hospital was obtained in 1928. Construction began shortly thereafter and, in 1930, the hospital was opened for patients. The timing was perfect, as the hospital had been virtually completed at the time of the great stock market crash of 1929.

During the years of work leading to completion of the hospital, Amelia Caroline matured professionally, and she came to realize that being aware of and involved in the political process was important if progress was to be made in any public sphere. Virtually every aspect of professional life, from her role as a county health nurse, to support of healthcare specifically for women and children, to establishment of the hospital, required an intimate knowledge of political views, attitudes and whims at the local, state and national levels.

Politics influenced all.

26

REDOING THE PHARMACY

The next years passed quickly for Papa and me. The hospital became a key aspect of life in town. Surgical cases increased dramatically and recoveries were less traumatic due to improved post-surgical care. Over time, we realized the promise of relief from many life-threatening situations.

On one particular spring day, five appendectomies were performed, thus assuring happy years in the future lives of as many families.

In addition, our attention to the care of pellagra patients became more focused. This was significant, as the disease continued to ravage the South. The number of cases locally became so large that a recommendation was made to dedicate a significant amount of space in the hospital to the care of pellagra patients. Although the need for care was great, local authorities were slow in accepting the research findings of Dr. Goldberger and the U.S. Public Health Service. The answer to the epidemic would come in the form of improved diet. This was particularly true for school children.

I was convinced that without proper nutrition, school children would not develop to their full potential. Lethargy was common among children from families in which pellagra had been diagnosed. The children were listless in school and studies were often neglected.

This situation was of particular concern to Annie Mae Woodside, who served as assistant superintendent of the schools. Though Annie Mae was older than I, we had become close friends. We shared a keen interest in the health and well-being of the community, and we both were dedicated to serving the good of others, particularly the children. So we decided to implement a program that would provide nutritious snacks and meals during school hours. Annie Mae contacted several influential people, and a fund was established to purchase milk for children to have with their snacks. Soon, in the face of deteriorating financial circumstances in the Depression, supplemental food distribution paralleling the school program was implemented by the government and extended to the county as a whole.

Working from my position as county nurse, I continued to draw on newly acquired political awareness. Over several years, my relationship with Annie Mae strengthened and we began to consider goals in addition to the school diets. By the end of the 1930s, Annie Mae had become the first female superintendent of schools in North Carolina. Using her influence in this role, we were able to extend our efforts to include basic healthcare in all the schools. We acted in accordance with one guiding premise: Well-fed and healthy children would learn under careful guidance.

Eventually, I turned my attention to the pharmacy. Products of questionable merit came under scrutiny, and soon many of them were gone from the shelves. Among the first to go was "Dr. King's Germentuer" which claimed a taste as pleasant as lemonade and was advertised as the ideal cure for all summer-based diseases of the stomach and bowels. Along with that went "Simmon's Liver Regulator," which claimed to be the best springtime medicine, and "Dr. Pierce's Favorite Prescription," which advertised that it could rob childbirth of its torture, terrors and dangers to both mother and child.

It wasn't long thereafter that the pharmacy no longer offered "Lydia E. Pinkham's Vegetable Compound." The Vegetable Compound had been endorsed by General Roger Hanson, C.S.A., as being effective in treating ills peculiar to the female sex. Included were extreme lassitude and that "all gone feeling."

Other than testimonials of such questionable authenticity, there was no evidence to support the claims. Deception was quite common among the manufacturers of patent medications. Mrs. Rosa Adams, a niece of General Hanson, who by that time was deceased, had made claims of having experienced tiredness, loss of energy and irregularity. Then after just two bottles of "Lydia Pinkham's Vegetable Compound," Mrs. Adams could "feel the buoyancy of my younger days returning. I became regular and was able to do more work. I continued to take the Vegetable Compound until restored to perfect health."

Cleansing and fortifying the blood were major themes among the patent medications. In the past, these claims had been of great appeal when workdays were long, diets were poor and people chronically felt tired and run-down. This was particularly true for women, who in addition to never-ending demands on their time and energy had to endure the experience of their "monthlies." "Pink Pills for Pale People" was described in advertisements as the "true blood food" and just the ticket to provide a needed energy boost.

Similarly, "Scott's Emulsion" was advertised as being effective in treating the ills of young women. As the ads said, "Young women in their 'teens' are permanently cured of the peculiar disease of the blood which shows itself in paleness, weakness and nervousness by regular treatment with Scott's Emulsion."

How could such claims be refuted? This was the question facing Papa and me. Clearly, the advertisements appealed to the people of town. They promised cures for so many illnesses and the cures were available at such reasonable prices. In many cases, such as with the Lydia Pinkham compounds, specific audiences were targeted through use of testimonials by prominent regional personalities. Accompanying endorsements by the medical community did not hurt matters, even when the testimonials were vague. Dr. F.L. Morris, M.D. of Brooklyn, New York, testified on behalf of Ayer's products: "Ayer's medicines have been satisfactory to me throughout my practice, especially 'Ayer's Cherry Pectoral,' which has been used by many of my patients, one of whom says he knows it saved his life."

But even when more specific, the testimonials were a stretch of the truth at best. Dr. T.E. Miller of Cross Plains, Wisconsin, expressed the opinion that "for obstinate cases of syphilis and scrofula, 'Ayer's Sarsaparilla' is unquestionably the most effective remedy known to pharmacy. Wonderful cures have resulted from its use." This was the same Ayer's Sarsaparilla that "will relieve and cure dyspepsia, nervous debility and that tired feeling."

And if those testimonials were not sufficient to guarantee sales, a claim was made for relief in cases of severe traumatic injuries. Dr. J.C. Ayer submitted a testimonial on behalf of a

205

patient who reported that he had injured his leg, "leaving a sore which led to erysipelas. My sufferings were extreme, my leg, from knee to the ankle, being a solid sore that began to extend to other parts of my body. After trying various remedies, I began taking 'Ayer's Sarsaparilla,' and before I had finished the first bottle, I experienced great relief; the second bottle effected a complete cure."

Yet Papa and I knew that, in many cases, money was being wasted on useless treatments. And diseases that could be effectively treated were not. I often talked with Mr. Berg and Papa about products that I considered ineffective or that advertised cures to simply deceive their customers.

"How can such testimonials be true?" I would ask my father. "And in the case of physician endorsements, don't these come under the category of 'criminal participation' to which you have referred so many times in years past?"

Papa, of course, had to agree.

The list of questionable products was extensive. Although Papa's pharmacy only carried forty or fifty patent medications at any one time, there were hundreds being manufactured, and they were distributed without either explanation of composition or evidence of efficacy. Virtually every ailment common to mankind was targeted.

The Bobbitt Chemical Company of Baltimore offered "Rheumacide," for example. They claimed it "is not a cure-all, but it cures Rheumatism in addition to removing impurities from the blood."

The distributor of "Pe-Ru-Na" claimed that "Healthy women praise Pe-Ru-Na as a cure for colds and a preventive of catarrh." Similarly, "Taylor's Cherokee Remedy of Sweet Gum and Mallein" was "nature's great remedy for coughs, colds and LaGrippe." "Wintersmith's Chill Cure" was advertised as "a medicine of merit, sold on a guarantee to cure chills, ague, dengue, La Grippe and biliousness."

I was armed with references from my training in New York to counter such claims. Plus, there were the publications Papa received from the American Medical Association's Chemical Laboratory. Papa, Sven Berg and I worked steadfastly and, over time, we became pleased with the impact our efforts were having.

Not all patent medications left the shelves, however, for there were some products that customers simply insisted upon having. "McElwey's Wine of Cardui," "Grove's Tasteless Chill Tonic" and "Thedford's Black Draught" for constipation and indigestion were always in demand, so they were retained. Others patents, such as "Scott's Emulsion" with cod liver oil, were fairly well defined and in many ways beneficial. Tonics and bitters, such as "Watson's Drug – Iron Tonic and Bitters" for indigestion, were innocent enough. These often were taken as general stimulants rather than to alleviate specific disorders.

We had to make value judgments for each product, but ultimately I became confident in my belief that all the products being sold through the pharmacy would be beneficial.

27

COLLEAGUES AND FRIENDS

Generally speaking, feelings of contentment extended into most aspects of Amelia Caroline's life. She had not resolved her disillusionment with religion and she still had mixed feelings regarding events of the war. However, these were deep-seated issues, and the busyness of life kept her from dwelling on them overly much. In the main, she was comfortable with her personal situation and found her professional activities as county nurse to be challenging and quite rewarding.

The status of women in town had evolved since the war, and the role of wife and homemaker was no longer seen as the only option. The number of women employed as career healthcare providers increased as the hospital expanded its services and as additional physicians chose to practice in the town or nearby in the county.

Those were challenging years, but I felt good about my efforts and their rewards. I had a number of peers with whom work could be shared. Among these was Beatrice Carson, who worked both as office manager for Dr. Dosher and as a surgical assistant at the hospital. Beatrice and her mother had relocated from their home in Clarks Summit, Pennsylvania, about two years after the First World War. Their move from Pennsylvania to Southport had not been entirely by chance, for Beatrice, as a result of her experiences working as a registered nurse during the war, had several contacts in our town. During the early months of the war, she had volunteered to serve in the U.S. Army Nurse Corps. Initially, she had been stationed at the U.S. Army Base Hospital at Camp Wheeler, which was located near Macon, Georgia. Then, in 1918, as casualties increased in Europe, she had been reassigned to the Army Base Hospital at Beau Desert, France, where she had met and worked for nearly two years with Dr. Dosher. It was largely this professional relationship that resulted in her move to Southport.

Beatrice and I immediately became friends. We shared career goals, but also personal ties evolving from the professional relationship between Papa and Dr. Dosher. In addition, much to my surprise, while Beatrice had been in France, she had met Susan Williams, who was also serving in the Army Nurse Corps. Though the two had not maintained close contact after returning from Europe, Beatrice was aware of Susan's position as head of nursing at the hospital in New York. She was delighted to learn about my training under Susan's watchful eye and to know of our family relationship. Within days of our meeting, Beatrice and I had lunch with Lelia, Susan's sister, who still lived in Southport. Through this association, Beatrice's acquaintance with Susan was renewed and a lasting friendship among the four of us developed over the ensuing years.

As the years passed and Papa aged, I assumed more responsibility for the pharmacy. Then, much to my disappointment, renewal of the Sheppard-Towner Act failed to pass in Congress. Consequently, the U.S. Public Health Service program in support of healthcare for women and children was discontinued.

My role as county nurse lost some of its political muscle, but I remained in that position for a few additional years, largely as a volunteer. Use of the hospital by physicians from surrounding communities was expanding and skilled nurses were in demand. So after nearly twenty years in public-health and clinic-based nursing, I joined the hospital staff part time as a surgical assistant. My role at the hospital paralleled the one filled by Beatrice Carson.

Though Amelia Caroline was fairly content with the course of her life, time does not follow a path devoid of sadness. She and her father were quite close and often, on warm spring evenings, they shared the evening's quiet and the pleasant breezes from the waterfront while sitting on the porch. On some evenings, particularly those that followed events involving great sadness for them both, there was little in the way of conversation, for a commonality in thought was between them.

Such was the case in the spring of 1939, for significant events over the previous months had brought sadness to both Amelia Caroline and her father.

Papa and I were deeply saddened by the loss of Dr. D.I. Watson. He had passed away at the age of eighty-two, having spent over a half century in service to the town. Dr. Watson's passing had come just weeks after the departure of Beatrice from town. She, along with her aged mother, had returned to their original home in Pennsylvania. Beatrice's decision to leave the town had followed the death just four months earlier of Dr. Dosher. Though remaining at the hospital in the role of head surgical nurse was an option open to her, Beatrice knew that her mother longed to return to their home place, where her final years could be lived among members of their extended family. So Beatrice moved and I was left with a void that was matched by the loss experienced by Papa.

The deaths of the two physicians weighed heavily upon Papa. Arthur Dosher had been both a lifelong friend and professional colleague, and Dr. Watson had served as advisor to Papa during his formative professional years.

For me, the departure of Beatrice Carson was particularly distressing, for over the years we had become best friends. We had, after all, been young women in the 1920s, living fairly independently as career-oriented females in a traditional male-dominated society. Each of us had chosen a role other than that of wife and mother, which was what society had expected. Our bonds initially had been career related, but over the years a relationship of a very close nature had evolved. We shared a commitment to women's causes, enjoyed days together away from work, and had numerous friendships in common, particularly the friendship with Susan Williams and her sister.

We had also shared great sadness when we received news of Susan's death in New York in late February of 1938. The day had been cold and gray when Beatrice and I journeyed to New York City to bid farewell to my mentor, teacher and great friend. The trip was my final one to that city.

These losses were particularly trying for Amelia Caroline. It is not that death was a stranger to her, for she had matured to the point of accepting death as an integral part of her profession. She also had experienced personal loss during the war.

In addition, it hadn't been too many years since the death of Mrs. Emma Wescott, her childhood nurse, nanny and substitute mother. Mrs. Wescott had been a "member of the family" for nearly twenty-nine years, and her sudden death at the age of sixty-three left Amelia Caroline with a great sadness. Yet over time, even that sadness had been tempered.

The more recent losses, however, impacted both her personal and professional lives. Dr. D.I. Watson and his pharmacy had graced the town for nearly six decades and Dr. Dosher had been a physician beloved by many for thirty-five years. Amelia Caroline realized this was just one year less than her father had been in practice, and the realization brought to mind her own mortality and that of her father. He was to turn sixty-seven that year and he was in reasonably good health.

But early in her life, Amelia Caroline had learned how quickly one's world could change!

While Papa and I sat on the porch that May evening in 1939, my mind, as frequently is the case following a sequence of emotionally traumatic events, drifted back to other disturbing events in my life.

I realized with these more recent deaths how quickly the lives of Joseph Miller, Bobby Mintz, James Bell, Elias Hewett, Thomas Gore and William Banes had changed. Along with their memories, long-suppressed questions once again came to my mind.

"Was there any relevance of religion to the actual events in life? Why was there such an apparent disconnect between the teachings of various religions and the daily practices of those who professed the religious beliefs?"

As my mind bounced around, other concerns were brought to the surface, concerns that had been put aside for many years. These were about the impact of the military and military-related activities on the lives of everyday people. The war of my teen years was focal to my thoughts, but I had learned over the previous two decades that the impact of the military was not exclusive to times of war.

Memory came to me of a scientific venture that had been carried out on Caswell Island some years earlier by the Marine Hospital Service, precursor to the U.S. Public Health Service.

The experiment was one that flew directly into the face of what I had been trying to accomplish through community education efforts. The plan involved establishing a research facility to study a deadly strain of typhoid germs on the island. The project was to be carried out under the direction of Colonel Charles Stiles, and it was designed to monitor the migration of the germs through the groundwater system of our community over a period of years.

Although public access to the research site was to be restricted and the site was to be located on an uninhabited stretch of beach, there existed a threat to the population of inadvertent -- yet massive -- exposure to the disease.

Since the war's end, young people had resumed day trips and picnics to the island. Fishermen plied the close-in waters for shrimp, flounder, clams and crabs. Innocent visitors to the island would be at risk, particularly if the scientists were wrong concerning their ability to contain the project. I was concerned about the ability of the military to fully secure the site.

These were very real concerns and they weighed on my mind. In addition, I was distressed and frustrated, for when the concerns were brought to the attention of local officials, the response was less than receptive. They argued in favor of the project because it would assure renewal of government interest and activity in the region. The research would bring national attention to the town once again and there would be a boost to the local economy.

By that time, Papa and I had become quite familiar with Colonel Stiles, his interests and his research efforts. It was he who had carried out the study of privies in Wilmington and reported on the relationship of poor sanitation to the prevalence of disease in that city. I had even drawn on data from those studies to argue on behalf of better sanitation measures in town.

Both Papa and I had high regard for his research, yet we persisted in presenting our concerns about the typhoid project. We tried every available level of government. The efforts had little influence on the decision to proceed with the research.

Politics at a higher level had come into play. The research project began the same year Elias Hewett died.

Recording Amelia Caroline's stories, as anticipated, had consumed my Sunday. Memories of soldiers, suffering, neglect and illness had come flooding back to her. They had remained with her throughout life and, over the past two days, she had brought them to me with each trip I made to the waterfront. Amelia Caroline had remembered those days in 1939 when she reached across the porch to touch her father. She also remembered that 1940 was just around the corner and another war was brewing in Europe.

The hour was growing late, and I had spent the entire weekend, nearly thirty-six hours, writing all of this in the journal. The process had left me both physically and emotionally drained. I needed rest, for the next day would be a busy one in the office. Monday always was.

Also, I was scheduled to meet again with Dr. Catherine Arrington after work. I still did not have a definitive answer to her question regarding the distinction between cryptic messages and recurring family memories. I did, however, know the direction in which I was leaning.

28

THE BELL TOLLS

"No man is an iland,
Intire of it selfe;
Every man is a peece of the Continent,
A part of the maine;
If a clod bee washed away by the Sea,
Europe is the lesse,
As well as if a Promontorie were,
As well as if a Mannor of thy friends
Or of thine owne were;
Any mans death diminishes me,
Because I am involved in Mankinde;
And therefore never send to know
For whom the bell tolls:
    It tolls for thee."

> John Donne
> 1624

Catherine met me in the waiting area, as was her norm. This had been part of our routine now for several weeks. We exchanged greetings then walked back to the office. As we entered, I glanced across the room where the window, located behind the two chairs and small table, looked out on the landscaped garden behind the clinic. It was mid-fall and the garden of azaleas, dogwood and camellias was no longer in bloom. I took my usual chair while placing some quickly scratched notes on the small table to the side.

"Mary Eliza, you seem a bit pensive this morning," commented Catherine. "Is there something in particular about which you are thinking?"

"I'm not certain how to begin, Catherine. My thoughts are so jumbled. The closest I can come to answering is that I am experiencing a blending of my own life with that of Amelia Caroline."

"When you use the word 'blending,' what do you envision in your mind?" Catherine probed.

"Sometimes I don't know where I end and where she begins!" I blurted out.

"Can you give me an example?"

"I'll try, but it may not make any sense," I responded and began to gather my thoughts.

"As you might recall, during our last session we talked about the thoughts I was having regarding my relationship with Amelia Caroline and I expressed the belief that perhaps I am part of her story. What I was experiencing at that time seems to have become more intense.

"'Intense' may not be the best choice of words; perhaps the word 'personal' might better describe what has been going on. During that session, I said that I knew Amelia Caroline's questions, I cried at her pains and I celebrated her joys. Although these experiences seemed intuitive on my part, that is they required no thought and were just spontaneous realization, I now am coming to believe that perhaps the events in her life are also events of my life. It is becoming difficult for me to tell where Amelia Caroline's experiences end and my own experiences begin. By experiences I mean both the actual events and the emotional reactions to the events in each of our lives."

I sat for a while, trying to think how to best describe, in more understandable terms, what was going on. I decided to begin with a hypothetical but rather extreme example. And I explained this to Catherine.

"Let's assume I've just returned from the Old Burying Ground, where I had been sitting for an hour or so next to the headstone for Amelia Caroline's Great-Grandmother. You will recall, Catherine, that I first came to see you after just such a day.

"Anyway, upon reaching the cottage and sitting at the computer, Amelia Caroline begins to speak. She describes having fallen from the porch and injuring her left ankle. In a typical relationship with a relative, friend, or even a patient, my reaction would be empathetic. The friend's emotional state following injury would be shared, but the injury itself would not be shared.

"However, my relationship with Amelia Caroline is unique. Amelia Caroline is no longer physically present in my life; yet even before the accident and the injury are described by Amelia Caroline, I look down and my ankle is inflamed and throbbing," I said, shaking my head as I put my disbelief into words.

Catherine responded with concern, "Your description is quite graphic, Mary Eliza. I understand that Amelia Caroline is no longer with you and, even if she were, you would not actually experience her injuries, at least injuries of a physical nature. So I'm wondering in what way you perceive the events of her life as part of your life?"

I said, "The most immediate example I can share pertains to those people who had left Amelia Caroline's life late in 1939. Her nanny Mrs. Wescott, her friend and mentor Susan William, and Doctors Watson and Dosher all passed away within a relatively short period of time.

"Each of these deaths left a void in her life. Seen from another perspective, each of the losses has taken something from her life. What comes to mind are the often-quoted thoughts written by John Donne in the early 17th century:

'Each man's death diminishes me, for I am involved in mankind.

Therefore, send not to know for whom the bell tolls; it tolls for thee.'

"Catherine, I don't know exactly what John Donne meant by being diminished, but I interpret his meaning to be similar to my use of the word 'void.' Each time the bells ring, there occurs a little place of emptiness in our psyche. From an experiential standpoint, acknowledgement of that emptiness, that is to say recalling the memory of those who have been lost, results in sadness.

"The voids, then, are those aspects of our being which Donne describes as diminutions. As I envision all of this, over time the voids or diminutions accumulate at the edge of an inwardly spiraling emotional vortex. When the number of voids increases, the force of the vortex is accentuated. Eventually, due to the increasing momentum, we are emotionally swirled toward the center of the vortex. There we encounter all the diminutions of the past.

" The bell rang repeatedly for Amelia Caroline, and the accelerating vortex took her to THAT PLACE where memories from her youth reside. Recollections of friends who were both lost and damaged came repeatedly, as well as recollections of the sufferings of war, her disappointment with the military and her disillusionment with religion.

"Finally, with respect to your question, it seems as if, during my conversations with Amelia Caroline, I have heard those exact same bells, and I was in THAT PLACE when she arrived."

The conversation was getting quite complex -- even for me -- so I sat quietly for a brief period. Then Catherine asked another of her poignant questions.

"Mary Eliza, several sessions back we talked about your brother Charles and his Army friend Louis Gabral. I know from your description that you and Charles were very close and, in a unique way, you had been quite good friends with Louis. You told me of the grief you experienced upon receiving the news that Charles had been killed in Vietnam, and you also described the sadness you shared years later with Louis's mother over his death. Did the news of their deaths toll the bells for you?"

I knew the answer even before the question had been asked. Once again, warm tears welled in my eyes. For I knew there had been these and other bells.

29

THE LANGDON FAMILY

My identification with Amelia Caroline was clearly becoming something of a second nature to me. After talking with Catherine Arrington, I was even more convinced, so much so that the following weekend, when I had those two days to write in the journal, Amelia Caroline came to me as if we were still sitting on her familiar porch and she in her beloved chair. I was not surprised, therefore, to have the same experience today as my mind went back to August 17, 2002, just before she passed away.

Amelia Caroline had been on the porch in deep reflection for some time. The morning shadows had shortened as the sun crept overhead and its rays no longer shined directly onto the porch.

The day was Saturday and Amelia Caroline was ninety-nine years, three months and six days old. Exactly how long she had been on the porch was neither known nor mattered, for Amelia Caroline could have spent the entire day in the rocker. After all, there just weren't many activities for someone who was well into her one-hundredth year of life. So time in the rocker while revisiting the past had become standard. However, the sound of my voice brought Amelia Caroline from her reflective state.

"Aunt Amelia?" I asked.

"I'm on the porch. Is that you Mary Eliza?" she responded.

"Yes. I'm just returning from the hospital. I awakened very early and decided to make a quick trip over there. I wanted to check on the status of Mr. Sellers. He had surgery on Thursday and, given his age, we decided it would be best if he remained in the hospital over the weekend. Have you been out here long?"

"Since early morning. I think it was just after you left. Last night was so hot; I only slept a short while. The porch is always comfortable this early."

"Have you been visiting with Great-Grandmother Amelia again?" I asked.

"No, but my mind has been going back to earlier days and I have been recalling some of the conversations I had with her in years past. We have had so many talks over the years and a lot of them still go through my mind. You know, don't you, that it was following those conversations that I finally dropped away from the church?"

"I recall your telling me about that some time back. You said the decision had been made following the conversation in which Great-Grandmother told her story of life during the Civil War. But you never really shared with me all she had said." I encouraged Amelia Caroline to tell me more.

"Yes, I remember talking with Great-Grandmother about those days. The conversations were so intense that recalling them has been strenuous, but let me think back," she responded.

"While you are thinking, I'll go in to the kitchen and make some tea. I see you've had your usual coffee, but I'm guessing you would enjoy a snack," I said, as I headed inside.

I actually knew much of Great-Grandmother's story already, as Amelia Caroline and I had talked about the family relationships on many occasions. But I also knew that Amelia Caroline wanted to talk again, and this three-day weekend had been arranged so we could spend a lot of time visiting on the porch, which I had also grown to love.

While I was in the kitchen, I pictured Amelia Caroline closing her eyes as she reached back in time. Upon returning to the porch, it was clear that her mind had not gone directly to the long-past conversation with her Great-Grandmother. Rather, she told me that her thoughts had drifted back over the family tree and her mind had gone to the relationship with my ancestral family. I was always pleased to learn more of the basis for the bond between us.

When I had poured the tea and placed the light snack on the table between our chairs, Amelia Caroline began to speak.

You know, Mary Eliza, the relationship between our families extends back to the early years of the 19th century when our families were linked through marriage. Your Great-

Grandmother several generations removed, Mary Eliza Everitt Langdon, was the sister-in-law to my Great-Grandmother.

As in the case of my ancestors, your family has been in the region since the earliest days of the 1800s. Although the two branches of the family had remained in the Eastern North Carolina, our nuclear families actually diverged for several years. The divergence came in 1835, following the decision by Richard Langdon to move inland and establish a plantation for farming northwest of the Cape Fear River near the small community of Magnolia.

To say that Richard and his family began farming is not exactly correct, for in those days virtually all families engaged in farming to one extent or another. Much of the farm activity was for subsistence, but in many cases it actually involved management of a plantation. Even my own Great-Grandfather Sterling Everitt, though a physician by profession, had partial interest in a rice plantation along the river just northeast of the town. In addition, he owned several properties both in the community and elsewhere in the surrounding county. The close-in properties, particularly those along creek bottoms and adjacent to swampland, were used to grow the food crops. These were primarily for family consumption and to meet the needs of the family's slaves. In contrast, the outlying investments, properties that were bought and sold, provided much of the family's income.

Originally, Sterling's sister Mary Eliza Everitt and her husband Richard Langdon lived in town where Richard was engaged in mercantile exchange and commerce along the river. Over time, as more commerce moved inland, so did Richard's interests. Cotton trade with England had become highly profitable, as was rice production in the tidal flood plains along the Cape Fear River.

Sterling had acquired several tracts of land that were located about fifty miles inland. The tracts were contiguous and all were located just a few miles from the headwaters of the Northeast Cape Fear River. This was important, for travel between inland plantations and centers of commerce at the coastal ports required access to navigable rivers. The land was reasonably priced and it had rich sand-hill soil that was well suited to growing cotton.

Richard, recognizing the economic advantages of expanding his interests, decided to purchase 1500 acres from

Sterling. There were a modest house and several outbuildings situated on the land. Therefore, the structures would afford enough comfort for the family to relocate, at least for a while, upriver toward Magnolia.

The Langdon land was heavily forested, with mature oaks and longleaf pines, the two trees of greatest value to the naval stores industry. So, upon relocation, the family farmed in order to meet their daily needs and those of the field workers, of which there were nearly twenty.

They also prepared the land for cotton production, which involved removing many mature trees. The resulting hardwood timber was milled and shipped downriver to Wilmington, where it was sold for use in the shipyards.

In addition, the abundant longleaf pines on the plantation were used to produce tar, pitch and turpentine for sale to the naval stores industry. Richard Langdon realized sizable profits even before the first cotton crops were harvested.

Much of this activity fell under the direction of overseers who had been hired to manage various aspects of the plantation's activities. Richard, meanwhile, drew upon his experience as a merchant in town, and he established a small store where those in the community and from neighboring plantations could obtain dry goods and imported foodstuffs, including fruits, spirits, herbs and spices. The store, which also stocked hardware and medical supplies for everyday use, remained a local institution for the next thirty years.

Following the Langdons' move to Magnolia, our two branches of the family maintained ties, but for the majority of each year, we lived in distinct spheres nearly fifty miles apart. This often was the case in isolated rural areas, where remotely located plantations had limited interaction with residents of the small, scattered towns.

Interaction between our families did occur on special occasions, however. Beginning the very year of their relocation, on holidays and during the hot summer season, the Langdon family would travel downriver to Wilmington,where a few days would be spent, then they would continue toward the ocean and to the town. Days and weeks would be spent here enjoying the waterfront and its ocean breezes.

The summer trips were not entirely for pleasure, however. The threat of deadly disease such as malaria or yellow fever during the hot, sultry summer weather that predominated *along the upper reaches of the river was widely recognized by plantation owners. With this threat in mind, the planters and their families often traveled to the coast where, for much of the summer season, ocean breezes offered some protection from the diseases. The plantations were left to the caretakers and the slaves, the latter of whom seemed to have some intrinsic resistance, at least to malaria.*

The journeys to the coast were always exciting as well as challenging. Travel would involve horseback or carriage rides along crude roadways to the river landing. Then three or four days would be spent on the river, with stops along the way to visit friends at neighboring plantations. Invariably, upon reaching Wilmington, several nights' stay would be arranged for the family at a boarding house, so time could be spent in the city visiting shops.

Referring to Wilmington as a "city" was a bit deceptive, for the community wasn't much at the time. It consisted of ramshackle buildings, warehouses and wharves scattered along a muddy riverfront. And just back from the water were small shops, taverns and businesses. For the most part, small three-room frame houses predominated, though a few stately homes and churches were beginning to appear on the higher ground overlooking the water.

When I was a young woman, I read the memoirs of Frances Anne Kemble an English actress who had married into the Butler family of Philadelphia. She had passed through Wilmington in the year 1838.

Frances Anne had been en route to the Butler family plantation along the coast of Georgia. Following her stay in Wilmington, her impressions of North Carolina in general, and the town of Wilmington in particular, were recorded and later published.

"......it (Wilmington) looked to me like a place I could sooner die than live in – ruinous, yet not old – poor, dirty and mean, and unvenerable in its poverty and decay."

Amelia Caroline paused for a short period, then with a smile on her face -- it was one of those times when she was smiling to herself -- she again spoke.

Mary Eliza, my mind took a side trip. I just recalled that this was the same Frances Anne Kemble and the same book that you and I had discussed some years back. We had been on the porch having a conversation regarding race relations when you mentioned the book and you also described a paper you had written on the topic of slavery.

I remembered that conversation. It was interesting how these memories pop in and out of our minds.

For a few moments we sat and mused at the thought of how the mind works. Then Amelia Caroline resumed.

Though I believe that Frances Anne Kemble's reactions to her experiences as she passed through the state reflected an opinion in the extreme, it must be said that Wilmington at the time was not a shining Mecca. This was particularly true when it was compared either to the large Northern cities or the more prosperous Southern cities such as Charleston, which had a population ten times greater than that of Wilmington.

Even so, Wilmington, with its population of more than 3500 residents, offered great advantage over the smaller North Carolina communities, and the Langdon family always looked forward to the stopover. Various items would be purchased as gifts to bring downriver, and orders would be placed with various merchants for necessities to be picked up on the return journey back to Magnolia.

While in the city, Richard would catch up on the latest political news. The growing dissatisfaction with the slave trade was of particular interest. This issue was being enflamed by an anti-slavery movement, one which had the sympathy of Frances Anne Kemble Butler.

As you know, living conditions on plantations owned both by her husband and his neighbors on St. Simon's Island, Georgia, were described in the book. Frances Anne Kemble's prose was anything but kind to the Southern way of life. Slavery as an institution was particularly attacked with an eloquence that spoke to the abolition movement. Though Frances Anne's journal was not published in America until after the outbreak of the Civil War, the slavery question -- and its growing opposition -- were of acute interest to virtually all who depended upon slave labor to offer their lives a margin of comfort. This included both the Everitt and the Langdon families.

The final leg of the trip was a day's sail by packet down the river from Wilmington to Southport, where the Langdons were welcomed into Great-Grandmother's household. Over a period of several days, the families would catch up and renew ties.

Meanwhile, the Langdon house in town, which had been maintained in their absence by resident caretakers, would be prepared for re-occupancy. Richard had insisted that they retain the house, for his full intent was to return here permanently as soon as the plantation near Magnolia became self-sustaining.

Beginning as early as 1836 when she was thirty-three years old and throughout this period, Great-Grandmother had assumed the role of family matriarch. This distinction was not due to age, as Great-Grandmother was nearly a dozen years younger than her sister-in-law Mary Eliza Everitt Langdon. But the fact that the Langdon family had moved away, whereas the Everitt family had resided continuously in town, conveyed special recognition.

This house became recognized as the family "home place." It was to the home place that the Langdon family came when they returned to town for their prolonged visits.

The town was integral to the family's roots. The presence of Great-Grandfather Sterling and Great-Grandmother served as a link to those roots, even for those who resided away from the town. It was this recognition that came to me over a century later, and this same linkage has drawn you, Mary Eliza, to the community.

Indeed, I had been been drawn both to Amelia Caroline and the town.

Since my first meeting with her in 1983, I had enjoyed being around my elderly relative; and following the summer vacation that year, I had looked forward to one day living in the waterfront community.

Fortuitously, as my final year of medical residency had begun, a position had been advertised by a small group of doctors in town. Their offices, at that time newly built across the street from the hospital, were located a short distance from Amelia Caroline's house. During my visits to town prior to completion of my residency, I had come to know most everyone in the practice. So I had been quick to indicate my interest in joining them.

Joining this practice had been my dream come true and, since Amelia Caroline's house had plenty of room, I had been

225

invited to move in. Actually, it is more accurate to say that my moving in had been expected. The arrangement had long been planned by Amelia Caroline, who had been alone for thirteen years following the death of her father. Having me share the house was something she had looked forward to with great anticipation. So as Amelia Caroline said, I returned to the ancestral "home place" exactly as my family had done one and a half centuries earlier.

Amelia Caroline's reaction to my decision regarding life in town had been immediate. She had been thrilled, for her Great-Grandmother's promise had come true. Not only was there family to share the house, but I would continue the family's tradition of physician healers. Amelia Caroline had been quick to point out that I was the first female in the family to become a physician.

My professional status was, in fact, the completion of a dream held throughout Amelia Caroline's adult life.

In the early months following my arrival, Amelia Caroline had repeatedly told me how much she enjoyed having me around and hearing daily reports from my practice. After all, at the time I had moved into the house in the mid 1980s, Amelia Caroline had already lived through more than eight decades, had experienced four traumatic wars and a great depression and, more importantly, had played a role in transforming the town from an early-20th-century village with 19th-century character to a modern community.

Our common bond of similar career paths solidified the relationship even further.

We had quickly become very close, for it had been clear that we shared many interests. I was one of the few persons in town who appreciated Amelia Caroline's lifestyle. Thus, in spite of my love for medical practice, I had looked forward each day to leaving the confines of the office and hospital and returning home to the open, airy house.

Many evenings had found the two of us walking on the waterfront. Often we would sit quietly listening to the waves while shorebirds played about them. Together we had awaited the homecoming of the fishing boats, and we had regularly purchased from the fishermen fresh flounder to broil, shrimp to steam, or oysters to roast in the backyard.

It was as if my presence had brought youth and energy to Amelia Caroline's years, whereas she clearly had brought the family roots to me.

Interestingly, we each had been named after a great-grandparent, though my namesake had been many more generations removed. After we had been together for some time, actually a few years, I began to feel a sense of continuity with the past. This had not been simply an awareness of and appreciation for history. It seemed to me, as we sat together on the front porch, that there was a direct bond with those who had been there before.

An ability to touch the past while living in the present was awakening in me; the ability was not unlike the one that Amelia Caroline had experienced since her earliest days. It was also the ability that had returned to Amelia Caroline in the early 1970s upon de-remodeling the house following the death of her father.

Over time, the acuteness of this experience had brought me to accept as reality the conversations between Amelia Caroline and her Great-Grandmother Amelia Caroline Potter Everitt.

We had by now finished our snack of toast, marmalade, fresh fruit and cool iced tea. Yet we continued to sit together watching the town move through its late-morning rituals.

30

CONVERGENCE

Mary Eliza, I've been recalling a conversation with my Great-Grandmother. The talk was one of several that occurred shortly after Papa's death. That awful war in Vietnam was still going on. I was quite distressed about the needless loss of life and the tragedy of war's wastefulness weighed more heavily on me than it had in years. It was such a burden and, from beneath the tremendous pressure, again came memories from the past. Memories that I was able to share with Great-Grandmother.

"Amelia Caroline, you seem unusually deep in thought today. Is it still the war?" Great-Grandmother gently asked.

"Yes. Great-Grandmother. I can't get away from all this continual emphasis on conflict and war. For my entire life, it seems the country has finished one war only to begin preparations for the next.

"And the people in town appear to celebrate the end of one while looking forward to the other. It takes them no time at all to forget the sacrifice, suffering and loss of lives. They wave flags and talk of destiny, and all the while delude themselves about having common bonds with the poor souls engaged in the carnage.

"Businessmen anticipate profit from military spending and investors look forward to sharing the rewards. National leaders dream of legacies based upon public service during years of war, and military officers look forward to the excitement of battle strategy. Engineers anticipate the challenges of battlefield logistics, while religious leaders speak again of God's Will. Then doctors go quietly to the front with hopes of saving just a few of those who have been sent to the slaughter."

"It is quite clear that you experienced much frustration and confusion during those days. But today there is also a lot of

anger in what you are saying, Amelia Caroline!" responded Great-Grandmother. "You previously told me about your experiences as a young girl, during what was your first war. And at that time you told me of your disillusionment, but when did the anger begin?"

"I'm not certain Great-Grandmother, because it just seemed to creep into my life gradually. But thinking back, disillusionment leading to frustration began shortly after I completed nursing training."

"As you know, I was very busy during those first years. Between calling on families to talk about ways to improve health and spending time in the pharmacy, I was perfectly happy, for my activities were having a visible impact. In several homes, the amount of sickness was reduced and, in those where illness did occur, the medications we offered were more reliable than they had been in years past. People were using less alcohol and opium disguised as medicine and, by cleaning up the neighborhoods, children suffered fewer skin and intestinal diseases.

"It was just as I was beginning to see the rewards of my efforts that the news came from Washington, DC about the plan to conduct the typhoid experiments on the island. Both Papa and I were concerned because the germs to be studied were extremely deadly. We felt quite strongly that the presence of the proposed experimental laboratory would place the entire community at risk.

"The government doctors and scientists and the politicians did not agree. The scientists were presuming safety based upon the design of the laboratory. Yet, paradoxically, it was that very degree of safety – the risk to communities following groundwater contamination -- that they were to be studying. The guarantee of safety, in a sense, was based upon a circular argument.

"The government doctors felt quite certain of their ability to control all aspects of the study. But in reality, scientific experiments rarely are absolutely perfect. Unknown or unanticipated factors often influence outcomes. And in this case, the experiments were not being carried out within the confines of a carefully designed laboratory. The laboratory was an open environment -- a low-lying sand-dune of an island where nature's forces can be unpredictable.

"No one seemed to care about the risks involved, so the project was just pushed forward. Like the war, the typhoid project had its own source of momentum. The proposal to conduct the experiments was a self-perpetuating energy field that swept people in and gained additional strength from their enthusiasm.

"I think that was the beginning of anger for me, Great-Grandmother. It certainly was my first realization that decisions made by others, or forces often beyond our awareness or control, moved events in our lives. I also came to realize that attempts to influence those decisions, or reduce the forces once they had gained momentum, were often futile, thus resulting in frustration. For someone living in a quiet, coastal resort and fishing village, that seems a remarkable realization, but it happened.

"As it turned out, nothing of great significance came from the typhoid study and, to my knowledge no one suffered. So in the end, it was just an isolated event that, for most people, was soon forgotten. But I did not forget.

"What stuck with me was the parallel between the public attitude toward the typhoid study and the one that had prevailed years earlier during the war. No one other than Papa, my friend Beatrice Carson and I seemed to care. Good people, neighbors and friends, who were not directly involved in either the study or the war, but who stood to benefit either directly or indirectly, supported the events. This support transcended what should have been their concern for others whose lives might be adversely affected.

"Over time, these kinds of thoughts began to encompass an even larger sphere, and it came to me that even poor-quality medications and ill-advised medical attention were often promoted for the same reasons. Furthermore, I began to believe that the responsible people, including some doctors and druggists, were as insensitive to the needs and dignity of their fellow man as those who arranged wars or conducted dangerous activities in our communities.

"Personal gain and profit seemed to be a common driving force, a force people blindly accepted, and this acceptance led to self-perpetuation of the system.

"Again, these thoughts stayed with me for many years, and I began to feel helpless about bringing change beyond that of my own actions or those of Papa or Mr. Berg. Perhaps the

231

anger grew out of frustration, but there were other events that also began to concern me.

"With the passage of time, I really began to notice and think about other events in town. Though the First World War had ended years earlier, the town was having difficulty moving away from its military legacy, and its historic role as a military center continued to be touted. Our July 4th celebrations focused less upon independence than they did upon the wars related to independence. Even the War Between the States, with its destruction and tragedy, continued to be recognized with regular meetings of the Confederate veterans.

"On the surface, these meetings were meant to remember lost colleagues, but honoring those who had died for the Confederacy was not the only intention. These men spent much time reliving the battles and falsely recalling glory on the battlefields. Their motto, 'the South will rise again,' bespoke a nostalgic longing for a return to those terrible times.

"Then other things began to happen. An airplane company, Aero-Limited, started to fly regularly between New York and Miami, and Southport became a scheduled stopover for fuel and rest. Soon the town became recognized for this attribute and developers began to envision another use of the town by the military.

"Both the U.S. Army and the Navy were expanding their fleet of seaplanes. Secure harbors would be needed to fuel and service the airplanes along the routes between distantly located bases, such as Norfolk and Miami. The suitability of our harbor was noted in 1939, when a U.S. Navy aircraft tender and five bombers were moored just off the waterfront near the quarantine station. The harbor had been selected as a sheltered temporary base while the seaplanes practiced bombing runs just beyond the coastal shoals.

"Realization that the government might have renewed interest in the area caught the attention of speculators who envisioned new and greater prospects involving both the town and the island. Following abandonment of Fort Caswell on the island, much of the government property had been sold to investors, who had several major schemes in mind.

"Initially, in the mid-1930s, the Caswell-Carolina Corporation opened a resort on the island. But other ideas were also under consideration, one of which was to establish a commercial seaplane air-service port there. Then, given the *topography of the island, such a seaplane port on the inland side of the island could be complemented with runways for land-based craft.*

"The schemes went so far as to imagine an internationally oriented facility. So anxious were the speculators during the late years of the Depression to have this transpire, that an offer was even made to a German firm to land its planes on the envisioned island base. Then, into the harbor came the U.S. Navy ship and the five seaplane bombers. The question was raised: Why not a permanent military air base of the same magnitude already envisioned for commercial flight?

"I began to feel the momentum building, as if life in a military camp was again on the horizon. And of course it was, for Congress was soon to pass -- and President Roosevelt was soon to sign -- an Arms Supply Act. The nation was preparing for war.

"I became uneasy as the 'Battle Hymn of the Republic' was sung again and again.

"Memories such as these increased over the years. Ultimately, they converged in my mind. The anger, I suppose, has grown out of this convergence.

"Now here I sit, nearly thirty years after that Second World War and twenty years after the war in Korea, being distressed by what is happening in Southeast Asia and here at home. After all these wars, people still ignore the carnage while they enjoy the profits. Though I see the news of outcry by young people in other parts of the country, I feel so isolated here with my thoughts."

As I paused in my long soliloquy, Great-Grandmother commented.

"Amelia Caroline, you are not alone, nor are your experiences unique. Perhaps it will help if I tell you the family's early story in its entirety."

With that, Amelia Caroline's demeanor changed ever so slightly. She continued to speak, but it was as if her Great-Grandmother were present and telling the story.

233

31

GREAT-GRANDMOTHER SPEAKS:
THE EARLY YEARS

I sat quietly as my elderly cousin began the tale. However, I soon realized that this wasn't just a story being told secondhand of a conversation that had taken place thirty or so years earlier. Rather, it seemed as if Great-Grandmother Everitt was again speaking to -- and through -- Amelia Caroline. It was as if Amelia Caroline's Great-Grandmother was actually present and the story was being told for its first time in her voice.

Amelia Caroline, there is a reason the town has had difficulty disassociating from its military aspirations. From the beginning, it was a simple military outpost. Your Great-Grandfather Sterling and his sister Mary Eliza were born in the shadow of cannons pointed toward the sea.

They had few childhood companions, so it was not unusual for them, along with the few other children from the town, to be entertained by young soldiers from the fort. The soldiers, often just out of their own childhood, taught the youngsters games, showed them how to whittle and included them in military drills. This all seemed natural, since there were many more soldiers in the fort than children in the town.

In addition, your Great-Great-Grandfather, beginning in the 1790s, was the surgeon to the troops at the fort. That was even before the town existed so, from the outset, the town and our families were entwined with the military.

As you know, Great-Grandfather Sterling was born in 1791, thirteen years earlier than I, so some of what I'm saying is based upon stories from his memory. But even in my early years, the fort was a major focus of our lives. Our houses clustered in open-ring fashion, about three quarters of the way around the fort, which being on the waterfront, closed the ring to the water. At that time, the waterfront strand was considered part of the fort, and the strand was used by the soldiers for their personal hygienic needs. The gun batteries were positioned on the small knoll just above the strand. It was a defensive position from which control was maintained over the maritime traffic.

Officers' quarters, barracks for the troops and the quartermaster's buildings were located to the rear of the fortifications. They were within a stone's throw of our porches, so we couldn't make a trip to the privy without half the garrison being aware of our whereabouts.

As children, we played on the waterfront adjacent to the fort, and seamen and sailors from merchant ships and warships kept us entertained.

It was an enjoyable time during those early years of the fort, for as I recall, the soldiers were just stationed here as a temporary duty assignment. Not much of a military nature other than routine activities like gun drills and daily formations took place. Typically, the soldiers were free to do as they pleased for most of their days.

On occasion, a foreign ship would enter the bay and every effort would be made to display military precision with the intention of conveying authority. But usually, the intruders were simply trading vessels from

Europe filled with goods such as fabric, spices, medicines or fresh foods to be exchanged for timber and naval stores.

The sailors, of course, were always anxious to put ashore, where they quickly gravitated to taverns and houses located at the western end of the town, beyond Boundary Street and adjacent to the swampland. Once there, the sailors generally kept to themselves, but not infrequently, the celebrants would drift into the center of the village and encounter an irate river pilot or townspeople concerned for their homes and families.

Before long, fights would break out, the military commander would exercise his authority, the blockhouse at the fort would be filled for the night and order would return to the town. However, none of this was particularly concerning and, for the most part, the town and the military comprised a comfortably integrated community.

Then, when I was about eight years old, things changed at the fort and the military activities intensified. Soldiers were less free to entertain us, as there was concern for renewed war with Britain. I was too young to remember exactly when things began to change, but it was in the winter of 1811 or the early spring of 1812.

As the prospect of war intensified, the number of soldiers increased and soon they outnumbered the town's residents. The fort was not large enough to accommodate all the new troops, so encampments began to form along the riverfront and in the woods behind the town. What had been a pleasant seaside village with a small semi-functional fort and a relatively small number of soldiers became primarily a military community. But it was one without a great amount of order, organization or discipline.

By that time, your Great-Grandfather Sterling had completed his apprenticeship as a physician and, along with his father, Reuben, he was treating the soldiers who were constantly ragged, dirty, hungry and sick. Rations for the soldiers were not abundant and living conditions in the various encampments were marginal.

The government, those people who sat in comfortable chambers and legislated, and those whose pockets stood to swell through government enterprise, were pushing young men into the military under the pretext of defending the nation's shores. However, they were doing so without making adequate provision for the needs of the troops. Soldiers at the forest encampments were sleeping in shabby tents, the houses initially proposed for their use having never been built. In addition to having six or more persons crammed into each tent, food was inadequate, clean clothing non-existent and medicine in short supply. Most of the soldiers went without blankets to help them survive the winters.

Before it all came to an end a few years later, camp diseases including cholera, dysentery and fevers known to be common among soldiers and sailors had crept into the lives of the villagers. Even my brothers, my sister and I, though well provided for by our father, repeatedly suffered illnesses. We were fortunate in that no one in our house died, but tragedy did strike our family with the sudden death of your Great-Great-Grandfather Reuben. He was fifty years old at the time of his death.

In many of the other families, children were particularly susceptible to the diseases and they died at an alarming rate. They were buried along with many of the young soldiers in graves that, for the most part, are now forgotten.

All of this deprivation and suffering for a war that really never materialized. Yet fear of conflict remained long beyond its reality, so our status as a military encampment remained, thus amplifying the tragic impact.

The presence of so many soldiers had a great impact on the town. Housing was nonexistent: Officers from the various companies expected comfortable accommodations, yet the officers' quarters at the fort were sufficient for only a few. So every available space, whether at the small inn run by my father, in one of the boarding houses or in a private home, was taken.

Privacy, which had always been limited due the town's proximity to the fort, became a rare luxury. Frequently there were newly arrived and undisciplined soldiers in the streets, always dirty, often drunk and disorderly, chasing livestock during the day and disrupting the tranquility of the night.

Normally, we would spend several months each year in the company of planters and their families, as they came to town during the summer season when fevers ravaged the plantations. But due to the great number of troops, it was impossible for many of the summer visitors to find houses. In fact, many of the planters who owned summer houses in town arrived only to find their houses commandeered by the military. Though it was often pleasurable for the more prominent families during that time to be entertained by the young officers, we were on the whole not disappointed to have the concern for war come to an end.

Amelia Caroline, your Great-Grandfather and I were married about four years after the threat of war ended. I was just turning sixteen and was swept off my feet by the attention of such a dashing young physician. I had known Sterling my entire life, at least as long back as memory served. He was much older than I; in fact, he was an adult studying medicine as an apprentice while I was still playing childhood games. However, I did grow up rather rapidly during the war years, as most young people matured fairly early in those days. Sterling began to pay attention to me shortly after my fifteenth birthday. In effect, we courted for a year, during which many hours were spent in the company of my mother on the porch of our house discussing our common interests. Sterling was unique among young men of the time, for he treated me as an equal and encouraged me to speak of all topics, including politics. Having shared the wartime experience, the events of that time were a common subject of discussion during our courtship, and those conversations ultimately shaped much of our lives together.

In the years after the war and prior to our wedding, Sterling established a small practice among the townspeople who then numbered about 300. Over time, the number of soldiers at the fort gradually decreased, finally reaching about fifty or sixty who occupied the fort at various times. During his apprenticeship and for a few years immediately after, Sterling had assisted his father, who was surgeon to the troops. However, following the death of his father and arrival at the fort of a new surgeon, Sterling no longer contributed to routine medical care at the fort.

I don't mean to imply that he was pushed to the side or that he had turned his back on the needs of the soldiers. He just did not wish to have his life tied directly to the needs of the military: he chose to be independent. However, when major emergencies arose, Sterling was always on hand to assist the post surgeon.

This was a change for the family as his father, Dr. Reuben Everitt, had been surgeon to the troops for nearly twenty years. He had initially served at the fort during the early 1790s, but toward the end of that century, Congress had decided to decrease the size of the standing Army. The position of surgeon at the fort had been eliminated. Reuben had then decided to move upriver to the town of Wilmington, where he entered partnership in an apothecary shop. This was important, for Reuben could both dispense medications and practice as a physician through the shop. The combination of these roles made up for the loss of his salary from the military. His tenure as an apothecary, however, was rather short.

As often seems to be the case, the government in Washington reversed its decision regarding the strength of a standing Army and, once again, Congress authorized more troops at the fort.

In 1805, while I was just a toddler, Reuben sold his share of the partnership in the pharmacy because he had been appointed by President Thomas Jefferson to once again serve as post surgeon at the fort. He had also been charged with establishing a hospital at the fort to serve both the troops and any seamen found ill upon their entering the harbor.

The hospital was to be part of a national network of hospitals being established by the Marine Hospital Service, an agency of the government that had been authorized through an act of Congress. The act had been signed into law in 1798 by President John Adams, and soon afterward hospitals were established at major ports, such as the one in Charleston. Although the hospital here was to be small, its presence called attention to the town and the fort as important for national security.

At the time of Dr. Reuben Everitt's return to town, tending the troops had been a great advantage, for the military surgeon received a comfortable government salary and was held in high regard by the community. And, of course, it was a time when few opportunities existed for employment outside of soldiering or piloting on the river.

Sterling's decision to disassociate from the military was not just because troop levels had decreased following the end of the war in 1814. As I have already said, your Great-Great-Grandfather died suddenly in 1813. His death occurred during the time of heightened military activity when troops were bivouacked everywhere around the town.

The cause of his death was somewhat of a mystery, but Sterling often suspected it was due to his father's constant exposure to sick soldiers. This suspicion weighed upon him, as did the loss of many soldiers and townspeople whose deaths could only be attributed to neglect and corruption on the part of those in government and among its suppliers, who should have advocated on behalf of the soldiers, sailors and marines.

Not having the responsibility for the poorly managed military was a relief to Sterling. His attentions could be focused in more rewarding directions. At any rate, as I mentioned, Doctor Bell, a military surgeon, arrived soon after Reuben's death and filled the position of post surgeon.

Reuben's funeral, as would be expected for a citizen of his stature, was attended by many, including all the prominent townspeople and both officers and soldiers from the fort. Following a procession to the town cemetery, an oratory was delivered by Captain Wilson who was commander at the garrison. Captain Wilson praised Reuben's contributions to the military, the community and his country.

Reuben had, after all, come to the fort in the early 1790s. That was even before the town, which at that time was named Smithville, had been chartered. Both of his children had been born and grown to adulthood in the shadow of the fort, and later he had become one of the town's founding citizens. In addition to the funeral oratory, a eulogy was delivered by your Great-Uncle Richard Langdon, who at the time was soon to be my brother-in-law. The eulogy called attention to Dr. Reuben Everitt as a man of compassion who was dedicated to the betterment of all.

Then the body was laid to rest in a brick-enclosed crypt. Reuben's burial plot was located very near the site in which a ceremonial urn had been buried following the death of General George Washington in 1799. This location carried particular significance, for following President Washington's death, it was Reuben who had led the honorary funeral procession and had delivered the oratory as the ceremonial urn was being buried.

The death of his father in 1813 marked a turning point in Sterling's life, for he lost not only his father but his medical mentor, role model and professional colleague. It was in the wake of this loss that Sterling charted the course that would be his life's path. A major aspect of his decision was to disassociate from the military, thus focusing his medical skills on the needs of the townspeople.

Now at the time, the practice of medicine was not highly lucrative, as physicians and their ministrations were viewed skeptically by many. Often, it was only in the most dire circumstances that the assistance of a doctor was sought, and in many of these situations the afflicted had little with which to pay for services.

Therefore, other sources of income were needed. Reuben had chosen the stipend of a military surgeon and, as I mentioned, he was also the proprietor of a small medicine shop for a short period. Sterling, however, chose to invest in real estate, a business at which he was quite successful. Because of this financial success, he was suitable in the eyes of my father as a husband.

We were married under the boughs of live oak trees on the waterfront on a beautiful summer evening in 1818. Following the wedding party, we boarded a schooner that was sailing for Charleston, where we enjoyed the gracious hospitality of the town as newlyweds.

The trip was a glorious occasion. Sterling was honored with an invitation to speak before the Medical Society of South Carolina. The timing was particularly interesting for Sterling, as the Medical Society, which had been in existence since the late 1780s, was considering establishment of a medical college in Charleston. Sterling was quite interested in their plans and he enjoyed numerous professional discussions with those who would comprise the faculty. In addition, we were entertained by many of Charleston's prominent families. Many evenings were spent walking at the waterfront near the battery. Many days found us sailing on the Cooper and Ashley rivers or enjoying pleasurable afternoons on the lawns of nearby plantations.

In all, we were away for six weeks, then following the return journey, we immediately took up residence in the house -- and I began to enjoy the rocking chair that Sterling commissioned as a wedding present for me.

Over the ensuing years, the troubling thoughts of the military died away. This was accompanied by further reduction in the number of troops. Life was quite comfortable -- that is, with the exception of having babies. For me, maternity began toward the end of the very first year of our marriage and continued at irregular intervals until your Grandfather Edward was born in 1839.

Your Great-Grandfather and I were fortunate in that the children, with the exception of George W. who contracted whooping cough and died during infancy, were healthy for the most part. And, as had been the case for both Sterling and me when we were young, the children enjoyed life along the waterfront. Fishing, sailing, bathing in the river, picnics on the beach, oyster-roasting parties and expeditions to the islands were regular events.

Of course, each of the children had chores as they grew. The girls primarily helped around the house, whereas the boys had responsibilities for the livestock. The latter routinely included several hogs, at least two milk cows, a passel of chickens and a few geese, most of which shared the small piece of property surrounding the house. Neither the cows nor the hogs could survive on such limited grounds so, as was the custom, they were allowed to roam the town along with other neighborhood livestock.

Your Great-Uncle Charles, as the oldest of the children, was given the responsibility to keep track of the larger animals and herd them back to the yard when necessary. The other children participated according to age. Some helped with the chickens, whereas others did little tasks around the house.

Now, carrying out the various chores was not a great burden for any of the children, for we had several slaves who actually did most of the labor. But the children had to participate primarily as a learning experience. And they were given the responsibility for seeing the chores to completion.

Most of our crops were grown upriver on one of the plantations, but several small gardens were maintained along the edge of the swampland and on the banks of Bonnet's Creek. The ground there was always fertile and sufficiency of water was never an issue. Also, it was from there that we obtained our herbs and several plants grown for medicinal purposes.

The swamp gardens were primarily tended by the slaves. This was because spending time in the lowland was known to be bad for the health of the family and, in some respects, there was danger. Poisonous snakes were not infrequently encountered. Children, whose minds were prone to drift, often were not alert to the threats. However, neither the risk of disease nor the danger of snakebite was of concern to the slaves. They were more experienced and seemed perfectly at ease working in the gardens.

For the most part, it was an enjoyable life. Sterling's medical practice brought esteem to the family, and his ventures in real estate as well as plantation investments provided a comfortable income with which small pleasures were obtained. We had a pianoforte in the parlor and the girls were all taught music, which became a frequent entertainment for the family and guests.

On several occasions over the years, academies offering instruction in Latin, Greek, Literature and Mathematics were opened in town and, whenever instruction was available, all the children were enrolled. A few times, specialized instruction in topics such as Geometry and Surveying was offered, and the boys always benefitted from such exposure.

Charles eventually elected to follow in the footsteps of his father and grandfather by studying medicine. After his initial tutelage under Sterling, he traveled to Virginia where he studied as an apprentice for three years. Then, in 1837, he enrolled in the Medical Department of Pennsylvania College. For each of the next two years, he spent three months attending lectures. Then, in 1839, he completed his thesis on gastritis and was awarded the degree of Doctor of Medicine.

It was a glorious time for the family; three generations had by now entered the profession, and Charles was the first in the family and from the town to earn a formal medical degree.

Life, however, was not without heartbreak. The very year, in fact within a matter of weeks, of Charles's completion of his degree, our second son, William Randolph, died at the age of twelve.

William Randolph had suffered with intermittent fevers for several months, and his condition was such that little response was obtained following the usual course of purges and bleedings. His constitution remained unchanged with administration either of calomel or opium, even when given under the most stringent conditions. Such sadness entered our family as the jaundice overtook his body and fevers eroded his strength. Nothing in the way of cure, either by his father or his brother, could be offered. He passed away on July 24, 1839.

The death of William Randolph was not our first loss. As I've already said, our young son, George Washington, had died in infancy eight years earlier, as was so often the case. He simply had no stamina and, from the first hours of life, demonstrated a weak constitution.

The situation was also complicated because I had little sustenance to offer him and he seemed unable to respond to the ministrations of a wet nurse. George became very weak, then the cough set in. Overall his death, though trying, was not the same as that of William Randolph, whose sparkling eyes, clever mind and boyhood charm had mesmerized the family and much of the town for more than a decade.

Another great personal sadness had come to me in 1832, when my sister Mary, who was married to Daniel Baker, died in childbirth. She was twenty-four at the time and I was just five years older. Mary and I had been very close, having been companions from the time she could walk enough to keep pace with the older children.

Then following my marriage to Sterling, Mary had become a regular house guest. With the birth of Charles, Mary stepped into the role of guardian aunt, a role that continued for the next nine years until her own marriage to Mr. Daniel Baker in 1828. I was so pleased when, following the wedding, Mr. Baker decided to remain in town to practice law, as their presence added strength to our family bonds.

Though she dearly looked forward to raising a family, Mary remained childless for the early years of marriage, so it was with great excitement and anticipation that she found herself with child.

There was a wonderful celebration when young John was born. However, the excitement was not to last, as the baby became ill and died before seeing closure of its first month. Mary was so distressed that we began to worry for her state. However, her melancholy did not last, and the family again found itself looking to the future when she was once more with child later in the year.

Through the months of winter and spring, carrying the child had been uneventful and Mary's spirits had remained high, but with the approach of her time, it became obvious that the birth could be a problem.

The baby was not positioned properly and little could be done by the midwife to correct the situation. As the hours of confinement passed, Mary's labor became progressively more painful. She tired first, then she became weak. All of this was distressing but not life threatening, until a hemorrhage occurred, at which time the midwife sent for Sterling.

He could do nothing other than offer laudanum to relieve Mary's burden; both she and the baby were laid to rest two days later. The year was 1832. I was twenty-nine years old, but already had experienced a lifetime of both joy and sadness.

With Mary's passing, I entered a prolonged period of melancholy. Had it not been for Sterling's kindness and the help of our house servants, the six children would surely have suffered neglect. At the time, Charles was thirteen and had already begun preparations for medical studies, so he was of minimal help with the younger ones, particularly Caroline, who was just three years old.

Marietta, however, was eleven and old enough to take a hand in directing many of the household activities, including supervision of the active younger children, Emeline, Julia, William Randolph and Caroline Amelia.

She became a great help to her father during the time of my trial; and following my recovery, she continued this support within the family until her death at the age of thirty-five in 1856. Though Marietta never married, her life was filled with family, including the youngest children, William, Caroline and Edward, born to me after 1825. With the birth of Edward, I had come to grips -- or at least thought I had come to grips -- with life's trials.

Following Mary's death, her husband, Mr. Baker, remained close to our family. Over the years, he and our Julia developed an attachment, though she was much his junior, which eventually resulted in their marriage. Paradoxically, the man who had been my brother-in-law became my son-in-law.

32

MILITARY MARRIAGES

It was in this manner, Amelia Caroline, that my married life passed for the first twenty or so years. Outside of everyday family events, most years were not particularly noteworthy. It was during this period that your Great-Aunt Mary Eliza and her husband Richard moved to the plantation in Magnolia. Though this created a void in our lives, we were thrilled each summer and on the rare holiday when they would return to town.

Throughout this time our children grew, some struck out to establish their own lives and others remained with us.

Storms occasionally ravaged the waterfront and ships often ran aground, bringing excitement to the town. For those who speculated in maritime salvage, among whom was my Uncle Robert Potter, the storms brought profit. Sterling continued to expand his financial interests, and among his acquisitions were a dry goods store, wharf and waterfront warehouse, all of which were purchased from Uncle Robert.

Sometime in the mid-1830s, activities began to increase at the fort. The garrison had been neglected for several years, during which time it had been staffed just by a minimal force. There were, however, troops on the island. Throughout the early 1830s, the government's interest in the town fort had decreased and attention had become focused upon fortifying Caswell Island. The island was better suited to the development of a major coastal installation with numerous gun batteries. Thus it was considered more important to coastal defense. Therefore, a majority of military personnel were there in support of that building effort.

But with the approach of 1835 , more troops began to arrive on a regular basis at the fort here in town. This build-up of troops, however, was not with the intent of maintaining a large force on the grounds. Rather, the garrison was being used as a stepping-off place for soldiers en route to Florida, where the government once again was engaged in war against the Seminoles.

As had been the case in earlier years, the increase in activity at the fort placed a strain on the town. Frequently, soldiers were disrespectful to both the townspeople and their military officers. Our small, sandy streets were often crowded with soldiers, wagons and mules. The woods were cluttered, as encampments were scattered about. While off-duty, the troops had little to occupy their time and this often resulted in mischief, particularly by the young and undisciplined recruits.

The attitude of the soldiers was not totally unjustified, for the historical pattern of poor planning by the Army prevailed. The men were poorly provisioned in all aspects. This was a constant source of dissatisfaction among those in transit to Florida. In spite of all the disruption, which extended over a period of five to eight years, the increased presence of soldiers became an accepted part of life, just as had been the case during my childhood years.

But there was a distinction: By 1845, there were many more townspeople. The population totaled nearly 600, which was greater than the number of soldiers at the garrison. Yet it became clear, based upon the prolonged war with the natives in Florida and the government's recent commitment to build more substantial fortifications on Caswell Island, that the soldiers were here to stay.

For the young women in town, this once again was an exciting time, as a constant stream of dashing young officers passed through the fort. While here, the young gentlemen were entertained nearly every evening by one family or another. This social pattern was welcomed, as many families had eligible daughters who were flattered with the attention bestowed upon them during the visits. Some of the young men even remained long enough to become more formally integrated into the local society, and two of them eventually became part of our family.

The first was the marriage of my Emeline in 1844, who was twenty-one at that time, to Captain George Taylor, a company commander at the fort. Emeline's marriage was a joyous occasion, for Sterling and I still had three daughters at home, and all of them were either at or approaching marriageable age.

That was a time when there were very few suitable young bachelors, other than military men, living in town. Many of the eligible non-military men offered little in the way of prospects for their future wives. After all, our girls had been raised in comfortable surroundings, had been well educated and shared appreciation for life's refinements like music and art.

These were characteristics associated with the more successful families, but rarely with the common folk. This is not to say that the less successful were undesirable people. It is just that they were dreadfully poor. They lived hard and somewhat barren lives on the edges of the community.

The match between Emeline and Captain Taylor was perfect. He had come from a good family up-east and, although just twenty-eight years old, his advancement in the military promised a rewarding career.

Even better, Captain Taylor was assigned semi-permanently to the fort, so the newlyweds were able to begin life together here in Southport in a house given to them by Sterling as a wedding gift.

The second marriage was of your distant cousin, Mary Elizabeth Langdon, the daughter of Sterling's sister and her husband Richard, to Lieutenant Sewall Fremont of the Army Engineers.

Lieutenant Fremont had first arrived in town following graduation from West Point in 1841. At the time of arrival here, he was still known by his birth name, which was Fish. However, during the early months following his posting to the fort, the lieutenant's name and that of his parents was changed from Fish to Fremont. We never learned why this change had been elected. The matter was not of importance to either Sterling or me, and we felt certain that those who were interested had been satisfied.

Lieutenant Fremont's first assignment had been to recruit and prepare troops at the fort for reassignment to Florida. Then, during the years following the Seminole War, Lieutenant Fremont was attached to the 3rd Artillery at the fort. He and Mary Elizabeth became acquainted during that period.

Mary Elizabeth was just entering young adulthood, about fifteen years of age, at the time of their first encounter. Lieutenant Fremont was a dozen years her senior. As fate often seems to take its turn, Mary Elizabeth's father had recently decided to return to town from Magnolia. The plantation was doing quite well and the family was anxious to resume life at the coast.

Then shortly following the family's decision to return, Richard was appointed by President Harrison to serve as postmaster. The appointment was an honor for the Langdon family, but it brought sadness, as well. Shortly following the selection of Richard for the post, President Harrison died. He had been in office for just two months.

The Langdon family, though in mourning with the nation, once again took up residence here in town, this time for more than the summer season.

Soon after their arrival, the Langdon home was opened to the young men from the fort. As one of the regular guests, Lieutenant Fremont took little more than a casual note of Mary Elizabeth. She, on the other hand, was just embarking on womanhood, and she was drawn to the young officer.

These feelings on the part of Mary Elizabeth were noticed by her parents. The prospects of a future match were discussed within the family. On more than one occasion, her mother sat with me and expressed reservations about the young lieutenant.

Mary Eliza knew from a lifetime of living in the shadow of the fort that the lives of soldiers were controlled by the needs of the nation. Often, even though posted at the fort, they would leave with their troops for duty in remote locations. Not infrequently, the reassignments would be prolonged, perhaps for years at a time.

Of greatest concern was the danger presented by a military career. Sometimes members of the troop would not return to their homes due to tragedies during the distant assignments. Mary Eliza had known many widows over her years of living in the shadow of the fort.

These were standard concerns any parent would have. But the match between Mary Elizabeth and Lieutenant Fremont carried other concerns, as well.

The lieutenant was known to be a bit brash. There was talk about town that at times he acted without first fully considering the ramifications of his actions. Some of this could be attributed to his limited experience as a young officer.

Mary Eliza acknowledged this, and she believed that allowances should be made for professional inexperience in most situations. However, one particular circumstance was acutely on the family's minds during this time.

The year was 1842 and several companies of soldiers, having served their duty in Florida, were assigned temporarily to the fort. As transients, the Florida troops were somewhat undisciplined. They had little sense of identity with the soldiers who were permanently assigned in town.

Complicating matters was the military's chronic lack of detail when providing for the troops who were passing through. Living conditions, as had been the case thirty years earlier in 1812, were insufficient for the large number of transient soldiers. Food was in limited supply and housing was totally inadequate.

Further complicating matters were diseases, including yellow fever, which were rampant among the enlisted soldiers. Consequently, desertions from the fort to escape the threat of disease were not uncommon. Many of those who remained had little respect for either their officers or the townspeople. There was a feeling of unrest in the town.

Then in late 1842, as conditions deteriorated even further, there was a major incident. A few soldiers got totally out of control and began to terrorize the town's residents. Lieutenant Fremont, who had responsibility for one of the companies, reacted swiftly. Three privates under his command were tied hand and foot, and corporal punishment was inflicted.

Lieutenant Fremont's action was effective in restoring order, but it was in violation of the military code of conduct. In response to an outcry on the part of the enlisted men, the matter was passed through the chain of command. Discipline for the young officer was recommended by the senior command.

In response, President John Tyler ordered a general court martial to be held at the fort. Under investigation was the charge that Lieutenant Fremont had acted illegally and had displayed unmilitary conduct.

Though the townspeople supported the action that Lieutenant Freemont had taken in his attempt to restore order at the fort, Mary Elizabeth's parents were sensitive to the extremity of the lieutenant's actions. They asked themselves whether this action was just due to his inexperience or if such extreme behavior would be expressed in marriage when times of stress arose. They knew that all marriages had trying moments.

The matter weighed upon them as they awaited news of the court's decision. However, in the end, both Mary Eliza and Richard knew that the outcome of the court would not influence their support for Mary Elizabeth's happiness.

The attraction between Mary Elizabeth and Lieutenant Freemont, as it turned out, was not an issue for the next few years, as the lieutenant and my new son-in-law, Captain Taylor, were dispatched to the Texas frontier along with the 3rd Artillery to participate in the war against Mexico.

This separation may have contributed in a positive way to the relationship between Lieutenant Fremont and Mary Elizabeth; during his absence, Mary Elizabeth sent him letters with news of life in the town. This correspondence was possible because military communications were dispatched from the fort to the troops assigned in the West. The family, by virtue of its prominence in town and the fact that Captain Taylor was a member of the family, was able to include personal correspondence along with the military dispatches.

Upon his return from the West, Lieutenant Fremont, whose service had by that time resulted in promotion to the rank of captain, soon resumed calling on the family, where the now young woman of nineteen drew his attention.

Before the year was out, a formal courtship began. The couple fully anticipated being married as soon as Lieutenant Fremont's long-term assignment to the fort was assured. Then in January 1847, the marriage plans were abruptly interrupted; Richard Langdon, Mary Elizabeth's father, died unexpectedly of heart disease at the age of fifty-four. Plans for a wedding were put aside with the intent of rescheduling later in the year after a time considered respectful.

The year, however, turned out to be particularly tragic. In May my father, your Great-

Great-Grandfather Samuel Potter, died in Wilmington. His death weighed heavily upon the family, for he was quite wealthy and conflicts arose regarding inheritance.

Then the very next month, while we were still in deep grief, news came from Massachusetts that Mary Elizabeth's brother, Richard Sewall Langdon, had died at the age of twenty-seven in New Bedford. His death had occurred five months to the day after the death of his father. With all this sadness, the wedding of Mary Elizabeth and Lieutenant Fremont was further delayed.

We all entered the following year with heavy hearts, but the healing had begun. Sterling and I provided support for Mary Eliza and the closeness that had characterized the family was enhanced.

Finally in April of 1848, Mary Elizabeth and Lieutenant Fremont were married. This was a small joy for Mary Eliza, who still grieved over the loss of both her husband and her son. The family closeness was particularly important for the newlywed couple. Although they were living in a rather tranquil setting here in Smithville, the nation as a general rule was experiencing great restlessness. This unrest frequently resulted in military action. We were, of course, still at tension with Mexico, but the residual conflict was a great distance away, so the tragedies for the most part had become abstract to us.

The town, however, was not totally without impact, for companies of soldiers recruited in the Carolinas continued to be dispatched from the fort to the West. As had been the case all along, the presence of so many transient soldiers brought medical problems. By 1850 nearly 200 boys died right here in town, many from yellow fever, typhoid, influenza and other camp diseases.

Luckily, neither Lieutenant Fremont nor Captain Taylor was ordered back to the West, although they and their companies were called upon regularly to assist with domestic matters. This included relocation of the natives from the Carolinas and Florida to the far Western frontier.

Following the discovery of gold in Western North Carolina, a crush of treasure seekers had invaded the region during the early 1800s. Decades later, ongoing disputes involving owners of plantations, newly arrived settlers, gold and gem prospectors, and speculators were common. Often troops were dispatched to settle the disputes. It was during such times of temporary military deployment and absence of their husbands that Emeline and Mary Elizabeth turned to the family for strength and support, which they received.

We also rallied around the wives and children of other families whose husbands and fathers were being dispatched elsewhere. In addition, we all found great strength in the sharing of faith and participation in church activities. So important was spiritual support to the community that troops and their families from the fort contributed mightily to the establishment of the town's first Anglican church.

About the same time, those of the Baptist persuasion had begun to congregate in the vicinity of Buck's Neck, and supporters of Wesley's teachings had arranged periodic visits of the Methodist circuit preacher.

We, of course, associated with the Anglicans through long-standing family tradition, but that association did not exclude our family from kindnesses of those whose persuasions differed.

Ultimately, it would be this extended community support that would bring the family through several of its most trying hours.

33

TRYING HOURS

Amelia Caroline sat quietly for a few minutes. She appeared to be deep in reflection, almost trance-like, so I sat patiently on the porch and watched the town go about its business. The midday traffic to city hall and the post office had slowed. Just a few folks were on the sidewalk across the intersection where Harrelson's Market had once been a hub of social activity. Now the old building was owned by the Baptist Church and it was being used as an annex for education programs.

Usually at this time of day, members of the church could be seen leaving for the noon hour, but on this particular day there was an uncharacteristic atmosphere of silence. It was as if the elements wished not to intrude upon Amelia Caroline's reflections.

I could hear the call of gulls from the waterfront, and a mockingbird cried out in a pestering tone from the dogwood tree in the yard next door. Mockingbirds were known for such intrusions.

Amelia Caroline stirred a bit, then she again spoke. But it was as if there were two persons engaged in conversation.

"Great Grandmother, are you still there?" she *hesitantly asked.*

Great-Grandmother responded, "Yes, but I've become distracted by memories of all that happened over those several years following the death of your Great-Uncle Richard Langdon. He was also, you know, Great-Grandfather several generations removed to your young cousin."

I nodded in acknowledgement, but remained silent, as Amelia Caroline responded to her Great-Grandmother.

"Yes, Great-Grandmother, both Mary Eliza and I have known that the marriage of Richard in the early 1800s to your sister-in-law, Mary Eliza Everitt, was the initial link between our families," Amelia Caroline observed.

"Oh, Amelia Caroline, that was so many years ago. But as I was saying, the tragedies following Richard's death seemed unending. For a period, they came in rapid succession. By that time, Sterling and I were getting on in years and we had experienced our share of grief.

Several children had died early in life, and I've told you of my sorrow following the death during childbirth of my sister Mary. But Mary was not the only loss among my siblings. Prior to 1815, two of my brothers and my sister Matilda had died from childhood diseases.

"Death was not a stranger to any family during those days. Yet what transpired during the middle years of my life and of the century now seem accentuated."

Great-Grandmother paused.

"Why do you feel they are accentuated now, after all these years?" Amelia Caroline gently probed.

"I believe that mixed in with all of my own life memories are the recollections you shared of the experiences during your youth. The deaths that began with young Joseph Miller, then continued with those of William Banes, Bobbie Mintz and Elias Hewett, along with other tragedies of war, came rushing upon you. You were not prepared for the impact those years would have on the rest of your life.

"Then a few years later in rapid succession was the loss of your colleagues and friends. Particularly trying for you was the death of Susan Williams. Then, the circumstances surrounding the passing of your father also were unanticipated.

"You had no counsel upon which to draw. Even your silent pleas to God were unanswered. Relief from your anguish was not to be found. Isn't this true?" Great-Grandmother asked.

"Yes, Great Grandmother. And when turning to the church, I realized that not only were there no answers to my pain, but those who professed the faith were insensitive both to the circumstances which caused the pain and to those who suffered."

"Amelia Caroline," said Great-Grandmother. "I lived long enough to accept certain truths regarding life and the *ending of lives. The passing of friends, family and loved ones from our lives -- and from this earth -- is always accompanied by grief.*

"Under normal circumstances, their passing is accepted as part of the natural order. We grieve, perhaps we turn to faith, and eventually we heal.

"In contrast, there are occasions when a death itself, or the circumstances at the time of a death, or the events that resulted in a death, or those that follow a death, are particularly tragic. Such occasions impact our lives forever. Such occasions we experience, but we do not understand. Furthermore, there is no true source to which we can turn for understanding. Consequently, we neither forget nor, depending upon the occasion, forgive.

"As I think back to the middle of my years and what transpired within the family, these truths apply. I also feel that the truths apply to some of the events in your own life."

Amelia Caroline quickly responded with a question.

"Great Grandmother, are you suggesting that faith failed you in your time of need? This seems contradictory to what you have just said about turning to the church and its teachings at life's most trying hours."

"That is hard for me to answer directly, but what I implied was that the family turned to an extended community for strength. Many of those to whom we reached out shared our faith, but this was not always the case. At any rate, at times, answers to my pleas could not be found.

Great-Grandmother continued, "Faith, though somewhat comforting, could not always bring relief. Distress over disturbing events stayed with me throughout the balance of my life. I remained unsatisfied, just as you have. Perhaps if I describe some of the events, you will understand more clearly."

Both Amelia Caroline and I sat quietly for a bit. Then Great-Grandmother Amelia Caroline Potter Everitt continued to speak through Amelia Caroline.

Toward the middle of the century, differences in social conditions and political interests led to disputes among the states as well as between individual states and the government in Washington.

Relationships had deteriorated and the call intensified for military intervention to contain the discord.

It seemed that Captain Taylor and Lieutenant Fremont were constantly gone. Tensions at the fort were running high and deployments were shifting. The military objective of relocating Native American Indians from Florida and the Carolinas to the West was reaching its completion and the focus at the fort was turning to more immediate regional matters. Primarily, this meant interceding with the political unrest being expressed by the citizens of South Carolina.

At issue were economic policies which were under consideration by Northern interests and the federal government, but which were generally not supported by the Southern planters. Objections to the proposed policies were being expressed also by merchants and other businessmen of the South. These were men whose livelihoods were based upon commerce through the Southern ports at Charleston and Savannah, where slaves were a primary source of labor.

Over time, the tensions evolved into a conflict between Northern and Southern financial interests. This brought the fort here in Southport to the foreground as a local means for enforcing federal policy.

Soldiers at the fort, including Captain Taylor and Lieutenant Fremont, who were now entwined with the townspeople, were being pitted against the interests of kinsmen and neighbors to the south. Needless to say, our own sympathies were aligned with those neighbors. The town, however, was being torn down the middle, with the government policies as enforced by those assigned to the fort on one side and the long-standing economic interests of the townspeople on the other.

For a number of reasons, some attributable to government policies which impacted the military and others due to personal decisions within the family, the late 1840s marked the beginning of a sad era for the family.

The sadness, as I have already said, actually began in 1847 with the death of Richard Langdon. It was compounded in a matter of months with the death of my father, Captain Samuel Potter. As I now think of that time, the two deaths influenced events both in your branch of the family and that of your young cousin, Mary Eliza.

Although born into modest circumstances, my father had been industrious and, in his later years, he came to be known as a self-made man. He had amassed a sizable fortune over the course of his life. This included ownership of a plantation known both as Peter's Point and Love Grove.

The land was on the river just north of Wilmington. The plantation, at the time of father's death, was managed by my brother, your Great-Great-Uncle Samuel. This was a great responsibility for, among other duties, Samuel had approximately eighty of father's slaves under his direction.

The plantation was a major source of income. In some years, the yield was several thousand dollars. When the plantation was combined with other properties in town, it constituted a sizeable estate. Some estimates of the value were as high as $130,000 just in property and slaves.

Unfortunately, my father did not leave a will when he died. Therefore, his estate was to be apportioned among his heirs as prescribed by law. My brother Samuel was appointed the executor. He was most familiar both with father's holdings and income. In addition, Samuel was fully aware of the family circumstances. By this I mean who was related to whom, and what each member was entitled to inherit under the law. Unfortunately, it was Samuel's use of this knowledge that eventually resulted in conflict among the family members.

Normally, settling an estate such as this would not have been a problem, but father had remarried twice following the death in 1815 of my mother, whose maiden name was Nancy Ann Wade.

Father's second marriage, to Rachel J. Golden, lasted about twenty years, but there were no children. His third marriage was to Mrs. Elizabeth A. Eyre, a widow from Philadelphia. They married rather late in father's life and they were still married at the time of his death.

Elizabeth Eyre had children and grandchildren as a result of her first marriage and, except for one of Elizabeth's granddaughters, the Eyre family and their descendants remained in the North.

Elizabeth, as my father's immediate widow, became heir to a large portion of the estate. In fact, the widow's portion of the estate encompassed one-third of the value of all the property plus a portion of annual income from the property. This was defined in law, so settling the estate should not have been a major issue. It simply should have been a matter of including the widow in the apportionment along with my sisters, Amy and Eliza, my brother Samuel and me.

But Samuel's knowledge both of the estate and the law led to events that created a legal conflict. Settling father's estate took over five years and required taking the case all the way to the Supreme Court of the United States. This was one of those post-death situations to which I referred, when events damaging to people and relationships, once initiated, seem to have a life of their own. As in the case of war, people suffer before resolution can be achieved.

On the day following our father's death, my brother Samuel, in the presence of his lawyer, convinced the widow Elizabeth to sign her entire portion of the estate over to him. The contract, agreed upon within hours of the funeral, specified that, in return for the vast fortune Elizabeth stood to inherit, Samuel would provide a home for her in addition to a small annual stipend.

This arrangement for the widow initially was presented as desirable, as Samuel was married to Elizabeth's granddaughter Marion. The argument was made that Elizabeth, in her advanced years, not only would be provided for but she would also be able to live in the house of her natural granddaughter, Samuel's wife. The arrangement seemed quite logical as presented by Samuel.

However, the legality of the agreement between Samuel and Elizabeth was challenged by Elizabeth's children and grandchildren. Shortly after learning of the agreement their mother and grandmother had made with Samuel, the widow's family from Philadelphia objected strongly.

There was great anger between the Eyre and the Potter families. Charges of deception, fraud and greed were made against us. Mostly, our family was humiliated. The situation had been created by Samuel. Yet by implication, we were all swept up in it. Included were your Great-Grandfather Sterling and I.

Within a month, the son of father's widow traveled south to take his mother back to Philadelphia.

That was the last we saw of her, but it was just the beginning of the legal fight.

The matter was taken to the Court of Equity in Wilmington. At issue was the fact that, for a relatively small amount of money in the form of annual support for the widow, his stepmother, my brother was to gain a significant portion of father's estate. Through this agreement, he would have controlling ownership in the plantations and the slaves.

Argument was made in court that the widow was approached by Samuel and his lawyer at a time when she was under great stress. It was the very day of her husband's funeral. She, it was argued, was not of a mind to enter legally binding contracts.

On the other hand, Samuel pointed out that his stepmother had made the agreement because she wished for her granddaughter to benefit significantly from the inheritance.

Witnesses before the Court of Equity presented testimony on both sides as to the state of Elizabeth's health at the time of father's death, her relationship with her granddaughter and her relationship to the Potter family as a whole.

A question was raised about the logic of Elizabeth's actions. Why would someone of sound mind relinquish such a large dowry in return for so little?

Ultimately, a decision was made in favor of my brother. The court ruled that, all things considered, the timing on Samuel's part was deemed questionable but neither coercion nor fraud were involved. Though clearly inequitable, the contract between father's widow and my brother was both legal and binding.

The matter, however, was not settled.

By the time of the ruling by the Court of Equity, father's widow had reaffirmed her own decision to request that the contract be nullified. Suspicions were raised that Elizabeth was being influenced by her original family, the Eyres of Philadelphia.

The case was appealed to the Supreme Court of North Carolina. In her petition, Elizabeth asked that her original decision and contract with Samuel be put aside. Argument was made that, at the time of the agreement with Samuel, Elizabeth did not yet own the property. Thus she could not legally transfer it to Samuel. In addition, Elizabeth argued that the gross inequity of the agreement was evidence of fraud on his part.

Elizabeth claimed that she did not remember the reasons why she had signed the agreement; but imposition, surprise and misrepresentation on the part of Samuel were implied.

So the inheritance of the estate was further tied up. My brother, meanwhile, filed a counter-lawsuit with the Supreme Court of North Carolina requiring that the heirs, including Sterling and me, immediately release the estate. This would allow Elizabeth's portion, particularly the land and the slaves, to be legally transferred to him.

The family was falling apart over the issue of father's estate.

Five years after father's death, the State Supreme Court passed a ruling in support of the lower court and in favor of Samuel. It was true that Elizabeth, on the day following father's death, could not sign her inheritance over to Samuel because she did not yet have the property. She could, however, sign a contract agreeing to transfer the property when it came into her possession. And the court felt that this is what she had done. As to the prospect of fraud, the court ruled that evidence to support the charge did not exist.

Ultimately, the Eyres of Philadelphia, Elizabeth's original family, became directly involved. They argued that the decision by their natural mother, Elizabeth, to give my brother Samuel her portion of the estate had indirectly deprived them of their inheritance.

Then Elizabeth died, which complicated matters. Father's estate became a legal mess. Six years following father's death, the case had gone all the way to the Supreme Court of the United States. At issue remained both the circumstances under which the initial agreement had been reached between Samuel and Elizabeth and the state of her health at the time of the agreement.

The Eyre family argued that Elizabeth's state of mind had been established only by the testimony of witnesses who reported acquaintance with her. Although these persons, including members of our family, argued for her health, the Eyre family disagreed. The fact that Elizabeth had agreed to give Samuel tens of thousands of dollars worth of property in return for a limited value of lifetime support was evidence both of an unstable state on Elizabeth's part and the possibility of fraud on Samuel's part. They further argued that Samuel's contention that the widow wished for her granddaughter to have the property could not be substantiated. First, nowhere in the agreement was the granddaughter Marion even mentioned. In addition, every woman in the state knew that under North Carolina law a married woman could not hold title to property.

In 1853, the U.S. Supreme Court supported the original decision by the Court of Equity and the ruling by the Supreme Court of North Carolina. It ruled in favor of Samuel.

The justices wrote that inequity of agreement, in the absence of other evidence, does not constitute fraud. The testimony of family witnesses as to Elizabeth's health was found to be acceptable evidence of her competence on the day of entering the agreement with Samuel. In addition, the court found evidence in the testimony of impartial witnesses that the widow had actually told several persons she wished the property to go to her granddaughter's household.

My brother prevailed and got title to Elizabeth's portion of father's property. Furthermore, since Elizabeth had died during the years of legal battle, Samuel did not even have to pay the annuity.

The entire experience was terrible and there was lingering resentment among the rest of us, since our portions of father's estate had been modest in comparison to what Samuel had arranged for himself. Then there was public humility for the entire family. In its ruling, the Supreme Court of the United States called attention to "the spectacle of a widow and a son bargaining over the unburied corpse of the husband and the father for the partition of his property -- a proceeding revolting to decorum."

Our family was never again to be a close as it had been prior to father's death.

In the middle of all this, gold was discovered in California and chaos ensued. In response to the chaos, military intervention was called for. This was to have an even more tragic impact on the family. Troops from the fort were dispatched to sail around the Straits to California. It was as a result of this relocation that our next trial began, for we were to lose our daughter Emeline and her husband Captain Taylor, as well as our son Charles, to events in that far-off part of the country.

Charles, by that time, was well into his medical career as a military surgeon, a role rejected by his father, yet one filled with distinction by his grandfather. Sterling had been disappointed with the direction Charles had chosen, but honored Charles's decision to serve as a military officer.

During the early years of his career, Charles's assignments had been at establishments along the East Coast but, as with many others, he had traveled to the West at the time of war with Mexico. Following the war, he was reassigned along with a company from the 3rd Artillery to the California Territory.

Charles wrote home with great enthusiasm about the promise of life in that land, yet it was so far from the family. I was always glad to have his letters, which were read and reread in front of the warm fires of winter and in the rocker on the porch during summer evenings.

However, the letters also brought sadness, as I knew that Charles would never again visit the town, his home and the family. And this was the case, for Charles died in that lawless land, near the gold fields of Mariposa, in November of 1852. One year later, we were to lose our Emeline.

34

THE SHIPWRECK

It was morning cold and gray when she was struck
A violent sea amidships carried the main saloon
Paddle-boxes, smoke stacks and lives all overboard
The hurricane deck fell to the cabin floor
And the angry sea rushed in to those below

The horror of the moment -- beyond description
Families gathered, clinging each to the other
Fathers, mothers, brothers and sisters
From the gray, seasoned veteran of the Army
To the child, nestled, weeping at mother's breast

Fearful the sight, to look upon dark angry water
There, not less than 100 human souls crying out
Clinging to spars, doors and such fragments
As could be obtained for preservation of life
Yet, fate's decision already had been sealed

The next wave, towering majestically above
Crashed upon ship and those in ocean's grip
And they were hurried with not a moment's notice
Into the arms of He who heard not their pleas
        Into the depths and eternity.

Amelia Caroline Potter Everitt
Fall, 1854

Amelia Caroline and I had been sitting quietly for several minutes following the story of Captain Samuel Potter's death. Amelia Caroline seemed to need space to herself, so I sat patiently. Then she resumed, and again it was Great-Grandmother speaking, but there was a tremble as she relived the tragedy.

"I am not sure how to continue, Amelia Caroline, for what transpired following the death of Charles is so tragic that it tests the limits of my ability to recall."

"We understand, Great Grandmother. Say what you may when you are ready to share," Amelica Caroline responded.

Again there were several moments while Amelia Caroline rocked slowly. Then Great-Grandmother resumed the tale.

The situation in California had become explosive and rumors about troop relocations circulated constantly. During the winter following Charles's death, the level of rumor was such that the entire town of Southport was in turmoil. Reports came of near anarchy in California with the burgeoning population of desperate miners. Finally, in response to the need for greater authority and protection for the population, the entire 3rd Artillery Regiment, including companies from the fort, was reassigned to California.

Given the magnitude of the relocation, this was to be a long-term change, so wives and families were to accompany the troops. Mary Elizabeth and her husband Lieutenant Fremont, Emeline and her husband, who had recently been promoted to the rank of major, were all to leave. The family was crushed, but we rallied around to provide comfort as best we could with the memories of Charles still fresh in our minds.

The relocation was scheduled for early November of 1853, with embarkation from New York on the newly built steamer *San Francisco*. This news of the deployment and orders to report for duty in New York reached the fort late in the summer so, for me and the girls, much of the fall season was spent helping Emeline and Mary Elizabeth with preparations. We recognized that they would be gone for years. So all things of comfort had to be prepared for them to take.

Finally, the day for departure was upon us. It was among the saddest days in my life and in the life of my sister-in-law Mary Eliza. We each would bid farewell to a beloved child. In addition, Mary Eliza's three young grandchildren were to sail with their mother. With a heavy heart, I hugged Emeline and Major Taylor that morning. Little did I know how much sadder I would become as events unfolded.

The regiment was to sail via Rio de Janeiro and through the Straits of Magellan. This was a hazardous journey under the best of conditions and would require several months at sea. The voyage of the *San Francisco*, however, was ill-fated, for on December 23rd, the engines of the ship failed in the middle of a gale. But I am getting ahead of myself.

The first letter from New York to Sterling and me came through the fort about November 25th. Emeline had been gone for nearly three weeks. She wrote that, upon reaching New York, they learned that the process of readying the steamship was behind schedule; thus, sailing from the city was delayed. This was of course not a source of disappointment to them, for all the families were apprehensive about beginning the long voyage.

The schedule change, therefore, served as a respite during which she, Mary Elizabeth, and the other military wives were able to enjoy the wonders of New York. Emeline said the officers and their families were very comfortable, the regiment having arranged accommodations for them in the Astor House Hotel.

In contrast to this pleasant news was concern shared among the officers about the steamship. This trip was to be its maiden voyage and the vessel had yet to be fully commissioned. Apparently, neither its seaworthiness nor its sufficiency in design had been certified.

Major Taylor had told Emeline that the ship's design was new. It incorporated features which raised questions in the officers' minds regarding the capacity to transport all the troops. This latter news was particularly distressing. Our lives had been spent in a town of seafaring men. We knew the challenges and dangers facing all who leave the security of shore.

Over the ensuing days, Sterling spent many hours talking with the well-seasoned sea captains who gathered daily at the waterfront here in town. Times and tales of life and boats and death and the sea were shared.

We heard nothing more of the matter until the next letter which reached us late in December, just after Christmas. The letter was dated December 21, 1853. The steamship *San Francisco* had been readied and all troops were to be aboard. Emeline described the accommodations they had been assigned. She felt that, although the stateroom was cramped and located on one of the lower decks to the rear of the ship, she and Major Taylor would be comfortable enough during the prolonged voyage. The one assigned to Elizabeth and Lieutenant Fremont adjoined Major Taylor's room, so the family would be together.

Emeline also told of her surprise at the state of disorder on the ship when she boarded. Sea trunks and troops were described as cluttering every surface and corner of the ship. Having little experience with the newer ocean-going steamships, I was surprised to learn from Emeline that the ship, although designed to accommodate 500 passengers, was actually to transport over 700 passengers.

Emeline wrote there were so many soldiers aboard that accommodations in sheltered cabins were insufficient. Consequently, tent-like structures were being arranged for the soldiers on the exposed upper deck of the ship. She learned that 200 soldiers were to live in temporary shelters amidst all the trunks and military equipment on the upper decks during the long winter voyage.

Her letter was brief, as the major had arrived on board. Emeline had just been informed that the major was attempting, by way of his rank, to change their accommodations. He desired more spacious quarters in the upper saloon. The letter closed with love.

This was the last communication we had from them. We later learned that the ship sailed the very next day. Neither Mary Eliza nor I expected additional news until the ship put into one of the more southerly ports, where letters from passengers on the *San Francisco* could be transferred to other ships that were sailing north.

So the Christmas season passed, winter began and we wondered of Emeline's voyage. Then, in mid-January a shocking message came to us.

On Thursday, January 5, a telegraphic dispatch had reached New York City from Liverpool, Nova Scotia. A Captain Freeman of the sailing ship *Maria* reported encountering the steamship *San Francisco* in the midst of a severe gale on the 26th of December. The steamship was described as being completely disabled. Her boats were gone and her decks swept away.

Captain Freeman noted that the storm was severe and the seas running extremely high. Consequently, approaching the disabled vessel was impossible. During the night, the vessels became separated, both being at the mercy of the storm.

The following day, with seas still running high, Captain Freeman attempted to relocate the *San Francisco*, but he was unsuccessful. News of the cable was reported in *The New York Times* on January 6th. The residents of that city knew of the disaster for several days before a packet that sailed from New York brought the news to the fort on January 12. That news, however, was just the first announcement which had been published by *The New York Times* on January 6th: there was no other information. We were immediately distressed with worry over the safety of Emeline, Mary Elizabeth, their husbands and the children.

"Oh, what of my beloved child Emeline," I cried?

We were upset to the point of becoming frantic, but additional news could not be obtained. We had received our first news seventeen days after the initial sighting of the *San Francisco* by Captain Freeman. Where was the ship? What of her passengers? Soldiers had been assigned to live on the decks that were described in Captain Freeman's cable as being swept away. What of them? What of the family?

These questions brought me near to a state of shock. I could do nothing. Had it not been for our loyal household help, the family would have gone totally neglected.

But I was not alone, for Mary Eliza also was in shock. Her daughter and her three grandchildren were on that ship, and she was a widow. Were her life's remaining years to be spent alone?

The fort could be of no assistance. Even the residual troops who were stationed at the garrison as a maintenance force could get no news of their comrades. We waited, grieved and wept.

Our wait, though nearly unbearable, was not prolonged for, on January 22, 1854, a letter from Mary Elizabeth reached her mother. The Fremont family -- Mary Elizabeth, Sewall and all three children -- had been rescued from the wreck on December 28th, the fourth day of the storm. On that day, they had transferred to the bark *Kilby,* along with 102 other officers, families and civilians. Although his small ship was also damaged and they were short of supplies and water, Captain Low of the *Kilby* agreed to take as many from the *San Francisco* as his ship would hold. It was over the next several hours that transfer of the first passengers took place. Nightfall came, so rescue activities had to be suspended until daylight, at which time other passengers from the *San Francisco* were to be transferred to the *Kilby.*

Then during the night, as had been the case several days earlier with the *Maria,* the storm strengthened and the two vessels became separated. No further contact between the *Kilby* and the *San Francisco* was made. Captain Low, realizing his ship was taking on much water and was at risk of foundering, decided to sail for the nearest port.

The forces of nature were not kind, and the small bark *Kilby* drifted for the next sixteen days, an experience that Mary Elizabeth described in the most distressing terms.

Tragic though Mary Elizabeth's experience was, it was not the most devastating news. My Emeline and her husband Captain George Taylor had been swept into the sea on December 24, 1853.

Little did we know on that Christmas Eve, as we sat comfortable and warm before our fires and surrounded by our younger children here in the house, that Emeline was to breathe her last as she sank into the cold, dark depths of winter's ocean.

Amelia Caroline, God then turned a deaf ear to my pleas for understanding. The church had no answers, but those who formed our larger community brought care and love. For the longest time, I was unsure that healing would ever occur but, in most aspects, time has leant its salve. There are, as in your own case, scars which will never abate.

Mary Eliza was much consoled after receiving word of the safe return to New York for Mary Elizabeth and the children, and she awaited anxiously for their return to town.

In subsequent letters, Mary Elizabeth shared some news of the proceedings in New York. A military Court of Inquiry was assembled at the headquarters of General Winfield Scott a few days following the arrival of the *Kilby* in New York. The goal of the inquiry was to determine the events related to the *San Francisco's* failure.

Mary Elizabeth also sent articles that appeared daily in *The New York Times*, so by early February we learned that the final 400 men, women and children who had been left behind on the *San Francisco* following the initial transfer to the *Kilby* were heroically rescued by Captain Robert Crighton and the crew of the ship *Three Bells*.

By the time it encountered the *San Franciso*, the *Three Bells* had been at sea for nearly two months and was en-route from Glasgow, Scotland to New York. We also learned from *The New York Times* that the events of the *San Francisco's* voyage and those of the rescue operation brought great criticism to the Army. In addition, disparagement was cast upon the officers who were in command of the regiment. This included Mary Elizabeth's husband, Lieutenant Fremont.

The storm had arisen on the second day out of New York and, during the initial rough seas, the engines failed. The failure was due to the breakage of an engine part, one of the new designs being first tested on the *San Francisco*.

Without power, the ship was left at the mercy of the seas, which became more violent as the storm increased. The day following engine failure, waves began to wash across the open decks, placing the soldiers there at great risk. The masts and much cargo were washed away. Yet nothing was done to ensure the safety of the troops.

Then on December 24th, a massive wave -- described as mountainous -- towered over the ship and crashed onto the decks. The upper saloon, the engine paddles and nearly 140 souls went into the sea and to their deaths.

Dear Emeline and Captain Taylor, who had demanded rooms in the upper saloon, were among those carried away. The wife of Colonel Gates reported that Major Taylor and Emeline were last seen with life preservers around them, clinging each to the other in a desperate attempt at survival. But the frigid waters won out and, slipping beneath the waves, they succumbed to the final call.

One of the issues brought before the Court of Inquiry was related to the design of the ship's engines and whether the design had been fully studied by the military prior to engaging the vessel. A second issue was why provisions had not been made to properly accommodate the soldiers aboard the ship. By extension, had the ship been so overburdened by the military with passengers and baggage that its capacity had been exceeded?

These latter questions reflected upon Lieutenant Fremont. He was both acting as adjutant and serving in the capacity of quartermaster for the regiment.

Other major questions brought before the court were related to conduct of several regimental officers during the rescue operations. Why had the great majority of the officers, including the commanding officer, Colonel William Gates, left the wreck to board the *Kilby* at the first opportunity? Why was the majority of the regiment left behind to cope as best it could? Being aboard the *Kilby* was of great advantage, for it assured safety away from the damaged *San Francisco*. Had the officers, all trained leaders, abandoned their troops and their responsibilities in favor of personal safety and the safety of their families?

The New York Times reported that Colonel Gates had chosen to be in the first boat to leave the *San Francisco*. He then ordered that, in accordance with rank, the other officers and their families were to be transferred.

Lieutenant Fremont had his family removed from the *San Francisco* during the day, but he personally remained actively involved on the wreck until the final boat left for the *Kilby*, just prior to the onset of darkness.

Lieutenant Fremont was among those in that final transfer boat. Some hours after he reached the *Kilby*, the seas rose. The hawser binding the ships together broke and they separated.

The circumstances aboard the *Kilby* were disastrous. The ship drifted, unable to reach port for sixteen days. Elizabeth described a shortage of food, water and sanitation. Many of the military passengers and several from the crew of the *Kilby* died from cold and disease. Most deadly was cholera. The disease was rampant under the crowded conditions. And it was no different for those who had been left behind on the hulk of the *San Francisco*.

In the end, the overall death toll exceeded 200, including Emeline, Captain Taylor and the other 138 souls who had been washed into the ocean on the first day.

With regard to the family, there was one particular incident on the *Kilby* that brought dishonor. The initial agreement between Colonel Gates and Captain Low was that, in light of limited supplies onboard the *Kilby*, it was the responsibility of the Army to transfer provisions sufficient to meet the needs of the survivors from the *San Francisco*. Yet no such arrangements had been made either by Colonel Gates or Lieutenant Fremont. So tensions ran high regarding use of the ship's galley and its limited provisions.

After being adrift for nearly fourteen days, and provisions having reached a critical level, the military posted guards at the galley and took control of its use. This angered the ship's crew, for the galley was theirs, not the military's.

On the day in question, Lieutenant Fremont, as officer of the day, entered the galley and found two sailors. He ordered the sailors to leave. They refused, saying they were not under military control. The threat of violence followed: Lieutenant Fremont was determined to enforce military authority.

Reportedly, Captain Low defused the situation, and he had to remind Lieutenant Fremont that the military held no authority on the ship other than to maintain order among themselves. In addition, he pointed out that any further such action by the lieutenant would precipitate a mutiny by the entire ship's crew. All of this was reported in one of *The New York Times* articles sent home by Mary Elizabeth.

Mary Elizabeth decided to leave New York early in February. The military court was to continue for a prolonged period. There was no reason to keep the children in the city. Sewall, on the other hand, was under orders to remain for the rest of the inquiry, and he did so.

Late in the month, the court found great disfavor with the actions of Colonel Gates and several of the junior officers. Its findings on February 24th were forwarded to Washington, DC for the War Department to take action as it would see fit.

Shortly thereafter, Lieutenant Fremont resigned from the Army of the United States and returned to town. Sewall and Mary Elizabeth ultimately took residence along with Mary Elizabeth's mother at the Langdon plantation in Magnolia.

The *San Francisco* incident brought great sadness in addition to embarrassment to the family. The entire nation, including our neighbors here in town, knew of the family's involvement in all phases of the disaster through articles published in *The New York Times.*

We were to lose much of our respect for the military and, over the months, we became distanced from those stationed at the fort. This was less difficult for Sterling than for me. He had, after all, inwardly carried a distrust of the military since the death of his father in 1813. Life was never to be the same.

Amelia Caroline sat for several minutes in the rocker. Tears glistened on her cheeks, and her eyes gazed fixedly at the massive live oak tree on the road's edge just beyond the sidewalk. The tree's age was unknown, but it had been there throughout Amelia Caroline's life. She recalled her father's tales of playing in the giant tree as a very young boy. She remembered hearing stories told of the celebration held beneath the boughs of the tree in 1819, when Sterling Everitt celebrated the birth of Charles, his first child.

Stories also told about a celebration of a different nature under that tree, one that took place later, in 1865. It was on the day the family slaves were informed of their freedom by Lieutenant W. B. Cushing, commander of the federal troops that had recently re-occupied the fort.

The tree had been there, steady and dependable, throughout nearly two centuries of family history. It had witnessed the building of the house, arrival of the rocker, births, deaths, sadness and joy. It knew Amelia Caroline and it had known her Great-Grandmother. It also knew what was yet to come in the story.

35

SUNSET

Amelia Caroline remained quietly rocking, her tear-filled eyes fixed trance-like on the small patch of water barely visible in the distance. A warm August breeze passed across the porch and moved the oak branches ever so slightly, but enough to catch her attention and awaken her soul from its tearful journey. She knew, of course, that life's trials had challenged her Great-Grandmother and others in the family who had struggled to establish and maintain life in the small isolated town. But the intensity of the struggles became clear only during these moments in the rocker when she felt the presence of those from before.

Amelia Caroline also wondered how they had endured the death of children, the diseases for which there were neither understanding nor cures, the constant disruption of military intrusion and the pursuit of war, and the reports of people gone to distant places, many of which were names not yet on common maps.

And while she sat there, I knew that her heart cried out for her father, whose life had drawn to a close at the hands of a young physician, highly professional yet lacking in the subtleties of life's experiences. Her father's passing had been in the hospital, a familiar setting, and he died among those who knew him; but the setting was, by necessity, institutional. Thus in the end, he had been separated from his grounding, and this separation had caused emotional pain that Amelia Caroline continued to experience these many years later.

Her heart cried also for her Great-Grandmother, with whom so much of the past had been shared.

The moment was one not unfamiliar to me, for often I found Amelia Caroline lost in memory. Yet in spite of this prior experience, I still felt the need to step into the solitude.

"Aunt Amelia, are you all right? You have been quiet for some time," I observed.

"Yes, Mary Eliza, I'm fine, just a bit distracted in my thoughts. There is so much to remember, but I am also beginning to feel a bit tired," she replied.

"I know that recalling these memories has always been a drain for you, Aunt Amelia. Perhaps we should take a short rest. Later in the day, a walk along the waterfront might be nice. We could sit in a swing and enjoy the sailboats on the river. There probably will be several young children feeding the gulls, and you have always found pleasure in their joy.

"I noticed this morning while returning from the hospital that the *Cape Jen* was moored in the yacht basin, and I was told that Captain A.J. would be selling shrimp from the boat. How would it be if I pick up some shrimp while you are resting and make a light dinner to share before going to the river? I can also make a brief stop at the hospital to check one more time on Mr. Sellers while you nap," I suggested.

"You are right, Mary Eliza. A nap would be pleasant, and later today I will look forward to some time at the waterfront. However, I feel compelled to continue our conversation. Perhaps we should plan to talk some more this evening."

It was late in the day when I returned to find Amelia Caroline up and about. She was dusting the sideboard and the dining table in preparation for dinner. The evening meal for Amelia Caroline had always been a time for the family to gather and share events of the day. As was the habit of many in her generation and generations before, setting a formal table was a requisite. This ritual had become special for me also, for Amelia Caroline regularly displayed fine linens, china and silver, all of which had been in the family for several generations. The evening meal was, in fact, one more tie to those in the past. Without fail, setting the table brought a renewed sense of connectivity, one which had become as meaningful to me as it was to Amelia Caroline.

"Oh, Aunt Amelia. The table is lovely," I said.

"Thank you. I see you have a package from Captain A.J.'s boat. I prepared some slaw and sliced one of those nice tomatoes while you were out. I've also laid out ingredients for making hush puppies to accompany the shrimp. You know, don't you, that the recipe is from my mother's cookbook. It was handwritten, so I don't know it's actual origin; but Papa often spoke of having hush puppies with fish when he was a child. That would have been years before the turn of the century. So there has long been a family recipe, but from how far back I don't know.

"I do, however, remember a conversation I had with Great-Grandmother in which hush puppies were discussed. That would have been thirty or so years back. The conversation was one in which Great-Grandmother was speaking about the near famine conditions during the war over slavery. Cornmeal was being used everyday as a major staple. She mentioned that among the routine dietary items were cornbread balls, which were either baked in the fire or fried in lard.

"My response to her was 'those sound like the hush puppies I've eaten all my life!' Then Great-Grandmother told me of first hearing the name hush puppy just after the war when Union troops were occupying the fort. Those Yankees often joked about how 'Southerners enjoyed eating fried corn, a food that was fit only to hush the puppies.' " Amelia Caroline chuckled as she remembered the story.

I smiled. It was a story told regularly, but hearing it once again simply endeared Amelia Caroline to me. I knew she was spending more and more time living in past memory.

We then entered the kitchen and, without words, worked as one in preparation of the meal – each of us doing a part, in concert, as if in a well-rehearsed play, one that came to the curtain without prompts.

Later that evening, the sun was just above the marina in the western sky as Amelia Caroline and I arrived by car at the waterfront park. A few low clouds were on the horizon and their presence promised a spectacular sunset. It was to be one which, like evening primroses, would splay deep pinks, reds and purples across the evening sky.

The display, however, was several minutes away and this gave us an opportunity to walk on the strand. The short walk was always special for, if one was lucky, pottery shards and other treasures from the past would be found. After all, the waterfront had been host to visitors for nearly four centuries and the townspeople had enjoyed the strand for over two hundred years.

So we walked in silence; together, yet each of us in a private world. These worlds were special places in our minds which we entered only when at the water's edge. It was that mystical, mesmerizing affect of the waterfront, where fragments of shells -- conch, oyster, clam and mussel -- crunched softly beneath our feet, complementing the gentle whisper of the water on the shore.

Nearby, shorebirds, gulls and sandpipers scurried ahead of us, running into and out of the water as they searched for morsels and treats from the river. The walk was not far and certainly could not be considered robust exercise. But that wasn't the purpose; rather the intent was to just be in this place where all the beauty and peace of nature flowed together. When experienced at its fullest, the waterfront gives a feeling of wholeness, an awareness of the soul and perhaps its renewal.

After a short while, I spoke.

"Aunt Amelia, the sun is about to go down, but I think we have just enough time to reach the pier."

The distance to the city pier was not great which, considering Amelia Caroline's age, was an important consideration. So we slowly walked the few yards down the strand, climbed the six wooden steps to the pier, then walked about a hundred feet over the water to a point where the full glory of the setting sun could be viewed without interference from surrounding buildings, docks or boats.

Upon reaching our favorite spot, which was a small wooden bench attached to the side railings of the pier, we sat and watched as the sun, by that time a bright reddish-orange ball, slowly sank over the salt marsh and disappeared beneath the horizon. The colored display over the next thirty minutes was as spectacular as we had anticipated, and it was as we had experienced innumerable times in the past. Every day was essentially the same, yet each sunset was uniquely different from those before.

Amelia Caroline then spoke.

"The evening is particularly pleasant today. The breeze is just enough to move the flag at the garrison, yet it is sufficient to control the pesty gnats and mosquitoes. We have shared so many equally beautiful evenings."

"Yes, Aunt Amelia. And I have loved every one of them," I answered.

Amelia Caroline continued, "Mary Eliza, I know you have thought of how your life here will be when I'm gone. We have been together nearly every day since completion of your medical training. That was over eighteen years ago, and we have been in each other's life since your first visit to the house in 1983. I knew from that very first visit that ours would be a special relationship." She paused, waiting to hear if I shared her feelings.

"The thought of being alone, without having you here to share my days, is with me every day, Aunt Amelia, and I do wonder how the emptiness will affect me. My work is extremely satisfying, and it asks for more of my time than currently I wish to give. Perhaps that demand will help.

"Regarding companionship, I have no interest in marriage. Between colleagues at the hospital and friendships both here in town and those I have maintained since college and medical school, my social needs are well met. I have been extremely fortunate in these relationships.

"There was a time when marriage was a consideration. I don't remember if I ever mentioned it to you, but it was toward the end of medical school. John Rhodes and I were quite close. Basically, John and I were good friends, sort of soulmates who supported each other during the rigors of medical school. Everyone accepted our relationship as that of close friends; but between us, particularly during the final semester as graduation approached, something more seemed to be emerging. I began to ask myself if marriage was of interest.

"The question, however, became moot in March of our graduation year. That was when our residency matches were announced. I was to do my training in North Carolina and John was assigned to Southern California, where he would begin to serve a commitment with the U.S. Navy. During his second year of medical school, John had entered a program through which his medical school expenses were paid by the military. In return, he had a commitment to serve six years as a medical officer. This was the same sort of arrangement that my brother Charles had made. The years in the Navy would serve both as John's internship and his specialty training.

"So upon graduation our worlds separated and I soon became immersed in my residency. Medicine and my years here with you have been my life. I now suspect that the balance of my years will continue to parallel your life in nursing and the years you had here with your father."

Again we sat quietly on the pier. Several seagulls were perched on the roof peak of Potter's Restaurant, while a large flock called noisily as they chased after pieces of bread being thrown into the water by two small children. A flight of pelicans, eight in number, passed gracefully overhead. Evening continued to settle.

I broke the silence.

"Aunt Amelia, I know your life has been both full and satisfying. But did you ever have thoughts of marriage?"

Amelia Caroline sat for a few moments before answering. Then in the fading light, her eyes showed a sparkle and a quiet smile came to her face.

She began, "I once had a fantasy. It was totally unrealistic; yet it was alive in my mind. Mary Eliza, I am going to share with you something I've never told anyone before. The story is one that normally remains hidden deep in the pages of a most personal diary. It is a story about dreams of the young."

As you already know, my first encounter with boys that would suggest a serious relationship came when I was approaching fifteen years of age. It was during that terrible war, and the boy was William Banes. Our association was brief, and primarily encompassed the time when he was so sick. That was when Papa and I were spending time on the island to help treat the troops.

Well, fifteen is not very old, but in those days many girls were married at that age, so as William and I became closer friends, thoughts came to me of love and the prospect of life with someone like William. These thoughts were not unusual, for all my girlfriends were in the same stage of life.

But the dream resulting from these thoughts was totally unrealistic, as William and I were from different worlds. My life was that of a schoolgirl and his life, at least in the immediacy, was slated to be that of a soldier. Still, I fantasized.

Then William died and I was disillusioned. Through his death, I had lost a friend, but not a lover. I did, however, lose a dream of love.

Over the next decade, school, nursing, the pharmacy, serving the community and my partnership in medicine with

Papa were fully satisfying. Then, just by chance in 1928, there was the most unexpected event.

August had begun with unstable weather and, on August 8th a gale began to blow, forcing several ships into the harbor. Among them was the yacht, Blue Heaven, *owned by the singer Gene Austin. The town was abuzz. One of the country's most famous crooners was right here at our waterfront. Shortly after the arrival of his boat, word came to Papa that Mr. Austin's wife Kathryn was aboard the yacht and was ill. Could he come to assist? Well, of course he could, and he asked me to accompany him on board.*

Mrs. Austin, as it turned out, was just ill from being on the rough seas. Nevertheless, Papa administered some medicine to relieve her discomfort. We assured her that with a few days in port she would be back in peak health. We then had a pleasant visit with Mr. Austin, during which Papa extended an invitation for Gene and his wife, when she felt better, to join us for dinner at home. The very next day, we received word that Kathryn was much better and they would be delighted to accept our hospitality.

How exciting! I could not wait to tell Beatrice Carson. Papa, however, suggested that perhaps Beatrice and her mother would like to join us, so we had a dinner party of six. During dinner, the conversation ranged over a variety of topics, with much time spent sharing experiences of New York City.

Kathryn then asked Beatrice about her background, and Beatrice mentioned moving to town following her experience as a nurse in France during the war. Gene Austin said he had been in France during the same period, so they began to exchange stories. Then, just as if directed by fate, Gene asked if by chance Beatrice had been involved with any of the soldiers who suffered from shell shock. Beatrice said no, that she had been primarily a surgical nurse. But she asked why this was of interest.

I almost fell from the chair upon hearing Gene Austin's response.

Apparently, one of his close companions, who was a member of General Pershing's expeditionary force to France, had been injured and sent for hospital care, but the friend never returned to the front lines. Gene had often wondered what had become of him.

As the story unfolded, we were told that Gene and his buddy had been together in Mexico during the campaign to capture Pancho Villa. Gene explained that he had grown up helping in his stepfather's blacksmith shop in Gainesville, Texas, so early in life he had become quite expert at handling horses. Consequently, in 1917, the Army had assigned him to the cavalry, where he became a member of General Pershing's special cavalry squadron. It was while in the elite squadron that he had met his friend, who at the time was a private first class.

Within the year, their unit was again mobilized and sent to France, where his friend was promoted to sergeant and became a squad leader. Soon thereafter, the sergeant was injured while crossing No-Man's-Land in an attempt to overrun the German positions. Upon his rescue by the medics, the sergeant was sent to the rear for hospital care. Word among the troops was that in addition to physical wounds, Gene's friend had been suffering from severe shell shock.

By that point in the conversation, I was not breathing. So I asked the question, "Was your friend Elias Hewett?"

Gene Austin looked as if he had been struck by lightening. "How did you possibly know?" he asked.

So I told him a bit of my childhood and that of Elias. And I closed with the story of Elias's return to town and the tragedy of his death. Bonds of which we were totally unaware had been formed between Gene Austin and me.

The evening continued as stories were shared. We laughed a lot and agreed that the world, though physically large, was a small place indeed.

To close out the evening, Gene offered to sing for us. Kathryn went to the piano, for my playing would have been no accompaniment at all. She played Gene's newest hits, "Bye Bye Blackbird" and "My Blue Heaven." Then Gene and Kathryn took their leave and we all agreed to stay in touch. The yacht Blue Heaven sailed from the harbor two days later.

We shared letters of appreciation over the next months, but life drifted back to the normal routine and we indeed lost touch. However, Papa and I often listened to broadcasts of the songs sung by Gene Austin while sitting in the parlor near our new Echophone radio. And surprisingly, as I closed my eyes and dreamily listened to that beautiful voice, my mind drifted and I allowed myself, for those brief periods, to experience a "what if" fantasy world.

Then without notice, nearly three years to the day, the Blue Heaven *again arrived at the waterfront. I was in my late twenties by then. Gene Austin was approaching thirty-one, and he was no longer married to Kathryn. Once again, time was spent over dinner and we renewed our friendship.*

Gene stayed in town for several days, during which time he visited with several families. Toward the end of his stay, Gene performed from the deck of the Blue Heaven. *The concert was his gift to the entire town. He was spectacular and he was my very special friend; for I knew him both as Gene Austin, the world-renowned singer and as Lemeul Eugene Lucas, the cavalry soldier and friend of Elias Hewett. Such is the stuff of which dreams are made.*

However, I was no longer a child, and I was aware of the difference in our worlds. I also knew the gap was to become greater. Within a few weeks of leaving town, Gene Austin relocated from New York to California where, along with other great singers such as Al Jolson, he became a star in films.

I redoubled my nursing activities here in town. Gene's second marriage in 1933 to Agnes Antilline was featured in all of the film magazines. In 1934, I saw Gene's first film, "Belle of the Nineties," right down the street at the Amuzu movie theater.

The chapter of my life with Gene Austin came to a close in March of 1939 when he consented to travel from California to do a special benefit performance at the Amuzu. The theater was packed to capacity and the show was beyond expectation. Everyone in town wished to see him perform, but the theater simply could not handle that many people. Therefore, as an encore, Gene gave select performances in several homes. Collectively, our hearts were his forever.

It was wonderful seeing him, but life in Hollywood had brought changes. I'm sure that I appeared changed to him, as well. We parted as friends. Over the years the fantasy has faded, but the question "what if?" has been with me ever since.

I moved a bit closer and put my arm around Amelia Caroline. There was so much yet to learn from and about my elderly cousin. But there was so little time.

We remained at the waterfront until the glow had waned and the sky began to darken just enough to show the early evening stars. Amelia Caroline was tired. The day had been long, so upon arrival back at the house she excused herself and went to her room for the night -- but only after promising to resume her Great-Grandmother's story the next day.

The following morning, Sunday, I found Amelia Caroline again in the rocker on the front porch. She had slept in a bit so, by the time she walked out onto the porch, the sun had already risen over the water, giving a golden glow to the early-morning bluish-grey sky. A slight breeze rustled the oak leaves, which spoke in their unique fashion, announcing a day that would be slightly cooler than the previous days had been.

Amelia Caroline knew that temperatures at that time of year were variable, but summer days typically ran on the warm side. She sat in the chair and gently rocked while listening to birds flitter from tree to telephone line and back. Early morning was always special as finches and sparrows flew in and out of the porch. Occasionally, they nested on top of the porch posts beneath the roof or set up housekeeping in the lush ferns which hung in baskets from the eaves. Every now and then we would be honored by the visit of a tufted titmouse as it passed on its way to the local swamps.

This morning, however, she was amused by a mockingbird, which was playfully toying with a pair of young squirrels as they dashed and chased each other across the ground and into the tree limbs.

"Good morning, Aunt Amelia. How long have you been awake?" I asked through the screen doorway.

"Oh, good morning, Mary Eliza. I've been here just a few minutes. I'm enjoying the birds, particularly that old mockingbird that is giving fits to the squirrels. He's always such a rascal, swooping and diving, and calling out to beware of his antics. He has been around so frequently and is so protective of this area. There must have been a nest in one of the nearby trees. The breeze this morning is very comfortable. Why don't you join me?" she invited.

"I will, but first a cup of tea. Perhaps one for you, also," I answered with a smile.

A few minutes later, I reemerged carrying a tray with two cups, a teapot and a small plate of scones. As we sat enjoying the tea, a neighbor, Mrs. Carson, came down the sidewalk and stopped at the front steps for a short time.

The town, though in existence for a couple of centuries, had not been formally platted until ten years prior to Amelia Caroline's birth. At that time, the town leaders decided that all streets would be lined with "conversation" sidewalks. In most cases, these passed just at the base of the front porches. It was difficult to approach any house without stopping at least for a minute to share greetings.

Such was the case that morning. Mrs. Carson, in the usual fashion, inquired into Amelia Caroline's health and asked me about plans for expansion of the hospital. This was not a singular thought on her mind, for numerous changes had taken place in the town since she and Amelia Caroline had been young.

"Times now are quite different from when I was a young girl," was the lead-in to her question.

Although Mrs. Carson was twenty years junior to Amelia Caroline, they both had attended the old schoolhouse in the town square. Now there were separate schools for youngsters, those in junior high school and those in senior high. The new schools were nice, but they lacked the feeling of community engendered during the early years, when students ranging in age from six to seventeen all attended classes in the same school building.

The hospital had also changed. Once a small community resource, it had been expanded to include laboratories, three surgical suites, and a nursing unit to care for patients who required prolonged care. In many ways, the new hospital brought comfort to the residents, as they knew most medical conditions could be treated right in town.

On the other hand, as in the case of the schools, a certain familiarity was lost in the expansion. Certainly, patients could no longer look out the window as had Amelia Caroline's father to see Mr. Perry leaving the Ford dealership at precisely ten minutes before noon. Both the dealership and Mr. Perry had long since departed and, with earlier additions to the hospital, patient rooms were relocated to the rear of the building where window views overlooked oak and pine trees in the back property.

Aware that too much detail was not of interest to Mrs. Carson, I simply mentioned the newly planned emergency room with adjacent x-ray facilities. The majority of my comments pertained to the redesigned entry at the hospital, which would be more welcoming to patients and visitors alike.

After a bit, Mrs. Carson said she was on her way to the new bakery, one that had recently been opened by a pastry chef who had been trained in Paris. This was common knowledge, as during the previous year everyone in town had waited on pins and needles for arrival of the special ovens that had been ordered from France. It seemed that signs announcing that the ovens were on their way had been posted in the bakery window forever.

The bakery turned out to be wonderful, as promised, and a daily walk for morning treats -- such as the scones we were enjoying -- had become almost a ritual for many folks. Mrs. Carson was among them, so she soon went on her way.

Once again Amelia Caroline and I sat in thought, each respecting the other's space. Then after a bit, Amelia Caroline spoke.

"I have been thinking about the conversation with Mrs. Carson. So much has changed over the past ten years or so. Life is different, even here in town. You and I can still enjoy pleasures at the waterfront in the evening, and the town still has a quiet atmosphere reminiscent of earlier years in the early morning hours. But by mid-morning, Howe Street is frantic with activity. There are tourists, cars, school buses, crowds, clutter, and even sirens as emergency vehicles rush out of the fire station down the street.

"I know that life, although simpler in earlier days, was not all a bed of roses. Yet on balance, it seemed more satisfying. Simple pleasures seemed to suffice. We were happy with rowboats and sails, picnics on the strand, walks in the park and afternoon stops at Mr. McKenzie's ice cream store. Now it is big boats with loud engines, movies in Shallotte, and houses larger and much more grand then even the most elegant hotels when I was young.

"But as you know, my youth was also colored by events over which I had no control. The same was true a hundred years earlier for Great-Grandmother.

"It is time I resume her tale."

36

WAR'S TRAGEDY

Amelia Caroline's mind began to settle on the conversation that had taken place thirty-plus years earlier with her Great-Grandmother.

"You know, Mary Eliza, I often think of Great-Grandmother when I walk on the waterfront and read the new signs calling attention to the historic Confederate Trail. My reaction is that folks can't give up on what was a tragic experience for all. It seems that all the publicity is an attempt to glorify the conflict, whereas little notice is given to the suffering that took place during the war and to the poverty that extended for decades afterward.

"The town seems quite prosperous now, but it is only in recent years that economic stability has been enjoyed. Even when I was a young girl, the economic aftermath of the War Between the States was felt.

"Yet attitudes on the part of the local folks indicated they would be willing to resume fighting for Southern independence. Nowadays there is that group, the United Daughters of the Confederacy, whose members wish to immortalize the women who endured the war. Although this is a good thing, the group seems to focus excessively on heroism, self-sacrifice and dedication to the cause.

"But as I know from conversations with Great-Grandmother, heroism and self-sacrifice were not the full story. On the contrary, the conditions under which they struggled resulted in deprivation, starvation, disease and death. In fact, shortly after the war's end, the town was described in Mr. Frank Leslie's newspaper as one of the most dilapidated villages in the South. But that is getting ahead of Great-Grandmother's story."

THE BATTLE IS LOST

The battle is lost; and our loved ones
Who freely have given their lives
For independence of the South,
Have they died in vain?

Clearly, the noble cause for which
They gave themselves is lost,
But without question they did not,
In futility, offer up their lives.

That which is honored by death
Was before God most righteous.
And, even though tragic at its end
We will celebrate the sacrifices.

But, those among us who remain
To see the end of that cause,
The fight for which was so proud,
What have we now? More suffering?

The deprivation would be nothing,
Had the outcome been different.
We have suffered hunger, and disease
Survived winters, tho' poorly clothed

We have been left alone and lonely,
And have endured so much more
Than anyone could believe -- except
Soldiers of the Southern Confederacy.

And at the end of it all, what is left?
Our desolate homes; shrouds of black;
Memories of Fathers, Daughters and
Sons, gone; and tears which remain!

Amelia Caroline Potter Everitt
Fall 1865

I sat quietly as Amelia Caroline seemed to drift. Again
Great-Grandmother spoke.

Our lives began to change quite noticeably following the deaths of Charles in 1852 and Emeline just one year later. Sewall Fremont retired his commission with the U.S. Army following the *San Francisco* misfortune and became employed as supervisor for the Wilmington and Weldon Railroad.

Your Grandfather Edward also joined the railroad a few years later. Edward, unlike Sewall, had not attended college, but he was ambitious. Within a short time, he became a conductor on the line.

About this same time, Sterling decided to withdraw from the practice of medicine. Coincidentally, a young physician named Dr. Walter Curtis arrived in town from New England. He was an energetic young man, from a good family and anxious to begin practice. Sterling, having thoughts of leaving practice, befriended Dr. Curtis and introduced him around town. At first the two practiced together, then after a couple of years, Sterling decided to relinquish the practice entirely and turned it over to Dr. Curtis.

Dr. Curtis was a capable young man and, although not a graduate of medical college as our Charles had been, had completed several years of apprenticeship and attended one full session in medicine at Harvard College in Boston.

However, although his medical expertise was fairly current, it offered little more in the way of relief or cure than had been provided by earlier doctors. This professional limitation soon came to bear on our family for, in 1855, just two years after stepping away from practice, Sterling became ill with dropsy and died. He was in his sixty-forth year and we had been married thirty-seven years. The emptiness following his loss was compounded the following August when our daughter Marietta contracted typhoid. She was just thirty-five.

Dr. Curtis provided relief, but a cure was beyond medicine's capacity.

I don't mean to be critical of Dr. Curtis. In fact, my memories of him as a physician are favorable. Yet there were limits to the medical profession in those days. These were limitations that we had known all our lives and which we had previously experienced in the deaths of our two young sons, George Washington and William Randolph. Childhood death was so common.

Three months following Marietta's passing, sadness entered the home of Elizabeth and Sewall. Their young daughter Ellen Mae, who had survived hunger, thirst and disease at sea on the bark *Kilby*, died from diphtheria at the age of seven. At the time of her death, Ellen had been under the care of Dr. Curtis for several weeks. She, along with many other children, had been experiencing a severe catarrh. Ellen eventually lost all desire for food and became listless with the fatigue. These signs were a concern, for most of the children began to improve after a few days of illness.

Then toward the middle of November, inflammation appeared in Ellen's throat and she passed away two weeks later. Our final resort was to prayers, which went unanswered.

At this same time, changes were occurring more rapidly both locally and in the South in general. Activities at the fort were sporadic. The government at various times would send Army engineers to shore up fortifications, then there would be periods of inactivity. There was, however, a constant undercurrent of unrest, as rumors of rebellion against the government were fueled by ongoing discontent in

South Carolina. Although security in the region seemed to be a concern for the government, troops other than engineers and a few caretaker soldiers were not stationed here.

Locally, our neighbors for the most part were passive with respect to the unrest in the region. They were content just making do in life. After all, it was hard enough to get by without dealing with the disruption of the Army.

Then early in January of 1861, the federal ship *Star of the West* was fired upon by cadets from the Citadel while sailing into Charleston harbor. This action by the Citadel cadets sent waves of concern up and down the Southern coastline. There was alarm over the prospect that the federal government would respond to the assault by sending more troops to discipline the South. In response to this concern, several local planters, in conjunction with planters from upriver and residents of Wilmington, met to form an unofficial force which they named the "Cape Fear Minutemen." Their intent was to defend the region from any retaliatory action by the federal government.

The dissatisfaction in Charleston continued to grow, and a feeling of discomfort began to permeate those of us here in Smithville and those who lived upriver toward Wilmington.

Though most of us were still reluctant to abuse the relationship with the federal government any more than had already occurred, war fever was running high among the militia volunteers. Within days of formation and under the leadership of Captain John Hedrick, the Cape Fear Minutemen decided to take control of both Fort Johnston here in town and the fortifications on Caswell Island. The reasons for this occupation were not clear; it just seemed that some men were on a mission to precipitate war.

Occupation of the forts, however, was not for long. Governor John Ellis soon sent word that the action had been taken without authority from his office. He acknowledged that the Minutemen had acted out of a sense of patriotism to the state, but he insisted that they withdraw. Within days, the two installations were returned to federal control and they remained so for the next three months.

Then following the siege of Fort Sumter in Charleston harbor early in April, war did ensue. On April 4th, the local militiamen -- primarily the Minutemen -- were reorganized into the Cape Fear Light Artillery and, on April 17th, Governor Ellis ordered the unit to join the 30th North Carolina Militia and recapture both the garrison and the Caswell fortifications. Thus the garrison and the town became occupied by Confederate forces and it remained so for years to follow.

The presence of troops, when combined with events of the long war, ultimately left the town and those of us who lived here in shambles.

The first activities undertaken by the Confederate soldiers involved improvements to reinforce the fort. This work was done at the expense of kitchen and backyard gardens. Earthen gun batteries were built along the riverfront using soil gathered from throughout the town. The new batteries were not very substantial, but they could accommodate the light artillery field guns which were intended as support for the larger cannons at the garrison proper.

Hundreds of slaves, laboring under the eyes of newly appointed military masters, pushed wheelbarrows through the streets to deliver needed dirt. Virtually every garden was stripped of soil, leaving barren, non-productive ground behind, thus ensuring poor harvests for years. This, of course, was done with consultation and support of the local residents, most of whom by that time were women and children: the men were busy preparing to serve as soldiers.

The town once again became an encampment. Following completion of improvements at the garrison and along the waterfront, soldiers began to arrive from throughout the state. Initially, the troops were not to be stationed here on a permanent basis. Rather, the fort was designated as a "camp for instruction" where new recruits would be sent for their initial training. Secondarily, the region was to serve as a holding place for those troops awaiting shipment elsewhere. Everything and everyone seemed transient.

But it wasn't long before the Cape Fear River and the town of Smithville became recognized for their full military value. Following the state's secession from the Union in May of 1861, emphasis expanded beyond just improving military fortifications and strengthening the garrison for training purposes. The town, with its deep harbor, became a shipping and receiving depot for supplies required to conduct the war elsewhere. It was in conjunction with this latter role that your Grandfather Edward and Sewall Fremont became involved in the war.

The Wilmington and Weldon Railroad was, in the words of General Robert E. Lee, to become the "lifeline of the Confederacy." On August 26, 1861, Sewall Fremont, newly appointed by Governor Clark to the rank of colonel in the 1st Regiment Artillery of the North Carolina Militia, reported for duty to General R.C. Gatlin, the commanding officer in Richmond.

Sewall, now Colonel Fremont, became chief engineer of the defenses of Cape Fear and the surrounding coast. Defending the railroad "lifeline" and safeguarding the ports here and in Wilmington were in his charge.

This heightened awareness by military leaders of the region's strategic value to the Confederacy precipitated substantial changes in town. Even more soldiers were to be permanently assigned here. In September of 1861, General Joseph Anderson took charge of all the Confederate forces surrounding Wilmington. By that time there were nearly 900 soldiers hereabouts. Four hundred were posted on the island at the Caswell fortifications, and the other 500 were assigned to the garrison in town.

We were honored to have such recognition: the town would shine through its dedication to and support of the cause. The war would highlight the harbor. In addition, those of us remaining in town, though not soldiers, would be seen as patriots in support of the cause.

Then to our surprise, the local commanders began asking for substantially more troops. They suggested that 5,000 soldiers should be dispersed partially at the fort in town and partially on Caswell Island.

This suggestion was worrisome to us, for the initial companies of soldiers had already begun to place some strain on resources. Fresh food was in short supply. The region was quite swampy, so areas to bivouac were limited and sanitary facilities were not available.

The military expected that, in part, provisions would be provided locally. Well, it was beyond reason to assume that a small village of 600, which in the past had marginally provided for itself, could support the needs of that many soldiers. Still, many in the town out of bravado insisted they would do their part. However, as we all soon learned, bravado does not grow crops, nor does it cure bacon.

Nevertheless, troops began to arrive. Companies of volunteers raised in Pender, Sampson and Columbus counties marched into town and joined the local boys. Before the year's end, nearly 1,000 additional soldiers were camped in the woods, at the edge of the swamps and on the island.

Each company had its own name that reflected hometown pride. There were the "Fair Bluff Volunteers," the "Holmes Riflemen" and the "Duplin Grays."

There even was a company known as the "Cabarrus Black Boys" assigned to this region. I doubt if many of the members of this troop were volunteers, as most probably were mustered out of slavery.

Few of the troops were actually at the fort, for the garrison grounds had just a couple of buildings other than officers' quarters. The town was overrun and soldiers were more plentiful than residents.

War fever in that first year was so pervasive that even Dr. Betts, a member of the ordained clergy, left his church, accepted a commission and was assigned as an officer at the garrison. When questioned about his faith and the decision to join the war, he insisted it was God's Will, for he became a soldier only after much deliberation and prayer.

One of the great tragedies of this period was displacement of local men by those who came into town. Shortly after the governor issued orders requiring that all able-bodied men report to signing stations, the young men, husbands and fathers from the town were shipped north to join the Army of Virginia. The town became a shadow of itself, being comprised of women and children and a few old men considered too feeble to serve in the military. All the while, strangers -- soldiers from elsewhere -- were being posted here. It was chaotic.

It wasn't long before local resources became overly strained and conditions deteriorated. Food, though sufficient in the beginning, became short and medications were soon to follow.

These conditions were not publicly acknowledged beyond the town limits. In fact, military commanders encouraged the boys who could write to send letters home reporting how well they were doing. So the letters contained glowing reports of life in the camps and newspapers reported morale to be high among the soldiers. Support of the townswomen was described as admirable. Soldiers told of dinners with beef, bacon, turnips, chicken, turkey and cakes of all kinds. Yet in reality, our livestock, except for a few milk cows and laying hens, had been depleted. We were getting by on wild greens from the swamps and what little fish we could catch and keep from the hands of the soldiers.

When the war began, we had had such beautiful gardens. There were spring bulbs, then camellias, azaleas, summer's roses and hibiscus. Our kitchen gardens had been bountiful with fresh vegetables in each season. We had spring peas and delicate greens, summer squash, beans of different varieties and tomatoes, and in the fall there had been cabbages, collards and pumpkins. Grains grown by those with larger properties had been plenty for our needs and those of the livestock. But all that had changed with time.

However, the gardens had been damaged nearly beyond salvage during construction of the defenses. Later in the war, any crops not taken from our yards during the night were trampled by the troops during the day.

Soldiers were bathing in the creeks and sewage was left behind. It flowed into the river. Oysters, those which had not been destroyed by over-harvesting the beds, often made us sick. Rice crops from plantations along the river were reduced, and that which was grown went mostly to the Army. Cornmeal from crops grown inland remained a staple, but its use changed. We no longer had eggs, milk, butter and sugar in sufficient amount to prepare treats like cornbread or sweet cornbread balls. Cornpones of meal, salt, flour and a bit of shortening were fried or baked in a skillet.

Coffee tested our limits. As supplies dwindled, the beans were mixed with dried, roasted and ground sweet potatoes or parched rye. Then there was sorghum, always sorghum.

We were not consulted as to our opinions on conditions. No one asked about the health of the sick elderly or the pain of watching young children go hungry. Except for the few entrepreneurial river pilots, who earned gold in return for running blockade ships, poverty was pervasive. Our money became worthless, while at the same time speculation ran the cost of basic provisions beyond the means of all except the most fortunate.

Credibility was truly stretched by suggesting that troops were eating sumptuous meals when the cost of bacon was approaching ten dollars a pound and flour was several hundred dollars per barrel.

Then came the chronic camp diseases. Mumps, measles, scarletina, fluxes and catarrh were always present, and an epidemic of each seemed to accompany the arrival of every new regiment of soldiers.

Distressing as this was, it paled in the face of smallpox, which quickly swept through the troops following arrival in town of a Confederate soldier who carried the disease from Richmond, where an epidemic raged. To our great distress, there was no *vaccinia* available and soon virtually every family in town was afflicted. It was a terrible state, with children disfigured and the elderly lost.

Fortunately, some of the townspeople had been vaccinated during youth and this treatment conferred a limited degree of protection. Such was not the case with the majority of soldiers, for most were boys from isolated small communities and farms where vaccination had rarely been practiced. Hundreds were debilitated, and the dead nearly overwhelmed capacity for burial.

The fearfulness that gripped the town in the face of smallpox waned as the epidemic passed. But in the aftermath, a great sadness overshadowed the town. And this general gray cloud remained into the following year, when word of yellow fever came from up the river. Several cases had appeared in Wilmington over the course of a few days, then the disease spread with fury throughout the community. Residents were fleeing the area, and many of them came downriver with the intention of waiting out the disease.

The arrival of the refugees in town fueled fear among residents and soldiers alike. Before long many of the residents, including Dr. Lorenzo Frink, a physician, went inland to escape from people who had been exposed to the disease and to remove themselves from the miasma of the swamps.

The soldiers were less fortunate, not being at liberty to protect themselves. But the fear of yellow fever and its near-certain promise of death had a greater influence than military protocol on several of the soldiers who chose to abandon their assignments. The outcome of their desertion was nearly as tragic as having remained on duty and risked illness.

Rewards for their return, payable in gold, were posted by the commanding officers. This promise of real money was more than some could resist and soon neighbor turned on neighbor. Many of the soldiers who had deserted were caught and, upon return to the fort following capture, they were imprisoned, where they were ruthlessly punished.

Some were not brought back, for desertion was a capital offense punishable by death. We heard many reports of deserters being captured by companies of soldiers sent out as trackers. The captured men were simply tied to trees then, under the order of the young officers in charge, they were shot by a squad of former comrades.

As it turned out, fewer people in town died from yellow fever than expected, but the number of deaths upriver was in the hundreds. It wasn't until the following spring, five months after the first scare, that we felt the epidemic was truly over.

Relief, though sweet, was short-lived. The very next summer, a ship arrived in the harbor with an infected sailor. Before knowing of his condition, military officials boarded the ship and, by week's end, yellow fever was again among the troops. Death simply would not leave us at rest.

The fear of yet another yellow fever epidemic quickly swept through the town, yet the general effect was less than anticipated. However, the new wave of disease was tragic for the family. Early in September of 1863, our daughter Caroline Amelia was taken ill and died. The circumstances of her death were particularly distressing. She had been sickly most of her thirty-four years but, prior to the war, signs had indicated that her constitution was strengthening. I had great hopes that, in time, she would have the stamina to more freely enjoy life.

These hopes were dashed as the war placed strains on our family and, when the fever came, she had not the ability to resist. The tragedy continued, for we had no more than placed Caroline Amelia at rest when sad news came from Magnolia: Mary Eliza Langdon, sister to my husband, had passed away.

Unlike Caroline Amelia, Mary Eliza had lived a full life, but the hardships of the war had taken their toll. She died in her seventy-first year. No physician was in attendance, for the few doctors who were willing to risk exposure did so only at great cost to the afflicted. The expense was more than most could afford.

These conditions -- war, disease and deprivation -- remained for nearly four years, by which time the town was a ghost of its former self. Most houses had been taken over by the military. The sick and wounded were housed throughout the town, as capacity at the small military hospital had been exceeded during the early stages of the war.

Then word came that Union forces were mounting a major assault on Fort Fisher, just up the river. It was widely known that if Fort Fisher fell, the war effort would also be lost. So in early January of 1865, the soldiers stationed at our fort and in the woods surrounding the town moved upriver to reinforce Fort Fisher.

The town became silent. It was truly a ghost town occupied by downtrodden women, frail elderly and infirm soldiers.   We walked the streets nearly dumbstruck at the void. Following departure of the soldiers, word got around that the quartermaster from the garrison had left stores behind. What ensued was near riot as the hungry and cold besieged the storehouse to take what could be had during the absence of the military. Such change had come about since the bravado of the war's beginning. Yet we had to survive.

The day following withdrawal of the Confederate forces, the U.S. Navy warship *Monticello* entered the harbor under the command of Lieutenant W.B. Cushing. Marines and sailors from the ship immediately captured two of the Confederate blockade runners, then they took control of the fort. Lieutenant Cushing and his officers moved into the garrison headquarters. The war for us was brought to a close.

The Union assault on the Confederate forces upriver at Fort Fisher and at Fort Anderson, which was located on the west bank of the river directly across from Fort Fisher, did not last long. In the waning days of the war, General Lee had stated that if Wilmington fell, the South would lose. And that was the case. The fortifications designed and built under the direction of Sewall Fremont had finally yielded, but only to the largest coordinated naval and land assault of the entire war.

Within days, a large flotilla of Yankee ships entered the harbor unmolested. Several thousand Union soldiers disembarked. We again were occupied, but this time by an enemy force which viewed us with some hostility.

Initially, the soldiers and sailors were set at liberty in the town, and they proceeded to pillage the courthouse, Masonic Lodge and other buildings as seemed worthy of their attention. In the process, the sailors destroyed legal records that predated the Revolutionary War. This activity slowly subsided as they learned there was not much of value left in town.

During the years when Confederate forces controlled the fort, our grand houses had been abused, the furnishings destroyed or taken, and most items worthy of sale had been confiscated to support the war effort. It did not take long for the Union occupiers to realize our plight, so an amicable agreement was reached. We co-existed without further animosity.

Life, though remaining harsh, did stabilize. In town, we had to endure a formal surrender of the fort and the few remaining Confederate soldiers, primarily captives, were required to denounce the South and pledge loyalty to the United States. Julius Dosher was the first to do so. Afterward, he was a free man and soon resumed his occupation as a river pilot.

One month later, on April 3, 1865, Sewall Fremont was captured by his former classmate at West Point, William Tecumseh Sherman. Sewall was placed under house arrest in Richmond and kept there until after surrender of the Confederate forces. He was considered by General Sherman to be a particular threat to the Union cause and, for that reason, was retained in captivity for several weeks following General Lee's surrender.

Sewall was a very proud man. He fully believed in and was firmly committed to the Southern cause. For this reason, he initially refused to renounce the Confederacy. In one regard, it was this steadfast loyalty to the South that made him an ongoing threat in the eyes of General Sherman.

Edward, meanwhile, had both made the renouncement and sworn loyalty to the Union, so he was free to return home and resume his life. However, upon learning of Sewall's situation, Edward traveled to Richmond where he met with Sewall. Though sharing Sewall's beliefs, Edward pleaded on behalf of the family. It was time, he argued, to begin rebuilding all that had been destroyed during the war. Ultimately, Sewall agreed to renounce the Confederate States of America. Then, along with Edward, he returned to town and the family.

Over the next few months, there was a decrease in the number of Union soldiers stationed locally as the troops moved inland in pursuit of fleeing Confederate forces that refused to recognize the surrender. After a couple of months, an entirely new regiment comprised of Colored troops from the Northern states was assigned to the garrison. Their presence was resented by the townspeople; but the occupation, which lasted for nearly a year, was without incident.

The year was not to end without family sorrow, however, for in August my granddaughter Caroline Baker, the daughter of Julia and Mr. Baker, died at the age of thirty-one. I was watching my family slowly succumb to conditions created by war.

The relative calm at the fort was not to endure, as near anarchy existed in the surrounding counties to the west. Therefore, the federal government decided to keep troops at the fort with the intent of dispatching them when necessary to maintain civil order.

This task proved to be more than the soldiers could accomplish. In the absence of authority, marauding bands of former Southern soldiers raided government establishments, taking what they could and destroying what they couldn't. The war was officially

317

over, but unofficially it continued to be fought by the actions of the lawless. Attempts to bring order and justice were frustrated.

In general, the people were sympathetic to the marauders and they held in contempt the Colored Union soldiers, who had been given the task of restoring order. Tension gripped and maintained its hold on the region and this tension eventually soured relations with the Black soldiers here in town.

We were, of course, aware that Mr. Lincoln had proclaimed an end to slavery during the middle years of the war, but this announcement did little to affect relations here. We simply retained our slaves. Given the harshness of the times, it seemed inconceivable that life could be bearable without help around the house and in the gardens.

But upon surrender of the town, Lieutenant Cushing, the commander of the Union forces, had gathered all the Blacks at the waterfront and informed them they were no longer bound and that their freedom would be ensured by the federal troops.

This pronouncement resulted in a spontaneous celebration, as many of the Negroes, much to the chagrin of their former masters, paraded through the streets waving Union flags. It wasn't long thereafter that a school for Blacks was established in the abandoned Episcopal Chapel, and instructors from the North were sent to teach rudimentary skills and principles of citizenship.

Our former slaves simply walked away.

We were impoverished.

The shock of having nothing other than sorrow and our desolate homes was not to our liking, but there was little to be done. So the months passed into years, and we slowly learned how to rebuild our lives.

Meanwhile, the new citizens slowly became politically active. This was both facilitated and enforced by the federal government and its representatives, the soldiers at the fort.

Over time, two opposing political parties evolved. One of these was comprised of radical Whites who were principally outsiders and Blacks who were both newly freed Negroes and Black men who had been independent prior to the war. There were many such freemen here and in surrounding counties. Many of these were former slaves who, prior to the war, had benefitted from the benevolence of their former owners, but equal in number were those who had earlier immigrated to this country as free men.

The other political party was populated by townsmen who had returned from the war. Needless to say, these war-weary veterans had little use for either the occupying forces or the newly enfranchised former slaves.

This division proved to be disastrous and, in 1867, a riot of street fights broke out during a political rally. Prominent among the radicals were Black soldiers from the fort. Their presence was not related to maintaining order, rather they were intent upon inflaming the situation by siding with their Black brothers. Once again, the military had injected itself into and disrupted our lives.

The year 1867 thus ended in turmoil and social unrest, an unrest that would continue into the next year when the radicals swept the election on behalf of the Republican Party. It seemed that the federal government was doing all in its power to turn control of the town over to the Negroes. Bitter was the pill we were required to swallow.

The following year was distressing for the family and for me in particular. Mr. Baker, husband to my Julia, became ill with pneumonia and died in April. Then, six months later in October of 1868, the same fate befell Julia.

The death of Julia left me with a great emptiness. Your Grandfather Edward was the last of my children to survive and he was no longer in town. After returning from the war, Edward had taken residence in Wilmington, where he again worked with the railroad. Sewall had also resumed his pre-war role as a supervisor for the Wilmington and Weldon Railroad. Once again, he and Edward were working together. Edward, recognizing that I was a bit out-of-sorts, asked that I join him and his young family for a while. In December of 1868, I went to Wilmington.

Except for several weeks in the summer, I spent most of the next years away from town. In my absence, the house was being looked after by my niece Mary Elizabeth. She and Sewall were mostly residing in town, though they also kept a house in Wilmington. The Wilmington place was used frequently by Sewall when he was working.

Mary Elizabeth and her siblings had inherited both the Langdon house here in town and the Magnolia property following the death of their mother. The plantation had been ravaged during the war, so Mary Elizabeth rarely visited.

Edward and his wife, your Grandmother Emily, held several rental properties here in town, though they lived in Wilmington. Periodically, particularly during the nice weather of spring or fall, they would take the steamer down from the city. On some of those occasions, I would travel along.

Edward would check on the rental houses while Emily and I would visit with Mary Elizabeth and her children. I, of course, looked forward to spending a few days in my own house.

These trips were not entirely for pleasure, as the town was still experiencing post-war unrest that resulted in criminal activity. Property damage, theft and arson were not infrequent. No properties were exempt, including ours. In fact, several of Edward's houses were destroyed during the great fire of 1869. The losses included a house that was occupied by Dr. Thurston, a new military surgeon at the garrison. There seemed no relief to the struggles that life was presenting to our family.

But life did go on and, after a period in Wilmington, I returned in 1871 to the house I had long known. Shortly thereafter, Both Edward and Sewall resigned from the Wilmington and Weldon Railroad, then took employment with the Wilmington, Charlotte and Rutherford Railroad. Edward was scheduled to spend a substantial amount of his work time in Charlotte, so Emily, who was with child, decided to join me in the house.

Your father Reuben, my grandson, was born under this roof. Reuben's birth marked the high point of the post-war period. Being with him and sharing his first year brought joy and a sense of restoration.

My closing days were spent on the front porch in the rocking chair that had been purchased for me by your Great-Grandfather, my beloved Sterling, over a half-century earlier.

The chair had experienced much in my lifetime.

37

REFLECTION

I sat quietly for a few moments before speaking, for I had learned over the years that Amelia Caroline often remained distant following communication with or about her Great-Grandmother.

The air was becoming still and the sun, now high in the sky was radiating the warmth that would call younger folks to the waterfront where the ice cream truck would be parked. The swings, located in the shade of old cedars and oaks, undoubtedly were filled with tourists who had come to the ancient shore to watch the gulls, admire the boats and enjoy a cool treat. These were simple pleasures of the kind Amelia Caroline had known for her entire life, but ones which now were rare for most people and were enjoyed primarily by those fortunate enough to have a day of leisure at the shore.

Finally Amelia Caroline looked over at me and spoke.

"Great-Grandmother died in 1873 while Grandmother Emily and Papa, who was an infant, were living with her. Then, following Great-Grandmother's death, Grandfather Edward thought it would be best to maintain residence here rather than pack everything off to Charlotte. After all, Grandfather had been raised in this house. So, they remained.

"However, since Grandfather was working much of the time out of Charlotte, he and Grandmother maintained a small house for some years in that city. Papa, therefore, spent a bit of time in Charlotte, but he lived most of his early life in this house, right up until he left for medical training in Louisville. Grandfather and Grandmother, by that time, had chosen to be in Charlotte full time to make working more convenient for Grandfather who was getting on in years.

"This house was often very quiet during the time they were in Charlotte and Papa was away at school. But with medical school approaching completion, Papa and Mother were married in Louisville in 1902. Then upon Papa's graduation,

323

they left Louisville and moved back here. The house has been occupied continuously now for one hundred years."

My thoughts flowed along with hers as I responded.

"Aunt Amelia, I see great parallels between your experiences and those of Great-Grandmother. Particularly evident are the tragedies resulting from war times. But you said it was a conversation with your Great-Grandmother that led to your decisions about the church. I still don't understand, for Great-Grandmother indicated the family had turned to religion for strength during times of crisis."

"Yes, that is true," Amelia Caroline explained. "The family did turn to the church at the time of Charles's death and again when Emeline and Captain Taylor were lost at sea. It was the simple kindness shown by church members on those occasions that gave Great-Grandmother strength.

"But the town was very small and most church members were also neighbors. So the support could have been the result of simple neighborly kindness. Ultimately, the number of tragedies experienced during Great-Grandmother's lifetime was overwhelming. Children died at early ages from diseases without cures, and young men were lost to wars being fought both here and in distant lands. Lives in town were disrupted by the constant comings and goings of military personnel at the fort and on the island.

"She lived with all of this, plus the never-ending threat of epidemics. Yellow fever, typhoid and smallpox were always promising to take lives, many of which had already been compromised by malaria. Hardly a year went by without some tragedy befalling the family.

"Religion sometimes offered relief, but rarely provided answers. Great-Grandmother came to question, as did many others."

"So do you think Great-Grandmother turned inwardly seeking answers?" I asked.

"I'm not certain," said Amelia Caroline, "but I know from her stories that the churches were often empty and the clergy frequently absent. In the early years of her life, the only clergy were itinerant preachers who visited the town on rare occasions. Periodically, a minister would move here, mostly from the North. But within a short while, the climate and constant threat of disease, which everyone believed came from bad air in the swamps at the time, drove them away.

"Folks in town and soldiers at the fort learned to fend for themselves when it came to matters of the soul. I suspect that Great-Grandmother began questioning early in her life and answers -- if there were any -- came from within."

I continued to question, "But what about neighborly kindness? Great-Grandmother referred to that. Didn't it stem from teachings of the churches?"

Amelia Caroline thoughtfully continued, "Its roots may have been in their teachings. However, you know from your own experience as a physician that kindness, compassion and caring are intrinsic to the lives of many. You would treat illness even in the absence of the church. In situations involving disease beyond medicine's reach or when death ensues despite your best efforts, where do you look for answers? Do you turn to science, to God, or within yourself?

"Working alongside Papa during that early war and over the ensuing years, I began to look inside myself for both strength and answers. It wasn't until after Papa's death that the conversations with Great-Grandmother resumed, and those conversations brought me to fully acknowledge what had been my pattern, one that had begun during World War I nearly a half century earlier. Not only was I looking inward, but I was relying on the conversations with Great-Grandmother to help me understand or at least come to grip with those circumstances, situations and events which were beyond understanding."

"I see what you are saying, Aunt Amelia, and there are many times I search within myself for understanding. Why is it, I often ask, that with all the technology and expertise available to us, we still cannot bring relief to many who suffer? At such times I do question, but for the most part, I find the dogmas of the churches to be irrelevant.

"I also have realized that conversations with you in the evenings and those with colleagues during the day are a big help to me," I finished with a smile.

Amelia Caroline smiled at my admission in return. "You see, Mary Eliza, we have that in common with each other and with Great-Grandmother. When we are in pain, either physical or emotional, pain that takes us beyond our inner resources, it is to family and neighbors we turn, regardless of their religious inclinations. This was the realization that came to me during the conversations with Great-Grandmother."

I asked again, hoping for still further clarification, "But why did you turn away from the church? Could you not have just continued to participate?"

"I suppose so, Mary Eliza, but the separation was not just because my most fundamental questions were going unanswered. I began to realize that churches had become more concerned with self-perpetuation than with helping folks find answers to life's ultimate questions.

"Preachers simply referred to age-old texts and offered antiquated rituals in response to questions. More attention was being given to financing grandiose sanctuaries than to solving mysteries or helping those who were down and out.

"Of course, they all made big productions at Thanksgiving or on the various religious holidays, but then they quickly reverted to raising money to pay construction costs and heating bills for the buildings.

"For me, the institutions had become empty and irrelevant. I had no need to participate."

Amelia Caroline and I sat thoughtfully for some time and watched as the noon traffic moved through the streets. Several cars were heading for Bay Street, where they would park along the waterfront. Many of the drivers would open lunch bags and enjoy a few moments of respite from their busy days.

Others turned toward the post office, hoping to get letters posted before the one o'clock pickup. The post office was located next to the city hall on the site where, at one time, a high school had been located. This school was not the one attended by either Amelia Caroline or her neighbor Mrs. Carson, for their school had long preceded it. Rather, the school in question was one that had been built in the late 1930s and burned thirty-five years later. The cause of the fire remained a mystery, but fires had been common in those days, particularly in the winter months when coal and wood were used to heat many buildings.

After a while I spoke again, raising a question I had longed to ask for some time.

"Aunt Amelia, you have often spoken of your memories from the First War, and you have described as you did today the reactions you had during the Vietnam War. But you have rarely spoken of the Second World War, and I know the town was involved at that time."

The question did not surprise Amelia Caroline, for it was one she often asked herself. What was it about those years that precluded her from speaking of them? Having asked the question of herself numerous times, Amelia Caroline felt she now could respond. And she did.

Of course the town was involved, as was the entire nation; and I, too, played a role. My involvement, however, seemed different from either the war of my teen years or experiences of Great-Grandmother. In both of those earlier situations, we --Great-Grandmother and I --had to suffer the tragedies of the times, but we were not direct participants in the war. I realize this is somewhat convoluted, but I'll try to explain.

The conflicts in those earlier years, by which I mean as far back as the early- to mid-1800s, brought the military, soldiers, guns, depravation, hunger, disease and death right here to the town. During Great-Grandmother's day, the town was essentially a military establishment surrounded by a small non-military population.

The same situation evolved during the war of my youth. Over time, the number of soldiers and sailors came to exceed the local population. The military and war activities became, at various times, the focus of life.

This was particularly true for Great-Grandmother. Both her father-in-law and later her own son served as military surgeons. The husband of your distant cousin, Mary Elizabeth, was a graduate of West Point. And late in her life, Great-Grandmother's youngest son, my Grandfather Edward, was an officer in the Confederate Army.

So the military dominated much of her life and, as you now know, the military was responsible either directly or indirectly for many of her life's struggles. In my case, Papa assumed responsibility for treating troops during World War I. As a young girl, I was struck by the toll the war had taken on my young friend William and other soldiers out on the island. In addition, I have long remembered the young men from the town who returned from the war never to be whole again.

The Second World War differed in that the number of soldiers and sailors stationed locally was relatively small. Therefore, our lives were not compromised by the constant arrival of outsiders. Furthermore, disease due to the concentration of troops was not a major concern. Those entering the military were immediately vaccinated against most of the common diseases that had plagued soldiers in earlier times.

While here, the troops were well provisioned. This was a major change from the past. Although the spread of polio became a concern late in World War II, as had been the case in 1917, the total number of cases nationally was just a few thousand, and it never became an issue here.

All of this having been said, the town did assume a military character. Even before war was declared, preparations were being made both in town and on the island. Several months prior to the assault on Pearl Harbor, the Navy bought nearly 250 acres on the island with plans to establish a coastal battery and training center. Shortly thereafter, Congress authorized nearly $35,000 to build and furnish a USO Center on the garrison grounds. We knew that the military soon would arrive.

By early fall of 1941, the town had taken on a military appearance. Squads of sailors from the naval ship moored at the government dock conducted daily drills at the fort, and warships, both our own and British, were constantly in the harbor. When arrangements were made to upgrade the town's power plant, with the intent of providing electricity to troops on the island, we knew war was not far off.

And in December, war was declared.

I don't remember how many soldiers and sailors came to town, but it was far fewer than at any previous time. The total was probably just a couple of hundred. The Navy had less than one hundred men stationed at the new base on the island, and the Army transferred from Fort Bragg only a small number of soldiers. They occupied the old CCC Camp just north of town.

As a general rule, the troops blended in with the town's people. After all, for the most part they were citizen soldiers who had been called to serve. They had come from farms, towns and cities and had left behind their homes, wives and families. While here, they were appreciative of opportunities to be with and share the lives of townspeople. Whenever possible, families of the servicemen moved here to be with their loved ones. This influx of new residents was welcomed. Many of the homes in town were converted to duplexes or triplexes, and the spare rooms were rented to the military families. They were viewed as new neighbors.

328

I interrupted her with one request for clarification.

"Aunt Amelia, are you saying the wartime had just a small effect on the community, and for that reason you were less distressed than you had been in the earlier war? "

No, Mary Eliza, quite to the contrary. The war changed virtually every aspect of life. But the changes were different from what they had been previously. For one thing, men and women alike were involved. During Great-Grandmother's time and, to some extent, when I was young, war was an activity of men. Women either were left at home on their own to cope, or they played minor supportive roles. In Great-Grandmother's day, the women who were left behind struggled to manage farms or family resources without guidance or support. Often their efforts were in vain, as marauding bands of vagrants, misfits and military, seeking to take advantage, ravaged the farms and stole family treasures.

Women and children were at the mercy of these elements, their husbands, fathers and brothers having gone afar to fight in the war. The weak were victims.

In the Second World War, women became partners in the effort. Civilian defense groups were organized. Coastal patrols kept an eye for enemy aircraft and ships offshore. More importantly, women were recognized for their knowledge, abilities and skills. Accordingly, they were recruited to fill roles in business and industry, roles vacated by the men who had been conscripted to fight. This fact alone took women out of their historic passive position and they became full partners in the enterprise.

Certainly there were sacrifices, as the needs of the war dictated rationing, but this also was seen as a contribution. Great-Grandmother also made sacrifices, particularly during the early part of the War between the States but, within a short time, all local resources had been exhausted and there was no answer to the suffering during the years that followed.

In our case, the government entered the war in 1941 with a plan, one to be shared by the entire nation. Lavish lives were not lived during the years of that war, but neither were deprivation, starvation and disease the norm.

Having said all of this, Mary Eliza, I still have not answered the question you asked regarding my reluctance to speak of that war. My hesitation has been due to the fact that, for many years following the war, I had conflicting emotions related to my involvement. It has taken a long time for me to work this out, but I now know what caused the emotional conflict.

Mary Eliza, it is the fact that I was an active participant. And after the war ended, I began once again to question my values. How was it possible, in view of what had transpired during my teen years, that I could become part of a war twenty years later?

There were groups and individuals who staunchly opposed becoming involved. War at any cost to them was considered an ultimate evil. In support of their perspective, they presented logical arguments. Many of their points impressed me. Yet I still found myself involved with war-related activities, although my contributions were indirect.

As you know, I had become quite active at the hospital by that time. I was both supporting Papa's patients and serving on the surgical service. When the war build-up began, I fell back upon my community outreach experience and I resumed the educational activities which had been the focus of my efforts shortly after nursing school.

I began teaching classes. The Red Cross had made a commitment to produce bandages for use overseas, and our local chapter felt it could make as many as 20,000 bandages each month. This became an activity of nearly every church group. My role was to explain both how the bandages were to be made and how they would be used to treat the wounded. The information was greatly appreciated by the women who were to do the work. It gave them a sense of playing a direct role in helping the boys overseas.

With time, my activities expanded and I began teaching classes in first aid to Civil Defense volunteers and members of the Red Cross Disaster Relief Committee. All of these efforts were natural extensions of the various roles I had played in town over the years.

Paradoxically, what I was doing seemed unrelated to the war. Other women, those who were in the WAVES and stationed on the island and those who became members of the Coast Guard Women's Reserve, were really involved in the war. I was just doing my regular jobs.

Yet the war was here and I was part of it. Soldiers were on the island and military ships were often in the bay. The town was under blackout conditions at night and the shore was under constant surveillance during the daylight hours.

We were also reminded of war's destructive power each time the Navy closed the local waters to shipping and fishing so that the coastal defense batteries on the island could conduct firing practice.

Then there were German submarines patrolling our shores. On several occasions, ships were torpedoed in coastal waters. Survivors of such attacks were brought to town by our local seamen and the injured were treated in the hospital. Fortunately, such events were few.

In many respects, though we were participants in the war effort, we were also isolated and insulated from its worst tragedies. Even at the local theater, the newsreels shown before each feature focused upon the positive. They highlighted the jobs women were doing at home and showed children contributing to war recycling efforts or selling Defense Bonds. And the combat footage emphasized the heroism of our troops.

That is what made the war different. Most likely, that is also what allowed me to be involved, and to do so without questioning. It was a safe and secure war for folks here in town.

Even today, nearly sixty years after World War II, many recall those years with fond memories. Dashing young men and women in uniform, exploits of the flyers, dances at the USO, and wartime friendships are remembered.

Such was not the case in Great-Grandmother's day when poverty, disease and tragic family deaths plagued the town. Nor was it the case following that first war of my youth. Even now I recoil at the thought of men dying -- hungry, cold and diseased -- in mud-filled, rat-infested trenches. The memories of young men less than whole returning from "over there" remain with me.

So, Mary Eliza, I internalized all of this and, because I did not know how to resolve my own conflicting questions, I have not spoken of those times.

I began to realize that even the horrors of war and constant military activity may be supported, depending upon circumstances. Although I was aware of the suffering taking place elsewhere in the world during the Second World War and, to a lesser extent, during the Korean Conflict, my isolation here in town made it possible for me to contribute. Yet during my youth, I had personally experienced the pain of war.

331

I wrestled with that dichotomy for many years, until Vietnam brought war back into our lives through the power of television. Death and destruction were graphically displayed. It was then, when the nation was so torn over Vietnam, that I spoke again with Great-Grandmother about my distress.

Yet to this day, I ask myself the question, "Under what conditions is military activity with its guarantee of death and destruction acceptable?"

Still the answer eludes me.

We had been on the porch a long while, and it was time for a meal, the lunch hour having passed earlier in the conversation. I turned again to Amelia Caroline.

"Aunt Amelia you are looking drawn, perhaps it is time for us to go in."

"Yes, I have enjoyed the conversation, but now, the time has come," she replied.

I asked if she would enjoy a light snack.

Amelia Caroline replied, "I would like that perhaps a little later. I am very tired just now."

With that, Amelia Caroline eased herself from the rocking chair and entered the house that had been her home for her entire life. She went into the parlor, relaxed into a favorite lounge chair and picked up a book, the newest mystery written by Anne Perry.

Amelia Caroline enjoyed stories based upon life during the Victorian Era and Anne Perry was currently one of her favorite authors. Typically, she would read for thirty minutes or more; but on this day, she was fast asleep within minutes. She remained in a deeply relaxed state for several hours.

Amelia Caroline awoke to find me at the desk working with my laptop computer. I often did chart work at the house, as it gave me more time to be with Amelia Caroline. At present, I was just completing the charts of recently seen patients. One particularly rewarding aspect of practice in the small town for me was having an opportunity to intimately know my patients. As I sit at the computer transcribing my hand-written clinical notes into the electronic record, each patient comes clearly to mind.

"Mary Eliza?" I heard Amelia Caroline calling.

"Yes, Aunt Amelia. May I help you with something?"

"No. Not with anything in particular. I'm thinking about warming some of that leftover chicken soup. Would you care for some? We still have a bit of that nice farm bread to go with the soup."

"That would be enjoyable, Aunt Amelia. But how would it be if I prepare the soup while you wash for dinner? Later, we can listen to the evening programs on NPR. The repeat of yesterday's Prairie Home Companion will be on soon."

So the evening went. Amelia Caroline and I shared the meal outside in the cool summer evening air. Then we retired once again to the parlor to enjoy the Sunday-night radio programming.

About eight o'clock, I turned to Amelia Caroline with a question.

"Aunt Amelia, you have not said much about your Grandmother Emily or her family. Why is that?"

Interesting that you should ask at this moment, for family relationships were just going through my mind.

It has long been my impression that dynamics within the family changed following the death of Great-Grandmother. During her time, family relations were focal to life and, from the earliest years, Great-Grandfather Sterling and Great-Grandmother were at the hub of the family. Great-Grandmother, by virtue of the fact that she remained here in the house, became the matriarch. Others in the family came and went. They lived in town or lived elsewhere, but always with the security of knowing that Great-Grandmother would be here. Her presence provided the family fold to which all could return. She provided stability, security and love. Several of her own children, my great-aunts, never married. They simply remained within the fold.

The family was not the same following her death. Society had become more mobile and children moved away. There was less cohesiveness. And it was into this atmosphere that I was born. As I have already told you, Grandfather Edward and Grandmother Emily had moved to Charlotte by the time of my birth. And I was just two years old when Grandfather passed away. Grandmother Emily, having few ties to Charlotte, left that city and moved back to Wilmington rather than return here. She had always been more of a city person, and

Wilmington was the largest and most dynamic city in North Carolina at the time.

What I've not told you before is that Grandmother Emily was born and raised in Philadelphia. All her people, the McLaurins, were still in that area during the early years of the 20th century. They were Northerners, so you can imagine that we had little in common, given the regional animosity that still existed. So I have known almost nothing of that branch from my tree.

At any rate, right through my early teen years Papa and I would occasionally visit Grandmother. But she was not a particularly warm person, so the visits were short. After the onset of World War I in Europe and the preliminary military activities here and on the island, we hardly ever got to Wilmington. Grandmother died in 1916.

The other major change to the family following Great-Grandmother's death was the relocation of Mary Elizabeth. Sewall had become more involved with matters related to basic engineering in the city of Wilmington and this was keeping him away from town for much more prolonged periods. In addition, Sewall's long-held interest in agriculture grew in scope and he purchased a rice plantation named Clarendon on the upper river. So he and Mary Elizabeth closed their place here in town and moved to the plantation.

Thus, Mary Elizabeth followed the same path her mother, your Great-Grandmother Mary Eliza Everitt Langdon, had trod nearly a half century earlier. But the migration did not stop. Mary Elizabeth returned to town in the mid-1880s, for Sewall had accepted a government engineering position involving work near the city of Memphis. Mary Elizabeth died at the age of 58 in September of 1885. She had been back in her house just a short while before passing away. Sewall died six months later while in Memphis.

Following the deaths of Mary Elizabeth and Sewall, we – meaning Grandfather Edward and Grandmother Emily and Papa -- lost all contact with your branch of the family, Mary Eliza.

Ultimately, the result was that Papa and I comprised the entire family remaining in town. Then after his death, I was alone. So you can see why I was so excited when you came to me in 1983, Mary Eliza.

Within a few minutes of completing the story, about 9:00 PM, Amelia Caroline retired. That was her normal routine. She was after all, ninety-nine years, three months and seven days old.

38

NOT THE END

Amelia Caroline was still in bed at 6:30 AM when I entered the kitchen to make coffee on Monday morning. Sleeping to that hour was quite unusual for her, but I knew the previous days, though being spent exactly as she wished, had been both physically tiring and emotionally draining. Before retiring the previous evening, as we stood together in the front parlor, Amelia Caroline indicated that she would enjoy some quiet time by herself in the morning. Then just as she was about to leave for her room, she turned. We embraced and she told me how much love she had for me and how she had enjoyed our special weekend together. Later, while laying awake in my own room, tears, brought about by memories and love, streamed down my cheeks and onto the pillow.

When Amelia Caroline was not up and about on Monday morning I assumed she either was sleeping in or was enjoying the quiet morning she had requested. But the fact that she had been excessively tired over the last several days weighed on me.

Amelia Caroline and I had often discussed her advancing age and the accompanying frailty. As it turns out, I had greater concerns than she. Nevertheless, as a result of those discussions, we had come to an understanding regarding her care. I intended to honor our agreement, even though in some respects it ran counter to my training as a physician. I would allow Amelia Caroline the morning she wished. Love asks much of us.

Perhaps, I thought, this was an opportunity to run some errands, then return to the house for breakfast before seeing patients in the office.

Originally, I had planned to check in at the office about 8:15 AM, then go to the hospital about 10:00 AM. But under the circumstances, going in earlier seemed a better choice. My first patient in the office was scheduled for 11:00, so I had more than three hours during which I could go to the office and return the patient charts I had been working on over the weekend. Then I could spend a short while at the hospital before being needed in the office.

Mr. Sellers was still in the hospital, but he probably was doing well enough to be released. His grandson and great-grandchildren had come over from Raleigh to be on hand during the surgery and had remained for the weekend. Mr. Sellers wished to spend a few hours visiting at home before his grandson and the children had to return to Raleigh. I needed to check his chart one more time before authorizing the discharge.

So upon finishing my coffee, I drove to the office and left a note for Sarah with instructions to file the charts. At the hospital, I found Mr. Sellers in good spirits and anxious to be on his way.

I left the hospital about 8:30. Approximately two hours remained before I was required in the office, so I drove to the bakery. Fresh scones were just being placed in the display cabinet. Amelia Caroline was particularly fond of raisin scones, for they were similar to the ones prepared by the family as far back as her Great-Grandmother. So I purchased two raisin scones and, for a treat with tea later in the day, I added one of the spiced pumpkin scones. Upon leaving the bakery, I drove along the waterfront. Just a few cars lined the parking area, so I decided to stop for a few minutes.

The tide had just passed high and, with its ebb, the current swirled past the channel buoys, leaving them to strain against their anchors. The sun was well up in the southeastern sky, and its rays reflected from the water's surface which, except for the tide's pull, was glassy in the early morning hours.

In a small wooden skiff just offshore, an elderly man and young child sat patiently while their fishing lines bobbed in the water. I recognized Mr. Gore, one of my patients, and his grandson Eugene, who had come to spend a few delightful late summer days in town. We waved to each other as I started the car's engine.

Suddenly, as the car was leaving the curb, I experienced a sensation, one that was calling me to the house. The drive was less than two or three minutes. Upon opening the front door and entering the house, it was apparent that something significant had transpired. Even before checking Amelia

338

Caroline's room, I knew from where and I knew why the sensation had come to me.

A note lay on the bed table. The hand had not been steady, but the message was unmistakable.

Mary Eliza,

I enjoyed a glorious sunrise, the early rays shown brightly through the bedroom window and projected a golden glow on the wall beside the bed. While treating myself to the morning sounds of the birds, I heard the door close and I knew you were going to the hospital. So I decided to remain right here, enjoying the leisure and the coolness of the early day.

Then the words of Great-Grandmother Amelia came to me once again. "We will talk," she said. " I can tell you of that which has been. It will be up to you to live the present. The future will follow in its time."

I knew that my time to be with Great-Grandmother had come.

Thank you, my dear. Know that I am with you always."

Your loving Aunt and Cousin,
Amelia Caroline

A great sadness weighed upon me as I sat beside Amelia Caroline, who now rested on the bed in that state of eternal peace which eventually we all find. This was a day we had frequently discussed. I had known full well the wishes Amelia Caroline had for her final moments. Those wishes had been fulfilled. We had both been aware for the past few weeks of her failing health, and we had recently discussed her wish to depart life unburdened by medical interventions.

Whether Amelia Caroline and I had made the correct professional choice could never be determined. However, I believe, as had Amelia Caroline, that professional considerations should not come to bear on what is life's singularly most personal experience. Amelia Caroline's final moments had been as so many of us would wish for ourselves. Hers was a fitting close to a life that had lasted ninety-nine years, three months and eight days.

Some weeks later, the number not being important, I sat on the front porch of the house that now was to be mine. Amelia Caroline had been placed to rest in the family plot in the Old Burying Ground. Her resting spot was to the right of the graceful marble obelisk where her Great-Grandfather Sterling Byrd Everitt was buried. She would now -- and for eternity-- be with her Great-Grandmother Amelia Caroline Potter Everitt.

A gentle breeze stirred in the large live oak tree and shadows from its leaves danced on the ground. The dance had caught my attention, then left me in a mesmerized state. I remained deeply immersed in thought for several minutes.

The president had just announced that the country was to be at war in the Middle East, and my classmate, John Rhodes, was to be deployed. Upon completion of his initial commitment to the Navy following medical school, John had decided to remain in the United States Navy Reserve. He was a neurosurgeon and held the rank of lieutenant commander.

John would be in harm's way. Both the prospect of war and the deployment of a friend weighed heavily upon me. I kept thinking about how much of life is used just in living and so little time is spent finding answers.

As I sat on the porch rocking in that ancient chair, a voice spoke from the quiet.

"Mary Eliza?"

"Yes, Aunt Amelia."

And so our conversations resumed.

39

FINAL SESSION

Fall is in full bloom, and the late morning air is crisp, clear and comfortable at seventy-five degrees as I pull into the parking lot at Catherine Arrington's office.

Surprisingly, the lot is nearly full. Catherine's partner, Dr. Steven Jeffries, must have been delayed at the hospital, thus creating a backlog of patients in the clinic. With so many fall vacationers on the island and in the town, hospital emergencies are quite common and frequently result in delays at the offices of local doctors. Fortunately, the majority of vacation injuries are minor and can be handled in urgent-care offices. However, more serious cases end up in the hospital emergency room.

Local residents, including regular patients in Dr. Jeffries's office, or my own for that matter, are not immune. Although the hospital in town is fully staffed to handle such situations, whenever possible I try to be on scene when one of my own patients is involved. This is particularly true if I happen to be making rounds at the hospital at the time the emergency arrives. Dr. Jeffries shares this philosophy.

Despite the number of cars, several spaces are available, and among them are spaces facing the building as well as some facing the natural scrub area. I have made progress over the past months, and thrashing myself over a parking decision is no longer an aspect of my arrival. I simply pull into the nearest spot and enter the building.

"Good afternoon, Dr. Langdon. I see you are scheduled with Dr. Arrington," is the greeting I receive.

Nearly a month has passed since my last appointment. Even so, the receptionist recognizes and greets me as if my previous session had been just a few days back. Such personal recognition is something I stress with my own staff, for it goes a long way to ease concerns of patients while they await appointments with the doctor.

"Hi Susan, I'll take a seat in the waiting area," is my response.

The wait is not long, and soon I am sitting in the now familiar office. Catherine and I chat for several minutes just in greeting. We then shift to matters at hand and I begin.

"Basically, Catherine, I'm feeling quite at ease with myself. The treadmill of thoughts has subsided and the indecisiveness no longer keeps me tied in knots. I'm not saying that distressing thoughts and the treadmill are entirely gone, but they no longer are in control.

"Occasionally, unresolved issues regarding communication with Amelia Caroline, Charles, Louis or Great-Grandmother do come to mind, and I fully expect that to be the case for the remainder of my life. Of course, the Fats Domino tunes still come out of the blue and remain longer than is necessary, but for the most part the troublesome aspect is behind me."

Catherine observed, "I'm pleased for you, Mary Eliza. Do you have any ideas regarding when the resolution came about?"

I know it is time for our discussion to shift to Amelia Caroline, Great-Grandmother and my journal. I am feeling quite comfortable, even though I speak of Amelia Caroline and Great-Grandmother as if they currently are active in my life.

"I think that, perhaps, completion of the journal has brought me to accept experiences and events for which there have been no clear explanations. By this, I mean my being drawn to the town, the introduction to Great-Grandmother through Amelia Caroline, and my sense of communication with Charles and Louis.

"I have reached a point where I'm no longer confused or concerned and I attribute this to writing the journal. As the journal took form, I realized there is a commonality between my life and the life of Amelia Caroline and, by extension, the life of Great-Grandmother. I say there is a commonality among us, but actually the association is much more. I feel we are linked directly, as if our three lives in reality are one life extending over a period of two centuries.

"Catherine, you and I talked many sessions back about the Universal Mind. I don't fully understand this from a philosophical standpoint, but I have come to embrace it from the experiential perspective. The form in which communication comes to me from Charles, Amelia Caroline, Great-Grandmother or even Louis no longer is a concern for me. I accept Amelia Caroline's thoughts as my own, and I embrace whatever comes from Charles, Louis or Great-Grandmother.

"Whether the communications are cryptographic messages or voices I now realize is not relevant to the experience. I just open myself to the forces, spirits or souls and accept what comes, for I know they are part of me and I am of them.

"Amelia Caroline and I continue to have discussions in the evenings when I sit in the rocker on the front porch. These are quite real to me and I always look forward to being with her. Perhaps the journal has helped open me to this. For certain, the journal, in combination with the conversations, has opened my mind to my own life.

"This is not to say that I have been oblivious to the direction in which my life was going. Nearly twenty years with Amelia Caroline has taught me much about being in the world and being proactively self-directed.

"Some of this, however, I misplaced following Amelia Caroline's death. When I first came to you, my thoughts were focused on trying to comprehend what was and had been happening to me. I felt compelled for some unconscious reason to understand the mechanism, the how and the why, of my experiences.

"Over the past few months, the folly of this attempt to understand the mechanism came to me. I realized that I was attempting to understand the delivery system; yet all the while, I was missing the messages.

"As the journal unfolded, I was struck by the realization that Amelia Caroline did not question how or why she was able to talk with Great-Grandmother. She simply accepted the reality. I have come to share Amelia Caroline's acceptance. Consequently I now ask, 'What does this experience tell me of myself and the future?' The messages come from yesterdays of the past; they are from those who are now gone. I realize that yesterday and yesterday's yesterday have much to teach me about tomorrow and tomorrow's tomorrow.

"These realizations have helped me refocus on living today for today, while at the same time accepting what comes from the past as guidance for the future. This may sound trite, but I see myself undergoing evolution both from the perspective of insight and of how I live each day. Even my medical practice is undergoing change."

Catherine spoke, "Yes, Steven mentioned that you have become actively involved with the new Community Free Clinic."

I continued with pleasure, "I have. In fact, I've decided to devote thirty percent of my time to the Community Free Clinic. We, meaning the office staff and I, actually have set aside blocks of time to see the less-fortunate patients. The entire staff seems enthusiastic about pitching in.

"I've also accepted an adjunct faculty appointment in Family Medicine with Wake Forest University Medical School. The agreement will allow residents from the medical school to spend time in my office as part of their training. In addition, provisions have been made for third- and fourth-year medical school students to do family medicine rotations with me here in town. All of this is purely optional on the part of the residents and students, but I'm excited about the prospect of involving them in the Community Free Clinic."

"That sounds wonderful."

"Yes, it is. You know, Catherine, I think this is all part of a dream that Amelia Caroline and Great-Grandmother had throughout their lives. Amelia Caroline and her father had dedicated much of their professional time treating those of limited means. In addition, Amelia Caroline provided community-health and nutrition education through her role as county health nurse.

"My new efforts will continue and extend that which they championed. And Great-Grandmother's life was entwined with medicine, so her life will also continue through mine.

"I, in return, will be with them as I sit on the front porch in that ancient rocking chair."

ADDITIONAL CHARACTERS

Abbott, Ira, Supreme Court Justice, New Mexico Territory
Adkins, J.J., Captain
Alexander, Annie L. MD
Anderson, Joseph, General CSA
Austin, Gene (Lemeul Eugene Lucas)
Austin, Kathryn
Bell, Egbert Haywood, Dr.
Berg, Jens.
Betts, A.D., Rev.
Blackwell, Elizabeth MD
Bickett, Thomas, Governor
Boeck, William, Dr.
Bonney, William (Billy the Kid)
Broadway, R.E., MD
Bynum, J.M., Rev.
Carson, Beatrice, RN
Casal, Don Pedro
Childs, Thomas, Colonel
Clark, Henry T., Governor
Clark, Walter, Captain
Clark, Walter, Justice, NC Supreme Court
Cranmer, E.H., Judge
Crighton, Robert, Captain of ship Three Bells
Culton, James
Curtis, Walter, Dr.
Cushing, W.B., Lieutenant
Davis, Anna
Davis, David
Davis, Henry
Dimock, Susan, MD
Dosher, J. Arthur, M.D.
Dosher, Julius
Early, H. B.

Earp, Wyatt
Eggleston, Cary, MD
Ellis, John, Governor
Frink, Lorenzo, Dr.
Garrett, Pat, Sheriff
Gates, William, Colonel
Goldberger, Joseph, MD
Goley, W.R., MD
Hallyburton, E.M., Sergeant
Hancock, Bessie
Harrison, William Henry, US President
Hedrick, John J., Captain, CSA
Holloway, Lloyd, Rev.
Jackson, Andrew, US President
Jones, John
Kemble (Butler), Frances Anne
Larson, Laura
Lee, Robert E., General CSA
Low, Captain of ship Kilby
McGlamery, G.W. (Mack)
McKenzie, Willie
McLaurin, Aleine
Miller, Joseph
Miller, Leonhard
Newton, Caroline
Parker, Linette A., RN
Perry, E.L.
Pershing, John, General
Piver, Lillie Drew
Price, Carrie
Reaves, Upshaw
Ruark, J.B.
Scott, Winfield, General
Sherman, Wm. Tecumsah, General
Smith, Dorothy
Smith, Ella Mae
Spencer, Vida
Stiles, C.W., PhD, Colonel
Stiffler, B.F.
Stride, Robert, Colonel
Stuart, Kate
Swain, Eddie

Thompson, Thomas
Thurston, S.D., Dr.
Trax, Lola
Tyler, John, US President
Vickers, Thomas, Rev.
Villa, Pancho
Watson, Duncan I, MD
Williams, James, Captain
Williams, Lelia
Williams, Susan, RN
Wilson, Victor
Wood, Leonard, General
Woodside, Annie Mae

SOURCES

American Medical Association Chemical Laboratory. Propaganda for Reform. 9th Edition - 1916, Reprinted from Jounal of American Medical Association. 1916.

Anderson, George B. History of New Mexico; Its resources and people. Los Angeles. Pacific States Publishing, 1907

"Arsenal Explosion at Frankford Plant". New York Times Archives. September 9, 1917

Blakey, Frederic Arch, et al. Rose Cottage Chronicles. Gainsville,FL. University Press of Florida. 1998.

Bollet, Alfred J. MD. "Politics and Pellagra", Yale J. of Biology and Medicine,v65(2).1992.

Bryan, Mary Norcott. A Grandmother's Recollections of Dixie. New Bern, NC. Owen G. Dunn, Printer. 1912.

Carson, Susan S. Joshua's Dream: A Town With Two Names. Wilmington, NC. Broadfoot Publishing Co. 1992.

Chin, Eliza Lo. MD. This Side of Doctoring: Reflections from Women in Medicine. Thousand Oaks, Ca. Sage Publications. 2001.

Clark, Walter Jr. North Carolina in the War: An Address Delivered before the North Carolina Bar Association at Blowing Rock, NC. July 5, 1923. Charlotte, NC. Charlotte Chamber of Commerce. 1924.

Cravens, Hamilton. "Sheppard-Towner Maternity and Infancy Act". Encyclopedia of Children and Childhood in History and Society. Paula. S. Fass, Ed. New York. MacMillan. 2003.

Culbreth, David M.R., MD. Materia Medica and Pharmacology. Philadelphia. Lea & Febiger. 1927.

Curtis, Dr. Walter G. Reminiscences of Wilmington and Smithville-Southport. 1848-1900.
1905. Second Edition. Southport, NC. Southport Historical Society. 1999.

Daniel, Peter V. Eyre v Potter/Opinion of the Court: 53 U.S. 42: United States Reports-v56: Decisions of the United States Supreme Court. Washington, DC. 1853.

Dickson, Samuel Henry. Dickson's Elements of Medicine. Philadelphia. T.K. and P.G. Collins, Printers. 1855.

Ford, Joseph H., Colonel. The Medical Department of the United States Army in the World War. Washington, DC. US Government Printing Office. 1927.

Green, Elna. "Why North Carolina Didn't Give Women the Vote". Tarheel Junior Historian Magazine. Raleigh. North Carolina Museum of History.1994.

Green, Elna C. Southern Strategies. Chapel Hill. University of North Carolina Press. 1997.

Henderson, Archibold. "North Carolina Women in the War". Raleigh. North Carolina Literary and Historical Association, 19th Annual Session, 1920. Chapel Hill. Women's History.Documentation of the South. University of North Carolina Library. 2011.

Hyams, Charles W. Sergeant Hallyburton, The First American Soldier Captured in the World War. Moravian Falls, NC. Dixie Publishing Co. 1923

Iredell, James. Reports of Cases in Equity argued in the Supreme Court of North Carolina. Volume VII. Raleigh. Seat Gales Publishers. 1851.

Joyce, John St.George. Story of Philadelphia. Philadelphia. Rex Printing House. 1919.

Kestenbaum, Lawrence. The Internet's Most Comprehensive Source of U.S. Political Biography. Political Graveyard.com. 2011.

Kemble, Frances Anne. Journal of Residence on a Georgian Plantation in1838-1839. Athens, GA. University of Georgia Press. 1984.

Lee, Lawrence. The History of Brunswick County North Carolina. Charlotte, NC. Heritage Press. 1980.

Lefler, Hugh Talmage. North Carolina History as Told by Contemporaries. Chapel Hill. University of North Carolina Press. 1934.

Lemons, J. Stanley. "The Sheppard-Towner Act: Progressivism in the 1920's". Journal of American History. v55(4). 1969.

Leon, Louis. Diary of a Tar Heel Confederate Soldier. Charlotte, Stone Publishing Co. 1913.

Lewis, Jon C. & Susan S. Carson. Joshua's Legacy: Dream Makers of Old Southport. Southport, NC. The Southport Historical Society. 2003.

Malburne-Wade, Meredith. "North Carolina and the Struggle for Women's Suffrage" Chapel Hill. Women's History. Documentation of the South. University of North Carolina Library. 2011,

Martin, Sanford. Public Letters and Papers of Thomas Walter Bickett - Governor of NC 1917 -1921. Raleigh. Edwards and Broughton, Publishers. 1923.

Meads, Manson, MD. The Miracle on Hawthorne Hill. Winston-Salem. Wake Forest University Press. 1988.

Mitchel, Cora. Reminiscences of the Civil War. Providence. Snow and Farnham, Co. 1916.

Moore, Frank and Edward Everett. The Rebellion Record.1861-1868: A Diary of American Events. New York. D. Van Nostrand, Co. 1867.

Moorhead, James Howell. "Religion in the Civil War: The Northern Perspective." Divining America -Teacher Serve. National Humanities Center. 2012.

North Carolina. General Assembly. House of Representatives. Telegram to the Tennessee Legislature and the Sixty Three Members of the House Who Signed it. Raleigh, NC. The House. 1920.

Parker, Linette A. Materia Medica and Therapeutics. Philadelphia. Lea & Febiger. 1926.

Pepper, William, MD. A System of Practical Medicine. Philadelphia. Lea Brothers & Co. 1885.

Pierce, Franklin. Report of the Mint of the United States: Message from the President of the United States. Washington, DC. US Government Printing Office. 1856.

"Plot in Powder Blow-Up: Eddystone Plant". New York Times Archives. April 11, 1917

Reaves, Bill. Southport (Smithville): A Chronology: Vol. 1-4. Southport, NC. Southport Historical Society. 1992.

Richardson, Joseph G. MD. Medicology. Philadelphia. University Medical Society. 1907

Salley, Eulalie. "Class and Regional Identities Among Female Activists". Chapel Hill. Oral Histories of the American South. Documentation of the South. University of North Carolina Library. 1997.

Saxon, Elizabeth Lyle. <u>A Southern Woman's War Time Reminiscences</u>. Memphis. Pilcher Printing Co. 1905.

Smith, Margaret S. and Wilson, Emily H. "The Importance of Women's History." <u>Women's History: An Online Workshop.</u> Raleigh, NC. The North Caolina Museum of History. 2011.

Stackpole, Edouard A. <u>The Wreck of the Steamer San Francisco</u>. Mystic, CT. The Mystic Marine Historical Association, Inc. 1954.

Stiles, Charles W. "The Surface Privy as a Factor in Spreading Hookworm Disease and Typhoid Fever." <u>Journal of the American Medical Association. v53(8).</u> 1909.

Stout, Harry S. "Religion in the Civil War: The Southern Perspective." <u>Divining America - TeacherServe.</u> National Humanities Center. 2011.

The United States War Department. <u>War of Rebellion: A Compilation of the Official Records of the Union and the Confederate Armies</u>. Washington, DC. US Government Printing Office. 1880-1901.

"The Wreck of the San Francisco". <u>New York Times Archives</u>. Jan 6, 1854-Feb 25, 1854

Walker, John Otey. <u>Official History of the 120th Infantry "3rd North Carolina" 30th Division from August 1917- April 1919</u>. Lynchburg, VA. J.P. Bell, Co. 1919.

"Wildcats Never Quit: North Carolina in World War One." North Carolina ECHO Project. Raleigh, NC. State Archives of North Carolina. 2009.

Williams, Ann. <u>Your Affectionate Daughter, Isabella</u>. Asheville, NC. Historical Images. 2001.

Wilson, John and Wilson, Ashley Lefler. <u>North Carolina Nurses: A Century of Caring</u>. Research Triangle Park, NC. UNC-TV ONLINE. 2002.

ACKNOWLEDGEMENTS

The research behind this story and the evolution of the work into a book involved the support and contribution of many individuals and institutions.

Initial background research must be credited to the faculty and staff at the Wellcome Institute Library for History of Medicine in London, where I had the privilege to study some years back.

Then staff members at the Margaret and James Harper Library in Southport, North Carolina, provided assistance over several years – with great patience -- while I ferreted out historical jewels from microfilm, printed works and family genealogies.

Similarly, staff members at the North Carolina Historical Archives in Raleigh and folks in the office of the Brunswick County, North Carolina Register of Deeds were extremely helpful as I was sorting through dusty documents from the past.

Archivists at the Latimer House in Wilmington, North Carolina, were particularly adept at finding treasures that missed my inexperienced eye in the archives of the Historical Society of the Lower Cape Fear.

Special acknowledgement must be given to the staff at the Coy Carpenter Library, History of Medicine Collection, at Wake Forest University School of Medicine in Winston-Salem.

355

I am much indebted to the staff at University of North Carolina Library in Chapel Hill, whose program *Documenting the American South* has provided access to numerous and invaluable historical records, documents and personal stories.

Many thanks go to friends, as well: Margo Roberts, Jerry Miller and Judith Roderick, who provided feedback and encouragement upon reading early versions of the work.

I credit Ms. Susie Sellers Carson, historian and friend, for kindling in me an interest in the history of Southport, North Carolina.

Special thanks to Kris Pfeifer for help with the cover design and to Chris O'Shea Roper, whose editorial talents moved the manuscript from the state of rough draft to that of a polished work.

Finally, to my wife Pat Harrison Lewis, whose artistic talents resulted in a cover portrait reflective of times past, I give much credit. Had it not been for her continual support, encouragement and love this work would still be a collection of electrons on my computer hard drive.

ABOUT THE AUTHOR

Dr. Jon C. Lewis, Emeritus Professor of Pathology, has been affiliated for thirty-five years with Wake Forest University School of Medicine in Winston-Salem, North Carolina. A native of Southport, Connecticut, Dr. Lewis was awarded the Bachelor and Master of Science Degrees at the University of Houston in Texas and his Doctoral Degree from the University of Kansas. Following several years affiliation with the University of Minnesota Medical School at the Mayo Clinic in Rochester, Minnesota , he relocated to North Carolina in 1977.

The author of over 200 professional publications pertaining to cardiovascular disease, Dr. Lewis's professional foray into history began in 1997 when studying at the Wellcome Library and Institute for the History of Medicine in London, England. Upon retirement from the active faculty at Wake Forest University, Dr. Lewis moved to Southport, North Carolina, where he worked closely with historian, Susan Sellers Carson. Their collaboration culminated in 2003 with publication of the book, <u>JOSHUA'S LEGACY</u>: <u>Dream Makers of Old Southport</u>.

Dr. Lewis, though continuing pursuit of his interest in North Carolina history, currently resides in Placitas, New Mexico.